THE BLADE OF THE FLAME

"What is this Black Fleet?" Makala asked.

"Pirates who fly under no flag," Yvka said, "they ply the Lhazaar Sea, plundering villages and ships. But their main prey is people. Young, old, men, women . . . it doesn't matter. They take gold, but it's said what they really want is blood."

Diran Bastian, priest of the Silver Flame, has thwarted assassins, banished demons, healed the sick, and brought justice to the oppressed. But when he returns to the land of his birth, he must face his greatest challenge yet . . .

THE THIEVES OF BLOOD

THE BLADE OF THE FLAME
Tim Waggoner

Thieves of the Blood

Forge of the Mindslayers

Sea of Death
(February 2008)

TIM WAGGONER

THIEVES OF BLOOD

BLADE OF THE FLAME

BOOK 1

THE THIEVES OF BLOOD
The Blade of the Flame · Book 1

Cover art by Raymond Swanland
Map by Rob Lazzaretti
First Printing: May 2006
Library of Congress Catalog Card Number: 2005935537

9 8 7 6 5 4 3

ISBN-10: 0-7869-4005-0
ISBN-13: 978-0-7869-4005-9
620-95536740-001-EN

U.S., CANADA,	EUROPEAN HEADQUARTERS
ASIA, PACIFIC, & LATIN AMERICA	Hasbro UK Ltd
Wizards of the Coast, Inc.	Caswell Way
P.O. Box 707	Newport, Gwent NP9 0YH
Renton, WA 98057-0707	GREAT BRITAIN
+1-800-324-6496	Save this address for your records.

Visit our web site at www.wizards.com

ACKNOWLEDGEMENTS

Thanks so much to Mark Sehestedt. His brainstorming, suggestions, and editorial feedback throughout the writing process made this a far better book than it otherwise would've been.

DEDICATION

To the Warner brothers: Joshua, Brandon, Cory, and Trent. All fine young men.

CHAPTER

ONE

Two men walked side by side down a narrow street in Port Verge. One was human, tall, thin, and garbed in black. The other was half-orc, taller, broad-shouldered, thick-limbed, and wearing a breastplate that had seen hard use over the years.

This was one of the older sections in the city, and the buildings here were weathered and in disrepair. They'd been constructed so close together that in some places the only reason they remained standing was because they leaned against one another. The streets were unpaved and worn by the feet of thousands of pedestrians over the years. Most of the people here were seafolk—sailors and fishermen—but there were a few low-level merchants and sellswords in the mix, along with street vendors hawking cheap tidbits made from shells and the like. Humans were the predominant racial group, followed closely by gnomes and half-elves. There were a handful of dwarves, elves, and halflings around as well but no orcs or half-orcs, except Ghaji, that is, and he received quite a few stares as he and Diran moved through the crowd. Ghaji was used to getting such looks, but that didn't mean he liked it.

"So . . . what's in Port Verge?" the half-orc asked. For the last several weeks they'd been wandering the Principalities, moving aimlessly from one place to another. Ghaji didn't want to admit it to his friend, but he was beginning to get bored.

Diran shrugged. "The usual. Restaurants, wharfs, warehouses, shops, smithies, drinking holes . . ."

Ghaji scowled. "I mean, what's *interesting?*"

Diran opened his mouth to reply, but then he closed it and frowned. He stopped walking and nodded toward a sailor standing near the mouth of an alley across the street from them.

"How about him?"

The sailor didn't strike Ghaji as out of the ordinary. He was medium height, stocky, with curly black hair and a clean-shaven jaw. He wore a white shirt with the sleeves rolled up to the elbows, black trousers, sandals, and a crimson sash belted around his waist. He carried a blade—from the look of the scabbard, a bastard sword—which rode on his hips just below the sash. This detail did strike Ghaji as a bit odd. Though he wasn't native to the Lhazaar Principalities, he'd been traveling among its islands for the last several weeks alongside Diran, and from what he had seen of sailors in the Principalities, a bastard sword wasn't a common weapon. The man looked dazed, eyes half-lidded, a dreamy smile on his face, and he swayed from side to side, as if he were having difficulty maintaining his balance—that or he was swaying in time to music only he could hear.

"Look at his *hands,*" said Diran.

Ghaji focused his attention on the sailor's hands, frowned, then blinked several times as if to clear his vision.

"They're backward," the half-orc said. They looked as if they'd been twisted all the way around, though the man showed no sign of injury or pain.

Diran's lips stretched into a small, thin smile. "Exactly. Come, Ghaji."

The two companions stood on the opposite side of the street from the backward-handed sailor. Diran, without pausing to see if Ghaji would follow, stepped into the street and started heading for the man at a brisk pace. Ghaji had been traveling with Diran long enough to know that when the priest thought he was on the trail of some unearthly menace, he could be more determined than a starving swamp lion tracking wounded prey. With a sigh, the half-orc followed.

Diran Bastiaan cut quite an impressive figure as he crossed to the alley, and the pedestrians who clogged the street parted before him, almost as if they sensed who he was and what business he was about. He wore a black leather armor vest over a black shirt, black pants, black boots, and a black belt with sheaths for a pair of black-handled daggers. He had long black hair that he wore loose, and the breeze coming off the Lhazaar Sea caused his locks to trail out behind him. He wore a black traveler's cloak, with the hood down, but despite the breeze, the cloak did not billow outward. Ghaji knew this was because it was weighted down by numerous daggers Diran kept in hidden pockets sewn into the cloak's inner lining.

It wasn't his manner of dress that caused the crowd to back away as he approached. It was his eyes, arctic blue, piercing and set into a gaunt face with lean, wolfish features. Those eyes glittered with penetrating intelligence. Ghaji had seen strong men tremble when caught in the fierce, dispassionate scrutiny of Diran Bastiaan's gaze.

Diran could move quite fast when he wanted to, and Ghaji, though well over six feet tall, had to lengthen his stride and push himself to catch up. He managed to do so, and the two of them got there at the same time.

"Good afternoon to you," Diran's tone was pleasant enough but with a subtle hint of underlying challenge.

The man's eyes rolled in Diran's direction, but they couldn't remain focused on him and kept rolling away to stare off into space.

"Afternoon? Already?" The sailor paused, and Ghaji noticed that the veins in his eyes, and there were plenty of them visible, were tinted purple.

The sailor frowned. "Still summer, isn't it? I wasn't in there *that* long . . . was I?"

The man's voice was breathy, his words slurred to the point where it was difficult to understand him. The idiot had obviously overindulged in one substance or another, though it was difficult to say what. Ghaji smelled no alcohol on the man's breath or clothes, but there was any number of intoxicants available for a price, especially in a busy seaside town like Port Verge.

"Too much urchin-sting, eh?" Diran said. "How long you were in whatever establishment provided the toxin for you, I can't say, but I can confirm that it's still summer, though late enough in the season for there to be a chill in the air. Summers are all too short in the Principalities, aren't they?"

The priest's words were friendly enough, but his tone

remained emotionless. He was staring hard at the sailor with his ice-blue eyes.

Ghaji had seen that look numerous times, and he knew what it meant. Trouble. The half-orc carried a hand axe tucked into his belt, and he reached down and took hold of the handle just beneath the axe-head, though he made no move to draw the weapon. He did, however, decide it was time to make use of the more bestial half of his heritage. He scowled, prominent brow furrowing, the nostrils of his flat broad nose flaring, lower lip curling back to expose large lower incisors. Ghaji kept his black hair in a wild, shaggy tangle to better accentuate his orcish ancestry, and he sported a thin vertical strip of beard in the middle of his chin that served to highlight his teeth even more, like a black arrow pointing right to them. Add to this numerous scars on his face, neck, and hands, souvenirs of his time as a soldier in the Last War, and Ghaji could present quite a fearsome aspect when he wished, and he so wished now.

The sailor chuckled. "You've got that right, Blackie. I've never been to anyplace else that . . ." The man trailed off. He stared at Diran for a long moment, peering hard into the priest's eyes. "You're awful talkative, you know that?"

Diran ignored the man and nodded at his backward-twisted hands. "You really should go easy on the urchin-sting. You obviously can't handle it, or you'd never become so intoxicated that you forgot to keep your hands twisted around while masquerading as human."

"My hands?" The sailor held up his hands and tried to focus his bleary eyes on them. "Ah, I see what you mean!" The man's hands twisted around and returned to their natural position.

"There, all better. Thank you for pointing that out. Now if you don't mind, I'm due to meet some friends of mine."

The sailor attempted to push past them, but Ghaji put a large hand on the man's chest and pushed him back. "My friend and I haven't finished talking to you."

The sailor scowled, but he made no further move to depart. He looked back and forth from Ghaji to Diran, and though the man's gaze was still clouded, his voice was steady as he spoke. "What do you want?"

Diran's right hand blurred and he pressed a silver dagger to the man's throat. Ghaji was well aware of how swiftly the priest could move when he wanted to, but he doubted he'd ever get used to it.

Ghaji drew his axe and grabbed the handle tight. "What's wrong with him? Is he possessed? Undead? A card-cheat?" Despite his joke, the half-orc knew Diran had a good reason for confronting the man. He always did.

"The current races that rule Eberron weren't always the world's masters," Diran said. "Millennia ago, another race held sway . . . cruel, evil beings who called themselves rakshasa."

Ghaji felt a stab of fear. He'd battled numerous threats alongside Diran, but they'd never faced anything as powerful as a rakshasa before. The half-orc examined the sailor's face more closely. His features remained human, but the face had taken on such a fierce expression that Ghaji had no trouble imagining the man to be some manner of fiend in disguise.

Diran continued speaking in the calm, detached tone of a lecturer. "The rakshasa lost their hold at the end of the Age of Demons, and over the centuries their numbers decreased. Still, some survive to this day, disguised in human form and working evil wherever and whenever the opportunity presents itself." Diran pressed the point of his dagger harder against the sailor's throat and a bead of dark blood welled forth from the man's flesh. "And the rakshasa are known for possessing reversed hands."

The sailor looked at Diran for a long moment before bursting out in laughter. "A rakshasa? Is *that* what you think I am? If I were, you'd be a fool to continue harassing me."

Diran looked a bit taken aback by the sailor's amusement, but he forged on. "I am Diran Bastiaan, priest of the Silver Flame. It is my sworn duty to destroy evil wherever I find it."

The merriment left the sailor's eyes. "I don't have time for this foolishness. If you think I'm a raskahsa, then fine. That's what I am."

The sailor's form shimmered and though he wore the same clothes, he was now a humanoid tiger, with a tawny orange coat, black stripes, savage fangs, and feral cat eyes. The man-beast growled as his left arm swept up in a blur and knocked Diran's dagger away from his throat. Equally as swift, his right hand grabbed hold of his sword hilt and drew the weapon from its scabbard.

Off balance, Diran lost his footing and fell to the ground. His hand sprang open when he hit and the silver dagger skittered out of his reach. Ghaji knew the creature wasn't about to wait for Diran to get back on his feet before attacking. The half-orc also knew that he didn't have time to raise his axe and swing it, not fast as this being was. Ghaji rushed the rakshasa, angled his left shoulder at the creature, and slammed into the man-beast's side as hard as he could.

Ghaji didn't expect the rakshasa to be a pushover, but hitting the man-beast was like ramming his shoulder into a brick wall. The impact jarred Ghaji to the roots of his teeth, while the rakshasa didn't budge. In response, the tiger-man lashed out at Ghaji with the claws of his free hand, but he only raked the half-orc's battered breast-plate, adding a fresh set of furrows to the numerous marks that scored its surface. The blow was strong enough to make Ghaji stagger backward, though he didn't fall.

Pedestrians had cleared the street to give them room to fight, but they hadn't gone far. The entertainment value of a street fight was too much to resist. They stood in doorways, in the mouths of alleys, on street corners, anywhere they could see but still have a fast means of escape should the fight end up becoming more threat than amusement. In a better section of the city, there might have been calls to summon the City Watch but not here. No one wanted the authorities to interfere and spoil their fun.

The rakshasa glared at Ghaji. "I think I'll slay you first." His fur-covered fingers tightened around the hilt of his bastard sword.

Diran lay on the ground where he'd fallen, still as a statue, looking up at the rakshasa with his cold, calculating gaze.

Ghaji couldn't help it. He laughed.

The rakshasa frowned. "Did I say something amusing?"

"More than you could ever know," Ghaji said.

The rakshasa started to reply, but his eyes flew wide as Diran hurled a dagger toward him. The blade struck the creature in the throat, but only partially penetrated. The flesh there was no longer covered in tawny fur. Instead it appeared rough and bumpy, as if it had been in the process of transforming into lizard-scale when Diran's dagger hit. Blood trickled from the wound, but far less than would have if the scales hadn't appeared. What had been intended as a killing strike had become only a flesh wound.

Diran quickly hurled two more daggers aimed at the creature's chest. The blades struck the creature, but instead of sinking into flesh, they bounced off and fell to the ground. The creature's shirt was ripped where the daggers hit, and hard lizard-scale was visible underneath. Ghaji stared as the gleaming scales began to spread across the creature's body, replacing tiger fur. The creature's feline features began to soften, blur, and rearrange until it no longer resembled a rakshasa but a lizardman. Ghaji was confused. Rakshasa were reputed to be powerful sorcerers, but were they shapeshifters as well?

The creature, who was now completely a lizardman, tail and all, raised his bastard sword, clearly intending to bring it down upon Diran. Ghaji started forward, intending to intercept the blow, but before the half-orc could strike, a feminine voice shouted out from the crowd.

"Hey, Scale-Face!"

The lizardman turned his head toward the voice. There was a loud twang, and a crossbow bolt slammed into his left eye socket. The creature stiffened and took a stumbling step backward. Armored its body might have been, but its eyes were a different matter. It reached up and clawed weakly at the bolt in an attempt to dislodge it, but it was too late. The damage to the creature's brain had already been done. The being turned to Diran and glared at the priest with its remaining eye.

"Tonight the streets of Port Verge will run thick with blood, yours included, priest."

Then a gasp escaped the creature's throat as it released its last breath and slumped to the ground, dead. Slowly its form began to change. The lizard aspect of its features melted away until the being appeared humanlike once more. Its skin was now pale grey, its hair thin and ivory-colored. The wide staring eyes had no pupils, only whites, and the face possessed only the merest hint of nose and lips.

Diran rose to his feet and looked down at the dead creature. There was no satisfaction in the priest's eyes, no delight upon seeing an enemy defeated. In fact, there was no emotion of any kind. Though Ghaji considered Diran a friend and would gladly lay down his life for the priest, it was at moments like this, the moment of the kill, when Ghaji found himself more than a little afraid of his companion.

"A changeling," Diran said.

Ghaji stepped to his friend's side. "So he wasn't a rashasa after all."

"I'd begun to suspect as much. Rakshasa are far more powerful. We'd never have been able to defeat a real one so easily."

"Easily?" Ghaji pointed to the crossbow bolt protruding from the changeling's eye. "Are you forgetting we had help?"

"Whom do we have to thank for aiding us with such a well-timed strike?" Diran asked.

Both companions scanned the crowd. Standing only a few yards away was a blond woman dressed a form-fitting leather-armor vest that left her abdomen bare, along with blue leggings, brown boots, and a dark-red traveler's cloak. She held a crossbow in her hands and wore and a quiver of bolts over one shoulder.

The blond woman stepped toward them, smiling as she came, but it was a strange sort of smile, one Ghaji had difficulty reading. It seemed to contain a mixture of happiness and sorrow, with more than a little regret tossed in for good measure.

Ghaji glanced at Diran and was startled to see an expression of wide-eyed shock upon his friend's face. In the time they'd known one another, the half-orc had never seen the priest shocked by anything. Together they'd battled horrendous creatures the likes of which Ghaji had never imagined could exist, and in all those battles, Ghaji had never seen Diran so much as bat an eye. The priest now appeared completely astonished and perhaps more than a bit afraid. For something to frighten Diran Bastiaan, called by some the Blade of the Flame, it had to be awful beyond all belief. Ghaji gripped his axe handle tightly and prepared to face whatever new threat the woman might present.

She stopped as she reached them, and she and Diran stared at each other for a long moment. Finally Diran said, "Thanks for the help."

The woman acknowledged Diran's gratitude with a nod. "It was nothing. You'd have slain him in the end. I simply helped matters along a bit."

"Don't be modest. You may well have saved my life."

The woman's smile was tender this time. She reached up and touched Diran's cheek. "It's the least I could do for an old friend."

Ghaji groaned. It looked like this woman was going to be just as dangerous as the changeling.

CHAPTER

TWO

"Why is it taking so long? We've been sitting here for almost half an hour!"

The woman, whose name was Makala, raised her hand in an attempt to capture the attention of the serving girl, but she continued past them to another table. A trio of sailors sat there, talking and laughing, and soon the girl was laughing along with them. One of the sailors, a man with red hair and a beard to match, laughed loudest of all, sounding more like a braying donkey than a human, Ghaji thought.

It was a typical dockside tavern in Port Verge. Wooden chairs and tables were sticky with spilled ale, their surfaces scored with knife-carved graffiti. The floor, covered with sawdust, soaked up whatever liquids might spill upon it. The room was lit by everbright lanterns, windows open to allow in the cool evening breeze coming off the sea. The sole ornamental touch was a fishing net strung across the ceiling with shells and dried starfish hanging in its weave. Instead of a minstrel, tonight's entertainment was an elf-woman who stood juggling in front of the empty stone hearth. She stood a touch over five feet, was slender, and had the pointed ears and elongated head common to her race. She wore her brunette hair in a pattern of complex braids, as was common in the Principalities, and was dressed in the typical garb of a traveling player: white blouse, brown tunic, green leggings, and brown boots. She was juggling ten red wooden balls in a circular pattern with graceful ease.

"Don't take it personally," Diran said. "Ghaji and I have encountered similar treatment before. People are often uncomfortable in the presence of priests, let alone one who killed a changeling only a few blocks from here."

"They're wondering if Diran really is a priest of the Silver Flame," Ghaji added, "or if he's just some lunatic who might well decide the next person who looks at him cross-eyed is a monster and start throwing daggers around the room. It doesn't help that he travels with me either."

Makala frowned. "I don't understand."

"People find us a rather unlikely pair," Diran said. "A priest and a half-orc . . . it gives them further reason to suspect I'm not truly a priest, or if I am, that I'm a mad, dangerous one."

"Well, you are dangerous," Makala said. "As for mad . . ." She trailed off, smiling.

"Forget about the others," Ghaji said. "They'll ignore us for a while and hope we get the message and leave. When we don't, they'll realize the best way to get rid of us is to serve us quickly. Then we'll drink, eat, and go, and everyone will be happy again."

"This is ridiculous, Diran," Makala insisted. "I'll go talk to

that wench and let her know that we'd like to be served—*now.*"
Makala started to rise, but Diran took hold of her elbow and
stopped her.

"Don't bother. The girl will attend to us or she won't. In the
end, it's of no real importance which she chooses."

"It's important to my stomach," Ghaji muttered.

The half-orc warrior didn't like how the evening was going.
So far, neither Diran nor Makala had seen fit to enlighten him
any further on the details of their shared history. Had they
once been lovers? Ghaji had no idea if Diran's order discour-
aged or even forbade romantic relationships. During the time
they'd traveled together, he'd never seen Diran show more than
a clerical interest in women.

Despite himself, Ghaji had to admit that Makala was an
attractive woman. Her features tended toward pretty rather
than beautiful, but she exuded a quiet strength and confidence
that drew all male eyes toward her. She was surely a warrior,
Ghaji guessed. That was no lucky strike she'd hit the changeling
with. Some men found women who were as strong, if not stronger, than themselves off-putting, but not Ghaji, and neither, it
seemed, did Diran.

How did Diran know her? Ghaji wondered. Had they met
during Diran's early days as a priest, before Ghaji had become
his companion, or had they met before, during the Last War
when Diran had served a far different master than the Silver
Flame? If so, just how dangerous did that make Makala?

Whatever the nature of their past relationship, Makala
had certainly disturbed the mental and emotional equilibrium
Diran normally maintained. The priest sat more stiffly than
usual, and when he spoke, his voice held an edge of tension.

His manner was friendly enough but guarded, almost as if he suspected Makala might be yet another creature of darkness that they'd have to dispatch, and he was waiting to confirm the fact before striking.

After they'd dispatched the changeling, an officer of the City Watch had finally appeared. He'd questioned Diran and Ghaji about the incident, but the man hadn't seemed overly concerned about the changeling's demise.

"Just another urchin-sting addict with poor judgment," he'd pronounced. The officer had taken down Diran and Ghaji's names then told them to leave.

"And try not to kill anyone else while you're in town," he'd added.

Ghaji hadn't replied. He didn't like to make promises he wasn't sure he'd be able to keep.

"What I don't understand is why the changeling acted the way he did," Ghaji said. "His kind usually prefer to avoid direct conflict whenever they can. Besides, when you mistook him for a rakshasa, all he would've had to do was show us he was a changeling, and we would've left him in peace. Instead, he transformed himself to appear like a rakshasa and attacked. Why?"

"He *was* intoxicated," Diran pointed out. "That could easily explain his erratic behavior."

"Maybe," Ghaji said, "but then what about what he said right before he died? 'Tonight the streets of Port Verge will run thick with blood.' "

Makala shrugged. "An empty threat. The man was dying and wanted to strike out at Diran one last time with the only weapon he had left: words. I've heard such words many times before, and they meant no more than than they do now."

"Last words always mean something," Diran said.

Makala looked at Diran as if truly seeing him for the first time. "You've really changed, haven't you, Diran Bastiaan?"

Diran smiled. "More than I could ever have imagined, but still not as much as I'd like."

Makala grinned. "Now *that's* the Diran I remember. No matter what, he's never quite satisfied."

Diran's smile didn't falter, but his voice became a trifle colder. "I like to think there's always room for improvement, regardless of the person or the situation. How about you, Makala? Have *you* changed?"

Makala's grin fell away, and Ghaji felt himself becoming extremely uncomfortable. Thus it came almost as a relief when one of the sailors at the next table, the red-bearded one, said, "Hey! Ugly!"

Ghaji ignored the taunt, so the man hurled another.

"Tell me, what's a beauty like her doing sitting at a table with a beast like you?"

Makala started to say something, but Diran motioned for her to remain silent. The other two men sitting at Redbeard's table laughed, but once again, Ghaji ignored the loudmouth, refusing to even look at him this time. A moment later came the sound of chair legs sliding on sawdust, and Ghaji knew Redbeard had stood up. The next sound was the clump of boots as the man walked over to their table and stood behind Ghaji.

"What's wrong, orc? You hard of hearing or just too stupid to understand?"

Though Ghaji's back was to the idiot, he could sense the man quivering with anger behind him. Still Ghaji didn't react.

Redbeard poked his index finger hard into Ghaji's right shoulder. "Hey! I'm talking to you!"

One of Redbeard's companions shouted, "Hit him, Barken! That's the only way to get an orc's attention!"

"Don't punch him in the mouth!" Redbeard's other friend said. "With those oversized choppers of his, you'd cut your knuckles to shreds!"

Laughter followed this comment and not only from Redbeard's companions. A good portion of the tavern's other patrons joined in this time.

Despite Diran's urging, Makala couldn't restrain herself any longer. "Shut your mouth before I shut it for you," she said. Her voice was cold and hard as steel, and her eyes glittered like moonlight dancing along the edge of a knife blade.

"Don't bother," Diran said calmly. "Let Ghaji have his fun if he wishes."

Makala looked at Diran as if he were crazy. *"Fun?"*

"Stop jawing and hit the ugly bastard!" someone called out.

"Not on the top of his head!" another added. "Orc skulls are supposed to be hard as rock!"

"I thought all the rock was *inside* their heads!" yet another person shouted, eliciting a fresh round of laughter from the tavern-goers.

Ghaji smiled as he stood and turned to face Redbeard. The man was short and stout, with curly red hair to go along with his bushy beard. He wore a leather vest, brown leggings, and worn brown boots. His hands were heavily callused and his face well weathered, indicating a life spent on the deck of a sailing vessel, but that was hardly a surprise. Folks in the Lhazaar Principalities viewed sailing the same way other people in

Khorvaire viewed walking. Indeed, many were more comfortable at sea than on dry land.

Redbeard carried no weapons, but his arms were thick, his chest broad and strong. Ghaji's axe was tucked under his belt, but he kept his hand well away from it. He'd been in similar situations far too many times in his life. He knew that if it so much as looked like he was reaching for his axe, Redbeard, both of his friends, and most of the people in the tavern would draw their weapons and attack the "foul orc" in their presence.

"May I help you?" Ghaji kept his tone neutral.

Redbeard stared for a moment, as if Ghaji were a dog that had begun spouting epic verse. He quickly recovered his bearings, though.

"Yeah, you can help me by hauling your stinking carcass out of here!"

More laughter from crowd.

Ghaji could smell more than ale on Redbeard's breath. Obviously, the man had been drinking stronger spirits, and Ghaji doubted the man had started his day's drinking here. Redbeard wasn't just drunk, he was seriously, dangerously drunk.

"Sorry, but I can't oblige you," Ghaji said. "I haven't been served yet, and I'm very thirsty."

"Oh, well, in *that* case . . ."

Redbeard grinned and stepped back to his table. He picked up a mug of ale, returned to Ghaji, and emptied it over the half-orc's head.

"There, that should quench your thirst!" Redbeard said.

Laughter spilled from the crowd again, but a bit more subdued this time. People were beginning to realize how ugly this situation was becoming. A few got up and began making their way toward the door, but most settled into their chairs, preparing to view the fight to come.

Ghaji stood calmly as ale dripped from his hair and ran down his face. He wiped ale from his face, then flicked the drops onto the sawdust-covered floor. "Not that it's any of you business, but my mother was orc, my father human."

Redbeard barked out a nasty laugh, but he was the only one laughing now.

"How in the name of all the Host did an orc woman manage to get herself with child by a human man? Was he ensorceled? Or just blind and lacking a sense of smell?"

Redbeard roared with mirth, holding onto his belly as if he feared his innards might burst out if he laughed too hard.

Ghaji turned to Diran. "I'm going to be busy for a while."

Diran smiled. "Of course. Enjoy yourself."

Redbeard was still laughing when Ghaji's hand fastened around his throat. The man's laughter was instantly choked off, and Ghaji lifted him off his feet. Redbeard grabbed Ghaji's wrist and tried to free himself, but strong as he was, Ghaji was stronger.

Ghaji grinned at the drunken sailor. "Why don't we continue our conversation outside?"

Ghaji hurled Redbeard through the air toward an open window. Patrons ducked as the man sailed over their heads, though the window, and out into the night. Ghaji headed for the door at an unhurried pace. All eyes in the tavern were watching him, but no one was laughing now.

Once Ghaji had departed, Diran looked at Makala. "As you might have gathered, Ghaji's had similar conversations before, and they always end the same way."

"With the other party sadder but wiser?"

"Sadder at any rate. I'm not sure anything can make that sort wiser."

The serving girl made her way through the maze of tables toward them, carrying a tray with two mugs of ale. She stopped at their table, placed the mugs before them, and said, "On the house." She waved a hand in the air over their drinks, casting a charm to cool them, then scampered off.

"Do you often get free drinks after one of Ghaji's conversations?" Makala asked.

Diran took a sip of cool ale, then set his mug down. "Sometimes."

Makala drank as well, and then said, "I must say that I'm surprised that you and Ghaji are friends. The two of you seem so . . . opposite."

"That's why we make such a good team," Diran said. He resisted adding, *Just like we did once.*

"I bet there's a story to how you met one another."

"Isn't there always?" Diran didn't add anything more. He didn't want to talk about Ghaji or himself right now. "Thanks again for helping us with the changeling. You're just as skilled with the crossbow as ever. Perhaps more so."

"You're just as deadly with a blade." She gave him a teasing smile. "I didn't realize priests were permitted to wield weapons."

"Weapons are merely tools in the battle against evil, though I'll admit that some tools are more effective than others."

Makala laughed softly. "Indeed."

"Actually, the favored weapon of my order is the bow."

Makala frowned. "You're not carrying one."

Diran smiled sheepishly. "I left it back in the room Ghaji and I rented at one of the nearby inns. I'm . . . still working on achieving proficiency with it."

"Which means you couldn't hit the broad side of a cow if it were three feet away from you."

"Precisely." He sighed. "Nevertheless, I continue to practice." A pause in the conversation came then, and both Diran and Makala took the opportunity to drink more of their ale.

When they'd put their mugs down, Diran said, "I assume you haven't come to the Principalities to kill me. You had a perfect chance to send a crossbow bolt into my back during the fight with the changeling, but you didn't. You could've simply let the creature claw me to death, but you didn't do that either."

"Perhaps I didn't want to take advantage of you while you were distracted."

"Perhaps, but I doubt it. You were never one to hesitate, Makala, no matter the reason, no matter the target." Though he tried, Diran couldn't keep bitterness he felt out of his voice.

Makala looked him in the eyes and softly said, "I've changed, Diran."

"Have you? How much?"

Makala paused to take a drink of her ale, and Diran knew she was stalling for time so that she might frame her reply to her best advantage. He knew this because he would've done the same thing. It was how the two of them had been raised.

"I know what you're asking, and the answer is I'm free, just as I assume you must be, unless the Order of the Silver Flame has taken to ordaining possessed priests."

Despite himself, Diran smiled. "You always had a way of approaching the most serious of subjects with humor."

She smiled back. "Is there any other way?"

"Your assumption is correct. The dark spirit that once shared my body was cast out some time ago." He almost said, *A spirit you enticed me into accepting*, but he didn't, though it took an effort to hold his tongue.

"As was mine," Makala said.

"Then you'll have no objection to my making certain."

Makala continued to smile, but her eyes narrowed. "What's wrong, Diran? Don't you trust me?"

"If our places were reversed, would you?"

Makala's smile faded. "What must I do?"

"Give me your hand."

Her smiled returned. "If you wanted to hold my hand, Diran Bastiaan, all you had to do was ask." She reached across the table and Diran gently grasped her hand.

It was the first time that their flesh had come in contact in years, but Diran remembered the soft smoothness of her skin as if they'd touched only yesterday. For a moment he savored the sensation of her hand in his, and though he was tempted to look into her eyes and see if she felt the same, he didn't. He had a task to perform.

He closed his eyes and concentrated, opening both his mind and his spirit, searching for some indication that Makala's own spirit wasn't the sole inhabitant of her body, but he sensed no other presence.

He opened his eyes, but didn't let go of her hand right away. "It's true; you *are* free."

"Told you." Makala allowed him to hold onto her hand a moment longer before she withdrew it.

"There must be a story there," Diran said.

The tavern door opened and Ghaji came striding in, the unconscious form of Redbeard slung over his shoulder. Despite the man's girth, Ghaji carried him easily across the common room to his table. The tavern fell silent as Ghaji pulled Redbeard off his shoulder and placed him in his chair. The man remained upright for a moment, eyes closed, face and lips swollen and already beginning to bruise. Then he slumped forward and his forehead hit the wooden tabletop with a loud smack.

Ghaji nodded to Redbeard's two companions, then turned and started back toward his own table.

"Feel better?" Diran asked as the half-orc took his seat once more.

Ghaji nodded. "We had a nice, civilized discussion and came to a mutual understanding."

Redbeard's associates were glaring at them, faces contorted in expressions of murderous fury. The serving girl came by again, this time with a mug for Ghaji. She cooled the ale, gave Ghaji a wink, then departed. Ghaji watched her go, his gaze lingering on her swaying hips. Diran didn't blame him; they were an impressive sight.

Makala took Diran's arm and pulled him to his feet. "It's getting stuffy in here. I think I'd like to go outside and cool off in the night air."

Diran glanced around the tavern. More than a few of the patrons were scowling in their direction, and some had their hands on their weapons. Whoever Redbeard was, he was evidently well liked in Port Verge, or the other patrons were simply bored and looking for a fight to entertain themselves.

"Sounds good to me." Diran tossed a few coins on the table as a tip for their server. "Coming, Ghaji?"

Ghaji looked around before replying. "I think I'll stay here and finish my ale, if you don't mind. That'll give you two a chance to get reacquainted. Who knows? Maybe I'll make some more new friends." The half-orc grinned, baring his lower incisors.

"Very well, but if you do, try not to play rough," Diran said. "I'd rather not return to discover than a justicar arrested you and shipped you off to Dreadhold."

Ghaji chuckled. "I'll play nice." The half-orc glanced toward Redbeard's table. The loud-mouthed sailor was still unconscious, but his two companions had their hands in easy reach of their weapons. "Well . . . nice enough, anyway."

CHAPTER

THREE

Once Diran and Makala were outside the tavern, Makala didn't take her hand from his arm, and he made no move to pull away from her. Though it was full night, everbright lanterns mounted on iron poles illuminated the streets. The light was a soft yellow-green that gave off an eerie glow, especially when, as now, mist from the sea rolled in. There were others on the street—couples like themselves, drunken revelers who'd likely been thrown out of one tavern and were searching for another, beggars who sat against buildings, holding forth wooden bowls and asking for whatever small coins passersby could spare.

Though it was summer, the night air was cool, and Makala drew her cloak around herself and walked closer to Diran, her hip pressed against his. Diran tried not to think about how good her body felt next to his, but he failed dismally.

"You still haven't told me what you're doing in Port Verge," Diran said.

"Neither have you," she countered.

Diran smiled. "True enough."

An awkward silence fell between them, and they continued to walk for several moments without saying anything. Finally, Makala said, "Port Verge is a pleasant town—not so large or modern as Regalport, perhaps, but it has its charms."

"Prince Kolberkon wouldn't agree with you, I'm afraid," Diran said. "He's somewhat jealous of Regalport's standing as the jewel of the Principalities. Rumor has it that he desires to build the town up until it challenges Regalport's claim to the title."

"What a shame," Makala said. "I rather like it the way it is."

Diran stopped and pointed northward. "Do you see that manor high on the northwestern hill overlooking the sea?"

The land Port Verge proper was built on was flat for the most part, with a gradual slope down to the sea, but the nobles who lived there—Prince Kolberkon chief among them—lived in luxurious manors in the hills that lay just outside the town limits. While the manors themselves were little more than shadowy shapes at this distance, lights burned in their windows, dotting the hills with points of illumination.

Makala looked where Diran was pointing and nodded.

"That's the manor home of Prince Kolberkon. It's said that from up there he can keep an eye on the entire town as well as the sea beyond."

"There are few lights burning in the prince's manor," Makala said. "I doubt he's keeping watch on much of anything tonight."

Diran smiled. "Probably not."

Though he hadn't planned it, Diran realized they were headed for the eastern docks. The tang of salt in the air grew stronger, accompanied by a slight fishy odor that Diran, who'd spent his early childhood in the Principalities, though not in Port Verge, knew came from the old fishing boats moored at the docks. Since Port Verge was a seatown, the docks were the main hub of all activity. The eastern docks were where the fishing boats put in, and numerous fish markets were located nearby. The central docks were reserved for merchant and trading vessels, with warehouses and shops located a bit further inland. The western docks were where the town's higher-ranking merchants and noble families kept their private vessels, and past those were the prince's docks, where not only Kolberkon's personal vessels were berthed but also the ships of his fleet, the aptly named Diresharks.

As they continued toward the docks, it was Diran who first broke the silence.

"So . . . why are you here?"

"Believe it or not, looking for you."

Diran was momentarily taken aback. Of all the answers she could've given, he hadn't anticipated that on. He tried to keep his tone light as he replied.

"I thought you said I wasn't a target."

"I did and you're not. Just like you, I'm no longer an assassin. Well, not *just* like you. I haven't entered into the priesthood or anything, but I no longer work for Emon."

Emon Gorsedd was a mercenary warlord who specialized in training assassins that he would then hire out to the highest bidder. Actually Emon did more than merely recruit his trainees; he acquired children, sometimes through legal means, most often not, and made them his slaves. He then trained them ruthlessly in the art of killing, transforming them into highly skilled and completely amoral murderers. To solidify his control over his young charges, Emon manipulated them into allowing evil spirits to share their physical forms. These spirits not only helped dampen the children's natural empathy so they could kill more efficiently, they made it impossible for Emon's assassins to even think about leaving him.

Diran and Makala had both been among Emon's "children." They had grown up together, as close as brother and sister. When they reached adolescence, they'd become even closer, much closer, but soon after his last mission for Emon, they'd had a falling out. Once he was free of Emon's control and studying the way of the Silver Flame, he'd often entertained thoughts of returning to Emon's compound and attempting to free Makala, though he'd never acted on those thoughts. He'd still harbored hurt feelings over their parting, and more, he feared she'd only send him away or worse, try to kill him on sight. Now he wished he'd put his resentment and fear aside and at least made the attempt.

"How did you manage such a feat?" Diran asked. "I thought I was the only one who'd ever escaped Emon by any means other than death."

"You still are. Two years ago, Emon sent me to kill a rival warlord named Grathis Chessard who'd been stealing much of his business." She smiled grimly. "Since the end of the Last War, there isn't as much work to go around for assassins as there used to be. Somehow, Chessard knew I was coming—perhaps he had a spy in Emon's service—but whatever the reason, the warlord was prepared, and when I entered his bedchamber one night, the man slew me with a single sword-thrust to the heart."

"You look awfully good for a dead woman," Diran said.

Makala laughed. "I didn't remain dead for long. Chessard's sister was a priestess, and he had her resurrect me. His plan was to place me under his control and send me back to slay Emon."

Diran nodded appreciatively. "Sounds like a good plan. What went wrong?"

"When I died, the spirit that possessed me fled my body, so when I was returned to life, my mind and soul were once more my own. The priestess tried to cast some sort of control spell on me, but I resisted and the spell failed. I killed both the priestess and Chessard then fled the warlord's home. Afterward, I made sure the word reached Emon that while I'd succeeded in my mission, I'd died in the process. As far as I know Emon believes it. At least I've never had one of his assassins come for me."

"I wish I could say the same. I also wish it had occurred to me to fake my own death. It would've saved me a lot of trouble over the years."

They'd reached the docks by now, but instead of walking alone the shoreline, as if by unspoken mutual consent they stepped onto the dock and began walking down it. Makala let go of Diran's arm and took his hand. Diran didn't discourage her.

"I knew that you'd escaped Emon too, though I had no idea you'd become priest of the Silver Flame. Once I was free as well, I had nowhere to go, nothing to do, and no idea how to go about making a life for myself. I'd spent my entire childhood learning to kill people for my master. I knew nothing else."

Diran understood.

"I was tempted to continue working as an assassin—even went so far as to accept a job in Sharn, but without the spirit inside me . . ."

"You couldn't kill your assigned target," Diran finished.

"That's right."

They reached the end of the dock and stood looking out across the sea. The wooden dock bobbed gently beneath their feet as waves rolled in toward shore, and gulls drifted on the air around them, calling softly as if in deference to the night. While sea-mist hovered close to the water, the sky was clear and cloudless. The golden Ring of Siberys was clearly visible, as were a number of Eberron's twelve moons, some full and glowing bright, others only slivers. The illumination they cast down upon the ocean made the sea-mist seem to glow with soft, pulsing light.

Makala continued. "Do you ever miss it, Diran?"

Even though he'd been expecting it, the word hit him like a jolt. For an instant his mind and body remember what it had felt like to play host to another entity. How every fiber of his being, every muscle and nerve-ending, every thought and emotion, had been intertwined with his dark spirit. The strength, the confidence, the clarity of thought and purpose were far more intoxicating than any drink or drug.

"Of course not," Diran said. "You?"

"Never."

They each knew the other was lying, but they also understood why and chose to let the matter rest there.

"Once I was free, I could no longer do the only work I was trained for," Makala said. "I no longer *wanted* to do it, so I decided to try and find the only thing in my life that had ever been good." She turned to look into Diran's eyes and placed a gentle hand on his cheek. "You."

They stood like that, gazing into one another's eyes for a long moment. Then Diran leaned forward and kissed Makala. The kiss was slow and lingering, and he savored the sweet softness of her lips. He'd feared he would've forgotten their feel, their taste, but he hadn't. Finally they broke apart and Makala put her arms around Diran and lay her hand on his chest. Diran wrapped his arms around her and held her close.

"I knew you'd been born in the Lhazaar Principalities, so I came here, hoping that one day you might return and that our paths would cross once more. I've been in the Principalities for almost a year now, wandering around, taking whatever honest— or nearly honest—work I could find, waiting and searching. Now at last my search is over."

She moved in to kiss him once more, but he drew back, though without breaking their embrace. She frowned. "What's wrong?"

"I don't know. I still . . . care for you, but so much has happened since we last saw each other . . . we've both changed so much . . ."

Makala pulled out of his arms and took several steps away from Diran. She turned her back on him, folded her arms, and stared out at the glowing ocean mist.

"What are you saying? That you don't love me anymore?" Her voice was tight with anger, hurt, and fear.

Diran felt incomplete without her in his arms, but though he ached to go to her side, he remained where he was.

"I'm saying that I don't know if we can simply pick up where we left off." He stepped up behind her and put his hands on her shoulders. "You tried to kill me, Makala."

Her shoulders stiffened beneath his touch, but she didn't reply. He opened his mouth to speak, intending to say something, anything, but no words came to him. Instead, his attention was diverted by the sight of three large shadowy forms out on the water. At first he thought they might be a trio of creatures, sea dragons, perhaps, or even gigantic water striders, but as they came closer, he was able to make out their shapes more clearly and realized that he was looking at a trio of three-masted ships. The galleons were black, gliding across the glowing sea mist swift and silent. Huge towers rose from the stern of each vessel, supporting trapped air elementals bound into the form of rings. The elementals powered the ships, sending them across the surface of the water with great speed, the finlike structures that extended from the hulls of the ships slicing through the waves like finely honed blades.

The changeling's words came back to Diran then. *Tonight the streets of Port Verge will run thick with blood.*

"I think we should leave," he said. *And go get Ghaji,* he added to himself. He had a feeling the two of them would soon have work to do.

"Give up, orc!"

"*Half-*orc," Ghaji said through gritted teeth. With a surge of strength, he slammed his opponent's arm to the table.

The crowd of men and women gathered around Ghaji's table cheered, and more than a few coins exchanged hands as bets were settled.

Ghaji's opponent—one of Redbeard's companions, a blackhaired bear of a man with brownish skin who went by the name of Machk—sat back in his chair and rubbed his sore shoulder. "Best three out of five?" he said, almost begging.

"Nothing personal, friend, but I'm not sure your shoulder could take it."

Machk glared at Ghaji for a moment, then he relaxed and sighed. "Aye, you're probably right. Besides," he grinned, "this is my drinking arm, and I'm going to have further need of it tonight!"

The crowd cheered the man's good sportsmanship, and none cheered louder than Redbeard, whose real name was Barken. Ghaji grinned in appreciation of Machk's joke, though it was one he'd heard before, and with slaps on the back from Barken, Machk got up and headed back to his table. The crowd began to disperse as well, no one evidently game to arm-wrestle Ghaji after seeing someone as strong as Machk lose to him.

Ghaji drained the dregs of ale from his mug then set it down. Diran and Makala had been gone for a while now, and he wasn't sure whether he should continue to wait for them here. Makala had left her traveler's pack, crossbow, and quiver, and he couldn't just leave them here, but he didn't feel like sitting here arm-wrestling all night either. He was still trying to decide what to do when the brown-haired elf-woman approached his table.

"Mind if I join you?"

Ghaji had always liked elvish voices. They were warm and mellifluous, with a rhythm and cadence to the words that was almost like music.

"Please, but don't you have work to do? This lot might get restless if they're deprived of entertainment."

The elf-woman laughed softly, the sound putting Ghaji in

mind of wind wafting gently through branches covered with fresh green leaves.

"Believe me, after the entertainment *you've* provided them tonight, my juggling would only pale in comparison."

She sat down opposite Ghaji and looked at him with the piercing gaze common to her kind. Though she was but a traveling player, she nevertheless carried herself with a regal air, as if she were one of the lords of creation. It was this seeming haughtiness of elves that made others so uncomfortable if not downright resentful toward them, but Ghaji had been prejudged too many times in his own life to do the same to others.

"My name is Yvka."

"Ghaji."

"I was quite impressed with how you handled yourself tonight."

"What do you mean?"

"You started your evening here with people insulting you and wishing to fight you. After a relatively short time you've become, if not their friend, at least someone they respect enough to no longer taunt."

Ghaji smiled. "I guess it's just my sunny personality."

"I would say it was due to your keen observation of human behavior and motivation," Yvka said.

Ghaji shrugged at the compliment, though inwardly it pleased him. "Being half human does give one a certain insight, so for that matter does being half orc, but I can't take full credit. I have a friend who's far more observant than I. I guess some of his qualities have rubbed off on me during our time together."

"The man in black?" Yvka said.

Ghaji nodded. "Diran Bastiaan is his name, and a finer man I've never met, though if you tell him I said that, I'll deny it. Neither of us is big on sentiment."

"Your secret is safe with me. I saw both of you earlier in the day, though I doubt you noticed me. In the merchant quarter, near the warehouses?"

"I don't remember seeing you."

"I wasn't performing at the time, just going from one tavern to another, hoping to line up some more work for the next several days. Port Verge gets its fair share of visitors, but it's still a small enough town that outsiders get noticed, especially when they're as . . . intriguing as you and your friend."

Ghaji couldn't help but feel flattered, though he knew if the elf-woman felt any romantic attraction to either of them, it was most likely Diran.

The elf-woman simply seemed curious. Still, Ghaji's instincts urged him to lie, and he hadn't survived the battlefields of the Last War, let alone his battles alongside Diran since, by ignoring his instincts. "Diran's a scholar from Morgrave University. He travels throughout Khorvaire, gathering tales and legends from each region. He hopes to eventually collect them all in a book, perhaps even a series of volumes." The lie came easily, for it was a cover story that Diran and Ghaji used whenever their activities called for a certain amount of anonymity.

Yvka's smile might or might not have held a trace of slyness, as if she recognized the fabrication for what it was. "I see. And you?"

"I protect him. He is, as I said, a scholar and not a warrior."

"Strange. He certainly seemed to have the mien of a warrior to me."

"Can't always judge by appearances."

Ykva nodded. "Indeed not."

At that moment, as if Diran had somehow known what Ghaji had said and had decided to prove his friend a liar, the tavern door burst open and the priest rushed in, followed by Makala.

"Arm yourselves!" Diran shouted. "The city is under attack!"

The taverngoers fell silent upon hearing Diran's dire pronouncement. Some of the customers looked to the priest while some looked to each other, all of them trying to determine if the man garbed in black was playing some sort of distasteful joke.

Ghaji turned back to Yvka and shrugged. He then jumped out of his chair and hurried to Diran's side, drawing his axe as he ran. Makala rushed past him, hurrying to their table to retrieve her crossbow and bolts.

"How bad is it?" Ghaji asked.

"Three elemental galleons, with at least twenty hands apiece . . . say sixty raiders in all. They've likely already made landfall." Diran turned from Ghaji to address the whole tavern. "Arm yourselves or flee! And someone tell the City Watch!"

Everyone sat in stunned silence for a moment longer, until Ghaji roared, "Move, damn you!"

They moved. Chairs and tables were overturned as men and women began running in panic for the tavern door. Ghaji stepped between Diran and the onrushing crowd, feet planted wide, axe held at the ready, lower incisors bared. The fleeing taverngoers parted around the orc and the priest like rushing river water around a boulder lodged in midstream.

The tavern was soon empty, save for Ghaji, Diran, and

Makala, who hurried over to join them, crossbow in hand, a bolt nocked and ready.

"Who are we up against?" Ghaji asked.

"I'm not certain, but I think it may be the Black Fleet."

Ghaji's expression turned grim. "Sixty raiders, you say?"

Diran nodded. "Perhaps more."

"One thing certainly hasn't changed about you, Diran," Makala said. "You never were one to be overly concerned about the odds, but three against sixty?"

"Four," Yvka said. She walked over after Makala. Instead of appearing afraid, the elf-woman seemed calm, though alert. Ghaji noticed that she'd taken a trio of red wooden balls from a pouch that hung from her belt, and though he knew the idea was ridiculous, he couldn't help but think that somehow she intended to use them as weapons.

Both Diran and Makala turned to look at the elf-woman, as if only just noticing her.

"This is Yvka," Ghaji said. "She's a . . . juggler."

Diran glanced at Ghaji and raised a questioning eyebrow.

"I'm an acrobat as well," Yvka said.

Makala rolled her eyes. "Both are *extremely* useful skills when you're fighting for your life."

"There's no need for sarcasm," Yvka said. "I don't see anyone else who's remained behind to help you."

It was true. Aside from the four of them, the tavern was now empty.

"What is this Black Fleet?" Makala asked.

"Pirates who fly under no flag," Yvka said, "they ply the Lhazaar Sea, plundering villages and ships. But their main prey is people. Young, old, men, women . . . it doesn't matter. They take gold, but it's said what they really want is blood."

Screams erupted from the street, followed by the sound of clashing steel. The raiders had come.

Without a word, Diran drew a pair of daggers and raced for the door. Ghaji ran after him, axe gripped tightly, Makala and Yvka close on his heels. The four of them burst out into the night and into a scene of complete chaos.

CHAPTER

FOUR

Dozens of raiders were attacking men and women in the streets. Steel rang as swords struck sparks off one another, and screams of agony pierced the night as those who had no weapons or possessed little skill in their use fell to the ground.

The light cast by the moons revealed the raiders to be of similar aspect. They were human, most of them bald and clean-shaven, garbed in black leather armor and black boots. Each carried a long sword in one hand and a wooden cudgel in the other. Both males and females were represented in their ranks, though since the women were also bald, it was difficult to tell the genders apart.

Directly outside the tavern, a male raider crossed swords with Barkan, the red-bearded man Ghaji had arm-wrestled. Barkan was fast with a blade, but the raider was faster, and he carried two weapons. The raider slammed his cudgel into the side of the other man's head, and Barken collapsed to the ground, unconscious or dead.

Diran's hand blurred as he hurled a dagger at the raider. The blade struck the bald man in the throat and blood sprayed the air. The raider dropped his weapons and reached up with a trembling hand to remove the dagger. Before his fingers could reach the hilt, a horrible gurgling sound escaped his mouth, and he fell to his knees, swayed, then slumped over onto his side next to Barken's still form.

One corner of Diran's mouth ticked upward in cold satisfaction. "It's like Emon used to say: 'You can always count on a well-honed blade.' "

A squad of raiders—three men and two women—had witnessed their companion's death. They broke off what they were doing and came running toward Diran and others, clearly intending to avenge their fallen comrade.

Makala's crossbow twanged and a bolt slammed into the left eye of one of the female raiders. Such was the force of the blow that the woman spun to the side and fell, dead before she hit the ground.

Four raiders were left.

Diran hurled another pair of daggers and two more raiders fell, leaving only two to press the attack. Unfortunately, they were too close for Diran to throw any more daggers or for Makala, who was still in the process of reloading her crossbow, to loose a bolt. That meant it was Ghaji's turn.

The half-orc stepped forward and swung his axe at the nearest raider. The man blocked the blow with his cudgel, and flashing a sharp-toothed grin, he thrust his sword at Ghaji's unprotected midsection. Ghaji twisted to the side to avoid the strike then swept his free hand, now curled into a fist, around in a vicious arc that connected with the jaw of the second surviving raider. The man's head snapped back, the motion accompanied by the sound of breaking bone. The second raider went limp and collapsed to the ground, neck broken, head lolling at an unnatural angle.

Ghaji didn't have time to savor his victory, for he had the final raider to deal with. The man still had Ghaji's axe blocked with his cudgel, and he'd pulled back his sword in preparation for a second strike. The man's cudgel terminated in a round ball, through it was slightly hooked toward the end. Ghaji tried to pull his weapon free, but the cudgel had caught hold of the axe head in its crook, and he couldn't easily dislodge it

Ghaji gritted his teeth and yanked his axe backward with all his strength. The raider was pulled off balance and was forced to relinquish his cudgel lest he lose his footing entirely. The raider still had hold of his sword, but without the cudgel, Ghaji was confident he could—

Before the half-orc warrior could make good use of his advantage, the raider bared his teeth and lunged. Ghaji didn't have time to think. He slammed his forehead against the raider's. The impact jarred Ghaji's teeth to their roots, but it had a far more serious result for the raider. His jaws clacked together and his teeth sliced into his lower lip. Blood splashed over the man's chin, and he let out a howl of pain.

Ghaji had earned another momentary advantage, and he wasn't about to waste this one. He swung his axe toward the raider's neck, and the man fell dead to the ground in two separate pieces.

Ghaji looked toward where Barken lay and saw Diran kneeling next to the man. Diran looked at Ghaji and shook his head. The man was beyond the priest's power to heal. Ghaji gripped his axe so tightly his knuckles ached. Barken hadn't exactly been his friend, but he vowed to kill as many raiders as he could tonight in the man's name.

Another squad of raiders came at them, seven of them this time.

"My turn," Yvka said. She stepped in front of the others and began juggling the wooden balls she carried. She started off in a slow circular pattern, but as she increased speed she shifted patterns. Soon the balls began to glow with a softly pulsing red light. The raiders stared at the crimson traces of light the balls made as Yvka manipulated them, almost as if the glowing light and ever-shifting patterns had hypnotized them. Ghaji found himself following the traceries of light the balls made. He had no desire to look away and wasn't in fact sure that he could.

"Close your eyes," Yvka said, then one by one she tossed the glowing red balls toward the assembled raiders in rapid succession.

As the balls moved away from them and closer to the raiders, Ghaji found the hypnotic pull of the glowing orbs lessening, and he was able to do as Yvka ordered. He closed his eyes just as the first of the balls exploded in a soundless burst of bright red light over the raiders' heads. So intense was the light-burst that Ghaji saw the crimson flare through his closed eyelids, as well as the two other bursts that followed. He also heard the raiders cry out in pain and surprise, the sounds of their distress all too human despite their appearance.

Ghaji opened his eyes. Crimson afterimages danced in the air before him, but he could see well enough, which was more than the squad of raiders could say. They'd remained mesmerized and wide-eyed as the balls came toward them, thus they got the full dazzling effect of the triple light-burst. They stood hunched over, rubbing tear-filled eyes as they moaned and cursed. Most of the raiders had dropped their weapons when the light-bursts occurred, and swords and cudgels littered the alley floor around them.

"Attack!" Makala raised her crossbow to her shoulder and loosed a bolt at the raiders.

Ghaji didn't need to be told twice. With a roar, he raised his axe, ran forward, and began fulfilling his silent promise to Barken's spirit.

$\bullet \ \bullet \ \bullet \ \circledcirc \ \bullet \ \bullet \ \bullet$

Pandemonium ruled the streets of Port Verge. People ran screaming as raiders pursued them. Some got away, but many more were clouted on the head by a raider's cudgel, picked up and carried away, unconscious. Officers of the City Watch fought raiders sword to sword, but though the watchers inflicted their share of wounds, they were no match for the savagery of the shaven-headed warriors. The city's defenders fell, one after the other. Those offices who valued survival over duty broke off the battle and escaped the deadly kiss of the raiders' steel, but most didn't, earning a sword strike in the back for their cowardice. Not all the citizens of Port Verge fled or remained barricaded indoors though. Men and women of varying races took to the streets, weapons in hand, and fought to repel the gray-garbed raiders, but though many of these brave people were experienced fighters, they fared little better than the City Watch. The Black Fleet raiders were simply too numerous, too fierce, and too skilled. Of the Prince's Diresharks there was as yet no sign. Perhaps they were on the water, attacking the galleons themselves, or, and Ghaji considered this most likely, word had yet to reach either Kolberkon or the commander of the Diresharks.

Ghaji, Diran, Makala, and Yvka continued fighting the raiders, and the half-orc lost track of how many they'd dispatched. The exact number didn't matter. As long as even one raider survived, there was still work to do.

Ghaji saw several raiders gang up on a half-elf sailor armed only with a long knife. While the other raiders attacked the sailor, another hit the sailor on the head with a cudgel hard enough to stun him but not hard enough to kill. The raider then hoisted the unconscious victim onto his shoulder as his or her companions went off in search of fresh game. At first, Ghaji had no idea what was happening, then he heard the sound of iron-rimmed wheels on paving stones as a wooden cart rounded the corner. Two raiders pulled it—large, muscular men as well they needed to be, for the cart was laden with unconscious bodies.

"Demon-scales," Ghaji swore. "They're *harvesting* people!"

"So it would seem," Diran said.

In unspoken agreement, the half-orc and the priest finished off the raiders they were fighting then sprinted toward the cart. Ghaji didn't look back to see if Makala or Yvka followed. He knew they would.

As the raider carrying the half-elf dumped the unconscious man on top of the other victims, Diran and Ghaji arrived. A moment later, the raider had been felled by Ghaji's axe. The two raiders pulling the cart reached for the swords sheathed at their sides, but a dagger from Diran and a bolt from Makala's crossbow stopped them. The two men dropped to the ground, as dead as their companion.

"Makala and Ghaji, stand guard while Yvka and I see to the unfortunates in the cart."

Makala frowned. "Diran, I don't remember you being quite so . . ."

"Commanding?" Ghaji offered.

"Bossy."

Diran smiled, and he and Yvka headed for the rear of the cart while Ghaji and Makala watched for raiders. The street was littered with bodies, many of them raiders dispatched by Diran and the others, but otherwise it was empty. The fighting had moved on to other sections of the city, but it hadn't moved far. Ghaji could still hear ringing steel, defiant shouting, and agonized screaming.

Diran and Yvka began pulling the raiders' unconscious victims out of the cart and laying them prone on the street. When only four more people remained in the cart, Diran said, "That's enough. We can arrange the others so they'll be comfortable enough where they're at." They did so then turned their attention to those on the ground.

Nine people altogether, Ghaji thought. He wondered just how many men and women the raiders would've crammed into the cart before deciding they finally had a full load.

Yvka began attempting to rouse a young woman barely out of her teenage years by patting her hands and cheeks, but the woman didn't respond.

"Allow me," Diran said. "Once her head injuries are healed, she should awaken without much difficulty."

Yvka looked up at the priest with a frown, as if she wasn't

used to being ordered and didn't particularly like it, but she moved away from the woman. Diran knelt. The priest placed his right hand on the girl's chest directly over her heart then bowed his head and closed his eyes.

No matter how many times Ghaji had witnessed Diran perform a healing, he never ceased to be awed by it. Most of the time he thought of Diran as just a man, albeit an extraordinary one, but when Diran invoked the power of the Silver Flame to turn undead or perform a healing, Ghaji was reminded that his friend wasn't merely some variant of magician. He was a conduit through which the holy force of Good could work its will in the physical word.

Diran's hand glowed with a soft silvery light, but before the healing could be completed, a voice cut through the night air.

"Take your hand off the girl, priest. She's our property now."

Ghaji turned to see a man striding toward them down the street. He was dressed like a common sailor—white shirt, black pants, boots—and carried a cutlass tucked beneath his belt. He was of medium height, stoutly built, bald, with a black beard shot through with gray. He appeared to be in his late fifties, though he moved with the confidence and grace of a much younger man.

The glow that enveloped Diran's hand winked out, and the priest stood to confront this newcomer.

"Who might you be?" Diran demanded.

The man's eyes seemed to smolder with crimson fire.

"Onkar, commander of the Black Fleet, and you four are interfering with our business."

CHAPTER

FIVE

Interfering in others' business is one of our specialties," Ghaji said.

Onkar came toward them, moving with a fluid grace that that seemed more serpentine than human. "So I've heard. Reports of you practicing your 'specialty' made it back to my ship. Seems you killed one of our people earlier today, a changeling. He was a good scout but something of a discipline problem. Liked his fun a bit too much, if you know what I mean. Still, problem or not, he was one of us, and I've come to settle accounts with his killers."

So the changeling that had masqueraded as the rakshasa had been one of the Black Fleet. It made sense they'd use a shape-shifter as a scout, Ghajhi thought. Too bad for them that they hadn't been able to find one that could hold his urchin-sting better.

Diran frowned. "Onkar . . . why does that name sound so familiar?"

The commander stopped within ten feet of them, and though he seemed relaxed, Ghaji could sense an underlying tension building in the man, as if he were a predatory animal readying himself to strike.

"Seeing as how you're all about to die, it doesn't really matter where you heard my name, does it?" Onkar reached for his cutlass.

Makala took a step forward, though she did not attack. Ghaji judged the distance to Onkar's head, preparing to hurl his axe and split the man's skull if need be.

Onkar looked appraisingly at Makala, then he took his hand away from his cutlass and smiled at her.

"You step forward to draw my attention in hope of distracting me from what your friends are doing. You're a spirited one, but I also see a coldness within your soul. You're one who's touched evil and been touched in return. Most interesting. I know someone who'd love to meet you." Onkar turned to Diran, then gestured at the cart which was still half full of unconscious men and women. "Keep this lot if you want. I'll be taking *her*."

The Black Fleet commander stepped toward Makala, grinning, his eyes blazing like twin crimson fires.

Makala loosed a bolt from her crossbow, but before the shaft could strike Onkar, his hand lashed out in a blur and plucked the bolt from the air.

Onkar grinned, baring his teeth and displaying a pair of ivory fangs. "Surprise," he said. He dropped the bolt. Moving almost faster than Ghaji's eyes could track, the man, the *vampire*, struck Makala with a backhanded blow. The impact knocked Makala off her feet, and she fell hard and didn't move.

"Makala!" Diran shouted. He started toward the still form of his former lover then stopped himself. He turned to face Onkar, features twisted into a mask of cold hatred.

While Onkar's attention was on Diran, Ghaji hurled his axe toward the raider commander's unprotected head. The weapon tumbled end over end as it flew at the grinning man. Though Onkar didn't take his gaze off Diran, his hand reached out and snatched the axe out of the air as easily as if it were hovering motionless before him. Without turning to look at Ghaji, Onkar returned the axe with a simple flick of his wrist. The weapon came spinning back toward Ghaji, and the half-orc barely managed to jump out of the way before the axe struck. The weapon continued flying past him and eventually came to a clanging, skittering stop in the street a dozen yards away.

Onkar didn't appear to move, but one moment he was just standing there and the next he had Makala tossed over his shoulder. "Well, it's been lovely, but I have to take my leave. The Black Fleet's style is hit and run, and now that we've finished hitting, it's time to start running."

"Hold, Onkar!" Diran raised his hand high and a silvery glow began to emanate from his palm as he summoned the holy power of the Silver Flame itself to repel the vampire. Onkar averted his gaze, but he held his ground.

"Before you do that, priest, take a look at the cart."

Diran, Ghaji, and Yvka looked at the bodies of the men and women who remained in the back of the cart. They were covered by a squirming, writhing blanket of rats, as were the victims lying on the ground.

"My little friends are just crawling right now," Onkar said, "but if you make even the slightest move against me, I'll tell them to start biting. Do you know how long it'd take that many rats to strip the flesh off their bones?"

Diran glared at the vampire commander, silvery light waxing and waning in his palm, as if it couldn't decide whether or not to be born. Finally, Diran closed his fist around the silvery spark and snuffed it out.

"Not long," the priest admitted and lowered his hand to his side.

"That's right," Onkar said. "Don't any of you try to follow me. My furry friends will keep watching you long after I'm gone." The raider commander inclined his head in a mocking manner. "A good night to you all."

The vampire turned, and with an unconscious Makala still slung over his shoulder, he began walking away. Though Onkar didn't appear to be hurrying, he moved far more swiftly down the street than he should have, and then the vampire turned a corner and was lost to the night.

Ghaji turned to Diran, intending to ask his friend what they should do next, but the priest was staring intently at the mound of vermin crawling over the unconscious men and women who remained in the cart. The rats seemed to stare back at Diran with their beady black eyes, and Ghaji wondered if the creatures truly would still bite now that the vampire had departed or if Onkar had been lying to them, in which case they were letting him get away for nothing.

"The rats are under evil's influence, though they are but pawns," Diran said. "The situation has some distinct parallels to possession, though it isn't precisely analogous. Even so . . ."

Diran raised his hand and this time the Silver Flame instantly blossomed forth from his palm. The power of the Silver

Flame blazed outward, casting its bright blue-white light onto the squirming pile of rodents. The rats screeched, squealed and began scuttling frantically over the raiders' unconscious captives. At first Ghaji feared Diran's ploy hadn't worked and the vermin were even now beginning to gnaw hunks of flesh from their victims' bodies, then the rats' exertions began to lessen until finally the small beasts stopped moving altogether and became calm.

Diran closed his hand into a fist and the silvery flame went out. A moment passed, then one by one the rats began jumping down from the cart and fleeing toward whatever shadows they could find. When the last rat was gone, Diran ran forward to examine the people remaining in the cart.

"It worked," he said with obvious relief. "Now for Makala!"

The priest took off running in the direction Onkar had taken, Yvka following. Ghaji paused only to retrieve his axe and then hurried to catch up.

● ● ● ◉ ● ● ●

Diran was standing at the end of the dock when the others got there. The priest was covered with sweat and breathing hard as he stared out to sea, shoulders slumped in defeat. The Black Fleet had set sail, the ships visible only as a trio of shadowy shapes melding with the darkness as they drew away from Port Verge.

They were too late.

Of the Diresharks there was no sign. If the Sharks didn't get on the water soon, they'd never be able to track the raiders. Makala, and everyone else who had been taken, would be lost forever.

"The question before us now is how best to give chase," Diran said. "Do we charter a ship, and if so, with what funds?"

"Maybe we could wrangle a berth aboard one of the Diresharks' vessels," Ghaji said. "They're bound to set sail in pursuit of the Black Fleet, and they might want to have a priest of the Silver Flame along with them when they finally catch up to the raiders, especially once they learn that a vampire commands the raiders."

"Perhaps," Diran said, "but there's a good chance Kolberkon will prefer to send a priest of his acquaintance along. He's bound to be distrustful of strangers after tonight's raid, so it would take some effort to convince him."

"I have a ship," Yvka interrupted.

Both Diran and Ghaji turned to look at her.

"She's not that large," the elf-woman said, "but she's fast."

"Fast is good," Ghaji said.

* * * ◉ * * *

Waves crashed against the rocks, sending sprays of seawater into the air. The footing was treacherous, and it didn't help that they were laden down with full traveler's packs. Ghaji had already fallen a couple of times, once cutting his forearm on a sharp outcropping so badly they'd been forced to pause for Diran to heal the wound. The half-orc was soaked from head to toe, and the wind coming off the Lhazaar Sea made him shiver. Both Diran and Yvka were equally as wet, and presumably equally as miserable, but neither of them showed it. The elf-woman picked her way carefully over the slippery rocks, moving with a steady confidence as if she wasn't concerned about the possibility of falling. Diran followed right behind her, and though as a human he couldn't match the elven grace with which Yvka moved, he too seemed confident, as if he scampered over wet jagged rocks every day.

Diran carried his blow slung over his shoulder, and his quiver of arrows nestled next to his traveler's pack. Given Diran's almost complete lack of proficiency with the weapon, Ghaji wouldn't have been concerned if Diran had chosen to leave the bow behind. He'd almost suggested as much to Diran before they left town, but the priest was determined to master the weapon favored by his order, and Ghaji knew he wouldn't listen.

Before long, Ghaji was breathing hard, and he wanted to ask Diran and Yvka to slow down a bit. After all, he'd been born and raised in the Shadow Marches, not the Lhazaar Principalities, and he couldn't scuttle over wet shoreline like some sort of giant crab. He was too proud to say anything, so he continued struggling along behind Diran, trying his best not to fall and hurt himself again, inwardly cursing the day he'd decided to give up his job as guard for a house of pleasure and accompany Diran on his journeys.

They traveled along a portion of the shore to the east of Port Verge. Here the ground was rocky and uneven, as the smooth sandy beaches of the town gradually gave way to the stony cliffs that dominated the far eastern side of the island. Ghaji had no idea how long they'd been negotiating the irritating terrain, but it was still night, though much closer to sunrise than it had been when they'd stood on the docks watching the Black Fleet disappear into the distance.

In between puffs of breath, Ghaji said, "Tell me again why . . . you keep your boat . . . hidden in a cave instead . . . of tied to the dock like any . . . sane and rational being would?"

Yvka called back over her shoulder. "My vessel is valuable, and I have no wish to tempt thieves by leaving her at the town docks."

"Nothing personal, but how . . . valuable can she be?" Ghaji's right foot slipped and plunged into a small tidal pool. Cursing, he extracted his foot and kept going. "From what I understand, juggling, while amusing enough, isn't exactly a profession that makes one rich."

"The craft is a gift," Yvka replied. "More of a loan, actually, which is an additional reason I'm so concerned about protecting her."

Ghaji ground his teeth in frustration. Diran had an exasperating tendency to, as the Lhazaarites put it, dive in head-first without bothering to check how deep the water was. Ghaji usually followed, despite his better judgment. He wasn't at all certain that they should trust Yvka. She was obviously hiding something. It was clear enough to Ghaji that the elf-woman wasn't a simple traveling entertainer, but what exactly she was he didn't know. Ghaji *hated* not knowing. It was more difficult to fight something—or some*one*—if you didn't understand your foe. Lack of knowledge had probably killed more men and women in the history of Eberron than all the swords that had ever been forged. Ghaji decided he'd simply have to keep a sharp eye on Yvka and watch for any hint of betrayal.

"Not much farther now," Yvka said.

Yvka continued to lead them along the shore until they reached a small cove. It was so small, in fact, that Ghaji didn't see how the elf-woman had managed to steer a ship between the outcroppings of rock without running aground. Yvka'd said her craft was small, but Ghaji figured she couldn't be any larger a common lifeboat. While she might be large enough to carry the three of them, Ghaji couldn't see how she could possibly be swift enough to catch up to the elemental galleons of the Black Fleet.

Yvka led them to the mouth of a cave that opened onto the sea. The elf-woman paused at the entrance to reach down and pick up a metal lantern lying just inside the cave. Yvka lifted the lantern's hood then and a warm yellow glow shone forth. Since she hadn't lit it by hand or uttered a spell, Ghaji assumed it was an everbright lantern.

Yvka turned to them and said, "She's here."

Ghaji peered into the cave. The light from Yvka's lantern did little to dispel the darkness within. If the elf-woman intended to spring some sort of trap on them, this would be the perfect place to do so.

"You hesitate," Yvka said. "What's wrong, don't you trust me?"

Ghaji was about to answer when Diran responded.

"Trust must be earned, and we haven't known you long enough to trust you. Besides, the only person I trust completely in this world is the man standing beside me."

Ghaji nodded his thanks to Diran without taking his eyes off Yvka.

The elf-woman didn't seem put out in the slightest by Diran's comment. "Very well. I'll go first." She turned and walked into the cave.

Diran and Ghaji exchanged looks, then the half-orc stepped forward, the priest following close behind.

The cave was larger inside than Ghaji expected. The walls and ceiling were rough and uneven, but they displayed unmistakable signs of having been carved by hand. This was no natural cave. A narrow walkway ran around the walls, providing just enough room for two people, and thin ones, at that, to walk shoulder to shoulder. In the middle of the cave was a pool of water and there, tethered by a rope tied to an iron ring set into the walkway, was Yvka's vessel.

Ghaji hadn't known what to expect, but this certainly wasn't it. The craft was larger than he'd anticipated, about the size of a sailboat, though narrower and sleeker, her bow tapering to a point almost like the tip of an arrow. A slim mast rose from the center of the sloop, the sail furled and tied down. Behind the mast was a small cabin barely large enough to accommodate a single crewperson, let alone three, especially if one of those three was a tall, broad, and slightly thick about the middle half-orc. The sloop rode several feet above water, resting atop a pair of runners that protruded from the bottom of her hull. A wooden column rose from the stern of the vessel, a thin metal ring bolted to its top.

"She's an elemental sloop," Diran said in wonder.

Yvka shone the lantern's light on the craft so they could get a better look at her.

"*Zephyr*'s something, isn't she?" the elf-woman said. "She was built by an artificer to carry supplies during the Last War. She was designed for speed in order to outrun and out-maneuver other ships, and her size allowed her to navigate past naval blockades."

"She's built from soarwood, isn't she?" Diran asked.

Yvka nodded. "It possesses magical buoyancy."

"Soarwood is quite rare indeed," Diran said. "Do you mind my asking how you came by such a singular craft?"

"I don't mind you asking at all," Yvka said with a smile, "provided you don't mind my not answering."

Ghaji frowned. "What sort of supplies could you transport with so small a vessel?"

"Dragonshards, of course," Diran said.

Yvka nodded. "Though since the war ended, she's served a different purpose."

"Which is?" Ghaji asked.

Yvka smiled again, and this time her eyes held a mischievous twinkle. "To take me wherever I wish to go."

Ghaji hated Yvka's evasiveness, but as maddening as the twinkle in her eyes was, it only served to accentuate her elven beauty. At least now he understood how she'd managed to navigate the treacherous waters of the cove. Her elemental sloop was doubtless far more maneuverable than any ordinary craft.

"Climb aboard," Yvka said.

Diran started toward the craft, but Ghaji took hold of the priest's arm and stopped him.

"A moment, Diran. I know you're eager to rescue Makala," when Diran frowned, Ghaji hastily added, "along with the other prisoners, of course, but this boat gives us all the more reason for suspicion. There's no way that a traveling player would be in possession of such a vessel." He glanced at Yvka.

"Undoubtedly," Diran concurred.

Ghaji regretted having to speak his next words, but he had no choice. "Yvka's not a simple juggler, and since she won't tell us what she *is*, we have no choice but to assume she's a criminal of some sort, a smuggler or perhaps even a spy for one of the other Lhazaar Princes."

"I am offering to help you," Yvka said with more than a hint of exasperation. "What more do you need to know?"

"At the moment, nothing," Diran said. He turned to Ghaji. "You're wrong, my friend, but not about being suspicious, though, for our elven friend is quite a mystery. You were wrong when you said we have no choice but to think her a criminal. There is another choice."

"And what's that?" Ghaji said, unable to keep the words from coming out in a growl.

Diran smiled gently. "To have faith."

Ghaji scowled.

CHAPTER

SIX

They had spent the hour picking their way through the night forest, slowly and deliberately, making no sound and disturbing none of the animals busy with their nocturnal foraging. They were shadows, creatures formed of air and darkness, phantoms flitting from tree to tree, silent and unseen.

Makala was impressed. She and Diran had been friends since childhood, and she'd known he was one of Emon Gorsedd's most talented charges. After all, hadn't it been *she* who'd told the warlord that Diran was ready for his final test? She'd never realized the profound depths of patience and concentration that her childhood friend was capable of summoning. Emon had chosen her to accompany Diran during his test and evaluate his performance, but though she was fifteen, two years older than Diran, and had passed her own final test *three* years ago, she found herself hard-pressed to match his stealth. Diran was going to make a great assassin one day, perhaps even greater than Emon himself. *If* he passed his final test, that is.

The woods were thick here, and the canopy of leaves above them blocked out all light from the moons and stars. The forest was so dark it was as if the air was filled with solid shadow, but after a time a glint of orange light became visible off in the distance. They headed toward the illumination, Diran leading, Makala following. The glint grew larger, the trees sparser, until they at last found themselves at the edge of a small clearing. Diran and Makala crouched behind a thick hawthorn bush and peered into the clearing. Actually, only Diran looked into the clearing; Makala was watching his face, waiting for him to react to what she knew waited for them here.

In the clearing, a man sat before a campfire, bedroll spread out beside him, an open traveler's pack on the ground nearby. He had no steed, which wasn't surprising given how dense these woods were, but what *was* surprising was the man's identity.

Diran's eyes widened and his lips parted as if he were about to say something, utter a whispered exclamation, perhaps, or turn to her and ask how such a thing could be possible. Sitting before the fire was their lord and master, Emon Gorsedd. To Diran's credit, he said nothing. He closed his mouth, and his eyes narrowed as he assimilated and assessed this unexpected turn of events.

As Diran's observer for the test, Makala had been the one to relay Emon's instructions, and they'd been clear enough. Enter the Wood of Erlaigne at midnight, make your way to the center as swiftly as possible without making any noise, and slay the person you find sitting before a campfire. Makala had given Diran no other information about his target, and he understood enough about the rules of the final test to know that she'd given him all the details he could and that any requests for further detail would go unanswered. Diran hadn't even known whether his target would be young or old, male or female, but now he knew. The target was male, middle-aged, medium height and somewhat stout, bald, with a thick black mustache and beard. He wore a dark crimson tunic with gold trim at the neck, sleeves, and hem, and black pants and boots made of the finest leather. Emon's weapon belt had been removed but lay on the ground within close reach.

It wasn't difficult for Makala to guess what Diran was thinking. She'd been his only contact for this "job." Perhaps for some reason known only to her, Makala was using him to assassinate Emon and this wasn't his final test at all. Maybe the test wasn't to see if he would kill Emon but rather spare him, to show that Diran didn't blindly follow orders and could think for himself. Perhaps it was simply a test of his ultimate loyalty. In the end, was his loyalty to the job or to Emon Gorsedd?

Bird and insect song drifted on the cool night air, occasionally punctuated by the pop and crackle of the campfire. Diran had paused for several seconds so far, and Makala expected him to hesitate further. She herself had paused nearly an entire minute before finally acting during her test, but Diran waited no longer. He drew a dagger from his belt, gripped it in a throwing position, then stood. His hand blurred as he hurled the blade toward Emon Gorsedd's unprotected back. The knife hissed through the air, but before it could bury itself between Emon's shoulder blades, another dagger flashed out of the darkness and knocked Diran's off course with a loud clang of clashing metal. Both knives tumbled to the ground without doing any damage, and Emon turned and glowered in Diran's direction.

"Step out into the light where I can see you, boy!"

Without saying anything to Makala, Diran walked into the clearing until he stood within three yards of Emon Gorsedd. He didn't look back at Makala, and she didn't step forward to join him. Diran had to face this part of the test alone.

"What do you think you're doing? Who hired you to betray me?"

Though Diran was just beginning his teenage years, he stood before his master with the calm, relaxed dignity of a far older man. "No one hired me. I came here on my own to take my final test."

Emon stood, teeth clenched, face red, hand balled into fists. "You fool! Why would I order my own assassination?"

"You wouldn't," Diran said, "but then, you are not Emon Gorsedd."

There was laughter, deep and masculine, from somewhere in the woods. Diran didn't seem to notice it as he continued.

"Emon would never wear such a fine tunic for traveling, nor would he wear such expensive boots. He's far too practical a man. There's also one thing that Emon Gorsedd would never do as long as breath remained in him: he would never ever remove his weapons belt. Besides, only Emon is skilled enough with a dagger to deflect another blade in flight."

"Especially when it's hurled by one as skilled as you, lad!"

Emon Gorsedd walked into the clearing from the opposite side, beaming at Diran like a proud father. The warlord was garbed in a dark brown tunic and leggings, along with a hooded forest-green cloak. Makala took Emon's appearance as her cue to step out of concealment, and a moment later she stood near the campfire with Diran and the real Emon, while the other one looked on.

Emon clapped Diran's shoulder. "Congratulations, my boy! You've passed the test!"

As soon as those words left the real Emon's mouth, the features of his double began to blur and shift. A moment later, the being that sat before the campfire no longer resembled the bearded warlord. In fact, it no longer appeared human. It wore the same clothing, but it now possessed gray skin and thin, fair hair. It had large blank white eyes, but the remainder of its facial features seemed unfinished with only a hint of nose and lips.

"A changeling," Diran said upon witnessing the creature's transformation back to its natural form.

"You don't sound particularly surprised," Makala said.

"I'm not. Only a changeling could have assumed Emon's aspect so completely." Diran turned to the changeling. "I'm glad Emon was able to intercept my dagger, Rux."

The changeling's nearly nonexistent lips formed a vague suggestion of a smile. "As am I, Diran."

Diran turned back to Makala. "You knew."

Emon answered for her. "Of course she did, boy! The final test is always the same—will you be able to slay your assigned target no matter who it is?"

"What happens to those who fail?" Diran asked.

Emon's only reply was a feral grin.

"Whose task would it have been to deal with me if *I* failed?" Diran looked at Makala. "Yours?"

She wanted to lie to him, but she couldn't, not with both Emon and Rux here, so she said nothing.

"I see." A hardness came into Diran's eyes then, and Makala felt a surge of sorrow. He had just lost a part of his childhood, perhaps the last remaining part. He now understood that no matter how much he cared for someone, or someone for him, no one could be trusted, not entirely. It was a vital lesson for an assassin to learn if he not only wanted to be able to perform his job but stay alive while doing so, but Makala regretted having been instrumental in teaching Diran this cold hard lesson. The way he was looking at her now came near to breaking her heart.

Emon broke the mood by laughing. "Come, let us sit by the fire. We'll share some drink and a few lies before we must start back home."

As they settled around the campfire and Emon began passing around a wineskin, Makala tried to catch Diran's attention, hoping that she might somehow be able to signal her feelings to him through her gaze. Diran, who'd made a point of sitting between Emon and Rux, didn't look in her direction, nor did he look at her the rest of the night.

* * * * * * *

For a long time there was only darkness: black, cool, and soothing. Though the darkness remained, it was eventually joined by two other sensations. One was movement, a smooth, subtle sense of motion experienced primarily as a gentle vibration in the floor upon which she lay—rather pleasant, actually, until it was joined by the second sensation. Pain. Her whole body ached, but her head hurt worst of all. Her skull throbbed with every heartbeat, as if her brain was a forge, and some cruel blacksmith was furiously pumping the bellows until the heat and pressure became too much and the forge threatened to explode. The pain soon grew so intense that it drove away the last soothing shreds of darkness, and Makala opened her eyes.

She was lying on her left side, and while there was light, it was dim and she couldn't see through the tears of pain that filled her eyes. Her muscles felt as if they'd turned to jelly.

Where was she? How had she gotten here? Makala tried to remember, but the throbbing in her head made it so hard to think. She remembered dreaming about Diran taking his final test, and she also recalled something about a wooden cart filled with bodies. While that was strange enough, she also remembered seeing Diran, not as a thirteen-year-old boy, but as a man twenty years older, different in so many ways yet so much the same. Had that been a dream, too? It was all too confusing, and she decided it was best not to worry about it for now. She closed her eyes and attended to her other senses.

The air was thick with the mingled smells of sweat and fear. She could hear people whispering and crying softly, bodies shifting in a vain search to a more comfortable position, chains clanking as they moved. She was a prisoner, that was clear enough, but where? Why?

She remembered the words of Emon Gorsedd, the man who had once been father, mentor, commander, and lord to her.

If you ever find yourself captured, sweetmeat, the first thing you must do is assess your situation, for only by knowing who and what you're dealing with do you stand a chance of survival.

Makala hated Emon, hated what he'd made her become. Despite her feelings about the man, she'd never rejected his teachings. They'd saved her life too many times over the years. Best to start off small, she decided. She tried to move her hands, but she discovered they were bound at the wrists. She twitched them and heard the soft jangling of chains. Manacles. No surprise there. She tried to move her feet, and as she suspected, her ankles were encased in manacles as well. Was she also chained to the floor? If not, she'd have the capability of movement, however restricted it might be, and a length of chain stretched between two wrists could make quite an effective weapon if employed properly. She attempted to sit up. The throbbing in her skull grew more intense, and a wave of weakness overcame her. She started to collapse, but instead of falling to the floor, she slumped back against a wall that she hadn't realized was there and managed to remain sitting.

She remained still to conserve her strength and breathed deeply and evenly. After a time, the pain in her head lessened until it became manageable, though it didn't go away entirely. Her tears dried and she opened her eyes once more. The light was dim, but it was enough for her to make out the shadowy forms of a dozen people or more sitting on the floor around her. Though she couldn't discern their individual features, she could tell by their sizes and shapes that they were a mix of men and women, adults, youth, and children. She had no doubt they were all wearing manacles and chains just as she was.

Makala was still dressed, though her crossbow had been taken from her or perhaps was lost somewhere along the way. The various smaller weapons she kept concealed on her person were gone as well. Though she'd been trained to kill a target with her bare hands as easily as she could with a weapon, she still felt naked, far more so than if she *had* been undressed.

She was trained in hand-to-hand combat, but what good were such fighting techniques when she could barely move?

"Poor girl. The raiders handled you pretty rough, did they?"

Makala was startled by the voice, and she turned toward it too fast, causing her head to throb anew. The voice was that of an elderly woman, but all Makala could see was a blurry outline of her form. Makala squinted, but her eyes refused to focus.

Knowledge can just be as powerful a weapon as any made of steel. Sometimes more so.

Emon's advice again, and again Makala decided to heed it. "Where am I?" she asked, her voice coming out as a dry croak.

"You're aboard one of the Black Fleet ships," the old woman said. "I believe this one's called *Nightwind*, though I don't know for certain. I overheard a couple of raiders call her by that name, but my hearing isn't what it used to be, so perhaps I'm mistaken."

Black Fleet? Raiders? The words sounded familiar, but . . .

With a rush, Makala's memories returned. Port Verge, Diran, Ghaji, Yvka, the raiders, and Onkar, who, it seemed, was a vampire. Obviously she'd been rendered unconscious and brought to the hold of this ship and put in manacles, along with the rest of the captives, but for what purpose? To be made a slave? She thought once more of Onkar's glistening fangs and another more terrible possibility occurred to her. Maybe she, along with the others around her, were meant to be *food*.

Her vision had cleared to the point where she could make out the old woman's features. She wore a simple white blouse, brown skirt, and a knit shawl over her shoulders. She had a lean face, wrinkled, but not overly so, along with curly white hair. Her eyes seemed to be yellowish, but Makala was certain that had to be a trick of the light or perhaps her own still-addled mind. The woman also had a pair of what looked like gray sideburns running down to the edge of her jaw. There was something about those eyes and sideburns that seemed significant to Makala, but she couldn't think what it might be at the moment. Besides, she wanted to know about Diran and the others.

"Have you seen my companions? Were they captured, too?" Makala gave the old woman a quick description of Diran, Ghaji, and Yvka.

The old woman thought for a moment before answering. "I was conscious when the raiders brought me aboard, though I'm not sure I count that as a blessing. I don't recall seeing any of your friends as the raiders packed us into the hold. It's possible that they're being held on one of the other two ships, but I have no way of knowing."

So there was no guarantee that Diran and others had escaped the Black Fleet raiders, but then again, there was no indication that they'd been captured either. Until she had any evidence to the contrary, she would assume they were still free.

"Tell me, grandmother, what's your name?" Makala asked.

"Zabeth. I work—worked—as a fish packer in one of the prince's own warehouses. After the fish were filleted and smoked, it was my job to pack them in salt so they would be ready to travel. I had finished my work for the evening and was on my way home when the raiders struck." Zabeth's voice became low and dangerous. It was nearly a growl as she said, "When I was younger, they'd never have taken me alive. I'd have clawed their stinking guts out with my bare hands!"

Makala was taken aback by the woman's sudden burst of anger, but then she realized—the fuzzy sideburns, the yellow eyes . . . Zabeth was a shifter. An elderly one, but a shifter never-theless. Makala wasn't all that comfortable around shifters. One never knew when the bestial aspect of their heritage would come to the fore, as witness Zabeth's sudden outburst, but Zabeth had shown Makala kindness as she'd struggled to regain conscious-ness, and Makala decided to trust the elderly woman, for now, at least.

"So how does it look?" Makala asked.

Zabeth gave Makala a puzzled frown. "Excuse me?"

"Our situation," Makala said. "How many of us are there? How many raiders? Are all of us shackled hand and foot? Is there a ladder or a set of stairs that will allow us to climb out of the hold? I assume they keep the hatch locked, but then again, they might not, not if they expect these shackles to keep us from trying anything."

"*Trying* anything?" Zabeth said. "Like what?"

Makala couldn't believe what she was hearing. "Like an escape, for pity's sake!"

"Escape?" Zabeth sounded both surprised and amused. "You must be joking! That, or your brains were scrambled when the raiders hit you on the head. There's no way we can escape. We're chained, and from the smell of blood in the air, I can tell many of us are wounded, and many more are afraid. Even if we somehow could get out of our shackles and reach the upper deck, we have no weapons and we're on the water, so there's nowhere to flee. Whether you like it or not, dear, and believe me, *I* don't, there's little we can do until we reach whatever destination the raiders have in store for us. Perhaps then an opportunity for escape shall present itself . . ." Her voice grew softer. "Perhaps."

Makala realized that she still wasn't thinking straight. Just because Zabeth was a shifter didn't mean she was a warrior. The elderly shifter's assessment of their situation struck Makala as right on the mark. There really *wasn't* anything they could do right now, save perhaps rest, heal, and regain their strength while they waited for the Black Fleet to make port. Wherever they were going, since they traveled within the belly of an elemental galleon, they should get there soon enough.

"Maybe you're right," Makala said. "I should rest."

"I'll do the same," Zabeth said with obvious approval. The old woman settled back against the wall of the hold, folded her hands over her stomach and closed her eyes.

Makala did likewise, and if she hadn't been a prisoner chained in darkness, she might've found the gentle vibrations in the wood she lay against soothing. Before too long Zabeth was snoring softly, but despite what she'd told Zabeth, Makala refused to sleep.

It was as Emon always said. *When you can't do anything else, you can still think.*

As the raider vessel *Nightwind* glided swiftly across the Lhazaar Sea to wherever it was bound, Makala thought. She thought through different escape scenarios and their various permutations so that if and when an opportunity presented itself at last, she would be ready.

Mostly she thought about Diran.

CHAPTER

SEVEN

I don't suppose that one of your priestly abilities allows you to locate sailing vessels?"

Diran's eyes were closed and his arms crossed over his chest, but Ghaji knew he wasn't sleeping. Without opening his eyes, the priest replied, "I'm afraid not."

The *Zephyr* was headed southeast, and the first light of the coming dawn pinked the horizon just above their port bow. The sloop glided swiftly across the calm surface of the sea, her soarwood runners barely kicking up any spray. Ghaji didn't particularly care for sea travel, but this trip was so smooth he was actually beginning to find it boring.

"We need to do something," Ghaji said. "We've been sailing for hours without any sign of the Black Fleet. It's a big sea, Diran. I doubt we'll just happen to bump into Onkar and his crew out here."

"Of course you're right," Diran said, eyes still closed, "but then we won't need to. Since we've left Port Verge, our mysterious benefactor has been heading on a steady course southeast into what, on the seacharts, at least, is open water, but I believe Yvka has a specific destination in mind."

Ghaji turned to look back at the elf-woman. She sat in the same position as she had for hours, one hand on the tiller, the other resting in the depression on the arm of the pilot's chair that allowed her to control the air elemental that powered the *Zephyr*.

"Is this true?" Ghaji asked. "Don't bother lying to me. I'm tried and hungry, and the only thing meaner than a tired and hungry half-orc is a tired and hungry full-orc."

"It's true," Yvka confirmed. "When we didn't pick up the Black Fleet's trail right away, I realized we'd need some help to locate them. I'm taking us to see a friend of mine who might be able to provide us with some useful information."

"Thanks *so* much for letting us know when we first set sail." Ghaji's voice dripped with sarcasm.

"I'm not one to indulge in idle conversation," Yvka said.

"Idle?" Ghaji growled. He reached for his axe as he started to stand, but Diran, still not opening his eyes, gently took hold of his friend's wrist.

"Unless you know how to control an air elemental, I suggest you sit back down."

Ghaji ground his teeth, but he removed his hand from his axe and did as his companion suggested.

"So we just sit here like good little boys and allow Yvka to take us wherever she feels like?"

"Unless you have a better suggestion."

Ghaji glared over his shoulder at the enigmatic elf-woman, but she merely looked back, silent and unconcerned. He turned back to face the bow, folded his arms over his chest, and closed his eyes. "Wake me when we get there."

"Ghaji, we're here."

The half-orc's eyes snapped open, and he regretted it as they were stabbed by bright daylight. He half-closed his eyes again and squinted at Diran. The priest was shaking Ghaji's shoulder and none too gently, either.

"Danger?" Ghaji asked in a voice barely above a whisper.

"No. Nothing immediate, at least."

Ghaji nodded and slowly opened his eyes all the way once more and took in their new surroundings. The blue sky was filled with puffy white clouds, and a cool breeze blew across the water. He and Diran were still aboard the *Zephyr*, though there was no sign of Yvka. The sloop had dropped anchor a few dozen yards from mound of black rock the size of a small island, perhaps one hundred yards across, one hundred twenty at the most. Other vessels surrounded the tiny island on all sides—one-masters, mostly, like the *Zephyr,* though there were a few two-masters and even one three-masted frigate. The craggy obsidian surface of the island was bereft of plants and animals, but it was hardly lifeless. A few dozen sailors crowded the tiny island, most standing about and talking, but some had set up small wooden tables and were loudly hawking one product or another. Gulls floated on the breeze, circling the island and keeping a sharp eye out for any morsels of dropped food they might be able to swoop down and snatch.

"Flying rats," Ghaji muttered.

Many of the people on the island cast interest-filled glances at the *Zephyr,* while others gaped at it with undisguised avarice. Could be trouble, Ghaji thought. They'd have to keep a close eye on the elemental sloop as long as they remained anchored here.

Yvka stood in the midst of the crowd, talking to a gnome dressed in the white shirt, black pants, and head scarf of a common sailor. Yvka evidently asked the gnome a question, for he pointed toward the water, and she nodded. The elf-woman then turned away from the gnome and began picking her way through the crowd toward shore. When she reached the water's edge, she dove in without hesitation and swam over to her sloop. She treaded water on the vessel's starboard side as she spoke to them.

"My friend's here, but he's out fishing right now. We'll have to wait a bit." Without pausing for them to reply, Yvka turned and swam back to the obsidian island.

"Looks like we're going to get wet, my friend."

Diran took several daggers from their hidden pockets in his cloak and slipped them into his boots. He then removed his cloak, rolled it into a bundle, and stored it in the open compartment under his seat. He then sat on the port railing and allowed himself to fall backward into the water. Diran might have been taken from the Principalities as a child, but he still possessed a Lhazaarite's grace in the water. He swam quickly and confidently to shore, barely disturbing the water as he went. As Diran climbed onto the island's craggy surface, he glanced back at Ghaji and raised a questioning eyebrow.

Ghaji sighed. Best to get this over with.

He removed his breastplate and slid it beneath the seat next to Diran's cloak. He then climbed up onto the railing and jumped off. As he hit the water, sudden shock ran through his body, for the slate gray sea was so cold here that it felt as if he'd plunged into the deepest depths of an arctic ocean. The splash he'd made upon entering the water was so loud and the spray so voluminous that everyone on the obsidian island turned to look. One wit shouted, "There she blows!" and laughter rippled through the crowd. Cold seeped into Ghaji's bones as he swam for shore, and his limbs began to feel slow and heavy. He emerged from the frigid sea, swearing and shivering.

Both Diran and Yvka stood waiting for him, and the elf-woman gave him a look as Ghaji joined them, cold water dripping off him like freezing rain.

"Don't say a word," the half-orc snarled through chattering teeth.

"Not a peep," Yvka said.

Neither Diran nor Yvka seemed affected by their time in the chill water, but then both were Lhazaarites and presumably used to the cold sea.

"If the water's this bad in summer," Ghaji said, "what's it like in winter?"

"Deadly," Diran answered without the slightest trace of humor. "Winter storms churn the sea, and the water is so cold that if one falls in unprotected and isn't quickly rescued, death occurs within moments."

"Delightful," Ghaji muttered and tried not to shiver anew as a breeze wafted over his wet body. He noted a number of rowboats that had been pulled onto the shore around the small island, the craft no doubt having provided passage for those from the larger vessels anchored nearby. Not everyone was forced to swim to shore. Lucky bastards, Ghaji thought.

Waves lapped at the shore, and the black rocky ground was littered with bits of seaweed, shells, and the carcasses of small crabs.

"Depending on the tides and the season, the isle is sometimes submerged," Yvka said, stepping over a dead eyeless fish. "Don't worry, though. This time of year, the isle won't be underwater again until nightfall."

"What exactly *is* this place?" Diran asked Yvka.

"Nowhere," the elf-woman replied.

"If you're trying to make a joke," Ghaji said, "it's not funny."

"I'm not joking. That's what this place is called: Nowhere. As Diran guessed earlier, it appears on no chart, not because it's unknown to mapmakers, but because the Lhazaar princes wish it that way."

Diran frowned. "I don't understand."

"This small isle is neutral ground and has remained thus for centuries. Legend says that Lhazaar herself originally established it as a place to meet in secret with other princes, as well as to broker political and business deals with representatives of other powers. Anyone can come here to talk about anything without fear of discovery or reprisal."

Ghaji looked around. "So all these people . . ."

"Aren't here officially," Yvka said. "At the moment there are representatives present from Princes Ryger and Mika, various Dragonmarked Houses, as well as a group of merfolk who are meeting beneath the waves."

Diran looked impressed. "And no violence breaks out?"

"As I said, this is neutral ground and those who come here are dedicated to keeping it that way," Yvka replied, "though, as with so much else in life, Nowhere isn't perfect and the tradition of neutrality is sometimes breached. We must remain on our guard at all times."

"Tell me," Diran said, "among those currently present on the isle, are there any representatives of the Shadow Network?"

One corner of the elf-woman's mouth lifted in a half-smile. "Perhaps."

Ghaji looked at Yvka. "Since Diran and I first came to the Principalities, I've heard talk—mostly whispers spoken in the backrooms of taverns—about a secret organization of spies and assassins called the Shadow Network. I'd thought the stories nothing more than lies told to pass the time and impress outlanders."

Diran didn't take his gaze off Yvka as he replied to his friend. "Perhaps because that's what the Network prefers people to think."

Yvka's mouth stretched into a full smile but she didn't comment otherwise.

Their mysterious elf friend had just become even more mysterious, Ghaji thought.

"Who have you brought us here to meet?" Diran asked.

Yvka was about to answer when there was a loud splashing just offshore.

"Him," the elf-woman said, pointing.

Diran and Ghaji turned toward the commotion and saw a large gray figure emerge from the water and come trudging toward shore. The cause of the commotion was readily apparent. The gray figure had hold of a shark's tail and was dragging the thrashing beast behind him.

"Shark," Diran said. "Twelve, maybe fourteen feet long."

The being that dragged the very unhappy shark behind him was warforged, an artificial construct created to fight in the Last War and imbued with intelligence and sentience. Like all warforged it was constructed from a composite of materials: iron, stone, silver, obsidian, and darkwood. It had three-fingered hands and two-toed feet, and its face possessed glowing green eyes and a hinged jaw to form a mouth. In addition, this particular warforged was larger and bulkier than most and had obviously been built for strength. Crusty growths dotted the surface of its body, and Ghaji realized they were barnacles. Evidently this construct spent a significant amount of its time underwater. The warforged had to have some sort of protection against the corrosive effects of seawater, and Ghaji wondered if the creature had been adapted for underwater maneuvers by some artificer during the Last War. Ghaji had fought alongside and against numerous warforged during his years as a soldier, and he'd seen many built for specific tasks, but he'd never seen one like this. As big and strong as this warforged looked, Ghaji had no trouble imagining it striding across the sea bottom and ramming a fist into the hull of a ship to sink it.

The construct stepped onto shore and continued onto the island, dragging the writhing shark behind him.

The people gathered on the island, whether to barter, argue, persuade, threaten or simply exchange information, broke off their separate conversations and turned to watch as the warforged dragged the shark into their midst. They wisely backed away to give the thrashing shark plenty of room, for the creature's jaws snapped open and closed continuously, as if it didn't want to miss a chance to sink its teeth into whatever target might present itself. When the warforged reached the center of the small island, he released his hold on the shark's tail. The fish flopped about on the rocky black surface of Nowhere and with lightning speed twisted around and fastened its jaws on the warforged's left leg.

The construct displayed no sign of pain or distress as he bent down and slammed his fist hard onto the shark's head. The beast quivered from nose to tail but didn't release its hold on the warforged's leg. The construct hit the shark two more times before the creature finally ceased moving. The warforged then pried the fish's jaws from his leg and stepped free of the animal's mouth. Several triangular teeth were embedded in the wooden portions of the warforged's leg, primarily in his ankle and calf, but he didn't seem to notice.

"This shark was disturbing the merfolk down below, so I thought I'd bring it on up and see if anyone would like it. I'd rather not throw it back since it's likely to just draw more scavengers now that it's dead."

The warforged spoke in the measure emotionless tones common to its kind, with a hollow metallic quality to them, similar to what a flesh and blood being might sound like speaking through an armored helmet.

A male shifter wearing only a pair of deerskin pants stepped forward.

"I'll take it," he said in a guttural voice. "Our cook knows how to do up a shark right."

Ghaji looked to Diran to gauge his friend's reaction to the shifter. Shifters were descendants of humans and lycanthropes, and while they couldn't transform into true animals, they could assume a more bestial aspect that granted them greater strength and speed when they wished. The priests of the Silver Flame had long ago hunted pure lycanthropes to the point of near extinction, and the Church's current position, at least as far as Ghaji understood it, was that shifters were *not* true lycanthropes and thus *not* intrinsically evil. Even so, some of the more radical priests of the Silver Flame were still suspicious of shifters, if they didn't outright despise them. Diran had never evidenced any prejudice toward shifters since Ghaji had known him, but then again, he didn't seem overly fond of them either. Aside from a slight pursing of his lips, Diran showed no reaction to the shifter's presence.

The warforged nodded to the shifter and picked up the dead shark as if it weighed nothing, though Ghaji guessed the beast must weigh a thousand pounds or more. The construct followed the shifter over to one of the rowboats resting at the shore's edge. The shifter pushed the boat back into the water and the warforged waded into the surf alongside it, still holding onto the shark. The shifter tied a rope around the tiger shark's tail and then the warforged placed the dead fish in the water. The shifter began rowing toward one of the two-masted vessels anchored offshore, towing the shark behind him. As the shifter rowed past the *Zephyr*, he gave the elemental sloop an appreciative, and Ghaji thought somewhat covetous, look. The shifter continued past the *Zephyr*, rowing with swift, strong strokes, no doubt wishing to get the shark to his vessel before any other hungry sea creatures were attracted by its corpse.

The warforged turned and headed back to shore, and Yvka stepped forward to greet him.

Warforged had no facial muscles with which to express their feelings, but the construct's voice contained hints of both surprise and pleasure as he said, "My friend! What are you doing here?"

The elf-woman stepped up to the warforged and reached up to put her hand on his shoulders in greeting. The warforged made no move to touch her, which Ghaji thought wise. The construct might well crush the slender elf-woman if he tried to embrace her.

"I got tired of trying to find work in Port Verge, so I thought I'd try Skairn, and if that doesn't work out, maybe Tantamar. I tell you, Flotsam, it's getting damned difficult for a juggler to find honest work these days."

"Indeed," Flotsam replied. He lowered his voice before continuing. "Your employment situation must be most dire for you to risk bringing the *Zephyr* out into the open."

"It is," Ykva said. "I thought I'd stop here along the way on the off-chance you'd be about. I'm glad I did."

"As am I." Flotsam turned his head to look at Diran and Ghaji. "I saw you standing next to those two a moment ago. Friends of yours?"

Ghaji detected a deeper question beneath the warforged's words, and he sensed that if Yvka said no, Diran and he would be in big trouble.

"They are." She led Flotsam over to Diran and Ghaji. "These two gentleman were in need of passage, and I was happy to give them a ride." She smiled. "For a fee, of course."

"Naturally," the warforged said.

Ghaji frowned. Yvka had made no mention of a fee before this.

"I am pleased to meet you, Flotsam," Diran said. "My name—"

" —is Stendar," Yvka quickly said, "and his half-orc companion is Thon. They are agents of a Sharn merchant who specializes in importing unique and exotic items. They've been traveling the Principalities searching for new wares to add to their employer's stock."

The warforged nodded. "I see. It is good to meet both of you. Any friend of Ardella's is a friend of mine."

Flotsam stuck out a large three-fingered hand for them to shake. Diran did so, then Ghaji. Touching the warforged's hand was like touching that of a living statue, but at least Flotsam was careful to keep his grip gentle.

"How has your trip been?" Flotsam asked. "Have you met with much success?"

"Some," Diran said, "but not as much as we'd like."

"Ah. Well, perhaps your fortunes will change for the better now that you travel with Ardella. She's something of a good luck charm."

"Really?" Ghaji muttered. "I hadn't noticed."

Flotsam turned to look at Ghaji, the green fire in his eyes burning more intensely.

"He's jesting," Yvka said. Then in a mock-whisper, she added, "In truth, I think he has a crush on me."

Ghaji blushed but said nothing.

Flotsam looked at the half-orc a moment longer before the green glow in his eyes dimmed to its normal intensity. The warforged turned to face Yvka once more. "What news do you bring from Port Verge?"

"Bad news, I fear," Yvka said. "Last night the Black Fleet struck the town."

Though Yvka kept her voice quiet, a number of the other

people on the island turned in their direction, and the news was quickly picked up and spread throughout the crowd.

"Bad news indeed," Flotsam said. "Were Prince Kolberkon's Diresharks able to capture any of the raiders?"

"Not that I'm aware of," Yvka said, "but then we departed soon after the raid ended."

"I see. I'm glad that you three managed to escape the Black Fleet," Flotsam said.

"One of our companions did not," Diran said grimly.

"You have my condolences."

"We'd like more than that," Yvka said. "Might you tell my friends the stories you've heard about the Black Fleet?"

Flotsam hesitated for a moment before responding, as if he were carefully considering his reply. "I was under the impression that you, as well as certain mutual associates of ours, had discounted those tales."

"We had," Yvka said, "but last night I saw some things that cast new light on your information."

"Ah! In that case, I'd be more than happy to tell you what I know. Let us sit and talk."

Ghaji eyed the craggy surface of Nowhere doubtfully. Simply sitting down might be fine for Flotsam; he didn't have a flesh-and-blood behind. The large warforged sat, and so did Diran and Yvka, so Ghaji did as well, grimacing as he settled onto the hard, uneven rock.

"As Ardella may or may not have told you, I spend a great deal of my time on Nowhere, either atop the island's surface or beneath the waves. I see and hear many interesting things . . . things that often prove of value to my friends."

Ghaji was beginning to understand. If Yvka was a member

of the Shadow Network, then perhaps Flotsam was too. What better place to station a spy than here, an uncharted island in the middle of the Lhazaar Sea where powerful people from across Khorvaire and beyond met to deal and scheme under the protection of neutrality?

"I would think your constant presence wouldn't go unnoticed by those who come here," Diran said.

"It doesn't, but as the story goes, I was marooned here toward the end of the Last War. I found this location soothing after so many years of conflict, so I rejected any offers of rescue from passing vessels. After a time I came to be considered the unofficial caretaker of Nowhere, a role I do my best to fulfill."

Diran smiled. "As the story goes."

Flotsam nodded.

"And some of the interesting information you've acquired relates to the Black Fleet," Diran said.

"What I have to tell you was cobbled together from bits and pieces of stories told by dozens of travelers. Keep in mind also that Ardella's and my friends ultimately discounted the information, but judge for yourself. The tale begins over forty years ago, with a man called Erdis Cai."

"The explorer?" Ghaji said. Even he'd heard of the legendary sailor Erdis Cai who'd adventured throughout the world's seas.

"The same," Flotsam confirmed. "Forty years ago, Erdis Cai and his entire crew were lost when their ship, the *Seastar,* disappeared in the harsh waters of the north. Erdis Cai and his crew were never seen or heard from after that, and all were presumed dead. Decades passed, and one dark night three elemental galleons flying black sails appeared on the Lhazaar and began raiding small seaside villages, taking little of value save for the people that lived there."

"The Black Fleet," Ghaji said.

"The Fleet always struck at night and chose a different target every time," Flotsam continued, "but their raids, as swift and devastating as they were, left behind survivors—not many, perhaps, but enough. They told of raiders dressed in gray and black, men and women with shorn heads, and they told of the fleet commander, a man named Onkar."

Diran slapped his hand on his knee. "I *knew* that name was familiar! Onkar was the name of Erdis Cai's first mate!"

Ghaji frowned. "Are you saying that the Onkar we faced was the same man who sailed with the *Seastar* forty years ago? That would make him eighty years old at least!"

"If Onkar is a vampire, his age would be irrelevant since he would not physically grow older," Diran said. "You should know that by now, Ghaji, given how many undead you've slain at my side."

"True," Ghaji said, "but then again, Onkar isn't all that uncommon a name. *Our* Onkar doesn't have to be *the* Onkar, if you know what I mean."

"It could be coincidence," Diran allowed, "or a simple mistake on the part of the survivors. Terrified people don't always make the best witnesses."

"I cannot dispute your words," Flotsam said. "I can only pass along what I have learned."

"Let's assume for a moment that Erdis Cai is behind the Black Fleet raiders," Diran said, "perhaps as the master vampire with Onkar as his disciple?"

Ghaji shrugged. "I suppose Erdis Cai and his crew wouldn't

be the first adventurers to stumble upon a nest of vampires." The half-orc let out a snorting laugh. "Look how often it happens to us."

"Except when they stumbled out again, they were transformed," Diran said, "and not for the better."

"So Erdis Cai and his crew are vampires and the other raiders are their human servants?" Ghaji asked.

"I believe so," Diran said. "Perhaps Erdis Cai has promised to reward them with immortality if they serve him well."

"If all this is true," Ghaji said, "why go about raiding as the Black Fleet? Why draw attention to yourself at all? If the Lhazaar Princes were to pool their resources and go after the Fleet, which they will likely soon do if the raids keep up, the Fleet would be crushed. There has to be an easier, less risky way for Cai to obtain their food."

Diran thought for a moment. "Perhaps they aren't abducting people for their blood, or at least, not only for it. Perhaps they have another reason, one that's worth the risks they take."

A dark scowl came over Diran's face, and Ghaji knew he was thinking about Makala and wondering if she was still alive. Ghaji wished he could say something to reassure his friend, but he could think of nothing.

"That makes sense," Yvka said. "Over the months the Black Fleet has been striking at increasingly larger targets. Port Verge was the largest so far."

"Maybe the raiders are simply getting more confident," Ghaji said.

"Perhaps they're working to some manner of timetable," Diran said, "and they need to abduct as many people as they can as swiftly as possible."

"This talk is all well and good," Ghaji said, "and who knows? Some of it might even be true, but what use is it to us? If Erdis Cai is the vampire lord of the Black Fleet, how does knowing this held us find him?"

"It doesn't," Yvka said.

Flotsam cocked his head in a way that made him seem as if he were thinking. "I believe I might know of someone who might be able to lead you to Erdis Cai. He is a human named Tresslar, an elderly artificer who serves on Dreadhold. According to rumor, as a young man he sailed with Erdis Cai. If anyone could tell you more about Cai, it would Tresslar. Assuming the rumors are true, of course."

"Very well," Diran said. "Then we shall set sail for Dreadhold at once. Thank you, Flotsam, for . . ." The priest broke off, his eyes widening. "The shifter is trying to steal the *Zephyr!*"

Ghaji, Yvka, and Flotsam turned to look seaward. Sure enough, the shifter who had taken the shark from Flotsam was now aboard the *Zephyr*, swiftly hauling up the anchor. Two others stood on the deck of the sloop: A barechested, dark-skinned man covered with brightly colored concentric tattoos and a half-elven female with long blond hair who wore a green skirt and a top that left her midriff bare. They were all dripping wet, and it was no great leap of logic to guess that the shifter and his compatriots had swam silently from their ship to the *Zephyr* and stealthily climbed aboard. As the shifter worked to bring up the anchor, his two companions, both armed with bows, kept watch. The message was clear: if anyone tried to stop the thieves, they'd make the sudden acquaintance of the business end of an arrow.

Flotsam started to rise, but Yvka grabbed his arm and pulled him back down.

"Why did you do that?" the warforged asked, sounding more puzzled than angry. "Arrows can't harm me."

"True," Yvka said, "but you'd never reach the *Zephyr* in time. They can't activate and control the air elemental, but they can use the oars to row the boat far away enough that you won't be able to get to it."

Ghaji figured the thieves would tie the *Zephyr* to their two-master then tow the elemental sloop someplace where they could sell it for a handsome price.

"They can't have it," Diran said. "I need that craft if I'm to have any hope of finding Makala." A wild gleam came into Diran's eyes then, and Ghaji groaned, for he knew his friend had just had an idea.

Without taking his gaze from the thieves, Diran said, "Ghaji, your axe is still aboard the *Zephy*r, isn't it?"

"Under one of the seats," the half-orc confirmed.

"Get ready to grab it as soon as you're back aboard."

Before Ghaji could ask his friend just what he was talking about, Diran spoke to Flotsam. "When I give you the signal, I want you to pick Ghaji up and hurl him onto the *Zephyr*. Are you strong enough to do that?"

"Yes," Flotsam said, without any hint of ego or boasting, merely stating a fact.

"Well then," Diran said, "get ready."

Ghaji wished they had time to discuss alternative plans, especially ones that didn't involve him being thrown like a ball by a barnacle-encrusted warforged, but there was no time. A quick glance showed Ghaji that the crew of the two-master was already frantically scurrying about, preparing to set sail and leave Nowhere, and the rightful owner of the *Zephyr,* far behind.

"Now!"

Diran stood, drawing a pair of daggers from the leather strap around his chest as he did. As he straightened to his full height, he hurled the daggers toward the *Zephyr* and the thieves who now trod her decks. Ghaji presumed the blades streaked toward their targets, but he didn't see if they did, for Flotsam scooped him up with his thick metal and stone arms as if the half-orc were but an infant. The huge warforged spun around twice to build up momentum, then he released Ghaji into the air.

The world became a rushing blur as Ghaji ascended, and it felt as if his stomach sank to the bottoms of his feet. He straightened his arms out before him, his legs behind, as if he were preparing to dive into water. Though there was plenty of the wet stuff for leagues in all directions, he was hoping to land on a soarwood deck. He reached the apex of his flight and began to plunge downward. Now his stomach felt as if it were pressing against the back of his throat, perhaps in a desperate attempt to escape before the fool who controlled their mutual body managed to get both of them killed.

Ghaji saw the deck of the *Zephyr* rapidly approaching. The tattooed man clutched the hilt of a dagger protruding from his left shoulder, blood streaming from the wound and pouring over his fingers. The half-elf had crouched down to make herself a smaller target and was swiftly drawing arrows from her quiver, nocking and loosing them with speed and grace. If she'd been wounded by one of Diran's daggers, she showed no sign of it. The shifter had gotten the anchor up and was now fitting the oars to the oarlocks. Of the three thieves, Ghaji would've liked to take out the half-elven archer first, but his trajectory wasn't carrying him toward her. It was, however, taking him straight toward the wounded man.

Flying half-orcs can't be choosers, I guess, Ghaji thought, then he balled his hands into fists and slammed into the tattooed man.

The dark-skinned thief howled in pain and fury as he and Ghaji crumpled to a heap on the deck. Ghaji heard the harsh, brittle sound of snapping bones, and he hoped they weren't his. The impact had, however, knocked the wind out of Ghaji, and gasping for breath, he rolled off the tattooed man and reached for the compartment where he'd stowed his axe. He managed to close his fingers around the haft just as he heard the twang of a released bowstring. He rolled to the side as an arrow sank into the wooden deck after passing through the space where his throat had been an instant before. As he came up onto his feet, he brought the flat of his axe head up and deflected another arrow.

The half-elf stood facing him, already nocking another arrow. Ghaji was about to throw his axe at her, when her eyes went wide and she stiffened. She released her grip on her bow and it clattered to the deck, arrow undrawn and unreleased. The woman took a step toward Ghaji, her mouth working but no sound coming out. She pitched forward, and as she fell to the deck, Ghaji saw the hilt of a dagger protruding from between her shoulder blades.

Ghaji knew he had Diran to thank for saving him, but he had no time to spare for even a grateful wave. He heard a growl and turned just in time to meet the shifter's charge. The man had assumed his more bestial aspect; his eyes were feral yellow, his teeth longer and sharper, fingers now hooked into deadly

claws, and his body hair had grown wild and shaggy, more like
wolf fur than human hair. Often the mere sight of such a transformation was enough to startle a shifter's opponent, causing
him or her to hesitate for one fateful second . . . and a second
was all any shifter needed.

Ghaji had faced many shifters on the battlefields of the Last
War, and he'd fought far more fearsome foes since joining up
with Diran. Thus the half-orc didn't hesitate as the shifter came
lunging toward him. He didn't have time to swing his axe, but
he was able to bring it up in time for the shifter to slam face-first
into the flat of the axe-head. The shifter staggered back, nose
gushing blood.

"Leave now and I'll forget I ever saw you," Ghaji offered.
"Stay and die."

The shifter glared at Ghaji with his amber eyes and licked
at the blood covering his upper lip.

"Big talk from a half-breed," the shifter snarled.

Ghaji's grip tightened on his axe. "Now *that* was the wrong
thing to say."

He stepped forward and swung his axe in a vicious arc at
the shifter's neck. The shifter leaned backward just in time to
avoid having his throat sliced open. He countered with a swipe
of his claws aimed at Ghaji's face, but the half-orc brought his
left arm up to block the blow. Ghaji had allowed the momentum
of his failed axe swing to bring the weapon around, and now
he brought the axe up over his head and slammed it down on
the shifter's. The sharp blade sliced through the shifter's scalp,
shattered the top of his skull, and bit into the soft pulpy mass
within.

The shifter stopped fighting and stood looking at Ghaji,

blinking several times in an expression of bewilderment, as if he couldn't quite understand what had happened to him.

"Oh," the shifter said, as if something profound had just occurred to him. Then his eyes rolled white and he collapsed to the deck, his ruined brain making a wet sucking sound as gravity drew it away from Ghaji's blood-smeared axe-head.

Ghaji didn't pause to savor his victory over the shifter. He turned to check on the tattooed man, and good thing, too, for the wounded thief was on his feet and moving toward Ghaji, his features twisted into a mask of rage, Diran's dagger still embedded in his shoulder.

Ghaji waited for the man to get closer, and when he was near enough, the half-orc stepped aside from the railing. Unable to stop his approach, the tattooed man slammed into the railing, pitched over, and fell toward the water, bellowing his anger and frustration. His bellow didn't last long, however, for it was cut off as soon as he plunged into the sea.

Still holding his axe, Ghaji stepped back to the railing and looked over. A series of ripples spread out from where the tattooed man had sunk. Ghaji watched, waiting for the man to swim back up to the surface, planning to offer him the same choice he'd given the shifter. Ghaji waited . . . and waited . . .

A fountain of bubbling froth broke the surface, and an instant later the foamy white turned crimson. The tattooed man's head bobbed above the water, and his mouth opened wide to scream. Before any sound could come out, the maw of a large grayish-white shark much larger than the one Flotsam had caught rose up behind the man and snapped its jaws down on his head. The shark then disappeared beneath the water, taking the tattooed man with it and leaving behind nothing but a roiling mass of blood and seafoam.

Looks like the shark Flotsam caught wasn't the only one plying the waters around Nowhere, Ghaji thought. He had a sudden thought and turned to look at the dead bodies of the shifter and the half-elf. The corpses needed to be disposed of, so why not a burial at sea? Maybe the big shark had a few hungry friends.

Ghaji started toward the bodies.

CHAPTER

EIGHT

Interesting?"

Diran looked up from the large book spread open on the table before him. Makala stood on the other side, leaning forward, hands pressed to the smooth, polished surface of the table. She was wearing a low-cut white dress, and the way she was standing afforded Diran an excellent view. He tried not to look, especially because he suspected Makala *wanted* him to look, but he couldn't help sneaking a quick glance. Makala smiled.

"It's diverting enough," Diran said, instantly regretting his choice of words. Ever since he'd passed his final test almost a year ago, Makala had taken to teasing him in ways that made him uncomfortable, and he didn't want to make it any easier for her by providing straight lines like that.

For once Makala let the opportunity pass.

"What is it?"

"A history of the Lhazaar Principalities where I spent my early childhood. I suspect much of it's hyperbole, especially the more recent sections devoted to the exploits of the explorer Erdis Cai, but . . ." Diran trailed off as Makala burst out laughing. He scowled. "What's so amusing?"

"You," she said, her tone half-affectionate, half-teasing. "You always were something of a bookworm, but you've been spending so much time in here lately that you're starting to talk like one of these musty old tomes!"

Diran couldn't help smiling. "I like it here in the library. It's quiet and peaceful, and it provides an opportunity for me to gather my thoughts. It's somewhat like meditation for me, I guess." He shrugged. "Besides, you know Emon encourages us to spend as much of our spare time reading as possible."

"I know. 'There is no such thing as useless information, my darlings.' " She did a passable imitation of Emon's voice, and though Diran had heard her do it before, he laughed just as he always did.

"Sometimes I think you're more suited for the life of a scholar than that of an assassin," Makala said, clearly teasing now.

Diran didn't rise to her bait this time, for truth was, he sometimes thought the same thing himself.

The library was the second largest room in Emon Gorsedd's manor home, the first being the room where the warlord's charges trained in the deadly arts of assassination. Emon was a firm believer that a well-honed mind was an assassin's most important weapon, so he collected books and scrolls on every subject conceivable, and he expected his disciples to master the knowledge contained in the written word just as he expected them to master their blade work.

The library's walls were lined with bookshelves that reached all the way to the room's high ceiling almost thirty feet overhead. Numerous ladders were stationed throughout the library to provide access to reading material stored on the higher shelves. Painted on the ceiling was a detailed mural of the great dragons that represented the three parts of the world: Siberys, the Dragon Above; Khyber, the Dragon Below; and Eberron, the Dragon Between. Polished mahogany tables with soft leather chairs were spread throughout the room, but while there usually were at least two or three others present reading and doing research, today Diran and Makala were the only ones. In the middle of the room was a round table with an intricate map of Khorvaire carved into its surface. Whenever an assassin's mission took him or her far enough from the manor grounds, Emon would always brief them on their travel route using the map table. Though he'd passed his final test, Diran had never been assigned a mission that took him that far away from home, but perhaps one day soon . . .

"I bet I can think of something more interesting to do than reading history."

Makala came around to Diran's side of the table and sat on the arm of his chair. She crossed her legs, the motion revealing that her white skirt was slit up the side to her mid-thigh. This time Diran didn't even try to pretend that he wasn't interested in the sight of Makala's bare leg.

"What sort of things?" he asked.

Makala leaned forward and closed the book Diran had been reading. She then turned back to him and said, "I was thinking of something like this." She put her arms around Diran's neck and kissed him. The kiss was long and slow and altogether wonderful. Diran had no idea how long the kiss lasted; he only knew that he was sorry when it was over.

Makala pulled away, but she kept one arm draped over his shoulders.

"You'd better be careful," Diran said. "Quellin might suspend both of our library privileges if he catches us like this."

Quellin was an elderly scholar whom Emon employed to oversee and maintain his collection of volumes. He was a quiet man with a sour disposition who acted as if Khorvaire would be a much finer place if all the people vanished overnight so there'd be no one to get fingerprints on the vellum pages of his precious books or mis-shelve them once they were finished reading. There was something else about Quellin that bothered Diran, though he couldn't quite pin it down. Sometimes Diran would catch the elderly scholar looking at him with an expression of dark amusement, as if the man harbored a secret that he couldn't wait to share.

Since Diran was quiet and always careful with the books, most of the time Quellin left him to his own devices. Sometimes, like today, he'd even step out of the room for a time while Diran read. Where the old scholar went and what he did, Diran didn't know and didn't care. He was just grateful not to have Quellin hovering about, just waiting for him to crinkle or, Sovereigns forbid, tear a page.

"I think Quellin has more important tasks to attend to right now than come check on his favorite reader. C'mon." Makala slid off the chair arm, then took Diran by the hand and pulled him onto his feet.

"What are you up to?" Diran said suspiciously.

Makala gave him a sly smile. "You'll see."

She continued pulling Diran by the hand, leading him toward the back of the library. He had no idea what she had in mind. There was nothing in the back of the room except a wall of bookshelves crammed with reading material, but Diran didn't care. He felt a mounting excitement with each step further that Makala led him, and he knew that at this moment he'd follow her into a nest of basilisks if she asked.

When they reached the back row of shelves, Makala stopped and released Diran's hand. "You see that thick volume on the middle shelf . . . the one with the gold filigree on the spine?"

"Yes."

"Remove it."

Diran's earlier ardor began to wane. The last time Makala had led him somewhere was during his final test. There were no other rites of passage for Emon's students, at least none that he knew of, but this situation was starting to feel all too familiar. Still, he did as Makala asked and pulled the volume she'd identified off the shelf. As he did so, he glanced at the title: *From Beyond: Extraplanar Entities and Otherworldly Manifestations.* He didn't recognize the author's name, but the title was intriguing.

Makala reached past Diran and slid her hand into the space the book had occupied. She reached all the way to the back of the shelf and then pushed. There was a soft click and she quickly withdrew her hand.

"Step back," she warned, doing so herself.

Diran did likewise, and the bookshelf swung slowly outward to reveal an open doorway beyond, with stone steps leading down into darkness. He supposed he should've been surprised, but he wasn't. He'd been a ward of Emon Gorsedd too long to be surprised my much of anything.

"I take it we go down," he said.

"Of course. Put the book back on the shelf first, though. We don't need it anymore. The door will close when we set foot on the third step." She smiled. "Besides, Quellin would have a fit if you left it lying on the floor or worse, brought it with you."

Diran slid the volume back into its proper place on the shelf then followed Makala through the doorway. As soon as Makala's foot touched the third step from the top, the door-shelf began to swing closed. There was no light in the stairwell, and when the door closed all the way, they were left in complete darkness.

"Too bad I don't have a lantern on me," Diran said.

"We don't need any light. The way is safe and we don't have far to go. There's no railing, but it helps if you put both hands on the walls as you go down."

He heard Makala's footfalls as she started down the stairs. As she'd advised, he stretched out his arms, touched his hands to the walls on either side of him, and followed. Diran counted the steps, something that had been ingrained in him by Emon's training. After the thirteenth step they reached the bottom.

Makala's hand found his in the darkness and she gave him a gentle squeeze.

"We have but a short hallway to cross, then we'll reach another door. I can't tell you what lies behind it, but I can tell you this: be strong."

Diran felt her lips brush his, then she released his hand and started down the dark hallway. After only a second's hesitation, Diran followed. Twenty steps later, he caught up to Makala. He heard the click of a door latch, then bluish-white light spilled into the hallway. Diran squinted to keep his eyes from being dazzled after walking through total darkness. He didn't close them all the way, though. He'd been trained better than that.

The light was soft but enough to reveal the details of the

hallway, the open door, and Makala, who stood in the doorway, a solemn expression on her face. The hall was made of gray stone, the door oak with thick iron bands around the edges. Diran knew this place lay beneath Emon Gorsedd's home, but as to what it was, Diran hadn't a clue. He'd never heard anyone speak of an underground chamber, had never suspected its existence.

He looked at Makala for some hint as to what he should do next, but she just continued looking at him without expression. No real help there, but then, he supposed he didn't need any. He walked past Makala and through the open doorway.

Inside was a large chamber with smooth rounded walls and a domed ceiling. Light came from globes of mystic energy that hovered in the air near the walls. Curved wooden risers lined the walls on both sides of the chamber, and sitting on them were men and women, all looking at him with the same impassive expression Makala had worn. Many of the people were unfamiliar to Diran, but there were many that he recognized. All of them were older than he—some quite a bit so—and all of them were Emon's "children," as the warlord liked to call them: assassins who plied their trade for whatever clients Emon chose. Emon himself sat among them on the right side of the room, front row, center. There was an empty place beside Emon, and Diran had a good notion whom it was reserved for. His suspicion was confirmed when he heard the door close, then Makala walked past him and sat down next to Emon. The master assassin, unlike all the others, didn't affect a neutral expression. He was smiling broadly, looking for all the world like a proud father.

In the center of the chamber was a large obsidian table. The blue-white light of the mystic globes gleamed off its highly polished surface, making the table seem to glow with its own internal power. There were runnels carved along each side, and Diran didn't want to guess what they were for.

Standing behind the table was the librarian Quellin, though instead of his normal tunic and leggings he wore a hooded black robe. The old man usually displayed little emotion other than irritation or impatience, but the eyes beneath his bushy white brow shone with eager anticipation, and the mouth set in the midst of his full ivory beard was stretched into a dark smile. It was the first time Diran could remember seeing a smile of any kind on the librarian's face, but the most striking feature in the chamber lay behind Quellin. It was an altar that rose nearly to the ceiling, carved out of the same black stone as everything else in the chamber. Six figures rose from the altar's base, the statues rendered in crude detail, but no less recognizable for it. These were stone images of the Dark Six, gods of foulness and evil all: the Devourer, the Fury, the Keeper, the Mockery, the Shadow, and the Traveler. As with the table, the light from the globes played across the statues, gathering within their eyes and making it seem as if the Six were alive and staring at Diran, curious to see what he would do next.

No doubt the sensation the statues were watching him was solely due to his own imagination, but there were plenty of real eyes looking at him, Makala's and Emon's among them. Diran stepped toward the table and stopped when he reached it. He assumed he'd done the right thing, for Quellin's smile grew wider and more sinister. Quellin spoke, his voice pitched at normal volume but nevertheless echoing throughout the chamber.

"Diran Bastiaan, welcome to the Chamber of Joining. Today you will take your last step toward becoming a full member of the Brotherhood of the Blade." Quellin gestured toward the obsidian table. "Lie down."

Diran knew better than to ask what would happen if he refused. He would be slain, perhaps even by Emon himself, but Diran didn't want to refuse. Though he didn't know what this ritual might require of him, whatever it was, it would be worth it to at last be accepted into Emon's brotherhood. He climbed on top of the obsidian table and lay down. There was a smooth depression for the back of his head, and the cold, hard table made Diran feel as if he were a corpse laid out on a slab.

Quellin stepped around the table and stood by Diran's head. "Today you are going to receive a great gift, Diran Bastiaan. After this day, you shall be stronger than ever before, your mind will be clearer, your senses sharper, your resolve more firm and your heart cold as frost-covered steel. After this day, you shall never again be alone."

Obviously Quellin was much more than a simple librarian and scholar, Diran thought. Was he a wizard? A priest? A deluded madman? He supposed the next several moments would tell the tale.

Quellin turned and faced the ugly statues on the black stone altar. "We do the work of the Six, and to help us serve Them more efficiently, They imbue us with a small measure of Their own majestic darkness." The old man turned back to Diran. "You have been deemed worthy of being granted the gift of the Dark Six, Diran. Do you accept it of your own free will?"

A part of Diran, perhaps the deepest part of him, wanted to say no, but the word that came out of his mouth was, "Yes."

"Excellent," Quellin said, almost hissing the world. He turned back to the altar and lifted his hands over his head.

"Here me, oh Six! Your servant comes before You once more and asks that You crack open the Gates of Oblivion and permit Your shadows to join with this willing vessel. Diran Bastiaan has proven himself worthy. Under his master's tutelage, he has become a strong, swift, and cunning killer. All he lacks now is the touch of Your dark hands. I beseech You, reach out to this youth and grant him the fell blessing I ask, so that he might walk the face of this world as small reflection of Your own magnificence!"

As Quellin intoned his prayer, Diran had the impression of darkness gathering, pooling thickly around the base of the table, manifesting as a tarry black substance. The chamber grew colder, so cold that his breath came out as curling wisps of mist. Quellin stepped around to the table's side, and Diran was able to look at him without craning his neck. The elderly man leaned closer and whispered, "Whatever you do, do not resist."

Quellin straightened, reached between the fold of his robe and took out one of the daggers that hung from his belt. The old man pressed the blade's hilt into Diran's right hand.

"Two clean, quick cuts, one on each wrist," Quellin said, "not too deep, but enough to open the arteries. Once you've made the cuts, return the dagger to me, then place your bleeding wrists into the runnels carved into the sides of the table. Do you understand?"

Diran nodded and felt the familiar sensation of a dagger hilt resting in his right palm. He closed his fingers around it then hesitated. If he did as Quellin commanded, he might well bleed to death, but if he didn't do it, then he certainly would be killed for his defiance. He turned his head and looked at Emon and Makala. The master assassin was still smiling, but Makala's face remained expressionless, as did those of all the others nearby. Then Makala gave him a wink and he knew that, whatever was about to happen, it was going to be all right.

He was surprised by how little it hurt to make the cuts.

Quellin took the knife, and Diran lay back, putting his arms in the runnels as he'd been told. Seconds went by without anything happening as he slowly bled out his life's blood onto the obsidian table, but then he sensed the darkness pooled around table's base become alert, almost scenting the air like an eager hound. He felt it sliding up the side of the table, ebon tendrils probing as it came. He looked down at his feet. The runnels ended in shallow basins at the foot of the table, and the blood flowing from his opened veins had already filled them halfway. Dark tendrils stretched up over the edge and dipped into the basins, as if tasting the thick, red fluid they held. The darkness must've found what it tasted to be sweet, for it flowed up the sides, over the edge, and into the basins, splitting in two as it did so. The darkness absorbed the blood in the basins and then, hungry for more, flowed up the runnels, following the blood trail to Diran's cut wrists. He watched as tendrils emerged from the leading edge of the darkness to brush against his wounds, their touch freezing cold on his flesh.

On each side, tendrils wormed their way into his wounds, and Diran screamed as he experienced a pain more excruciating than anything he had ever imagined. It took several minutes for the darkness to finish entering his body, and he screamed the entire time, until finally his throat was too raw to make further sound. Then it was over.

Diran lay on the table, breathing slowly. The runnels were dry and clear; not a speck of blood remained on them. Diran sat up and examined his wrists. The wounds had healed with no sign of scarring. He felt healthy, strong, bursting with energy. He leaped off the table and landed lightly on his feet. He was hungry enough to eat a whale, and at the same time he felt ready to take on an army single-handedly, armed with nothing more than his wits and a sharpened stick.

He looked at Makala with new understanding. This was why she was seemed so different over the last year. She'd already undergone her Joining, and now so had he.

Emon Gorsedd stood and clapped. He was joined by Makala, then one by one all the other assassins. Even Quellin was grinning and clapping.

"Welcome to the Brotherhood of the Blade, Diran!" Emon shouted.

Diran smiled, and if somewhere in the midst of all the clapping and cries of congratulation he heard a small dark voice whispering to him from the most shadowy corner of his soul, he thought nothing of it. It felt natural, felt right . . .

Felt *good*.

❀ ❀ ❀ ◉ ❀ ❀ ❀

Diran's eyes opened. At first he didn't know where he was, but that didn't matter because for the first time in years he felt complete again. Like an amputee who'd gotten used to the loss of a limb, he'd forgotten how good it was to be whole.

All too soon the feeling began to fade. Diran felt wind rushing on his face, smelled salt in the air, heard the gentle whisper of soarwood runners cutting through water. He looked up, saw stars, moons, and the Ring of Siberys, all illuminating the night sky, and he knew that he had been dreaming. With that realization, the last lingering feelings of completeness vanished, and an empty space opened up in Diran's soul. He let out a long sigh.

"Uneasy dreams, my friend?" A woman's voice, coming from the stern. Yvka.

The last of the dream fog lifted, and Diran remembered everything: the Black Fleet, Onkar, the *Zephyr*, Flotsam and Nowhere, and most of all, Makala. He turned to Ghaji. The half-orc sat with his arms crossed, head down, snoring softly. Diran rose quietly so as not to wake his friend and moved back to sit cross-legged on the deck facing Yvka.

"At least Ghaji is having no trouble sleeping," the elf-woman said.

"Ghaji and I are both veterans of the Last War. One of the first things a soldier learns is to grab any opportunity for sleep. You never know when—or *if*—you'll get another chance."

The night air had grown chilly, especially with the wind kicked up by the *Zephyr*'s swift passage. Diran and Ghaji had broken out their bedrolls and wrapped them around their shoulders like shawls while Yvka was content to make do with a light traveler's cloak. She'd offered to let them sleep in the *Zephyr*'s cabin, cramped though it might be for two, especially when one of those two was as big as Ghaji, but the two companions had declined. Not only did they want to remain on deck in case of trouble, they still weren't sure how much they should trust Yvka.

"Speaking of sleep," Diran said, "you've been piloting the *Zephyr* without rest since we left Nowhere. I was raised in the Principalities. I learned to sail almost before I could walk. It's been a while since I sat at a tiller, but I think I can remember enough to take your place so you can get some rest."

"I'm holding up fine. My people don't need as much rest as yours. Besides, I want to maintain our best speed. The sooner we reach Dreadhold, the sooner we'll be able to track down Erdis Cai."

Diran looked at the column behind Yvka, atop which sat the metallic containment ring that kept the air elemental bound and servile. The interior of the ring glowed with shimmering blue energy as the elemental continued producing wind to fill the *Zephyr's* sails.

"Are you certain?" Diran asked. "I would think that an enchantment this powerful would take a great deal of energy out of the pilot."

"Controlling the elemental takes effort, but the magic's primarily in the ship itself," Yvka said. "The ring, the column, this chair . . . the hand-link carved into the arm has been keyed especially to me, though the spell could be broken by a wizard or even an especially skilled artificer. All I have to do is remain in physical contact with the hand-link for the elemental to stay active. It would remain so even if I slept, though I would be unable to work the tiller of course."

"Then I *can* take over for you," Diran said. "It would mean my standing next to your chair since I couldn't sit in it while you slept, but I—"

"Again, you have my thanks, Diran, but as I said, there is no need."

"You don't trust us, Ghaji and me, do you?"

There was enough moonlight for Diran to make out Yvka's features, and he saw her sad smile.

"It was how I was trained," Yvka said. "Trust no one. Surely *you* understand."

Diran frowned. "What do you mean?"

"You and Ghaji have been traveling in the Principalities for weeks now, and your presence has not gone unnoticed by the people I work for." Another smile, but one of amusement this time. "You and Ghaji don't exactly keep a low profile."

Diran couldn't help smiling himself. "I admit we have a tendency to stand out at times, so . . . how much do you know about us?"

"One of the primary goods my employers traffic in is information," the elf-woman replied. "It would be simpler for me to tell you what I *don't* know about the two of you."

"I see." Diran paused for a moment before going on. "In that case, yes, I had similar training, but I've learned how to trust over the years." He cast a glance back at Ghaji, but the half-orc was still asleep.

"You two make a good team," Yvka said. "Is Ghaji also a follower of the Silver Flame?"

"Ghaji tends more to the orcs' belief in the divinity of nature, when he thinks about religion at all, that is."

"I would think that might prove a source of conflict between the two of you."

"Why? My order believes that the Silver Flame is the source of all that is Good in existence and that in the end, all good things will rejoin the source from which they came and become one with the Silver Flame. Ghaji's belief in the sanctity of nature is simply a belief in one aspect of the Silver Flame. At least, that's what I keep telling him. I don't think he believes me, though."

Yvka laughed softly. "I've never met a priest like you before Diran."

Diran replied in all seriousness. "No, I don't suppose you have."

They sailed on in silence for a time after that, and Diran found himself thinking again of his dream. Though he was glad to be free of the dark spirit Quellin had implanted in him, part of him still missed its presence within his soul and always would. Not for the first time he wondered if by devoting his life to the Silver Flame, especially with its belief in rejoining the source of all good after one's death, he simply wasn't trying to replace the loss of his dark spirit with a different brand of spiritually. He knew what Tusya, his mentor in the Church and the priest who exorcised the dark spirit from his soul, would say.

When in doubt, look to your heart, Diran. Your heart is your connection to the Silver Flame, and you'll always find the answers you need there.

He also knew what Emon Gorsedd would say. *You've just traded one addiction for another, Diran, that's all. You've never truly been your own man and you never will be. You'll always be one of my children.*

To take his mind off these troubling thoughts, Diran resumed his conversation with Yvka. "Do you truly believe we're on the right track?"

"If you mean, will we find an old artificer named Tresslar working at Dreadhold who supposedly sailed with Erdis Cai's crew on their last journey, despite the fact that no other survivors had come forward, then yes. My employers have been aware of the man's claims since before he joined the warders of Dreadhold, but did the man truly sail with Erdis Cai, and even if he did, does he have any idea of where Cai may be holed up today? I don't know, but this is the only lead we have, so we must pursue it."

If anyone could lead them to Erdis Cai, it would be Tresslar, assuming the man wasn't a lunatic or a liar. The only way to know for certain was to sail to Dreadhold, the toughest, most isolated prison in Khorvaire, and see for themselves.

"Tell me, Yvka, why are you helping us? I was under the impression that the Shadow Network was completely mercenary."

"If by *mercenary*, you mean we look after our interests along with those of our clients, then of course. We're a business like any other, and you're not one to talk lightly about mercenary motives, Diran Bastiaan. Despite your earlier claim to be a soldier in the Last War, the truth is you were an assassin-for-hire."

The elf-woman's tone of derision stung more than her words.

"What you say is true, though for a time I deluded myself into believing that my actions served a greater good than profit. So you're saying someone has hired the Shadow Network to discover the secrets of the Black Fleet?"

"I didn't say anything of the sort. Your goals and my goals happen to coincide at the moment." She glanced at Ghaji's sleeping form. "Besides, I'm starting to grow fond of your cantankerous friend."

Diran smiled. "He does have a tendency to grow on you."

A large dark form broke the water's surface a dozen yards off the port bow. Both Diran and Yvka tensed, for many large aquatic creatures swam the depths of the Lhazaar Sea, and precious few of them were benign, but the dark shape released a spray of water from a blowhole, and both the priest and the elf-woman relaxed. Just a whale. The animal continued swimming close to the surface as the swift elemental sloop left it behind.

When they'd put a good amount of distance between themselves and the whale, Yvka spoke once more. "I have another question for you, Diran, but given my own reticence to answer yours, I'll understand if you prefer not to respond."

"Go ahead and ask."

"Back at Nowhere, when the thieves tried to steal the *Zephyr* . . ."

"Yes?"

"The way you killed that half-elf woman . . . given your former profession, I'm not surprised that you possessed the skill to slay her with such a dagger throw, but for a priest who supposedly reveres life . . ."

"You expected a little more mercy."

"I suppose so, yes."

Diran thought for a moment as he decided the best way to address Yvka's concern.

"Correct me if I'm wrong, but I'm assuming that you've received training similar to mine, and I wouldn't be surprised if you had occasion to use it."

Yvka didn't dispute this, so Diran went on.

"Then you know that it's much more difficult to subdue a foe than kill him. The half-elf was going to strike Ghaji with an arrow. If I could've stopped her without killing her, I would have, but at that range, and with her so close to releasing her arrow, I had to make certain she didn't harm Ghaji. The only way I could do that was to slay her."

"You don't sound particularly remorseful," Yvka said.

"The woman chose to attempt to steal the *Zephyr*, and she chose to draw her bow on Ghaji." Diran shrugged. "I chose to protect my friend."

"As simple as that, eh?"

A parade of faces flashed quickly through Diran's mind, the half-elf woman's the last in a long line. "Killing is never simple," he said softly.

"Does your faith make it any easier to deal with?" Yvka asked. "Do you truly believe in absolute good and absolute evil?"

"It does and I do," Diran answered.

"So certain creatures are just inherently evil and must be slain?"

"Since becoming a priest, I've encountered all manner of demons, spirits, and undead. Some were most definitely evil and had to be put down. Others fought the evil in their natures but ultimately failed, and there have been a precious few who, while suffering evil's taint, were able to keep the darkness within them from dictating their actions. Were these latter creatures evil? Some of the more fanatical in my order would deem them so, but I'm not certain."

"Have you ever spared any such creatures and later regretted doing so?" Yvka asked.

"Only once," Diran said, "and it nearly cost Ghaji and me not only our lives but also our very souls."

Once more, he heard Emon Gorsedd's voice in his mind. *You talk a good game, Diran, but we both know that deep down, you're nothing but a killer. It doesn't matter if you slay men or monsters, or whether you do it for money or for some abstract ideal called "Good." You enjoy killing and you're damn good at it. End of story.*

"Enough of such talk," Diran said, more to himself than to Yvka. "How much farther is it to Dreadhold?"

Yvka looked up at the stars and did a quick mental calculation. "I'd say another four hours, three at the earliest." She sniffed the air. "A storm's in the offing, though, and might slow us down some. In any event, you should try to get some sleep, Diran. You'll need your full strength when we reach Dreadhold."

"If it's all the same to you, Yvka, I'd rather stay up. It'll give you a chance to tell me what I need to know about Dreadhold."

"As well as prevent your having any more nightmares?" the elf-woman asked.

Diran smiled. "That too."

"Very well. Dreadhold was first established long ago by Karrn the Conqueror as a facility for exiling deposed rulers and courtiers that fell from favor. Over the centuries . . ."

CHAPTER

NINE

"Wake up, child. We've arrived, though I can't tell you where."

Makala opened her eyes to darkness. She started to panic, but then she remembered: the voice belonged to the old shifter woman Zabeth, and they, along with numerous others, were being held prisoner in the hold of the raider ship *Nightwind*.

Makala felt no vibrations in the wood beneath her. Zabeth was right: the elemental galleon had docked.

"How long did I sleep?"

If she knew, she might be able to make a rough guess how many leagues the *Nightwind* had traveled, though she wasn't certain what the ship's top speed was. Before Zabeth could answer her question, there came the sound of a lock pin being pulled back, then a rectangular patch of darkness above them was replaced by stars and a partial view of a moon as the raiders opened the hold's hatch. Nighttime—that meant she'd been on the *Nightwind* at least a full day, if not more.

A moment later, a rope ladder was tossed down. Makala entertained a brief fantasy of rushing over to the ladder, climbing up, leaping onto the *Nightwind*'s deck and strangling the closest raider with the chain between her two wrist manacles, but she knew she was too weak, and she was only one person. Even with all of Emon's training, she'd likely be killed before she could slay even a single raider, so she sat and waited, Zabeth crouched next to her.

Archers ringed the opening, providing cover for two of their fellow raiders who began climbing down. Neither of the raiders carried a lantern, and no one on the deck shone one into the hold for them. It was difficult to tell in the hull's gloom, but one raider appeared male, the other female. When they reached the bottom of the ladder, they stepped off and drew their swords.

"Up the ladder one at a time," the male commanded. "If anyone even looks like they're thinking of causing trouble, they'll taste steel."

"Or get an arrow through the heart," the woman added.

"How can we climb in these manacles?" one of the prisoners, a man, asked.

"There's enough slack in the chains for you to make it if you go slowly," the male raider said.

"What if we fall?" someone else asked.

"I suggest you don't," the female raider said. "Now move it!"

It took a little prodding from the raiders' swords, but the prisoners closest to the ladder began climbing. Some cried as they ascended, others mumbled prayers, but most were quiet, as if resigned to whatever fate awaited them topside. Since Zabeth and Makala were next to the wall of the hold, they were among the last to stand and start toward the ladder.

"After you, Grandmother," Makala said to Zabeth.

The elderly shifter gave her a smile, a wink, then started up the rope ladder with surprising agility for one of her years. Makala didn't like seeing that wink. Earlier, Zabeth had said something about waiting for the right moment to take action against the raiders. The old woman couldn't be foolish enough to try something now . . . could she?

Makala hurried up the ladder after Zabeth. She didn't think about the raiders still in the hold with their swords drawn, didn't think about the archers with their arrows nocked and aimed at her. Her only concern was to remain as close as possible to Zabeth so she could intervene if the woman tried anything heroic and stupid.

The cool night air deckside came as a shock after spending an unknown number of hours imprisoned in the *Nightwind*'s hold. At first Makala found it bracing, but then, weak from hunger and still hurting from the injuries sustained during her abduction, she began to shiver. The prisoners from the raid on Port Verge were already being offloaded one at a time, directed by armed raiders to "Move along now," in single file down a gangplank onto a wooden dock. There was enough light from the moons and the Ring of Siberys for Makala to get a basic idea of their surroundings.

She took her place in line and followed Zabeth down the gangplank. The three elemental galleons of the Black Fleet had docked next to a steep cliff that Makala estimated was a hundred feet high. She could make out the striations in the craggy stone of the cliff wall, as well as the silhouettes of trees lining the top. An opening in the shape of a half circle was carved into the base of the cliff, and the dock continued through the opening and stretched into the darkness beyond. All three of the ebon ships had dropped anchor and were disgorging their prisoners, all of whom were being herded along the dock and inside the cliff, prodded by the point of a raider's sword if they moved too slowly. People sobbed and chains jingled as the prisoners shuffled toward whatever waited for them within the darkness of the cliff. Makala glanced back over her shoulder. They appeared to be in a secluded cove of some kind, the cliff curving around to cut off the view of the sea and hide the Black Fleet's home port from any passing ships. Despite her current situation, Makala was impressed. This looked to be a perfect base of operations for the Black Fleet.

The light from the moons gleamed on the dark water of the cove. Makala had the impression of shadowy forms moving near the edge of the dock just beneath the water's surface, but perhaps it was just her imagination. The lingering after-effects of her head injury conspired with the night and moonlight to create an illusion. Still, she decided not to get too close to the dock's edge.

"Eyes front," a raider growled and pricked her lower back with his sword.

Makala had to bite her lip and curl her hands into fists, fingernails digging into the palms, to channel her anger so she wouldn't whirl around and break the sword-happy idiot's neck.

Ahead of her, Zabeth moaned and stumbled to her knees.

"Get up!" one of the raiders snapped.

Makala stepped forward to help the old shifter woman, but the same raider who'd pricked her back said, "Mind your place, missy, or you might find yourself taking a moonlight swim, and believe me, that's something you'd prefer to avoid."

The raiders nearby who had caught the comment laughed, and Makala knew she hadn't been hallucinating when she thought she'd seen something swimming in the cove.

As much as she wanted to go to Zabeth's aid, she knew the raiders would never permit it and that she'd likely just cause trouble for Zabeth and the other prisoners by attempting to defy their captors. She gritted her teeth and remained where she was while the sword-happy raider stepped around her. Zabeth knelt with her head hung low, trembling and swaying from side to side, as if she were going to faint any moment. The raider toed her in the rump, not gently, but not hard enough to be considered a kick, either.

"Come on, old woman, get on your feet. We're not going to carry you in."

"That's not a woman!" another of the raiders shouted. "Can't you see she's a shifter?"

"Nothin' wrong with that!" yet another raider called out. "Ernard likes 'em old and hairy!"

More raiders burst out laughing this time, and Ernard, less than thrilled at being the source of amusement for his companions, kicked Zabeth again, much harder this time.

There was only so much that Makala was willing to let pass. She started forward, intending to fulfill her earlier fantasy about wrapping her manacle chains around a raider's throat and strangling him. Before she could do so, Zabeth turned to look up at her tormentor, her face transformed into a more savage, bestial aspect. She bared her fangs, growled, and brought her claws up into the juncture between the raider's legs. The man screamed, blood gushed onto the dock, and Zabeth grinned.

Though the raider had been severely wounded, the man still possessed enough presence of mind to raise his sword so that he might strike back at Zabeth. Makala lunged at the raider and caught his sword arm with her manacle chains. She shifted her weight, yanked hard, and the bleeding raider dropped his sword as he spun off the dock and into the water. He hit with a loud splash and disappeared beneath the surface. Makala saw movement under the water as several large somethings swam from under the dock toward the spot where the raider had sunk. Everyone on the dock, raider and prisoner, watched the water now, and one of the raiders said, "That's it for Ernard, then," without the slightest hint of sorrow.

"Better this way," another raider said. "Who'd want to go on livin' after gettin' tore up down *there?*"

The water burst into a foaming froth as Ernard broke the surface, shrieking in agony and terror. Several large dark shapes had attached themselves to his body, and it took Makala a moment before she recognized what they were—crabs, but not ordinary crabs. These were much bigger, about the size of a large shield. The creatures tore vigorously as the raider's flesh, oversized claws cutting like razor-sharp blades through skin and muscle, all the way down to the bone. At the rate they were going, it wouldn't take long for them to strip Ernard's body clean.

The dock shuddered as if something huge moved beneath it, and a shadow slid out from under the dock toward Ernard, a *big* shadow.

"Looks like Mama's hungry," a raider said, and though the woman's tone was one of dark delight, there was an edge of queasiness to her voice as well.

The crabs, as if reacting to some silent signal, abandoned their prey and disappeared into the water. Still screaming and bleeding from dozens of wounds, Ernard sank beneath the surface, but he didn't stay down for long. Water roiled and Ernard burst back into view, caught within the claw of a gigantic crustacean. This, then, was Mama.

The claw squeezed and Ernard's screams were silenced as the raider fell back into the water as two separate pieces. The surface surged upward and Makala had the impression of a dark craggy shell, a pair of beady hate-filled eyes, and ferociously working mouth parts. Then Ernard was gone, and Mama submerged. The dock shuddered again, and Makala realized the gigantic she-crab had once again taken her roosting spot among the dock supports beneath their feet. How many of the she-crab's children clung to the supports along with the mother, hungry and ever alert, hopeful that another tasty morsel would fall off the dock and into their waiting claws?

No one made a sound as the ripples caused by the submerging she-crab slowly subsided, but once the water was calm again, one of the raiders stepped forward, grabbed Zabeth by the elbow, and hauled the elderly shifter woman to her feet. Makala expected Zabeth to attack the man just as she had Ernard, but her bestial features were gone. She was just a frightened, exhausted old woman who could barely remain on her feet.

"I don't know who captured you," the raider said, "but whoever it was is an idiot. We don't have any need for shifters, let alone any as old as you." With his free hand, the raider unsheathed his sword. "Ernard was no friend of mine," the man said with a slowly widening smile, "but I'm going to enjoy taking revenge for him."

"No!" Makala shouted.

She tried to put herself between Zabeth and the raider, but someone reached out and grabbed hold of the chain connecting her wrist manacles. The raider was female, and Makala recognized her as one of the pair that had climbed down into the *Nightwind*'s hold. Steel whispered and the woman pressed the point of a dagger to the underside of Makala's chin.

"Careful, you're about to make yourself more trouble than you're worth," the raider warned.

Makala wished her mind wasn't dulled by hunger and her reflexes slowed by weariness. She knew she couldn't just stand here and let Zabeth be slaughtered, but her brain refused to offer up any alternatives.

The raider who had hold of Zabeth raised his sword high, preparing to bring it down in a killing stroke. Makala hoped that Zabeth might be able to once more unleash the bestial side of her shifter, but the old woman just looked at the sword blade gleaming in the moonlight with tired resignation and waited for death to claim her.

"Hold!"

The voice echoed through the air, seeming to come from everywhere and nowhere all at once. The raider holding Zabeth froze, an expression of stark terror on his face. Makala glanced at the woman holding the dagger to her throat and saw a similar expression mirrored on her face. All the raiders looked scared, and they all stood motionless as statues, heads turned toward the entrance in the cliff wall where the dock disappeared into darkness. Makala turned and watched as two figures came striding forth from the shadows. She recognized the one on the left as Onkar. The raider commander was grinning, displaying his sharp vampire teeth, and his eyes glowed red like two smoldering fires.

At first she thought the woman walking next to Onkar was also a vampire. She was beautiful: tall, thin, and pale, with a slightly angular face and long raven-black hair. She was garbed in a red leather bustier and black skirt, but as Onkar and the woman drew closer, Makala could see that she was human after all. Her eyes didn't burn with crimson fire, and though her flesh was pale, it wasn't fish-belly white like Onkar's. While the sea captain moved with the fluid grace of a large predatory cat, the woman, graceful enough in her own right, couldn't match the vampire's eerie litheness

As Onkar and the raven-haired woman stepped before Zabeth and the raider holding his sword over the old woman's head, Makala thought she'd have to revise her estimate. Onkar's companion might be mortal, but the raiders had shied away from her presence as much if not more than Onkar's.

The man holding Zabeth slowly lowered his sword, as if he didn't want to risk making any sudden movements near Onkar or the woman. He bowed his head.

"Commander Onkar, Lady Jarlain," the man said in a quavering voice. "How may I serve you?"

"You can release the shifter woman," Onkar said, "unless you'd like to take her place."

The raider paled and shook his head. He released his hold on Zabeth, quickly sheathed his sword and scurried off to lose himself among his fellow raiders.

The black-haired woman—Lady Jarlain—turned to look at the raider holding the dagger against Makala's neck. "You, too, dear. Put the knife away and go before I decide you could use a session or two alone with me in my chambers."

Though there was no overt menace in Jarlain's tone, the raider made a terrified choking noise and pulled the blade away from Makala's throat. She sheathed the dagger, bowed low to Onkar and Jarlain, and departed at a near run.

Jarlain might not be a vampire, Makala thought, but she certainly inspired as much fear in the raiders as one.

Onkar turned to address his crew. "Stop standing around and get these prisoners inside!" When no one moved right away, he shouted, *"Now!"* in an inhumanly loud voice that made the wooden boards of the dock shudder beneath their feet.

That broke the raiders' paralysis, and they hurriedly resumed herding prisoners down the dock and into the cliff tunnel. After all that had occurred since they'd arrived, the prisoners gave their captors no trouble and went along quietly.

Makala put her hands on Zabeth's shoulders, intending to help the shifter woman rejoin the rest of their fellow prisoners, but Onkar held up a hand to stop her.

"Not you. You're not going to the holding pen with the rest of the rabble like this old wolf."

The vampire took hold of Zabeth's arm and shoved her toward the line of marching prisoners. The elderly woman stumbled and Makala feared she would fall, but Zabeth managed to maintain her balance. She gave Makala a last look, said, "Take care of yourself now," then fell into line with the other prisoners.

"You too," Makala replied, though she knew it would be far easier said than done for both of them. She turned to Onkar and Jarlain, trying not to look as frightened as she felt. "Where am I to go?"

Onkar's lips stretched into a smile wider than any human mouth could make, and his fangs glistened wet in the moonlight. "You've been granted a great honor," the vampire said. "You get to meet the master."

Jarlain's smile was smaller than Onkar's but no less sinister. "We're taking you to see Erdis Cai."

CHAPTER

TEN

Trembling with excitement, Ghaji crouched behind a tall tuft of swamp grass near an ancient elm tree. He could hear the snuffle-snorts of the wild boar that he and the others had been tracking all morning. *He* was the first to find it, and while this filled him with pride, he also felt a certain trepidation. Now that he'd found the beast, what should he do?

He couldn't signal Esk, Murtt, and Warg. If he made the least sound he risked scaring off the boar, and if that happened the others would be angry with him, especially given how many hours they'd already devoted to this hunt. He supposed he could attempt to bring down the boar himself. If he did, it would be an impressive feat, especially since the four of them had agreed at the outset of the hunt to use no weapons. Ghaji had only just entered his twelfth year, and though he had grown much in the last several months, he was unsure if he were strong enough to tangle with a swamp boar by himself. The animals had hides tough as boiled leather and dispositions mean as a swamp serpent with a bad case of scale rot, which was of course why hunting the boar barehanded was a favorite pastime of young orcs. This was the first time Ghaji had ever been allowed to come along on a boar hunt, and if he ever wanted to come again, he couldn't afford to mess this up.

Foliage was abundant here in the swampland: white cedars, red and silver maples, black spruce, elm and ash trees, along with ferns and numerous species of colorful wildflowers. Birds abounded as well: swallows, warblers, blackbirds, grackles, larks, and larger birds such as herons, egrets, and cranes. Ghaji loved it here. The swampland was alive and vibrant, bursting with energy but at the same time peaceful and tranquil. He could spend the rest of his life here and be content.

A cloud of biters drifted toward Ghaji, reminding him that even a place as wonderful as the swamp wasn't perfect. The annoying insects didn't much like the taste of orc. Unfortunately, Ghaji was only *half*-orc, and the pests loved to jab their needle-like mouths into him even more than they seemed to love doing so to humans. Ghaji sighed. It was the story of his young life; he always seemed to get the worst of both worlds. Maybe if he was lucky, the biters would pass him by for a chance to sink their needles into a fat, juicy swamp boar.

He wasn't lucky. It was a humid day, and to make matters worse, the sun's bright light was oppressively hot. Ghaji always seemed to sweat more than both orcs and humans combined, and perspiration was an irresistible lure for biters. Drawn by the beads of sweat forming on his greenish skin, the miniature swarm descended on Ghaji and began drilling greedily into his flesh. Swamp biters grew large as a man's thumb and their attack stung worse than being stuck by a black briar thorn. Ghaji gritted his teeth as the insects went to work, but maddening as it was, he made no sound and didn't attempt to shrug them off. An orc always wore his battle scars proudly, and though all Ghaji would receive were biter welts, he'd bear them with just as much pride as he would any other injury. Whatever the cost, he would not permit anything to interfere with the boar hunt.

Ghaji did his best to ignore the buzzing whine of those biters that had yet to select which portion of his skin they'd like to penetrate and listened for the boar. Its snuffling was muted now, and he could hear it scratching at the ground around the elm tree with its hoof not ten feet from the tall swamp grass where Ghaji hid. Swamp boars loved to eat grub worms, and one of the varieties they considered especially delicious lived in the soil near the base of elms—precisely the reason Ghaji had chosen this spot to hide and wait in the first place.

From the muted snuffling, Ghaji guessed the boar had already uncovered some worms and was busy gobbling them up even as the beast scratched around for more. Ghaji knew that if he had any intention of attacking the boar alone, he wasn't going to get a better opportunity. He tensed and visualized himself leaping out from behind the grass and running toward the boar, but as he was about do so, he heard loud shouting and the heavy pounding of feet. The boar squealed in alarm, and Ghaji stood just in time to see Esk, Murtt, and Warg converging on their prey from separate directions.

Each of the full orcs was a year or two younger than Ghaji, but they were already larger than he and better coordinated. They came at the boar like wild animals themselves, all three shouting and waving their hands in the air to confuse the boar so it would have no idea where to flee. The orcs had shaggy black manes and thick body hair. Their eyes were reddish, and their ears pointed. Their jaws jutted out more prominently than Ghaji's, and their lower incisors were larger and sharper. The orcs were garbed in simple tunics of brown, black, and gray, unlike Ghaji's tan one, and sturdy brown boots. Ghaji thought they were magnificent, and for perhaps the thousandth time he wished he looked like them.

Angered at having his plan ruined by the others but determined not to be left out, Ghaji pushed through the grass and dashed toward the boar. He didn't want the animal to run away from him. He wanted it to run *at* him, so he didn't wave his hands or shout. Instead, he would let the others drive the beast to him.

Ghaji had seen the boar while they were tracking it but only from a distance. Up close the animal looked even larger, and it had seemed big enough before. It was sixty pounds and likely heavier. The beast was dashing this way and that, foamy saliva bubbling past its snout and dripping from its long yellowed tusks. Its eyes shone with desperate fury as it cast its piggy gaze back and forth, searching for a way out of this trap it found itself in. Normally a boar would charge an attacker, but the orcs came at the beast from different directions, confusing it. Ghaji's companions closed in, still shouting and gesturing wildly, but Ghaji stood still, hoping to draw the boar's attention by *not* making a commotion.

His ploy worked. The boar saw a target for its fury and dashed at him, hooves churning the moist swamp soil, head swinging wildly so its tusks could do as much damage as possible. Ghaji's instincts screamed for him to assume a defensive posture—the thought of fleeing never occurred to him, for he was half-*orc*, after all—but he forced himself to stand calmly as the boar charged at him. Just as the beast was about to gore him, Ghaji jumped straight up. His plan was to come crashing down feet-first on the boar's head, driving its face into the ground, and if fortune was kind, breaking its neck.

Ghaji had never hunted swamp boar before, let alone killed one, and his inexperience caused him to misjudge the animal's speed. Instead of landing on the boar's head, he came down on its back. His weight caused the beast to stumble, but it had enough momentum to remain on its feet and keep going. For a moment, Ghaji managed to stand upright on the boar's back, then his right foot slid off the boar's bristly hide, and Ghaji fell to the ground, landing on his right side with teeth-jarring impact. The boar had had enough of this foolishness; it put on an extra burst of speed and raced away across the swampland.

Ghaji lay there for a moment, more upset than hurt. He'd been so *close* . . .

He looked up to see Esk, Murtt, and Warg glaring down at him with expressions of supreme disgust.

"You let it get away," Warg growled.

"Why did you jump on it?" Esk demanded. "You think you're a swamp hare?"

"You should've hit it!" Murtt said, slamming a fist into his open palm for emphasis.

Warg thumped his chest. "I would've tackled it!"

"Anything would be better than *jumping*," Esk said. "That was stupid."

Ghaji gritted his teeth as he sat up. He wanted to tell these three that if they'd tried using a little stealth and cunning, along with some teamwork, instead of relying on dumb brute strength, their families would've gotten to dine on roast boar tonight, but he said nothing. These were the closest things to friends that he had, and he didn't want to offend them, even if the idiots deserved it.

Ghaji rose to his feet. He didn't expect any of the others to help him up. That wasn't the orc way. Toughness, self-reliance . . . those were the things orcs valued.

Warg, the biggest of the three orcs, though he was the youngest, stepped toward Ghaji until they were standing almost nose to nose. For an orc, this intrusion into another's personal space was a major act of aggression and disrespect.

"The hunt has failed, thanks to you, Smooth-skin."

Smooth-skin was a slur used to insult half-orcs, since the latter typically had far less body hair than full orcs.

Warg went on. "You're a disgrace to your mother. You'd be a disgrace to your clan, too, if you had one."

As a half-orc, Ghaji wasn't permitted to be in a clan, not that any would have him. His mother, Aneen, had been raised in the Gliding Heron clan, but she had been ostracized after Ghaji's birth, and ever since had remained as clanless as her son.

Ghaji slammed his fist against his chest so hard that for an instant his heart seemed to skip a beat. "You cannot speak like that to me! I am orc!"

"No," Warg said, still standing with his face right in Ghaji's. "You're not."

The words cut through Ghaji more easily and with more force than any bladed weapon ever could.

Ghaji said, "Very well, I am half-orc."

The other three laughed.

Esk sneered. "Not to us, you aren't. To us, you're half-*human*."

The orc emphasized this last word as if it were a particularly noxious variety of swamp fungus, the kind that invaded the hidden recesses of body and made itself at home in the nooks and crannies that it found there.

Ghaji felt as if he'd been slapped in the face. Though he didn't want to risk driving away his companions, an orc would never let such an insult stand.

"I challenge you to single combat, Esk. Hand to hand or weapons. Your choice."

Esk laughed. "There is no honor to be gained from fighting a smooth-skin!"

Ghaji was so hurt and angry that he intended to push Esk to the ground and start pummeling him, whether the orc felt like fighting or not, but before Ghaji could make his move, Esk stepped away from him and turned his back. Murtt and Warg did the same, then the three young orcs walked away from Ghaji as if he didn't exist.

Ghaji stood and watched them go, too hurt and prideful to go after them and apologize for spoiling the hunt. Their insults echoed in his mind. *Smooth-skin . . . half-human . . .* but worst of all was the thought that he had disgraced his mother. Despite the fact that Ghaji had been the product of her rape by a drunken human soldier, Aneen had always loved and cared for him—the only person in the world who'd ever done so. Esk, Murtt, and Warg all belonged to Gliding Heron clan—Aneen's former people—and when they returned home, they would spread the story of how Ghaji had failed this day, thereby bringing further disgrace upon Aneen in the eyes of her one-time clan.

"I'm sorry, Mother," Ghaji whispered.

Tears welled in his eyes, and though orcs considered crying an unforgivable sign of weakness, he couldn't stop himself. Teardrops rolled down his cheeks, dripped off his jaw, and fell to the ground, only to be absorbed by the soft swamp soil.

❋ ❋ ❋ ◉ ❋ ❋ ❋

Ghaji felt a drop strike his hand, and he was surprised by how cold it felt. Tears were supposed to be warm, weren't they? He felt another strike his forehead, and now he was really confused. Since when did tears fall upward?

He opened his eyes and saw a full sail billowing before him and beyond it a pitch-black sky. Wind whistled through the sloop's rigging, and raindrops pattered onto the boat's wooden surface, only a few at first, then the sky opened up and rain poured down. It looked like the weather had taken a turn for the worse while he'd slept, but he was actually grateful for the storm since it had awakened him from that dream. He'd dreamed of hunting the swamp boar many times since that day, and he wished the storm had let loose a few minutes earlier so he might have awakened without having to relive his failure yet again.

He turned to Diran, but his friend was no longer sitting next to him. He looked over his shoulder, and by the soft blue-white glow of the ring-bound air elemental, he saw Diran and Yvka. They were talking to one another, both wearing the hoods of their cloaks up to keep off the rain. Ghaji shook his head. He didn't understand why they bothered. It was just a little water.

A bolt of lightning cut the darkness, and for an instant night became day. The lightning was followed almost immediately by a thunderclap so loud that Ghaji's eardrums rang as if his ears had just been boxed by a warforged.

Yvka shouted something, but Ghaji's ears rang too loudly for him to hear her. He didn't think she was asking him if he'd slept well, though.

The wind picked up strength and speed until it drove the rain sideways and sent it stinging into Ghaji's skin like tiny daggers of ice. The thought of wearing his hood up in a storm no longer seemed so amusing, and Ghaji pulled the hood of his traveler's cloak over his head and drew the fabric over his shoulders. The cloth had been treated to be water resistant, but that didn't make it waterproof, especially in a storm of this intensity. Rain began to soak through immediately, but at least the cloak continued to provide some meager protection against the wind.

Speaking of the wind, it was now blowing so hard that the slate-gray water of the Lhazaar Sea was rising and dipping alarmingly, and spray was breaking over the *Zephyr*'s guardrails and onto the deck. Ghaji had no idea if the elemental sloop was built to withstand such a storm, but he figured it was time he found out. He started back to the pilot's seat, doing his best to maintain his balance and ignore the nausea roiling in his stomach in response to the turbulent sea.

Another blinding lightning flash lit up the sky, and this time the accompanying thunder came so quickly it almost seemed to precede the lightning. Ghaji struggled to see past the glowing afterimages the lightning flash left in his eyes. He wasn't sure, but it looked as if the blue-white glow of the elemental bound within the metal ring mounted behind Yvka was flickering like a flame in a high wind.

Ghaji reached the pilot's seat. Yvka sat with her hands pressed tight against the chair arms, while Diran held onto the chair back, his head leaned close to the elf-woman's so they could hear each other over the storm. Ghaji took hold of the chairback and squatted on the other side of the pilot's seat. It seemed that Diran and Yvka were arguing about something, but even this close, Ghaji still had trouble hearing all their words through the howling wind and driving rain.

". . . can make it!" Yvka shouted.

"Not if . . . any worse!" Diran shouted back.

"Soarwood . . . strong enough . . . mast will hold . . . and elemental can . . . to get us through!" Yvka replied.

Ghaji understood the gist of their argument now. Yvka wanted to weather the storm while Diran thought it was too dangerous and likely wanted to detour around it. Given how badly Diran wanted to rescue Makala and the other prisoners captured by the Black Fleet raiders, the situation had to be dire indeed for him to suggest taking anything other than the most direct route to Dreadhold.

Ghaji leaned his face closer to Yvka's so she might hear him better. "Have you ever sailed the *Zephyr* through a storm this bad before?"

"Summer storms like this are common on the Lhazaar!" Yvka shouted. It was a strain, but Ghaji was able to make out all her words this time. "They blow themselves out within an hour or so!"

"That doesn't answer my question. Have you ever been through a storm like this?"

Yvka didn't respond right away. Ghaji couldn't see her expression since her features were concealed by her hood.

"No," she said at last, speaking so softly her voice was nearly carried away on the roaring wind. "I haven't."

"The storm moved in from the northeast!" Diran shouted. "Tack southwest! That should get us out of the worst of it!"

Before Yvka could respond, lightning flashed and thunder cracked once more. This time they could hear the sizzle of the lightning, and a charge ran through the air, making their hair, wet though it might be, stand on end.

"South it is!" Yvka shouted. "I'll work the tiller and keep the elemental going! Diran, you and Ghaji go forward and trim the mainsail! We'll be running with the wind at least partially at our backs, and the storm wind, together with that generated by the elemental, might be too much for the mast to bear!"

"Aye, Captain! No problem!" Ghaji said, though he had only the vaguest notion of what "trim" meant. He wasn't about to admit to that Yvka; besides, he was sure Diran could show him.

Diran reached over and clapped Ghaji on the arm. "Come, my friend! Time to begin your sailor's education!"

Ghaji scowled. He couldn't see Yvka's face hidden in the folds of her hood, but he had no doubt the elf-woman was grinning.

CHAPTER

ELEVEN

Makala, free of her manacles, tried not to shiver as Onkar and Jarlain escorted her down a cold, dank corridor. She was chilled and she was frightened, but she'd been trained never to show the least sign of weakness to an enemy. She visualized standing on a beach in the bright noon sunshine, and it helped . . . a little, anyway. The hall was shrouded in gloom and shadow, the darkness relieved only by the occasional placement of torches that emitted a greenish light that did little to push back the darkness. Still, it was better than nothing, if only just.

She experienced an unexpected longing for the evil spirit that had once shared her soul. If their essences were still intertwined, she wouldn't have to struggle to control her fear. The spirit had made her feel strong, confident, invulnerable.

The surfaces of the walls, ceiling, and floor were smooth and even, and every few dozen yards iron support beams had been erected to brace the tunnel. The corridor had obviously been carved into the interior of the cliff, and despite her current situation, Makala couldn't help but be impressed at the time and effort such a feat of engineering must have required. It was worthy of the dwarf miners of the Mror Holds, though she doubted dwarves were responsible for the construction of this place. She'd seen no sign of a mining operation so far, let alone any dwarves. Besides, the ceiling was ten feet from the floor. Why would dwarves build a tunnel with so high a ceiling?

They passed wooden doors reinforced with bands of iron, though since all of the doors were closed, Makala had no idea what might lay in the chambers behind them. Considering what she knew of this place's occupants, she didn't think she *wanted* to know. The corridor was deserted for the most part, though occasionally they encountered others, mostly men and women with shaved heads like the Black Fleet raiders, though these were garbed in simple black robes. Once a pair of shaved heads were escorting a group of a half-dozen prisoners who were shackled at the wrist and ankles just as she had been. Makala guessed that they had been here for a while, for their clothing was torn, tattered, and caked with filth. Their hair was long and tangled, fingernails broken or chewed to the quick, and the men all had beards in varying stages of development. The prisoners were cadaverously thin, looking almost like living skeletons with only a thin layer of pale-white skin stretched over their bones. Their eyes were sunken into their sockets, the flesh around them so dark it looked bruised. Their necks, arms, and legs were dotted with puckered round scars, as if they had been tortured by having needle-sharp spikes driven into their flesh. Makala knew the skin of these poor people hadn't been violated by metal but rather by teeth, hungry, thirsty teeth. Worst of all was the expression on their faces. Their features were slack, eyes half-lidded and devoid of the least sign of intelligence or awareness. It was as if their lifeforces—indeed, their very souls—had been bled out of them along with their bodily fluids. Was this the fate that awaited her, Zabeth and the others from Port Verge? Makala didn't want to think about it, and she was glad when they moved past the prisoners and continued on their way.

To try and get the lost, vacant expressions of the prisoners out of her head, Makala turned her thoughts to Erdis Cai. Could he really be *the* Erdis Cai, the legendary sailor and explorer? While growing up, she'd heard tales of his exploits, and she remembered how Diran had liked to read about Cai in the days when they'd both still lived in Emon Gorsedd's manor. She'd skimmed one or two of those books herself, just to get a feeling for what Diran was reading as a way of getting closer to him. From what she recalled of her reading, Erdis Cai, after more adventure than most humans saw in a full lifetime, disappeared along with his crew before his fiftieth year. That had been four decades ago. She supposed that it was possible that the man she was going to meet was indeed Erdis Cai, assuming that he'd remained alive and in hiding for the last forty years. The man would be in his eighties by now, unless . . .

She glanced sideways at Onkar. If *he* was a vampire . . .

Makala started shivering, and this time she couldn't stop herself.

The corridor continued on for a long distance, but finally the hallway began to grow wider, the ceiling higher, and the corridor came to a dead end at a pair of large metal doors. Two huge iron rings served as knockers, and Onkar stepped forward, lifted one, and let it fall. The ring slammed against the metal surface of the door with a deep, hollow boom that vibrated through Makala's bones. A moment passed, then two, and the doors slowly swung open. Makala expected to hear the protesting creak of ancient hinges, but the doors opened silently and smoothly, obviously well maintained. When they were open all the way, Onkar turned to her, and with a mocking gleam in his eye, made a sweeping bow.

"After you."

Jarlain smiled but said nothing.

Makala did *not* want to go inside. Every instinct she possessed screamed for her to turn and run back down the corridor as fast as she could. She knew that doing so would result in punishment or perhaps even death, but that didn't matter, just as long as she didn't have to pass through the doorway that lay open before her. Despite her terror, or perhaps in a strange way because of it, Makala held her ground. She took a deep breath, held it for a moment, then slowly released it. She crossed the threshold, Onkar and Jarlain following close behind.

The first thing that struck Makala about the chamber inside was its size. It was immense, so large that she couldn't see the far wall. The second thing that struck her was the stalactites hanging from the ceiling, and she realized that she wasn't standing in a manmade structure at all but rather a huge natural cavern. A series of black iron braziers were placed throughout the cavern, their flames burning with the same subdued green light that illuminated the corridors. Makala neither saw nor smelled smoke, so she assumed the green fires were magical. The cavern, despite its size, was far from empty. The uneven rocky floor was covered with all manner of objects, both large and small, mundane and esoteric, scattered about without any apparent thought to organization. There was so much crammed so close together that Makala couldn't comprehend it all. Certain items stood out, though, and caught her eye. Among these were a wooden barrel filled with cutlasses, each with a severed skeletal hand still gripping tight to the handle; the shell of a gigantic turtle, its hard surface covered with sparkling gems that appeared to have grown there naturally instead of being mounted in place by a jeweler's hand; stone tablets sitting upright, indecipherable runes carved into their surface, the marks seeming to blur, distort, and rearrange into new yet equally enigmatic shapes if stared at for too long; a ten foot chunk of amber, trapped inside the shadowy form of a humanoid creature with four arms and a long forked tail; a pair of polished curving mammoth tusks propped up next to a set of huge jaws that could only have come from a monstrous shark; a gold-framed upright mirror whose smooth surface displayed no reflection but instead a furiously roiling darkness; a trio of what Makala at first thought were statues, but which she realized were instead deactivated warforged, but none like she'd ever seen before. These were crafted to resemble human-sized spiders, four of their eight legs terminating in wickedly sharp scimitar blades.

Though these and other bizarre objects dominated the cavern, by far the most common items in the sprawling collection were piles of weapons: swords, pikes, battle-axes, spears, bows; mounds of jewelry—necklaces, medallions, rings, brooches, all wrought from precious metals; vases, goblets, bowls, platters . . . paintings, statues, musical instruments . . . and of course coins; platinum, gold, silver, copper—different sizes, shapes, and denominations. It was as if all the riches and wonders of Khorvaire had been gathered up and stored within this cavern.

Makala could only stand and stare, jaw hanging open, scarcely breathing as she struggled to cope with the staggering grandeur spread out before her.

"One tends to acquire quite a few possessions over the course of eight decades. I keep thinking that I really should get rid of some of it, but I can never bring myself to do so. Too sentimental, I suppose."

Makala heard the voice, but she didn't see the speaker. The sound seemed to come from right next to her, as if whoever it was had spoken softly in her ear, but when she turned to look, no one was there.

"I'm glad to see you've returned from your latest voyage, Onkar . . . and with a guest. She could use a bath and a change of clothes, but otherwise she's quite lovely."

Makala still couldn't see who was speaking, but she didn't appreciate what he'd said.

"At least I don't hide from an unarmed woman like a coward," she snapped. She instantly regretted her rash comment. She'd been trained to keep a tighter rein on her emotions.

There was no flash of light, no puff of smoke. One moment the space in front of her was empty, and the next a man stood before her. He appeared to be in his mid-forties, tall, broad-shouldered, with close-cropped white hair that tapered to a subdued widow's peak. An old scar ran from the top of his forehead, over his right eye, and down to his chin. Instead of marring his appearance, the scar only served to enhance it, making his handsome, patrician features stand out in counterpoint. His skin had a whitish-blue cast, though it was currently tinted green from the mystic verdant fires that burned in the braziers illuminating the cavern. His gaze was clear and sharp, blazing with both fierce intelligence and indomitable will. The eyes themselves were tinted red, but unlike Onkar's eyes they didn't glow with an inner crimson fire. Makala sensed the great power the man commanded, but she could also sense that he held it in check, controlling it, making it serve him instead of the other way around.

Though he wore no helmet, he was otherwise encased in full armor with curved spiked protrusions at the shoulders and elbows. At first Makala thought the armor had been forged out of some kind of black metal or perhaps that it had been painted black after it was made. The armor didn't reflect the greenish light from the braziers; rather, it seemed to absorb it, as if the armor had been wrought from some arcane shadowy substance. She thought one might reach out to touch the armor, only to find one's fingers sinking into the darkness as if it truly were nothing more than shadow, and a hungry shadow at that. The armor wasn't completely black, however. Emblazoned on the breast plate was a symbol, a large crimson teardrop shape that appeared to be emerging from the fanged mouth of a bestial copper skull. Hanging from the swordbelt around the man's waist was a black-handled broadsword in an ebon scabbard. Makala wondered if once the sword was drawn it would shine with a silvery metallic gleam or if the blade would be as black as the man's armor. She hoped she wouldn't get an opportunity to find out.

Makala could only stand and stare, heartbeat pounding in her ears loud as thunder. She couldn't move, could scarcely breathe, could only stand immobile before him like a small animal frozen in terror by the mesmeric gaze of a hungry snake.

"Welcome. My name is Erdis Cai."

He said nothing more, just continued to look at her with his piercing red-tinged eyes. Sensing he was waiting to see what she would do, Makala put on a brave front.

"Am I supposed to be impressed?"

Erdis Cai's eyes widened in surprise, then he threw back his head and laughed. His laughter echoed throughout the cavern, and Makala could feel the rock tremble beneath her feet in response to its master's mirth.

When he looked at Makala again, he was smiling. "How delightful!" He turned to Onkar. "I think I'm beginning to see why you brought this one to my attention."

Onkar smiled. "Her name's Makala, Captain. She helped those two I told you about kill Sagaj. She used a crossbow, but there's more to her than archery skills." The crimson fire in the sailor's eyes blazed more intensely. "A lot more."

Jarlain looked at Makala then, but there was no amusement in her eyes, no smile on her beautiful pale face. "Perhaps she should spend some time with me then." The woman reached up and stroked Makala's jawline with a long-nailed index finger. "You know how much I enjoy getting to know newcomers . . . peeling away their outer layers to discover what secrets lie hidden underneath."

As Jarlain stroked Makala's jaw, Makala felt a sudden surge of fear. Her breathing came in short, ragged gasps.

Onkar chuckled. "You mean we know how jealous you get whenever the captain shows an interest in anyone but you. The more you learn about her, the better you'll be able to compete with her, yes?"

Jarlain's eyes flashed, and she removed her hand from Makala's face. The physical contact was broken; the fear that had gripped Makala drained away, leaving her shaky and weak.

"Watch you tongue, Onkar. You may be commander of the Black Fleet, but *I* am the mistress of Grimwall!"

Before Onkar could reply, Erdis Cai interrupted, his voice cold as winter frost. "You both are who *I* say you are. No more, no less."

Jarlain and Onkar exchanged hate-filled looks before bowing to Erdis Cai.

"My most sincere apologies, my lord," Jarlain said, though in a tone that made it clear she wasn't sorry in the slightest.

"And mine," Onkar said. "I'll keep quiet if the 'Mistress of Grimwall' will."

Jarlain glared at Onkar but didn't take his bait.

Still unsettled from the lingering emotional traces of the sudden fear she'd experienced. Makala looked to Erdis Cai to see how the man felt about this exchange between his underlings. If she were to have any hope of escaping Grimwall, it would be because of what she learned about the place and those who ruled here. She knew, as Emon Gorsedd had taught all his, that knowledge was the ultimate weapon.

Erdis Cai's face might well have been carved from polished ivory for all the expression it showed. Makala sensed no anger in him, not even simple irritation. It was as if the man he'd seemed to be a moment ago had been but a disguise, one that he'd allowed to slip, revealing the true face underneath. It was as emotionless and cold as a reptile's face, inhuman and uncaring—the face of a being to whom the difference between life and death was so minor as to be meaningless, a being who saw others simply as either prey or not-prey.

Makala knew which she preferred to be.

Then, just as fast as it had been discarded, the disguise was back in place once more, and Erdis Cai smiled like a tolerant father.

"That's enough, you two. We don't want to make a bad first impression on our guest, do we?"

Both Onkar and Jarlain nodded, looking only slightly chastened.

Makala was beginning to feel the first faint stirrings of hope. If there was conflict between the three of them, then perhaps if she were clever enough, she might find a way to exploit it for her own advantage.

"Jarlain, since you're so eager to get to know Makala, why don't you take charge of her for a time?" Erdis Cai said. "See she freshens up, eats, and is provided with new clothing. See also that she gets some rest. Bring her to me again after sunset. I would like to . . . talk with her further."

Without saying farewell to either Onkar or Jarlain or giving Makala another look, Erdis Cai turned and strode off, making his way easily through the mounds of ancient artifacts, precious treasure, and arcane junk that crammed the cavern. Within moments the shadowy gloom of the cavern had swallowed him and he was lost to Makala's vision. Most of her was relieved to see him go, but part of her, the part that still longed for her dark spirit, wished he had stayed.

"Come, girl. You heard the master."

Jarlain grabbed Makala's wrist, and the woman nearly

panicked, recalling the horrendous fear that had gripped her previously, but this time Jarlain's touch didn't spark any reaction within Makala other than disgust.

Jarlain led Makala out of the cavern, Onkar following close behind. Once they had crossed the threshold, the metal doors swung shut and the lock engaged with a soft click. Back in the corridor once more, Jarlain turned to Onkar.

"As for you, Commander, go do whatever it is you do when you're not at sea."

Onkar glared and his hands twitched, as if he were considering wrapping them around Jarlain's neck and squeezing until her pale white face turned purple-black, but he made no move to attack the woman.

"I suppose I'll go check on the new prisoners before I turn in." He looked at Makala. "Have a pleasant day."

The vampire headed down the corridor leaving Makala alone with Jarlain.

"Let's us two girls go get acquainted, shall we?" Jarlain squeezed Makala's wrist in a grip just short of being painful, and Makala offered no resisted as Jarlain escorted her down the corridor.

● ● ● ◉ ● ● ●

As the metal doors shut, the green fire burning in the braziers throughout the cavern slowly dimmed until it was gone, leaving behind only the darkness. Erdis Cai strolled through the cluttered maze of his possessions, not needing any illumination to make his way. Even if he didn't have a vampire's eyes, even if he were still mortal, so well did he know the position of every item in the cavern that he could have gone blindfolded and still not have bumped into anything or gotten lost. He'd spent a great deal of his time in here during the last few years, too much of it, perhaps. He'd even taken to resting here during the daylight hours, something he knew Jarlain didn't approve of. She didn't think it was "healthy," whatever that meant.

He paused for a moment and stretched out his senses. Dawn would be coming soon, and though no light could penetrate the tons of rock that lay between him and the sky, nevertheless he would be forced to rest. It was one of the limitations of undeath, but he didn't mind. The power he possessed was far greater than anything he had known as a mortal man, and it was well worth whatever minor inconveniences accompanied it.

He continued touring his collection, occasionally reaching out to touch this or that object, as if by doing so he might relive the adventure during which it had been acquired. Though the memories came, they were empty, hollow, unsatisfying, but then Erdis Cai had never been one to settle for past glories. He'd always searched for the next destination, the next challenge . . . always looking for something but never quite finding it, until, that is, the day he and his crew had anchored offshore of a certain island in the far frozen north where they'd discovered a castle and what dwelled within its cold, dark halls. Erdis Cai had found what he'd truly been searching for that day, or perhaps, he mused, it had found him. Whichever the case, Erdis Cai had, like a caterpillar transforming into a butterfly, become something much greater than he'd ever imagined.

If that were so, why did he hold onto all these things? Why did he spend so much time among them while his fleet, under

Onkar's command, sailed the Principalities, working to make the final preparations for their next adventure, the one destined to be the greatest of them all?

He knew how Jarlain would answer that question, for she had spoken to him on the subject numerous times before.

You're in your eighties, Erdis. You're coming to the end of what would've been your natural life span just as you're about to see the fulfillment of a plan you've worked to bring to fruition for the last forty years. It's only natural that you should spend some time in contemplation and self-reflection.

Perhaps she was right. Jarlain possessed great knowledge and insight into the mysterious and often baffling ways of the mind. Certainly she had infinitely more understanding than he—who, at heart, was still just a simple sailor—would ever have.

Lately he'd begun to fear that something else was at work here, something darker and more complex than the simple melancholy of an old man. He thought Jarlain had gotten it right when she'd first pointed out that he was, at least in terms of years, at the end of his human life. More and more often it felt like the personality that called itself Erdis Cai, the man who had once been one of the greatest mortal sailors ever to ply the seas, was dwindling away, eroding, shedding pieces of itself, like a calving iceberg, and in its place remained only a cold, fathomless darkness, like the uncaring ebon depths of the most frigid sea. Forty years ago, his body had died and been reborn, but now it seemed his very *self* was dying, and what new being would arise from its ashes, he couldn't guess.

He grew tired of this brooding. He would just have to trust to the grand darkness that had transformed him so long ago. He pressed his hand against the crimson symbol on his breastplate—a symbol known as the Mark of Vol.

Thy will be done, Mistress, he thought.

He sensed the night dwindling outside Grimwall, felt the first light of dawn glowing gently above the eastern horizon. A dull, leaden weariness came upon him, and he knew it was time to rest. He simply lay down where he was, between a massive shield he had once stolen from a storm giant and a large clay jar. He didn't bother to remove his armor. He was well beyond the need for what mortals would consider comfort.

As the day's oblivion began to take hold of him, he thought of Makala. That she was something special, he had sensed right away. Just *how* special, though, remained to be seen. She would be the next mystery for him to explore, and he was looking forward to it immensely. That, at least, was something about him that hadn't changed.

He closed his eyes as in the outer world, the sun edged up over the horizon and a new day began.

CHAPTER

TWELVE

I think we're coming out of it."

Yvka looked drained, as if keeping the elemental active during the storm had taken a great deal of energy out of her. She was pale, her face drawn, and Ghaji feared she might pass out any moment.

Diran's suggestion had worked. By going southeast, they'd escaped the storm's fury, and the waters they now sailed were calmer, and the rain fell more gently. The wind was still blowing strong but nothing like the gales they'd experienced before. Diran and Ghaji stood next to the mast where they'd ridden out most of the storm, prepared to make any needed adjustments in the sails.

Ghaji leaned close to Diran and whispered, "Do you think she's going to be all right?"

Diran glanced back over his shoulder at Yvka.

"It's difficult to say. She claimed the magic that controlled the elemental was embedded in the pilot's chair and the containment ring, but our journey has obviously taken a toll on her. Perhaps it's simply fatigue."

Without waiting for Ghaji to reply, Diran headed back toward the pilot's chair.

"The wind's strong enough," he said in a gentle voice. "Perhaps it's time we gave the elemental a rest."

Yvka looked at Diran with half-lidded eyes. "The elemental doesn't need . . ." She broke off and gave Diran a tired smile. "I see. I *am* weary," she admitted. "I don't need more than an hour's meditation, two at the most. I am an elf, after all."

"Of course," Diran said. "Ghaji and I can sail the *Zephyr* while you rest. We'll call you if anything happens."

Yvka looked at Diran for a moment, and Ghaji thought she might change her mind about resting, but finally she nodded and lifted her hand off the chair arm. As soon as she did, the glow in the elemental ring faded, and the wind that had been issuing forth from it died away. Yvka flexed her fingers, the joints making soft popping sounds as she did. She then removed her other hand from the tiller and rose from the pilot's seat. Diran then sat and took hold of the tiller.

The rain had tapered off to a mild drizzle now, and Yvka removed her sodden cloak and hung it over the guardrail to dry. She then headed toward the cabin just as the clouds broke, revealing a hint of dawn. When she drew near Ghaji, she paused.

"There's both water and food in the cabin. Feel free to come in and get it. If you want it, that is." She smiled then continued on into the cabin.

Ghaji watched her go, admiring the smooth, languid way she moved even tired as she was. When she closed the cabin door, after giving him a last meaningful look, the half-orc turned to Diran. Diran smiled and waggled his eyebrows.

Ghaji sighed.

"Diran?"

"Hmm?"

"What's this stuff? It looks like seaweed, but it's thicker and it's all around us."

"Seaweed?"

There was something about Ghaji's words that set off a warning bell in the back of Diran's mind, though he wasn't sure why. He locked the tiller into its current position, rose from the pilot's chair, and moved toward the starboard bow where Ghaji stood looking over the guardrail.

The stormclouds were long behind them now, and the late morning sky was a rich, clear blue. The rain was a memory as well, and the breeze had done much to dry the deck, as well as their cloaks, which hung on the railing next to Yvka's. The elf-woman was still resting, though she'd been in the cabin longer than the two hours she'd claimed was all she needed. Ghaji had entered the cabin once, on the pretext of fetching them some breakfast, and he'd struggled to hide his disappointment was he returned and announced that Yvka was still meditating. Diran, to his credit, had managed not to laugh.

He joined Ghaji at the guardrail and looked down at the water. Just beneath the surface was a thready mass of greenery that indeed looked something like seaweed, and as Ghaji had said, it seemed to surround the starboard side of the *Zephyr*, stretching off into the distance.

"It's like this in front and on the other side, too," Ghaji said. "I checked."

"It doesn't appear to be slowing us down." Even without the elemental's aid, they were making good time, but Diran couldn't shake the feeling that this situation was familiar somehow. A mass of seaweed covering the water for miles . . . ships sailing right through it with ease, almost as if it parted to allow them passage . . .

"By the Flame!" Diran whispered as sudden realization struck him. "We're in the Mire!"

"The what?" Ghaji asked.

Instead of answering, Diran said, "Go get Yvka."

Ghaji scowled, but rather than questioning Diran further, he walked to the cabin. A few moments later he returned with Yvka at his side, the elf-woman looking rested and restored.

"Imagine my disappointment when Ghaji told something about a lot of seaweed in the water. Not to be rude, but where else is seaweed supposed to be?"

"I'm afraid we've blundered into the Mire," Diran said.

Yvka just looked at him for a moment, as if he'd just told the first part of a joke and she was waiting for him to deliver the punchline. When none was forthcoming, she said, "The Mire is nothing but an old sailor's legend."

Diran gestured toward the guardrail. "See for yourself."

Yvka walked over to the railing and peered out across the water. She stood there for several seconds before returning to them. "There's seaweed out there close to the surface, and a lot of it, but that doesn't mean this is the Mire."

Despite the elf-woman's words, her tone wasn't as confident as it had been a moment before.

"Whether we're in it or not, would either of you mind telling me exactly what this Mire is?" Ghaji asked, exasperated.

"My father used to tell me stories about the Mire—stories that he swore were true."

"With all due respect," Yvka said, "fathers tell their children spooky stories all the time, and they claim them to be true to make them even scarier, but that doesn't *make* them true."

"That still doesn't tell me what the Mire *is*," Ghaji complained.

Diran turned to his friend. "The Mire is a huge expanse of seaweed rumored to be thousands of square miles wide. According to the tales, ships have no trouble sailing into the Mire, but once inside, they become trapped and can never win free."

"It's just a fable," Yvka insisted, "a story told to explain ships that most likely went missing due to storms or other natural causes."

Ghaji glanced toward the starboard bow and pointed. "You mean ships like that one?"

Diran and Yvka looked in the direction Ghaji indicated. Off in the distance was a shape that appeared to be the partially submerged remains of a ship larger than the *Zephyr*—a two-master, perhaps, though it was difficult to tell since so much of it lay below the water's surface.

"Yes," Diran said dryly. "Precisely like that. Does it strike either of you as odd that we're heading directly for it, almost as if we're being guided there?"

Ghaji stretched out his arms then did a couple of torso twists to limber up. "Best get our weapons, eh?"

The half-orc didn't sound displeased at the prospect that they might be approaching danger.

Ghaji was probably getting restless, Diran thought. It had

been nearly an entire day since he'd had the opportunity to fight someone.

"Should I activate the elemental?" Yvka asked. "If we're going toward the vessel anyway, perhaps we shouldn't waste any time."

The elf-woman's meditation had restored her energy, and she was now wide awake and alert. Diran had no doubt she could summon and direct the elemental's power, but he wasn't certain it was a good idea.

"We don't know how thick the seaweed truly is. It's possible that the soarwood runners will be able to cut through the substance of the Mire without any difficulty, but it's also possible that by sailing at our top speed, we might end up entangling ourselves. We're making good progress at our current speed; I suggest saving the elemental for when we might truly need it."

Yvka considered Diran's words for a moment before nodding agreement. She returned to the tiller, and Diran and Ghaji armed themselves. The priest donned his cloak, though it was still damp from the rain, and retrieved his bow and arrows. Ghaji got his axe as well as a grappling hook. The points were sharp, and the rope looked strong.

The *Zephyr* continued sailing toward the half-submerged vessel, and before long they were within shouting distance of the derelict. Yvka locked the tiller once more and was about to prepare to put down anchor, when the wind died and the sloop began to slow down on her own. Diran peered over the side and saw that the seaweed was much thicker here, and instead of giving way before them, it now seemed to be pressing against the *Zephyr's* hull, as if purposefully retarding the vessel's progress.

When they'd come within a half dozen yards of the other ship, the *Zephyr* came to a halt.

This close, they could see that the partially submerged vessel was indeed a two-master, though the ship was tilted back so far the bow pointed skyward and the tip of the second mast barely extended past the water's surface. The sails were still up, though the fabric was sodden and torn in numerous places, as if someone had repeatedly slashed it with a sword. There were no visible signs of damage on the hull, at least not from their vantage point, and the vessel's name was clearly visible on the port bow, painted in faded black letters: *Proud Pelican*. The seaweed around the ship was so thick it resembled solid earth covered with wet green grass and a thin layer of water. It looked almost as if the plants were holding the *Proud Pelican* in place, and that the vessel would slip completely beneath the waves if they were to release her.

Evidently Ghaji was having similar thoughts, for he said, "Looks almost solid enough to stand on."

"Be my guest," Yvka said. "I'm not setting foot on that muck!"

"I don't blame you, lady!"

Startled, the three of them turned toward the direction the new voice came from. Perched atop the tip of the bow, straddling it as if he were astride a horse, was a halfling. Diran judged him to be three feet tall, an average height for his kind. He had an athletic build, ruddy skin, dark eyes—brown, Diran guessed, though it was hard to tell from such a distance—and straight black hair tied into a ponytail. As was common for halflings, he had pointed ears, though not so sharply pointed as Yvka's. He wore sailor's garb: brown leggings, bare feet, an orange sash around his trim waist, a white shirt with billowy sleeves, and a red scarf covering the top of his head as protection against the sun. Tucked beneath the halfling's sash was a long knife that, in his small hands, would look like a sword, and Diran guessed he wielded it as such. Though Diran had never spent a great deal of time around halflings, he judged this one to be a young adult in his early to mid-twenties.

"I guess we don't have to hail the ship now," Ghaji said.

"The name's Hinto," the halfling called, "and you can bet I'm glad to see you three! Tell me something, is your ship really made out of soarwood, or have I been alone too long and am starting to imagine things?" An alarmed looked came over the halfling's face. "Maybe I'm imagining this whole thing! The ship *and* you three!"

"Calm yourself," Diran said before the halfling could get too worked up. "We're real enough, though I fear we've wandered into the same trap that ensnared your vessel. You said you're alone, so I assume there are no other survivors."

"That's right, I'm the last one. That's because I know how to hide. When I put my mind to it, I can hide so good I can't even find myself!" Hinto chuckled at his own joke, then sobered. His eyes darted back and forth nervously, as if he were expecting to be attacked any moment from any direction. "I've been alone for days now, or maybe it's been weeks." He looked at them and smiled apologetically. "I've track of time out here."

"I don't think that's the only thing he's lost," Ghaji muttered, then he let out an *oof!* as Yvka elbowed him in the side.

"I'm Diran Bastiaan, priest of the Silver Flame. These are my companions, Ghaji and Yvka. Can you tell us what happened to your vessel and crew?"

"You mean can I tell you what's going to happen to *you*," the halfling said, an hysterical edge to his voice.

Diran was beginning to think Ghaji had been right: Hinto's mind was somewhat the worse for wear after being trapped alone in the Mire.

"It's this place . . ." Hinto began. "The Mire . . . though it's not really the Mire, not like the stories say it is. Oh, it *looks* like a mess of seaweed, but that's what it *wants* you to think. It's something else, something worse. Something . . . *hungry*."

Diran, Ghaji, and Yvka looked down at the seaweed between the *Zephyr* and *Proud Pelican*.

The half-orc shrugged. "Still looks like seaweed to me."

"Of *course* it does!" Hinto said. "Haven't you been listening to me? Don't you *get* it?"

Ghaji gripped his axe and bared his lower incisors.

Diran lay a hand on his friend's arm to calm him. "Can you throw that grappling hook so it catches on the *Pelican*'s bow?"

"I think so," Ghaji said.

Diran turned back to Hinto and explained their plan.

"Why don't I just climb over there?" Hinto asked. "Not that it's going to make any difference since you're all going to die."

"I'm afraid you may be too weak to hold onto the rope after being trapped here for so long." This was true enough, but Diran was also worried that Hinto's mental state made him so unpredictable that the halfling might well let go of the rope of his own accord for some reason before he reached the *Zephyr*.

"I appreciate the thought," Hinto said, "but I wouldn't try coming over if I were you. *It* won't like it, if you know what I mean."

"No, we *don't* know what you mean!" Ghaji shouted. "You don't make any sense! Now get out of the way unless you want me to bounce this thing off your head."

Hinto rose from his perch on the bow and scampered out of sight.

Diran and Yvka stepped back to give Ghaji room. The half-orc held the grappling hook in his right hand and the rope it was tied to in his left. He took a moment to gauge the distance and the direction of the wind, then he drew back his arm and threw the hook. The barbed metal object soared through the air, the rope trailing out behind it. The hook passed over the upraised bow of the *Pelican* and landed on the other side with a thunk against the ship's hull. Ghaji slowly pulled the rope until the hook caught on something. From the angle at which the *Pelican* was jutting out of the water, they couldn't see what the hook had taken hold of and whether that hold was strong.

"Hinto!" Diran called. "Can you check the hook to make sure it's holding fast?"

There was no reply for a moment, and Diran started to wonder if the mysterious *It* of which the halfling had spoken had snatched him when he was out of their view. Then Hinto, from wherever he was hiding, shouted, "It's caught tight against the bow roller! It's not going anywhere!"

The bow roller was the fitting over which the chain of the forward anchor ran. Good enough.

Ghaji tied the other end of the rope to the *Zephyr*'s guardrail. He then turned to Diran. "Which one of us goes first?"

"Of the two of us, you are the stronger."

"Where's Yvka?"

The two companions looked at the rope line that now

stretched between the two vessels. Yvka was walking across, hands held out to her sides for balance.

"She's a juggler and acrobat, remember?" Diran said.

"I've been thinking of her as a spy for so long, I'd almost forgotten."

Hinto's head poked up over the edge of the *Pelican*'s bow. "Be careful," the halfling said. "It's been awhile since *It* ate the last of my friends, and it's bound to be awfully hungry by now."

Yvka didn't respond to Hinto's warning, and she didn't look down at the surface of the Mire as she carefully made her way along the rope.

Diran and Ghaji, however, did look down, and they didn't like what they saw. Four holes opened in the thick seaweed, and from each a sinuous gray creature slithered. The serpent-like things had no features, save for openings on their rounded ends that resembled puckered mouths. The mouths gaped open to reveal circular rows of tiny sharp teeth.

"Watch out, Yvka!" Ghaji warned, then to Diran he said, "What *are* those things? Some kind of eel?"

"Eels can't raise up out the water like that, and their mouths look more like those of lampreys."

The four creatures, whatever they were, possessed no obvious sensory organs, but the lack didn't seem to impair them as they lunged toward Yvka, ringed mouths opening even wider. Diran reached for a pair of daggers, but fast as he was, the lamprey-like things were faster.

Just as they were about to fasten their hungry mouths on Yvka's legs, the elf-woman crouched down, bent her knees, and launched herself into the air in a forward roll. She tucked her chin to her chest and kept her arms held out straight as she spun around and landed lightly on her feet. The rope bowed beneath her weight and shimmied from side to side, but Yvka managed to keep from falling off.

The lamprey-things waved about in confusion at the sudden relocation of their prey, but Diran knew it wouldn't take long for them to attack again. He had only seconds to take advantage of their confusion. He drew two daggers and hurled them at a pair of the creatures, and before those daggers had time to strike their targets, he drew and released two more. All four daggers found their marks, but the rubbery gray hides of the creatures were so thick that the needle-sharp tips of the knives barely penetrated the flesh. The lamprey-things shook the daggers off, and the blades fell to the seaweed-covered surface of the water. Three of the four daggers landed on their side, but one fell point-first and embedded itself in the thick layer of plant material. The seaweed, dense as it was, wasn't as resilient as the lamprey-things' hides, and the blade sank up to the hilt. The seaweed surrounding the blade shuddered and the dagger popped upward, as if violently thrust by something below. The knife landed on its side this time, and its steel surface was coated with a viscous dark-green slime.

"Did you see that?" Ghaji asked.

"I did," Diran replied, but he had no time to consider the implications. He'd managed to distract the lamprey-things long enough for Yvka to keep walking across the rope, and she'd nearly reached the *Proud Pelican*. The creatures, as if sensing their meal was close to escaping them, turned in Yvka's direction and stretched for her.

Diran reached into his cloak for another pair of daggers, but these weren't like the others he'd tried—these had been specially prepared. The blades struck their targets with the same result as before, sinking into the creatures' hides only an inch of so, and just as they had before, the lamprey-things paused to shake off the blades before resuming their attack. This time instead of lunging toward Yvka again, they stiffened, the tiny wounds made by Diran's daggers rapidly swelling and turning an ugly black. Thick grayish-green ooze began bubbling out of the creatures' tooth-ringed maws, and their snake-like bodies shrank in on themselves as their hides grew wrinkled, dry, and leathery. Twitching feebly, the four desiccated creatures withdrew back into the holes they'd emerged from, and the seaweed filled in after them.

Yvka made it the rest of the way to the *Pelican* and crouched upon its upturned bow. Once more, Hinto was nowhere in sight.

"Hinto?" she called. "Are you hurt?"

At first there was no reply, and Diran feared that the halfling had been taken by other lamprey-things while hidden from view. Then Hinto called out, "I'm fine," and crawled into view.

Diran looked down at the surface of the Mire and saw that, while all four of the special daggers he'd thrown had landed on their sides, the seaweed around them had turned black.

"Interesting . . ."

Ghaji groaned. "I hate it when you say that. It often means we're in worse trouble than we thought."

Diran turned to his friend and smiled. "Aren't we usually?"

The half-orc smiled back. "I guess. Why should this situation be any different, eh?"

Diran glanced once more at the black patches of seaweed and noted they were slowly widening. He wasn't sure, but he thought the greenery surrounding the black patches was quivering, as if in pain.

Diran's smile fell away. "I'm afraid things *are* different this time . . . and if what I suspect is true, the situation is far deadlier than anything we've ever faced before."

"Worse than—"

"Yes."

"How about—"

"Not even close."

Ghaji looked over at the *Pelican* and sighed. "Now I *really* wish Yvka hadn't been meditating when I went into her cabin."

CHAPTER

THIRTEEN

Poison?" Hinto said. "I've never heard of such a thing. What kind of priest uses *poison?*"

"The kind that helped get you off that death-trap of a ship," Ghaji said.

Hinto looked at the half-orc as if he expected the big man to try to take a bite out of him. "Not that I'm ungrateful," he said to Diran. "Just surprised is all."

The four of them sat on the deck of the *Zephyr,* eating hardtack and drinking fresh water from Yvka's supplies. It wasn't the most satisfying meal Ghaji ever had, but he'd choked down worse during his years as a soldier. After Diran had used his poison-coated daggers to stop the lamprey-things, Yvka and Hinto had managed to cross back over to the *Zephyr* without incident. Ghaji figured that the poison had killed the creatures that had attacked Yvka and perhaps their deaths had frightened any others away, but when he'd said as much to Diran, the priest had merely grunted, and Ghaji hadn't pressed his further. He knew that Diran would share his thoughts with the rest of them when he was ready and not before.

"What can you tell us about the *Pelican*'s demise?" Diran asked Hinto.

The halfling bit off a chunk of hardtack and chewed as he spoke. "We set sail from Tantamar, carrying a hold full of spices and silks, bound for Port Krez. Well, that's a long voyage, and the captain and crew of the *Pelican* like . . . *liked* their drink, and it wasn't long before our supply of spirits began to dwindle, so when we spied another two-master on the horizon, we changed flags and set off after her."

"Changed flags?" Ghaji said.

"Life's hard in the Principalities," Diran explained. "Lhazaarites do what they must to survive. One day a ship might fly a merchant's flag, the next a pirate's. It's a matter of pragmatism."

Ghaji sniffed.

"I didn't say I approve," Diran added, "but that's the way it is."

"True enough," Hinto said. "A man has to live by his wits on the sea. Now, if I can get on with my story?"

Ghaji gritted his teeth. One moment the halfling acted terrified of him, then the next he was insulting. Another sign of the man's mental instability, Ghaji decided, but that didn't mean he had to like it.

Hinto continued, "We caught up to the other vessel and took the crew by surprise which, considering they were all drunk themselves, wasn't too difficult. The *Pelican*'s captain recognized the merchant's flag they were flying, and we couldn't believe our luck. The ship was likely carrying a hold full of

Regalport spirits, and the fact that the crew was more than three sheets to the wind meant they'd been sampling some of their own cargo. We subdued the crew, which mostly consisted of just tying them up. No need to hurt folks unless you have to, right? Then we set about emptying their hold of spirits and filling ours. When the deed was done, we sailed off, but only after untying a couple of unconscious crewmen so they could later free their fellows.

"The *Pelican* continued on her way to Port Krez, and the crew lost no time getting into the spirits." He grinned. "I have to admit to sampling a bit myself. That night most of us were dead drunk and sleeping it off." His voice grew softer then, and his tone hollow. "I guess we must've sailed into the Mire without realizing it, for when I woke up the next morning, half the crew was missing and the ship had a leak in the hold and was slowly sinking, though it never did go all the way under. Those of us left alive salvaged what food and water we could and broke out a couple of longboats. After the first one set off and the crew was devoured by those gray things, the last of us didn't bother launching the second longboat. Instead, we concentrated on keeping ourselves alive. Much good it did us. After the last of my shipmates was gone, I was alone in the dark, with those things out there, searching for me, slithering around what was left of the *Pelican*. I could hear their mouths opening and closing, hear the sound of their tiny needle teeth clacking together . . ." The halfling began shivering as if caught in a sudden cold breeze that only he could feel. "None of us will ever escape. *It* won't let us."

Yvka reached out and put a hand on Hinto's shoulder to comfort him, but the halfling let out a startled cry, and she quickly took her hand away. All they could do was sit and wait for Hinto to regain control of himself.

After a bit, the halfling's trembling eased, and he gave the others an embarrassed smile. "Sorry about that."

"Nothing to apologize for," Diran said.

Ghaji didn't want to disturb the halfling further, but they needed to understand as much about the Mire as they could. "You keep saying *It*, like there's only one great, powerful creature, but four of those seaworms attacked Yvka, and we got rid of them easily enough. Are you sure you're not making the Mire out to be worse than it really is?"

"I don't think our new friend is doing anything of the kind," Diran said. "I've been thinking a great deal about our encounter with those 'seaworms,' as you called them, Ghaji. I've come to the conclusion that they weren't separate creatures, but rather a single beast of some sort— one incredibly vast creature that is the Mire itself. That is the *It* of which Hinto speaks."

Ghaji had been expecting his friend to make some sort of statement about the nature of the seaworms, but he hadn't been expecting anything like this. "Didn't you say the Mire was reputed to be thousands of square miles in size? How could a beast that large possible exist?"

"If it did, how could it ever find enough food to feed itself?" Yvka added. "There's no way it could get enough nourishment solely by ensnaring sailing vessels and devouring their crews."

"I doubt the Mire subsists only on unfortunate sailors," Diran said. "It most likely preys on undersea life as well. As for the issue of its size, I believe that the vast majority of the creature—what appears to be mile upon mile of seaweed—is in fact some kind of sensory apparatus, lure, or camouflage, and quite likely a combination of all three. The heart of the creature lies here, at the center of the Mire."

"What where those seaworms then?" Ghaji asked. "Something like octopus tentacles?"

Diran nodded. "That's my guess, though with mouths on the end. Whether those orifices are for ingesting or merely grabbing hold of prey, I don't know."

Diran went on to tell them of his observations of how the "seaweed" had reacted to being stabbed by one of the daggers, how it shuddered when the lamprey-things had been poisoned, and how the toxic coating of the daggers had killed the surrounding seaweed when they'd landed upon it. They had all seen the large black patch of dead seaweed that had resulted. It covered most of the distance between the *Pelican* and the *Zephyr*. The daggers themselves had been retrieved by Ghaji with the aid of the grappling hook, now that the line between the two ships was no longer needed.

Yvka frowned as she considered Diran's words. "I suppose it makes sense. It certainly would explain why no one ever escapes the Mire . . . and it's difficult to believe that simple seaweed, no matter how thick, could really trap a vessel, especially one that's powered by an air elemental."

"If we're basically sitting on top of the thing's mouth," Ghaji said, "why doesn't it just swallow us down ship and all?"

Diran shrugged. "Who can say? If it could swallow an entire ship, or even use its tentacles to crush it, it surely would've done so to get at Hinto by now. Perhaps the Mire is like the larger whales who, for all their vast size, can only feed by straining water through their baleen and trapping tiny sea creatures within. The Mire feeds the way it does because it can feed no other way."

"It's a good thing too," Yvka said, "or else we wouldn't have a chance to escape." She rose from her seat and walked across the deck, heading back toward the pilot's seat.

Diran stood, but he did not follow her. "What do you intend to do?"

"I'm going to wake the elemental and get us out of here." The elf-woman sat in the pilot's chair, unlocked the tiller, then placed her palm on the hand link. A moment later, the containment ring behind her began to glow as the elemental awoke. Wind blew forth from the ring, and the *Zephyr*'s sails filled with air.

"Best take a seat, Diran," Yvka said. "We're going to be moving pretty fast in a minute."

From the expression on Diran's face, the priest didn't think this was a good idea, but he sat back down with Ghaji and Hinto and waited to see what would happen.

At first it looked like his worries were unfounded. The elemental sloop began to inch forward, slowly at first, then with increasing speed. Soon the vessel began to slow and it came to a jarring stop. The elemental continued to pour forth wind, but the *Zephyr* didn't move. Yvka concentrated and the wind blowing from the glowing containment ring increased in strength, but though Ghaji could feel the sloop straining to push through the Mire, it didn't budge. The wind grew more intense yet, whistling and roaring as if the elemental were summoning forth the power of a hurricane. Diran, Ghaji, and Hinto grabbed hold of their seats to steady themselves as the wind tore at their backs, but the despite the increased effort the vessel remained stuck.

Over the sound of the elemental's wind, Ghaji heard a

strained creaking, and he knew that they were in trouble. He turned around, closing his eyes against the buffeting wind, and shouted back to Yvka.

"The mast is breaking!" He yelled as loudly as he could, hoping the wind wouldn't muffle his words.

Yvka looked at the half-orc and frowned, so he shouted his warning again. A look of alarm came over Yvka's face, and she yanked her hand away from the chair arm. Instantly, the glow flickering around the containment ring vanished and the wind ceased blowing. The elf-woman leaped out of the pilot's seat and rushed to the mast to check the damage.

"How bad is it?" Diran asked.

"It doesn't look too serious," Yvka said, "but it would probably be best if we refrained from running at full speed from now on."

"I don't think that will be a problem," Ghaji said, "seeing as how it doesn't look like we'll be running at any speed for the foreseeable future."

"See?" Hinto said. "I told you we can't escape."

Diran ignored the halfling pirate and walked to the *Zephyr's* bow. Ghaji, after giving Hinto a quick glare, joined his friend. They looked over the rail, and Ghaji saw that the seaweed layer in front of the sloop looked as solid as green rock.

"The Mire might not be able to reach out and crush a vessel," Diran said, "but it can certainly keep us from going anywhere. At least, as long as it's healthy."

"What do you mean?" Ghaji asked.

In answer, Diran drew one of his poison-smeared daggers, to which he'd applied a fresh coat, and leaned over the railing. Holding tight to the hilt, he gave the blade a flick to shake off a few droplets of poison. Ghaji watched the seaweed where the drops hit turn instantly black, as if Diran had splattered them with dark ink, but more than their color change, the half-orc noted that the consistency of the substance softened and seemed to relax.

Diran replaced the dagger in his cloak, sliding it into the hidden pocket that Ghaji knew was specially treated to hold the poison he used. The priest then reached into the money purse hanging from his belt and withdrew two copper coins. He handed one to Ghaji.

"Throw yours onto the green section. I'll toss mine onto the black."

Ghaji nodded, took the copper, and did as his friend asked. Ghaji's coin hit the hardened seaweed layer with an audible clink and bounced several times before coming to a rest. Diran then tossed his coin. It hit the small black patch with a soft, moist splat and then slowly sank from sight.

Diran turned toward Ghaji and smiled.

❂ ❂ ❂ ❂ ❂ ❂ ❂

By mid afternoon they were ready to put Diran's plan into action. Ghaji stood at the bow, holding onto the grappling hook. His hand was covered with a crudely stitched glove made from the pockets in Diran's cloak where he had kept his poison daggers. The hook itself was liberally coated with glistening poison. Diran stood at the starboard railing, facing The *Proud Pelican*, bow in hand, arrow nocked and ready. The tip of Diran's arrow was wrapped in cloth that had been soaked in lantern oil. Yvka sat in the pilot's seat, ready to activate the elemental at Diran's command. Hinto crouched next to her, looking nervous, but ready to help if he were needed.

"Ready, Ghaji?" Diran called.

"Always," the half-orc replied. He had no idea if his friend's plan was going to work, but that didn't bother him too much. Finding out was always half the fun.

"Go!" Diran ordered.

Ghaji hurled the grappling hook as far as he could straight out before them. The opposite end of the rope was tied fast to the bow railing so there would be no worries about losing it. The hook hit the hardened seaweed layer and bounced a couple of times. When it came to a rest, Ghaji began hauling it in, being careful not to pull too fast so the hook wouldn't bounce much on the way back. The goal was not to simply retrieve the hook, but to poison as much of the green substance of the Mire as possible.

Ghaji watched the seaweed as he pulled in the hook. A black line of poisoned seaweed trailed behind the hook, almost as if it were a quill pen that Ghaji was using to etch a broad black line toward the *Zephyr*'s bow.

"Almost done!" Ghaji called out.

Diran nodded and using a flint and striker, ignited the oil-soaked cloth at the tip of his arrow. The cloth burst into flame, and Diran let it burn for several seconds before he drew back his string, aimed, and let the arrow fly.

Still pulling in the grappling hook, Ghaji watched Diran's flaming arrow arc through the air toward the *Pelican*. Diran had taken up the traditional weapon of the Order of the Silver Flame late in life and was still only minimally competent with it, but the target was large enough, and better yet, completely stationary, and the arrow streaked toward the *Pelican*'s upturned bow. Ghaji had already tossed a lantern full of oil over earlier, breaking it against the ship and soaking the wood with flammable fuel. Thus the arrow's fire quickly spread, and within seconds the *Pelican*'s bow had become a blazing bonfire, bright flames reaching toward the sky as they hungrily devoured the ship's wood.

Ghaji finished pulling in the hook, and he was careful to take hold of it with his gloved hand. The black line was widening as more of the seaweed, or whatever the stuff was, died. Now everything depended on whether what Hinto had told them was true. Inside the *Pelican*'s hold, which was only partially submerged, were crates filled with what remained of the Regalport spirits the crew had "liberated" during their ill-fated voyage. If the flames burned hot enough to ignite the alcohol in those bottles . . .

As if Ghaji's thought made it reality, the *Pelican* exploded in a fiery blast that sent flaming debris flying everywhere, including onto the *Zephyr*'s deck. Immediately following the explosion, a shockwave rippled beneath the *Zephyr*, and both Ghaji and Diran had to grab hold of the vessel's railing to keep from being knocked off their feet. Ghaji became aware of a low thrumming sound, one more felt than heard. It almost sounded like something was moaning in pain, something *huge*.

"Now, Yvka!" Diran shouted.

The elf-woman slapped her palm onto the hand link on the arm of the pilot's chair, and the containment ring flared to life. The elemental trapped within began producing wind, and the *Zephyr*'s sails grew instantly full. At first the vessel didn't move, but then she began sliding forward across the blackened path that Ghaji had created with the poisoned grappling hook.

It was working! Diran's plan had been to make a passage so they could sail out of the Mire and to burn up the *Pelican* to distract the great beast while they escaped. Of course, Diran hadn't mentioned anything about flaming debris raining down on the *Zephyr*. The elemental's wind extinguished the flames that had begun to eat at the mainsail, but a half dozen other small fires now burned on the sloop's deck. Hinto jumped up from where he crouched beside Yvka. Her traveler's cloak still hung on the railing where she'd earlier put it to dry. The halfling snatched up the cloak as he ran past then dashed into the cabin. When he came out, he carried a water skin, and he uncorked it and poured the contents over the cloak. Then Hinto went to work snuffing out the flames.

Ghaji looked back questioningly to the halfling, but the pirate said, "I've got it! You keep doing your job!"

Ghaji had to admit that for a man who was a few eggs shy of a full nest, Hinto didn't hesitate when it came time to act. Ghaji turned back toward the bow and hurled the grappling hook again, intending to create the next leg of their passage out of the Mire.

As Hinto slapped the sodden cloak on the deck in his effort to extinguish the flames, one of the Mire's lamprey-mouths lunged over the guardrail toward him. The halfling screeched in terror as the tooth-ringed maw came at him, but Diran dropped his bow, drew a poisoned dagger from his cloak and threw it at the lamprey-thing. The blade struck the creature in the mouth, and grayish-green ooze shot forth to splatter onto the deck, just missing the still shrieking Hinto. The lamprey-thing, already turning black from the poison, took

Diran's dagger with it as it slipped back over the railing and into the sea.

Diran started toward the halfling, but before he had taken two steps, he whirled back around. He drew another poisoned dagger as he spun and slashed the lamprey-thing that had just been about to fasten onto the back of his neck. The blade's edge was sharp, its poison strong, and the lamprey-thing's rubbery gray hide parted like wet vellum. The creature fell back into the Mire in two blackening pieces.

More of the lamprey-things came lunging over the railing after that, as if the Mire was desperately trying to keep them from escaping. Diran fought the creatures off wielding a poison-coated dagger in each hand, while Hinto continued putting out flames with Yvka's cloak, shrieking all the while. When the last fire was out, the halfling pirate ran back to Yvka's side, curled up into a ball, and shivered uncontrollably.

It was slow going, and the Mire continued to attack with its serpent-mouths as they went, but once they had gotten far enough away from what Ghaji guessed to be the Mire's central core, the lamprey-things came no more, and the *Zephyr* was able to make better progress. Come dusk, the sloop at last sailed out of the Mire and once more plied the open sea.

Ghaji tossed the grappling hook into the water to clean off the last traces of poison, then hauled it back in and dropped it onto the deck. His arm and shoulder ached like blazes from long hours of heaving the grappling hook and pulling it in, but the pain was a small price to pay for helping to win their freedom.

Ghaji walked over to Diran and gave his friend a weary grin. "Looks like we survived another one," he said.

Diran smiled and lay a hand on Ghaji's shoulder. Though the priest appeared to do nothing special, soothing warmth spread through Ghaji's shoulder and down along his arm, washing away his pain.

"Thanks," Ghaji said.

Diran gave Ghaji's shoulder an affectionate squeeze before removing his hand. "Anytime, my friend."

The two companions headed back to the pilot's chair were Yvka sat, Hinto sill at her side, though the halfling no longer shook with fear.

"I have to admit I was wrong," the halfling said. "The Mire *almost* got us, but it didn't, thanks to you three. I'm in your debt."

"You carried your weight well enough," Ghaji said. " 'Course, small as you are, there's only so much to carry."

Hinto grinned at the joke, taking no offense. "So where are you bound?" he asked.

"We're on an urgent mission," Diran said, "to save a friend of ours who's been abducted by sea raiders, along with all those who were taken with her. To that end, we're traveling to Dreadhold."

Hinto's eyes went wide. "Dreadhold? The prison island?"

"The same," Diran confirmed.

Hinto jumped to his feet and ran to the guardrail. He climbed up and launched himself into the air, clearly attempting to abandon ship. He would have succeeded too, if Ghaji hadn't managed to catch hold of him at the last instant.

"Let me go!" Hinto kicked and thrashed, trying to free himself from the half-orc's grip without success. "They don't kindly to resourceful sailors such as myself on Dreadhold!"

"You mean *pirates* like you," Ghaji said. He tossed the half-ling onto the deck.

"Don't worry," Diran said in a soothing voice. "What you may have done in the past is no concern of ours. We have no intention of turning you over to the prison's warders."

Hinto didn't look entirely convinced, but he didn't make another attempt to leap overboard. He drew his knees up to his chest and wrapped his slender arms around them.

"Tell me more about this friend of yours," he said.

CHAPTER

FOURTEEN

Makala awoke upon a soft mattress covered by a satin sheet that felt more luxurious than anything she'd ever known. The room was lit by the gentle glow of a lantern sitting on top of a dressing table of highly polished wood. A gold-framed mirror hung above the table next to a huge jewelry box with the lid raised. The box had to be kept open because of the massive mound of jewelry spilling over the sides: pearls, diamonds, rubies, opals, and shimmering crystals that Makala suspected might be miniature dragonshards. In the corner of the room was a tall wardrobe, its doors partially open to reveal the ornate gowns hanging inside. Other than these things, the room, hewn from the same smooth rock as the rest of Grimwall, was bare of furnishings and possessions.

This was Jarlain's room, though it seemed the woman wasn't here. After Erdis Cai had given Jarlain charge of Makala, the pale raven-haired beauty had escorted her though the corridors of Grimwall to her own quarters. She'd chatted along the way as if the two of them were old friends instead of captor and prisoner. When they'd reached Jarlain's room, a meal was waiting for them—shark steaks and white wine on silver platters laid out upon Jarlain's dresser. It had been so long since Makala had eaten that she couldn't keep from salivating as soon as she smelled the freshly cooked fish. She'd eaten her own portion and then, at Jarlain's insistence, the other woman's as well. With a belly full of food and too much wine, Makala had found herself becoming increasingly drowsy. She barely remembered Jarlain helping her undress and get into bed.

Had she been drugged? Makala wondered. No, she decided. She felt no ill aftereffects. Most likely she'd simply been exhausted due to hunger and fatigue.

She sat up, the sheet slipping down to reveal her bare chest. She glanced around the room but didn't see her clothes. Considering how filthy they'd become, that wasn't necessarily a bad thing. What *was* a bad thing was that she also didn't see any weapons. She supposed she could use the lantern if necessary, assuming it used fire and oil to produce light instead of magic, and if she rifled through the jewelry box she might find some brooches with sharp fastening pins. It wasn't much, but it was better than nothing.

She started to get out of bed, then the door opened and Jarlain entered. Despite her wardrobe full of clothes and her box overflowing with obscenely expensive jewelry, the woman was dressed in the same red leather bustier and black skirt she'd been wearing when Makala had arrived.

Jarlain smiled, unaffected by Makala's nakedness. "Good morning, or since the sun set a short time ago, perhaps I should say good evening." The woman carried a pile of folded clothing.

She crossed over to the bed and set the clothes down next to Makala. "I had one of the new servants launder them for you. The woman was given explicit instructions to take extra care with your outfit, but the fool still managed to tear a hole in one of the knees of your leggings. She repaired it, of course, under my extremely strict supervision, but I'm afraid she did only an adequate job."

"It's fine," Makala said without really looking at the leggings. "Fashion has never been one of my primary concerns, especially when I'm being held prisoner."

Jarlain smiled. "You amuse me, Makala. You really do."

"You can't imagine how happy I am to hear that." Makala threw off the rest of the sheet and began getting dressed.

"The wash-woman will be punished, naturally," Jarlain said. "Perhaps I made a mistake assigning the old shifter to laundry duty, but then I can only choose from those Onkar and his crew bring me."

Makala stopped dressing and turned to look at Jarlain. "This elderly shifter . . . was her name Zabeth?"

Jarlain gave Makala a quizzical look. "Perhaps. I don't know any of the servants' names. Once they come here, they no longer have any use for names."

Makala had to quell a sudden urge to lash out with her fist and break Jarlain's jaw, but as satisfying as giving into that impulse might be, she knew it wouldn't improve her situation. If she were to have a chance to survive Grimwall, let alone escape, she needed to remain calm and learn as much about this place and those who ruled it as possible. If she did find a way to escape, she vowed that she'd find Zabeth and take the old woman with her.

Makala finished dressing then checked her hair in the mirror—not much she could do with it without taking a long, hot bath first. She noted the reflection of Jarlain sitting on the bed, giving one more bit of proof that the woman wasn't a vampire.

Makala turned around to face Jarlain. "What now?"

"Erdis intends to give you a guided tour of our home a bit later, but he thought it might be nice if we had a chance to chat first." She patted the bed beside her, indicating that she wanted Makala to sit.

Makala pulled the chair out from the dressing table, turned it around so it faced the bed, and sat on that instead. If Jarlain was upset by this small display of defiance, she didn't show it.

"As you've no doubt ascertained by now, I am responsible for the day-to-day operation of Grimwall itself. Onkar commands the Black Fleet, and Erdis—"

"Commands both of you," Makala said.

Jarlain smiled, but her eyes glittered like chips of ice. "Indeed. I also have the honor of serving my master in one additional capacity. You see, Onkar and his raiders sail the Principalities to procure much-needed supplies for Grimwall, and chief among those supplies are people."

Jarlain said this so matter-of-factly that Makala felt a chill ripple down her spine. The woman might not be a vampire, but that didn't make her any less dangerous than one.

"We need servants," Jarlain continued, "and we also need a certain amount of nourishment for Erdis, Onkar, and the others."

Others? What others? The only vampires Makala had seen

in Grimwall thus far were Erdis Cai and Onkar, so who where these *others* of which Jarlain spoke?

"We also have need for . . . *special* individuals, ones who possess extremely strong spirits. It is my task to identify these people for Erdis."

Makala wasn't liking the sound of this. "And I'm one of these 'special' people?"

Jarlain shrugged. "Onkar thinks you might be, and so does Erdis, but that's for me to determine."

"Say you find out that I am one of these people you're looking for, one with a strong spirit, whatever that means. What then?"

Jarlain smiled. She rose from the bed and walked over to kneel next to Makala. Jarlain then reached out to take hold of her hands. "Now let's not get ahead of ourselves, dear."

Jarlain's grip tightened, and Makala tried to pull away, but she couldn't. It was as if she were no longer in control of her own body. She felt a presence in her mind, an intruder, like a thief who had broken into a locked home and was moving stealthily at first but with increasing boldness and confidence as he began searching for something of value to take. Makala hadn't felt anything like it since the day she had lain on the obsidian table in front of the altar of the Dark Six in the basement of Emon Gorsedd's manor. Part of her was terrified and outraged at this loss of control, but part of her, a part which had been so lonely since the exorcism of her evil spirit, welcomed it.

Then she felt herself falling into darkness. Down, down, down . . .

* * * ● * * *

THE THIEVES OF BLOOD

She hid in the shadows of the alleyway between two buildings, one belonging to a bookseller, the other a mapmaker. This
part of Sharn lay close to Morgrave University, and though it
was late, the streets remained crowded. That came as little surprise, since the City of Towers never slept. The pedestrians were
primarily students, Makala guessed, given their scholars' robes
and youthful age. They traveled in loud, laughing packs as they
searched for distractions on their various quests for amusement.
The noise and commotion of the students didn't bother her,
however. Quite the opposite. They would provide excellent cover
while she went about her work.

The alley was cleaner than she'd expected, with just a few
scattered bits of trash about—apple cores, crumpled vellum, a
few chicken bones that had been picked clean by vermin— but
there were no rats here now, and the ground was thankfully
clean of urine and feces. This wasn't the first time Emon had dispatched her to Sharn, but it was the first time that her assigned
task had brought her to this part of the city. It was certainly a
step up from the working-class section of Cliffside, where she'd
worked before. Maybe if she were lucky, the next time she was
sent to Sharn, she'd get the chance to work in the Skyway, where
only the wealthiest citizens lived.

The mapmaker's shop was closed, but Makala knew the
man was still inside, waiting for a courier who was due to arrive
sometime before midnight. Makala had no idea what the courier carried or why the mapmaker preferred to have it delivered
after business hours. Her orders were simple: when the courier
arrived, kill him before he entered the shop, take the leather
pouch he was to deliver to the mapmaker, and bring it back to
Emon, and that's precisely what she intended to do.

She heard nothing, but she felt air move lightly across the back of her neck, and she knew she was no longer alone in the alley. Without hesitation, she drew a dagger, whirled about, and threw it at the newcomer.

The blade flew straight at the man's heart, but he didn't so much as flinch. His hand swept up in a blur, and there was a metallic clang as he deflected her dagger with one of his own. Makala's blade struck the outer brick wall of the bookseller's shop, then fell to the ground, point dented, the knife now just one more bit of detritus in the alley.

Still holding onto his dagger, the man approached her. He was dressed all in black and wore a traveler's cloak with the hood pulled up to conceal his features. Despite the hood and the alley's gloom, Makala knew who it was. How could she not?

"Diran!" she whispered. Even the surprise of seeing him wasn't enough to make her break training and call out to him in a normal voice.

The man reached up with his free hand and drew back his hood. "Hello, Makala. Good to see you."

Makala wanted to rush forward and embrace Diran, but there was something different about him. His voice, his eyes . . . plus he still held that dagger.

"What happened to you?" she asked. "You disappeared after being sent to kill that magewright's daughter."

"She was but a child, and an innocent one at that," Diran said. "I couldn't kill her."

She couldn't believe what she was hearing. She'd feared Diran had met with foul play, though she'd still held out hope that he would return to her alive. Now, to hear that he'd purposely abandoned his assignment . . .

"She was nothing more than a job, Diran. Emon accepted a contract on her, and he sent you to carry it out."

Diran smiled sadly. "I couldn't."

"I could and I did. Emon sent me to finish the job."

Her words seemed to strike Diran with the force of a physical blow. Shock and sorrow registered on his face.

"Makala . . . she was no more than five . . ."

Makala shrugged. "And now she'll never reach six. Death comes to all of us eventually. It just came to her a little sooner."

"Don't quote Emon's words to me! I know them just as well as you!" He was almost shouting now, his hand gripping the dagger so tightly his knuckles were white.

"You've become so emotional, Diran, I don't . . ." She trailed off as she realized what had happened to him. "You no longer possess your dark spirit!"

"You mean, it no longer possesses me," Diran corrected, "but yes, I am free of the foul thing."

"Foul? Diran, the dark spirit is a great gift! It sharpens the mind, strengthens the will—"

"Hardens the heart," Diran said grimly.

She nodded. "Necissarily so. Without it, we would be lost."

"I am without it, and for the first time in a very long while, I don't feel lost at all. I've . . . found a new purpose, Makala, a new place to study, a new teacher . . . I've come to ask you to forget the man you've come here to kill, to forget the Brotherhood, forget Emon, and come with me. My new teacher freed me of my dark spirit, and he can do the same for you."

Diran sounded almost as if he were pleading now, and his display of emotional weakness disgusted her, or rather, it disgusted the dark thing that dwelled within her, but as there was little difference between her spirit and its, it amounted to the same.

"Don't be foolish, Diran. Let me finish this job, and then I'll take you back home. Perhaps Quellin can—"

"I'll never permit another entity to possess me," Diran said. "I'd rather die first."

Despite the fact that he still held the dagger, Makala moved closer and put her arms around his waist. "Diran, listen to yourself. The loss of your Other has unbalanced your mind. You're not thinking clearly." She gave him a quick kiss on the end of his nose before releasing his waist and stepping back. "Now just wait here and be silent. My target is due any—"

"The courier isn't coming," Diran interrupted. "In order to find you, I had to discover what your assignment was. I intercepted the courier before I came here and warned him off. By now he's likely aboard an airship and making ready to depart the city."

Cold fury surged through Makala. "I have never failed a job!"

"Until now," Diran said.

Kill him! She heard the thought in her own voice, but she knew it belonged to the Other.

I can't . . . It's Diran. I love him!

The fury continued to build inside her, overshadowing all other feeling, all other thought. When it was done, all that remained was the desire to slay a traitor to the Brotherhood of the Blade.

She reached for her sword, but she'd only managed to pull it halfway out of the scabbard before Diran reached into his cloak, brought out a dagger, and flicked it toward her with a smooth, graceful motion.

The last thing she remembered seeing was Diran's tear-filled eyes.

● ● ● ◉ ● ● ●

"How delightfully tragic!"

Jarlain let go of Makala's hands. Feeling weak as a newborn infant, Makala rose from the chair, staggered over to the bed, and flopped down onto the mattress. She immediately tried to rise again, but her body was too weak and refused to obey her.

Jarlain came over and patted her on the leg. "Don't worry. The fatigue will pass soon and you'll be able to move again."

Jarlain crossed to her dressing table, turned the chair back around, and sat down. She picked up a pearl-handled brush and began to run it through her long, raven-colored hair, gazing at her reflection as she stroked. The woman's normally pale face was slightly flushed and she wore a lazy, dreamy smile. Makala thought she looked like a woman who'd just experienced a most pleasurable session of lovemaking.

"Of course, Diran threw the dagger hilt-first, and you were struck on the head and rendered unconscious. When you came to, it was well past midnight and Diran was gone."

Makala was just barely able to make her mouth and voice work well enough to answer. "Y-yes."

"And that's the last you saw of him." Jarlain paused in her brushing to glance at Makala in the mirror. "For a while, at least."

Makala wondered just how much knowledge Jarlain had

pulled from her mind. Did she know of her reunion with Diran? Port Verge? Did she know Diran had become a priest of the Silver Flame, and even now he and Ghaji might well be on their way to rescue her?

Jarlain resumed brushing her hair with long, slow strokes. "I must say, this Emon Gorsedd of yours sounds like a most intriguing character, and the way he controls his assassins by implanting an evil spirit inside them is most ingenious, but like Diran, you no longer have your 'Other.' Unlike him, you didn't choose to give yours up. You lost yours."

Jarlain continued brushing in silence for several moments. Makala was beginning to regain control of her body slowly but surely, and she managed to push herself up into a sitting position by the time Jarlain put the brush down on her dressing table and turned to face her.

"Do you know why Erdis values my services? I possess the ability to reach into someone's mind and root out her most secret fears." She smiled. "Of course, I have other talents as well."

Makala thought of how Jarlain had touched her in Erdis Cai's vast trophy chamber, and how she'd felt a paralyzing, overwhelming fear.

"The little memory drama you were so kind as to share with me taught me a great deal about you, Makala. I now know what your two greatest fears are, and believe me, they're *juicy* ones. Would you like to hear?"

"Can I keep you from telling me?"

Jarlain laughed with dark delight. "Not at all! There are two main themes that are embedded in that particular memory. One is that of the dark spirits. Diran found the strength to give his up willingly. While you have been able to continue without yours, you miss its presence—the power and confidence it granted you. You fear that, like an addict who can no longer refrain from taking her favorite drug, you will one day return to Emon Gorsedd and plead to have a new spirit implanted within you."

Makala felt as if Jarlain had punched her in the stomach, but she fought to keep from letting the woman know how much she'd gotten to her.

"You said I had two fears."

"That's right. Your second greatest fear is of losing Diran for good. They're connected, you know. Your fear of losing Diran helps give you the strength to resist during those times when you feel the need for the Other. Imagine how disappointed Diran would be if you willingly returned to your previous life, but of course, one of the mean reasons you don't want to lose Diran is you hope his love will fill the empty space in your soul left behind when the dark spirit was exorcised. What if it doesn't? What if *nothing* can ever fill that space? Nothing except being joined to an Other again? It really is all too amusing!"

Jarlain laughed with almost girlish delight.

"I'm glad you find me so entertaining." Makala managed to keep her voice calm, but inside she was a turbulent mass of emotions. Fear, shame, anger . . . Jarlain had violated her in a way Makala had never imagined possible. Right then, Makala vowed that she would see Jarlain dead, even at the cost of her own life.

"I find you much more than that, dear." Jarlain's eyes glittered in the lamplight, beautiful, cold, and hard. "I find you *worthy*. That's going to come as good news to Erdis, very good news indeed."

● ● ● ◉ ● ● ●

"Thank you for agreeing to be my guest this evening."

Erdis Cai moved somewhat stiffly as he escorted Makala down the dimly lit corridor, and she wondered if it was because he was attempting to walk like a mortal man. If so, he'd lost the knack. He seemed more like a wooden marionette, with none of his vampiric grace.

"I wasn't aware that I had a choice."

The two of them were alone. Erdis Cai had come to Jarlain's quarters to fetch her, and now they wandered through Grimwall, seemingly without purpose or destination.

"Of course you had a choice." Erdis Cai gave her a closed-mouth smile, as if he didn't wish her to see his enlarged canine teeth. "But I don't think you would've enjoyed the alternative to coming with me."

"What would that have been?"

"Spending a few more hours as Jarlain's plaything."

Makala thought of the effortless way the woman had infiltrated her mind. "You're right. This is better."

Erdis Cai laughed and put an arm around her shoulders as if they were good friends. He still wore his black-metal armor, and it felt cold, hard, and heavy on her shoulders. More, it seemed to weigh on her soul, as if his touch were as much a spiritual burden as a physical one.

Makala had been trained in any number of unarmed combat moves that would allow her to render an opponent helpless, or should she wish to, kill him instantly, but she didn't seriously contemplate attacking Erdis Cai. Not only was the man a vampire, he exuded an aura of dark menace that spoke of just how powerful a vampire he was. Attacking him barehanded would not only be foolish, it might well prove suicidal.

"Speaking of Jarlain, she said she'd found me 'worthy.' What precisely does that mean?"

They came to a set of stairs, the first she'd seen since arriving at Grimwall. Erdis Cai removed his arm from her shoulders and gestured for her to precede him. The stairs led upward into darkness, but she knew that, one way or another, she would be going up them, so she chose to do so under her own power. There was no railing, so she kept her hand on the wall as she climbed. She couldn't hear Erdis Cai following behind, which was all the more impressive—and frightening—because he was garbed in full armor. Thus, when he spoke again, the sound of his voice coming so close to Makala's ear startled her.

"There will be plenty of time for us to talk about whether or not you're worthy—as well as for what—but keep this in mind: Jarlain only makes recommendations. It is I who render the final judgment."

Makala didn't like the way he seemed to stress the word *final*.

They continued climbing in silence for some time after that until finally Makala saw light ahead of them, however dim. They came to an open doorway, and Makala stepped through—

—and into wonder.

As large as Erdis Cai's trophy chamber had been, it was nothing compared to this. It was as if the entire cliff had been hollowed out inside, though how that could've been done without the entire place collapsing, she had no idea. There were vertical support beams visible, thick columns covered with runes engraved in a language she didn't recognize, but there were far too few to support the entire ceiling. Magic was involved somehow, but what sort and how it was applied, she didn't know.

Within the vast opening lay a small city with domed buildings of various sizes carved out of rock. The streets were lined with smaller columns atop which rested braziers burning with the same greenfire as had those in Erdis Cai's trophy chamber, and just like those, these produced no smoke, and Makala suspected, no heat. The streets were filled with men and woman garbed in black and gray—some dressed as raiders, others in robes or simple tunics. All of their heads had been shaven, and they ranged in age from late teens to early fifties.

"Impressive, isn't it?" Erdis Cai said. He stood beside her, hands clasped behind his back, looking out over the subterranean metropolis and its people like a proud patriarch. "The ceiling is three hundred feet from the floor, and the city itself is a square mile wide. Most of the structures follow the dome pattern that you can easily see is so prevalent. The builders didn't possess much imagination, but they surely were geniuses at architectural engineering."

"You didn't make this?"

"Of course not, lass! I find things, take them and make them mine, but I do not create them. However, that doesn't keep me from admiring the accomplishments of others and using them to suit my needs."

"What others? Who made this place?"

"Goblins," Erdis Cai said, "back when their kind ruled Khorvaire, before the invasion of humans from Sarlona. Though we've only been able to uncover a small portion of Grimwall's secrets, it is my belief that this underground city was built as a kind of refuge for their kind, a place where they could live in secrecy and safety, as well as a place where they could conceal their greatest treasure."

Erdis Cai's red-tinted eyes got a far-off look in them, and Makala sensed that he was picturing this fabulous treasure, whatever it might be.

"What treasure could be so valuable that a people would create an entire hidden city to safeguard it?" she asked.

"What indeed? Come now, we mustn't be late."

He started toward the city, with long, purposeful strides, and Makala hurried to keep up with him.

"My crew and I discovered Grimwall during one of our earliest voyages; although if truth be told, we blundered across it after losing our way in a dense fog. Still, a discovery is a discovery, eh? Grimwall was deserted then, its occupants having long ago departed. We decided to make this our home port, and it served us well for many years. No one but myself and the crew of the *Seastar* knew of Grimwall's existence, let alone its location, and that still holds true to this day."

As they walked among the black-garbed, shaved-head citizens of Grimwall, the people stopped what they were doing and turned toward Erdis Cai, prostrating themselves on the ground as if they were in the presence of a living god. Cai paid them no notice as he passed through their ranks, as if their obeisance was not only normal and expected but also boringly routine.

"You keep speaking of your crew, but so far the only member I've seen is Onkar. Unless some of the raiders—"

"None of those you see around you belonged to my original crew. These are all new recruits, culled from those whom Onkar brings me, though I confess that we've been doing this so long that some of these people are actually the children of those we first captured. Don't concern yourself about my former shipmates, lass. They're still around, as you'll soon see."

As they continued walking through the city, Makala kept her eye out for possible escape routes, but she saw nothing that looked promising—no tunnels, no other stairwells, nothing but domed houses with semicircular doors and no windows, and everywhere she looked, bald men and women who revered the vampire walking at her side as their lord and master.

For the first time since she'd been captured, she began to hope that Diran *was* coming to rescue her, for it certainly looked like she wasn't going to be able to get out of here on her own.

The domed buildings became fewer and farther between until they gave way to a large amphitheater carved into the ground. The greenfire braziers that ringed the top level of the amphitheater were larger and blazed more brightly than others in the city, no doubt to provide more light for whatever activities took place here. The circular stone seats were empty, save for one person sitting on the lowest level: Jarlain. Onkar stood on the smooth stone floor at the center of the amphitheater, holding the hollow curved horn of some large beast in his hand.

As Erdis Cai and Makala began to descend into the amphitheater, the undead explorer nodded to Onkar, and the vampire commander put the horn to his lips and blew a single long low note. He then walked over to Jarlain and waited for Erdis Cai and Makala to reach the bottom.

Makala heard noise behind them, and she glanced over her shoulder. The citizens of Grimwall were entering the amphitheater, summoned by the blast of Onkar's horn. Obviously something important was going to take place here tonight, but what? Whatever it was, Makala doubted it would be pleasant.

Erdis Cai reached Jarlain and sat next to her. He gestured for Makala to sit on his other side, and after a moment's hesitation, she did so. Onkar remained standing, though he set the horn down next to Jarlain, then grinned at Makala, looking at her with something too close to hunger in his eyes.

"I trust you're enjoying your stay so far? We've got a bit of entertainment for you this evening. Something special."

Erdis Cai flicked his gaze toward his former first mate, eyes glowing a brighter red, but his voice remained calm as he spoke.

"That's enough, Onkar. We don't want to ruin the surprise for her, do we now?"

Onkar glared sullenly at his master, as if he'd been sternly rebuked and resented it, but all he said was, "Yes, Captain."

They sat in silence for a while after that as the amphitheater seats slowly filled. Erdis Cai's subjects came down as far as they could, and they managed to occupy the entire bottom five rows before the last of them was seated. No one sat within twenty feet of Erdis Cai in any direction, however. While most of the citizens were men and women in the prime of their lives, there was a scattering of children and oldsters, though none of the latter appeared older than their early seventies. Makala wondered if any of them had belonged to the crew of the *Seastar*. Certainly they were old enough.

Onkar gave Erdis Cai a questioning look, and Cai nodded. Grinning, the vampire commander stepped into the middle of the stage area and raised his hands. The citizens had been speaking in hushed, excited whispers, but at Onkar's signal they quieted instantly.

"People of Grimwall! Tonight you have the privilege of being present to witness your master dishing out a well-deserved dose of justice! As you no doubt know, the Black Fleet and I came home yesterday after a successful raid on Port Verge!"

Onkar paused and the citizens, who counted the Black Fleet raiders among their number, cheered. When the cheers died down, Onkar continued.

"Of those we brought back with us, five have been found to be unsuitable for one reason or another. Tonight, they will be punished for proving unworthy of serving the master!"

More cheering, this time with a decidedly bloodthirsty edge to it.

Makala had a sudden sinking feeling in the pit of her stomach. She remembered something Jarlain had told her.

The old washer-woman will be punished, naturally. Perhaps I made a mistake assigning the old shifter to laundry duty, but I can only choose from those whom Onkar and his crew bring me.

Makala turned to Jarlain, but the woman just looked at her and smiled.

"Let the failures come forward!" Onkar commanded.

The audience had left space for a narrow pathway on the opposite side of the amphitheater, and now two raiders began walking down, escorting five people bound with wrist manacles. Three men and two woman, one of whom was, as Makala had feared, Zabeth.

CHAPTER

FIFTEEN

Makala tensed, ready to leap out of her seat, but Erdis Cai put an armored hand on her shoulder to keep her still.

When the raiders had marched their prisoners to Onkar, they turned and marched back. Other raiders sitting in the bottom-most row, a dozen in all, now stood. They were armed with bows, and they nocked arrows and took aim at the prisoners.

Onkar gestured at the archers as he addressed the prisoners. "As you can see, if you try to escape, the archers will fire upon you. Understand?"

The prisoners, including Zabeth, nodded miserably.

"However, Erdis Cai is not without mercy," Onkar continued. "Your punishment shall only last a short while. When it's done, should any of you survive, you'll get a second chance to serve the master, but I must warn you—it's been a while since we had anyone survive—a *long* while."

Scattered laughter among the audience, mostly from the raiders in attendance.

Onkar walked up to one of the male prisoners, a reedy fellow with red hair and a thatch of beard. "Hold out your hands," he ordered.

The man did so, the chains of his manacles jingling as he trembled. Onkar took a key out of one of his pockets and unlocked the man's manacles. They fell to the stone floor of the amphitheater with a clang, but Onkar made no move to pick them up.

He then handed Redbeard the key. "Unlock the others."

Blinking in confusion, the man nevertheless did as he was told, and soon the rest of the prisoners were free, their manacles joining his on the stone floor. Onkar then held out his hand. The man returned the key, and Onkar pocketed it once more.

"Stay right here," the vampire said, then he turned and headed back toward Erdis Cai, Jarlain, and Makala.

One of the other male prisoners took a step toward Onkar's unprotected back. The commander of the Black Fleet didn't turn around as he said, "Don't forget the archers, lad."

The short man hesitated and glanced at the raiders standing with arrows pointed directly at him. He lowered his head, shoulders slumped in defeat. Whatever punishment awaited him and his fellow prisoners, he had no choice but to see it through one way or another.

Makala tried to catch Zabeth's eye, if only to let the woman know she had a friend watching for whatever comfort the knowledge might provide, but if Zabeth saw her, the elderly shifter gave no indication.

Onkar sat next to Jarlain and then shouted, "Begin!"

Erdis Cai made a gesture with his hand. In response, there came a rumbling beneath their feet, and vibrations passed through the stone seats of the amphitheater. A seam opened in the stone floor running from one side to the other, neatly dividing it in two. The rumbling continued as the seam slowly widened, and Makala understood that the floor was retracting, sliding beneath the seats to reveal whatever lay underneath. The prisoners struggled to maintain their balance as the two sections of the floor slid away from each other. Three of them—the short man, Redbeard, and a petite woman who couldn't have been more than nineteen—stood on the left side of the widening gap. Zabeth, along with a man with long braided brown hair, stood on the right.

Within seconds, the floor had pulled back enough to reveal another surface beneath, though instead of stone, this one was constructed from crisscrossing iron bars, as it were the top of a huge cage. The space between the bars looked to be four or five inches wide, small enough to stand on yet wide enough to reach through. This latter quality became readily apparent as a mottled arm thrust upward between the bars, black-clawed hand swiping at the air. The hand was soon joined by another, and another, until dozens of them raked the air. Loud hissing filled the amphitheater, as if a pit of angry vipers had been stirred up.

"You asked what happened to the rest of my former crew," Erdis Cai said. "Now you know."

At the sight of dozens of clawed hands reaching through the iron grating, the five prisoners ran toward the seats, realizing that the only thing standing between them and the hissing creatures was a retracting layer of stone. There was nowhere to go, for the archers stood vigilant, prepared to loose their arrows on any prisoner who came too close to freedom.

The redbearded man tried anyway. He rushed for the steps, and the nearest archer released her arrow. The shaft slammed into the man's left shoulder, and he cried out in pain. He fell to his knees then reached up and gripped the arrow as if he intended to pull it out.

Onkar motioned to the raider who had wounded the prisoner. She nodded, lay her bow on the ground, then stepped quickly toward Redbeard. She grabbed the man's wounded arm and hauled him to his feet, eliciting a fresh howl of pain from him. She pulled him to the edge of the retracting floor and tossed him onto the iron grating. The man tried to sit up, eyes wide with terror, but before he could move, black talons tore into him and he screamed. The hands clawed furrows in his flesh, gouged out large chunks of meat, reached into red wet openings and pulled forth glistening organs. Blood rained down from the shrieking man's mutilated body. Naked, hairless creatures with burning crimson eyes and sharp teeth fought each other to stand beneath the grisly fountain they'd created and drink. Redbeard's screams ended, and all that could be heard was the scuffling of the savage creatures below him, and the ecstatic moaning of those lucky enough to catch some of the blood-rain on their tongues.

"The dark goddess granted undeath to all of the *Seastar*'s crew, but while Onkar and I became vampires, the others grew steadily more bestial and cannibalistic until I had no choice but to cage them." Erdis Cai spoke in a casual tone, as if the slaughter taking place before him meant nothing at all. "Still, ghouls or not, they are my comrades—or were, and I make sure to take care of them. Fortunately, they still prove useful.

Sometimes I wonder if this wasn't the purpose our goddess had in mind for them all along."

Little meat remained on Redbeard's corpse now, and the feral ghouls began snapping off bones and pulling them down into their cage. A moment later, all that was left of the man were smears of blood on the bars, and the ghouls were already licking those clean as best they could.

The stone floor ground to a halt, leaving only two five foot sections for the surviving prisoners to stand on. All of them, including Zabeth, stood right at the edge, looking back and forth from the ghouls to the archers, unsure about what to do next.

Grinning, Onkar said, "Quit stalling—time to get your feet wet!"

The archers stepped toward the prisoners. If the raiders were worried about moving closer to the ghouls, they still continued forward. Even confronted with the archers, the prisoners still did not move, and Makala didn't blame them. A swift death from an archer's bow was far preferable to what the obscene creatures that had once been mortal sailors would do to them, but the prisoners hadn't been brought here to receive swift, merciful deaths but rather punishment. The archers lowered their bows, reached out, and shoved the prisoners off the stone and onto the iron grating.

At least, they managed to shove three of the remaining four. Just as one of the raiders was about to push Zabeth, the elderly shifter spun around, snarling, eyes wide, fangs bared looking just as savage as any of the ghouls reaching through the grating. She grabbed the raider—a woman—by the arm and spun her off the stone edge. The woman screamed as she fell onto the interlocking bars, but she didn't scream for long.

Zabeth, her full bestial aspect upon her now, whirled around and started loping toward the assembled citizens of Grimwall, obviously intent on making a break for it. Archers lifted their bows once more and loosed their arrows, but Zabeth managed to evade the missiles, ducking and dodging as she ran, moving with far more speed than might be expected for someone her age, even a shifter. The other prisoners, without Zabeth's lycanthropic heritage to drawn on, were no match for the ghouls. Their deaths came swiftly, if not mercifully, their dying screams echoing through the amphitheater as Zabeth leaped onto the first ring of seats and continued running upward through the crowd.

Makala silently cheered her friend on, and she began to allow herself to hope that Zabeth might actually escape. Makala then felt a sudden breeze rush past her, and when the turned to look at Erdis Cai, she found he was gone. She looked back to Zabeth and saw that Cai now stood in her path. The shifter woman tried to veer around the vampire lord, leaping over a row of alarmed onlookers in the process. Erdis Cai didn't seem to move. One moment he was standing with his arms at his sides, and the next he had Zabeth by the throat, holding the woman in the air as if she weighed no more than an infant. Zabeth kicked, thrashed, and clawed at Erdis Cai's arm, but none of her exertions were enough to break the vampire's grip.

Erdis Cai looked at Zabeth, his brow furrowed and his upper lip curled into a sneer. All he did was open his hand, but Zabeth flew backwards as if he'd flung her violently from him. The shifter woman clawed the air as if she were trying to slow her descent toward the amphitheater floor, but there were no handholds to be found in empty space, and she slammed back, first into the iron grating with the horrible sound of snapping bones. Zabeth tried to rise, but she collapsed back onto the grating, moaning in pain. All the ghouls were busy at the moment fighting over the remains of the four other prisoners and the unfortunate archer Zabeth had served up to them. Thus Zabeth wasn't immediately attacked, but Makala knew it would only be a matter of moments before the ravenous ghouls went after her. Though shifters were known to be fast healers, there was no way Zabeth could recover in to time to avoid being dismembered and disemboweled.

Makala felt another breeze, and Erdis Cai was sitting calmly next to her again as if he'd never moved.

"It won't be long now," he said as if he were merely commenting on an approaching change in the weather.

Makala's gaze fell upon an object hanging on one of the grating's metal bars. It was a pair of manacles, one of those that the prisoners had been wearing when they'd first been brought in. Makala remembered Onkar freeing the prisoners from the shackles, but she realized no one had ever picked up the discarded manacles. When the floor had retracted, they'd fallen into the recessed pit below, but it seemed one pair hadn't fallen all the way.

Without thinking, Makala leaped up from her seat and started running across the iron grating toward the manacles. She didn't concern herself with where she placed her feet, didn't worry if black-taloned hands would come reaching toward her from between the bars. She trusted to her instincts and training and just ran. When she drew near the manacles, she reached down without pausing and snatched them up. She turned then ran for Zabeth, who was still trying to get up but with no more success then she'd had before.

In the back of Makala's mind, she knew that the archers could pick her off anytime, for skilled as she was, she hadn't a shifter's reflexes to help her dodge arrows. She also knew that if Erdis Cai chose to, he could intercept her whenever he wished and toss her about like a rag doll, just as he'd done with poor Zabeth, but she had no control over either of those things. Emon Gorsedd had taught her to ignore what she couldn't control, so she kept on running. Either she'd reach Zabeth or she wouldn't. At least she wouldn't simply have sat still and watched her friend be torn to pieces.

Up to this point, Makala had avoided looking through the grating, but as she approached Zabeth, she glanced downward. She saw dozens of hairless shapes moving like pale shadows beneath her, and she knew the ghouls were converging on Zabeth. Makala began swinging the manacles over her head as she closed in on her friend, just as the first mottled-fleshed hand came up between the bars and reached for Zabeth's left arm. Makala let out a battle cry as she swung the manacles with all her strength at the ghoul's grasping hand. The shackle smashed into the pale fingers, breaking the creature's claw-like fingernails. The ghoul screeched in pain and withdrew its hand, but more came to take its place—many more. Makala swung her improvised weapon with desperate, almost maniacal fury as she struggled to drive off the savage ghouls and save Zabeth, but there were too many of them and only one of her. Her arm and shoulder started to go numb, and despite her efforts, some of the ghouls had managed to wound Zabeth, and the shifter sobbed as her blood ran down into the pit below them, further exciting the ghouls. Makala refused to give in. She would fight to her dying breath and if possible beyond.

"Hold!"

The word echoed through the amphitheater like thunder, and the ghouls broke off their attack. They crouched below Zabeth, hissing softly as they cast covetous glances at the blood dripping from the shifter's wounds, but as much as they might long to, they made no move to feed. Makala stood panting for breath, the manacles dangling at her side. She turned to see Erdis Cai striding toward her. It might have been due to fatigue, but it looked as if the vampire lord walked several inches above the grating instead of on it.

"Congratulations, Makala." Erdis Cai stopped a few feet away from her, and if he'd been walking above the bars before, he stood upon them now.

"For . . . what?" she gasped.

"For proving yourself worthy."

Makala scowled. "You mean this was . . . a test?"

Erdis Cai smiled, and this time he seemed to have no qualms about displaying his sharp incisors. "Indeed, and you cannot possibly know how happy you've made me."

"You bastard!" Makala swung the shackle at Erdis Cai's face, intending to knock those damn teeth of his out of their sockets, but the vampire reached up and caught the chain with unnatural ease.

"The test is finished. There's no further need to prove yourself." Cai looked down at the ghouls crouching below.

"Finish the bitch," he ordered.

The ghouls shrieked with delighted lust, Makala shouted "No!" and poor Zabeth screamed. But not for long.

* * * * * * *

Now that the Mire was several hours behind them and the sun had set, Hinto seemed to finally be relaxing a bit, which was a relief to Ghaji. The halfling had held his own during the escape from the Mire, and Ghaji respected that, but he found Hinto's "emotional instability," as Diran put it, hard to stomach. During one of the halfling's low periods, he'd been standing at the port rail, weeping softly. Diran had taken Ghaji aside and explained that the trauma of losing his crewmates and surviving on his own in the Mire had taken a heavy toll on Hinto's mind. They needed to be understanding and patient with the halfling while he came to terms with what had happened. Ghaji was all for being understanding and patient as Hinto's wounded spirit healed, but did the halfling have to be so damn annoying in the process?

Hinto once more stood at the *Zephyr*'s port side, running his hands appreciatively over the surface of the railing.

"I never thought I'd ever get to see soarwood, let alone sail on a vessel made from it," he said. "It's so smooth that the hand slides over it as if it were ice. No wonder this craft can sail so swiftly."

Ghaji sat not far away, honing his axe blade with a sharpening stone. He didn't know if the halfling was talking to him or merely thinking aloud. Either way, Ghaji saw no need to reply. Tthen Diran, who sat next to him, restocking his cloak pockets with daggers he'd taken from the pack between his feet, gave Ghaji a look, and the half-orc sighed.

"She's a fine vessel," Ghaji said, then he shot Diran a glance that said, *There, are you satisfied?*

Hinto turned away from the railing and came over to join them, though the halfling didn't sit and Ghaji didn't ask him to.

"She'd certainly make an excellent pirate ship," Hinto said. "She's small enough that you could get close to other vessels before they had the chance to try and evade you, and she's fast enough that you'd be able to outrun any pursuit. She's too small to carry a large crew, though, so you'd have to choose your targets carefully so as not to find yourselves outnumbered, but—"

"We're not pirates," Ghaji said. "We're . . ." He trailed off, unsure precisely how to describe what he and Diran did.

"Pilgrims," Diran said.

A bit grand, Ghaji thought, but accurate enough, he supposed.

"Why are you trying to rescue that woman? Makala, right?"

Diran expression turned grim. He returned his attention to resupplying his cloak pockets from among his collection of daggers.

Hinto leaned forward and peered into Diran's pack. "You've got a lot of knives in there. Steel, iron, silver . . ." Hinto pointed. "Are those wood?"

"They are," Diran confirmed without taking his attention from his work. "The foul creatures that Ghaji and I battle have varying strengths and weaknesses. Some are affected by all metals, some only by certain kinds, while others aren't affected by metals at all. I must be prepared."

Ghaji knew that Diran had many more types of daggers beside those he'd already named. He carried blades fashioned from stone, ivory, jade, and crystal, most of which he'd fashioned himself. He also owned several daggers that possessed magical properties: a couple that had been given to him by Tusya, his mentor in the church, while the others had been acquired during various missions over the years.

"Must make for a heavy burden," Hinto said, eyeing the pack.

"In more ways than one," Diran said softly.

The halfling frowned. "I just thought of something. If your pack's full of knives, where do you carry your other supplies, such as a bedroll and the like?"

"He doesn't," Ghaji said. "I carry supplies for both of us in my pack. One of my primary duties is to serve as Diran's mule."

The priest looked up at him and smiled. "You're stubborn as a mule, I'll give you that."

Ghaji grinned. "And proud of it."

Hinto's eyes widened and he took two steps backward. At first Ghaji didn't understand why, then he realized he'd bared his teeth when he'd smiled. An orcish smile, even one half-orcish, was enough to give even the strongest warrior pause, let alone an emotionally disturbed halfling. Ghaji felt a sudden wave of shame. How many times in his life had he accidentally frightened people because of the way he looked? He wasn't above taking advantage of his appearance in battle—he'd done so many times during the Last War. Sometimes he forgot the effect his appearance had on others, forgot that too often it was a mistake to relax his guard and act like he was just another person talking, laughing, and smiling with friends. He wasn't "another person." He was a half-orc and always would be.

"Mind if I join you?"

Hinto started at the sound of Yvka's voice, and he stared at the elf-woman with a wide-eyed, terrified gaze.

Ghaji reached out and put his hand on the halfling's shoulder. "Calm yourself."

Though Ghaji's rumbling voice could hardly be described as soothing, Hinto nevertheless took a deep breath then let it out slowly. He then looked at Ghaji and smiled.

"Thanks, Greenie."

It took a monumental effort, but Ghaji managed not to tighten his grip and break Hinto's shoulder.

Diran looked up at Yvka. "Please, sit down."

"No thanks. I've been sitting in the pilot's chair for hours. I'd rather stand."

She put two hands on her lower back and arched her spine in a stretch. The motion caused her chest to bow outward and her head to lean back, her lips parting slightly.

Now it was Ghaji's turn to stare wide-eyed.

When she was finished with her display, which Ghaji thought went on a little longer than strictly necessary—not that he was complaining—she said, "The wind's blowing strong enough that we can do without the elemental for a short while without losing too much time."

"It's just as well," Diran said. "We need to make plans before we reach Dreadhold. How long do you think it will be before we're there?"

Yvka looked up at the stars glittering in the night sky. "Dreadhold is located off the northern reaches of Cape Far. We should arrive by midmorning tomorrow. Noon at the latest."

Diran nodded. "Do you have any friends on the island who can get us in to speak with Tresslar?"

"The Shadow Network is not without connections in Dreadhold," she said, "but I personally have no relationship with anyone there. I'm afraid I'll be of little help this time."

"Don't worry," Diran said. "Ghaji and I are used to providing people with reasons to let us enter where we're not always permitted."

"Or wanted," Ghaji added.

Diran grinned. "Indeed. I'm sure we'll be able to get inside, one way or another."

"Will we have trouble docking?" Ghaji asked. "The *Zephyr* isn't exactly an inconspicuous ship, and our arrival will be unscheduled."

"The dock is rarely used," Yvka said, "as there's little traffic coming and going from Dreadhold. Also, guards watch the sea carefully, ever alert for the approach of raiders who may be coming to help a comrade escape. We'll just have to make berth and hope we can talk our way past the dockmaster."

"Wouldn't it be easier to bribe him?" Ghaji asked.

"If it were anywhere else but Dreadhold, I'd say yes," Yvka said, "but the members of House Kundarak run the prison with rigid efficiency and unwavering adherence to the rules. They cannot be bribed."

Hinto sniffed. "I don't trust anyone who refuses to take an honest bribe."

"You could stay at Dreadhold," Diran said to the halfling. "The warders would surely help you return to the mainland if you wish, and if nothing else, you'd be out of danger."

"I thank you for your consideration," Hinto said, "but if it's all the same to you, I'd rather stay aboard the *Zephyr*."

Ghaji frowned. "Didn't you hear what Diran said? You'd be *safe* in Dreadhold."

"I'm safe right here. You three found me in the Mire, and

you three got me out. The way I see it, you're all good luck charms, and I'll be safe as long as I stick close to you."

Ghaji nearly groaned. It seemed Hinto had attached to the three of them like a stray puppy that had received a bit of food and a few kind words from a stranger. Wonderful.

"Since Tresslar works in the prison, I think we'll have an easier time getting in to speak with him than if he were an inmate," Diran said, "but we'll need some sort of cover story."

"Why?" Ghaji asked. "Why not just introduce ourselves to the warden, explain what our mission is, and ask to speak with Tresslar?"

"Ordinarily, that's just what we'd do," Diran said, "but there's one problem." He looked at Yvka.

"That problem is me," she said, "or rather, the people I work for. Officially, they don't exist. If we tell the warden the truth, he's bound to ask some uncomfortable questions, and though I am as committed to finding the Black Fleet as you are, I cannot reveal anything about my employers in the process, *especially* not to a representative of a dragonmarked house."

"I see," Ghaji said. "Then we go with a cover story."

"We'll make landfall on Dreadhold, and Ghaji and I will enter the prison while you and Hinto remain with the *Zephyr*," Diran said. "We'll speak to Tresslar and hopefully learn where Erdis Cai makes port. Once that knowledge is ours, we'll rejoin you and set sail once more. Easy as that."

Ghaji looked at his friend. "It's *never* easy."

"Try to be optimistic. Perhaps this will be the first time."

"Are you willing to wager on it?" Ghaji asked.

Diran thought for a moment. "No," he said with a sigh.

"However things go for us on Dreadhold, we'll need to be

well rested," Yvka said. "Diran, as long as the wind's strong, would you mind taking the tiller for a couple hours?"

"Not at all."

"Perhaps Hinto can keep you company," the elf-woman said. "He must have some absolutely riveting stories about his time at sea."

The halfling nodded enthusiastically. "That I do! One of my tasks aboard the *Pelican* was to serve as chief ratcatcher. Why, one time I caught thirty-seven rats in a single afternoon."

"Do tell," Diran said in a tone that indicated he'd like Hinto to do anything but continue.

"Oh, yes! It wasn't easy, mind you. The first seventeen gave me no trouble really, but after that—"

"If you'll excuse me," Yvka said, "I'll take my leave."

She looked at Ghaji's hands. He still held his axe and sharpening stone, though he hadn't been doing anything with them while they'd talked.

"You're obviously quite skilled with your hands, Ghaji," Yvka said. "There's something in the cabin that makes a squeaking noise and keeps me from falling asleep easily. I thought perhaps you might be able to find whatever is causing the noise and fix it for me. If you could, I'd appreciate it. Very much."

She gave Ghaji a look full of promise, then turned and headed for the cabin.

Diran smiled. "You'd better go, my friend. It's impolite to keep a lady waiting when she has a squeak that needs tending."

CHAPTER

SIXTEEN

The amphitheater was empty now. The stone floor was once again in place, for the punishment was over, and Erdis Cai's undead crew had been fed. The citizens of Grimwall had gone back to whatever duties were theirs to perform within their subterranean city. Even Onkar and Jarlain had departed, leaving only Makala and Erdis Cai. Makala sat staring at the amphitheater's stone floor, Zabeth's final screams replaying over and over in her mind.

The vampire lord stood looking down at her, head cocked slightly to the side in puzzlement. "Your friend fought most valiantly. You should be proud of her."

"What difference does it make how I feel? Zabeth is dead. Nothing can change that."

Erdis Cai continued as if she hadn't spoken. "The shifter would've proven most worthy if it hadn't been for her age. While strength of spirit is an important quality, youth and vitality are also necessary."

"You and Jarlain keep talking about worthiness," Makala said, unable to keep the hatred and rage she felt out of her voice, "but old or not, Zabeth was infinitely more *worthy* than any of you lot could ever be!"

The vampire lord's eyes flashed blood-red for an instant before returning to their more muted crimson color. "Perhaps you'd appreciate your friend's sacrifice if you understood what she died for." He considered for a moment before turning and beginning to ascend the amphitheater's steps. "Come," he ordered without looking back at her.

Makala had no intention of doing as Erdis Cai commanded, not caring whether her defiance would lead to her own punishment on the amphitheater floor, but as if of its own accord, her body rose to its feet, turned, and began following after the vampire lord. Makala struggled to stop, to make her body obey her once more, but it was no use. Whatever spell Erdis Cai had cast on her, she had neither the power nor the will to resist it.

She followed him out of the deserted amphitheater and through the city streets. At first she thought he was leading her back to the stairs they'd taken earlier, then she realized they were heading in the opposite direction. Before long they reached the far side of the underground city. The braziers were few here, the light dusk-dim. Erdis Cai continued walking until he came to a craggy section of cavern wall that hadn't been made smooth like so much else in Grimwall had. He stopped, and though he issued no command for Makala to do the same, she did anyway. She no longer knew if her body remained under Cai's spell or if she duplicated the action simply because she could think of nothing else to do. She watched as the vampire lord pressed his gauntlet-covered hand against the wall, and though she could see nothing to mark this section as different from the rock surrounding it, Cai pressed and was rewarded with grating sound of rock sliding against rock. He removed his hand as a door shaped in a half-circle slowly swung open in front of them.

"I can't tell you how many years I'd been using Grimwall as a base of operations before I discovered this door. I know I was still mortal at the time, though." He started to walk through the door, then paused and glanced back over his shoulder at Makala.

"This set of stairs spirals downward and can be somewhat tricky for mortals to negotiate. Remain in physical contact with me as we descend." He offered his arm in a gentlemanly gesture, but when Makala made no move to take it, he said, "Suit yourself," and passed through the opening in the wall. Makala, whether of her own desire or not, followed.

As they began going down, the door closed shut behind them, leaving Makala in total darkness. The stairs wound sharply and steeply downward, and it wasn't long before Makala found herself becoming dizzy. Despite her earlier reluctance to take Cai's arm, she now reached out and put a hand on his armored shoulder to steady herself, being careful to avoid touching the jutting spike there. She gasped as her flesh came in contact with the metal. It was freezing cold, so much so that it was painful to the touch. She tried to yank her hand away, but she couldn't pull it free no matter how hard she tried. She kept on trying as they wound down ever deeper into darkness but without success. After a time, the cold hurt so much it burned like fire, and soon after that, her hand began to go numb. By the time the darkness finally gave way to a flickering greenish glow, she couldn't feel any sensation from her fingertips to her elbow.

They reached the bottom of the stairs and stepped into a chamber lit by the same greenfire braziers as much of the rest of Grimwall. Makala's hand was still stuck fast to Erdis Cai's shoulder. As he came off the last step, she stumbled and nearly fell onto him, but terrified of what might happen if her body collided with his armored back, she gripped hold of the stairwell wall, tearing her nails on the rock.

Erdis Cai started to turn then, but the motion was awkward, and he realized that the flesh of Makala's hand had adhered to his armor.

"My apologies. I've worn this armor for so long that I often forget I have it on." He removed the gauntlet from his left hand, then reached over his shoulder and took hold of Makala's wrist. Gently but firmly, he pulled her free of the freezing-cold obsidian metal and then released her wrist.

Makala fell backward onto the steps, landing painfully on her rump. She cradled her useless right arm, unable to feel anything up to the shoulder now. When Cai had pried her off his armor, she'd expected the skin of her fingers and palm to peel off and stick to his shoulder in a raw bloody handprint, but her skin was intact—smooth, pink, and healthy—save for the total lack of sensation, of course.

Erdis Cai put his gauntlet back on. "You will recover in time. One of my armor's abilities is the power to drain the lifeforce of an opponent and feed it into me. It's more efficient than drinking blood, if not as satisfying, but we weren't in contact for long, and I did not consciously attempt to drain your lifeforce, so there should be no permanent effects."

"*Should?*" Makala said, though in truth she was already beginning to feel tingling in the tips of her fingers.

"Forget your arm and look around you, lass. We have arrived at the very heart of Grimwall, the site of the greatest treasure it has ever been my good fortune to discover."

The braziers here burned low, but at a gesture from Erdis Cai the green flames blazed higher, driving back the shadows and clearly illuminating the entire chamber. Once they had, Makala wished it had remained dark.

They stood at the outer edge of a circular stone chamber two hundred feet across. It was more roughly hewn than the rest of Grimwall, the wall, ceiling, and floor uneven and cracked in numerous places. Recessed areas eight feet high and four feet wide had been carved into the wall, and standing upright in each of the alcoves was a corpse garbed in full armor. Their flesh was dried, withered, and papery, drawn close to the bone. Though the creatures' bodies looked ancient, their armor appeared new and highly polished: breastplates, backplates, helms, shields vambraces, and gauntlets. Their weapons were also in excellent condition: swords, battle-axes, pikes, war hammers, spears, poleaxes. These were warriors of death, standing guard through the ages deep within the rock of Grimwall, but whatever they had been in life, they hadn't been human. They stood six-and-a-half feet tall, orange-red skins covered with dark reddish-brown hair. They had flat noses and chins, pointed ears, and sharp yellowed teeth. Worst of all, though their eyelids were closed, Makala had the impression that the desiccated things weren't so much dead as sleeping.

"Magnificent, aren't they?" Erdis Cai said. "There are twenty-five alcoves, each containing a squadron of eighty hobgoblin warriors."

"Eighty?" Makala imagined one armored corpse standing

behind another, and another and another . . . "That means there are—"

"Two thousand in all," Erdis Cai said. The vampire lord's voice held more emotion than Makala had heard since meeting him. He sounded excited, eager, almost like a small child impatient to open a long-anticipated present and start playing with it.

In the center of the chamber was a large circular pool full of a thick blackish substance that resembled pitch, though it didn't have the acrid smell. This liquid gave off a coppery tang than seemed familiar to Makala, though she couldn't identify it. There were four greenfire braziers in the chamber, set at regular intervals around the circumference of the pool. A narrow walkway stretched across the pool to the base of a stone dais engraved with strange runes located in the exact center of the chamber. The dais reminded Makala of the obsidian table in Emon Gorsedd's Chamber of Joining, and she feared the comparison might be too close for comfort. Shallow channels less than a foot wide had been carved into the floor—twenty-five in all—running from the edge of the pool and extending beneath the feet of the dead hobgoblin warriors, and presumably beyond so that all two thousand were connected to the pool of black liquid. However, the channels were dry, for the surface of the ebon liquid didn't quite reach up to floor level.

Then Makala realized that the substance in the pool wasn't black. It only seemed so because of the eerie greenish light given off by the burning braziers. The liquid that filled the pool was red, because it was blood. Gallons and gallons of it.

"The goblinoid empire lasted for eleven thousand years," Erdis Cai said, "but these warriors refused to perish along with their civilization. All two thousand of them sacrificed their lives so that they might enter into a state of living death, and here they have slumbered for centuries, waiting for the day when they would be called upon to fight once more." A sly smile twisted Erdis Cai's lips. "Of course, I'm sure they thought they'd be summoned to serve their own kind, but then death—just as life—is full of little surprises."

Makala turned to Erdis Cai. "You intend to wake these . . . *things*?"

"Of course. It's what I've been working toward for the last four decades, but I'm not doing it for myself." He touched the blood-red symbol on his chest and bowed his head in reverence. "I'm doing it for *Her*."

As if in response to the name, the blood within the pool bubbled for a moment then fell still.

Erdis Cai raised his head and when he looked at Makala, his crimson eyes gleamed with mad fervor. "Can you imagine it? The Black Fleet sailing under my command, holds filled with these warriors, all two thousand of them restored to life and ready to do whatever I ask of them. It shall be glorious!"

"Glorious? It's appalling!"

Erdis Cai went on as if she hadn't spoken. "The enchantment upon the warriors is a complicated one, however. In order to wake them, one life must be sacrificed for each warrior, and none shall so much as raise a hand until the two thousandth sacrifice has been completed."

Makala stared at the nearly full pool with a sudden sick feeling. "How many . . ."

"One thousand, nine hundred and ninety-seven," Erdis Cai said matter-of-factly. "The magic of this chamber keeps the blood fresh, and a good thing, too, for it's taken a long time to collect it all. We've had to be careful not to take too many candidates for sacrifice at a time, lest we anger the Lhazaar Princes enough to cause them to put aside their differences and come together to stop us. Not just anyone is suitable for sacrifice, otherwise we could've resurrected the warriors years ago. A sacrifice has to be a warrior as well, or at least possess the spirit of a warrior, but in and of itself, that isn't enough. One must possess—"

"Strength and vitality," Makala said as the awful implications of what Erdis Cai was saying began to sink in. "That's what makes a person—" she took a deep breath—"worthy."

Erdis Cai smiled, clearly pleased. "Precisely! That's why you should honor your friend's death. She gave her life so that we could identify the most important sacrifice of all." The vampire lord's smile stretched into a feral grin. "The last one."

Makala felt light-headed and she feared she was on the verge of passing out. "But . . . you said you'd only sacrificed one thousand, nine hundred . . ."

"And ninety-seven," Erdis Cai supplied. "That's correct, but to make matters even more complicated, sacrifices can only be made during certain times of the month. We identified two other worthy ones several weeks ago, but we've been waiting for the next time of sacrifice to arrive before . . . using them. Luckily, we found you before that time, lass, so now we can sacrifice all three of you together and complete the rite at long last."

"When?"

"Two night's hence."

"At midnight, I suppose." Makala's mind was working furiously. She couldn't allow Erdis Cai to sacrifice her. It didn't matter if she died, but she refused to allow her death to give Erdis Cai and his foul mistress control over an army of undead hobgoblin warriors.

"Half past, actually, though to be honest, I'd prefer midnight. It's much more dramatic."

Makala looked once more upon the blood pool. Erdis Cai had said a sacrifice didn't count unless it was performed at the right time. If she died *before* that time . . .

She started running toward the pool, intending to throw herself in and drown, but Erdis Cai reached out with inhuman speed, caught hold of her hair and yanked her backward, bringing her to an abrupt and quite painful stop.

"Don't make this any harder on yourself than it has to be," the vampire lord said. "You should take consolation in knowing that your death shall serve a higher purpose, that you will play a pivotal role in the history of the Principalities. Who knows? Perhaps the history of Khorvaire and even all Eberron itself!"

"Some consolation," Makala muttered.

She struggled to pull free of Erdis Cai's grip, but it was no use. She made up her mind to yank her head away from his hand hard enough to tear her hair out by the roots, then she remembered what had happened when she'd touched her hand to Erdis Cai's armor on the stairs.

Instead of pulling away from the vampire lord, Makala ran forward and threw her arms around him in a full body embrace. At first Erdis Cai just stood there, puzzled, then he roared with laughter.

"You're trying to drain your own lifeforce by grabbing onto my armor! How clever! Since I'm aware of your contact, I can keep my armor from taking more than a minuscule amount of your energy. You could hold onto me like this for an entire week without experiencing more than mild fatigue." He laughed again.

Swearing inwardly, Makala released her hold on Cai's armor and made a grab for his black-handled sword, but the vampire caught her hand before it could get close to the hilt.

"I had hoped you might appreciate the dark majesty of my plan," Erdis Cai said, sounding disappointed, "and perhaps even join us. I could use a woman with your spirit by my side, and I can find another sacrifice, even if it means waiting a bit longer to see my efforts come to fruition."

Makala tried to pull free of the vampire's grip, but it was no use. He was far too strong.

"I'd rather die than join you!" she said.

Erdis Cai looked at her for a moment, his expression unreadable. "Very well then."

The vampire lord's eyes began to glow with red flame. Makala tried to close her eyes, tried to turn her head, but she was unable to do either. She felt a great sleepiness coming over her, and though she struggled to stay awake, her efforts only made it worse. As her eyes closed, the last thing she saw Erdis Cai smiling at her.

"See you in two nights, lass. Rest well."

Then her eyes closed all the way and she knew only darkness.

● ● ● ◉ ● ● ●

"There it is!" Hinto said, pointing. "Dreadhold!"

"Aren't you supposed to say 'Land ho?' " Ghaji asked, but the halfling just stared at him.

Ghaji, Diran, and Hinto stood at the *Zephyr*'s bow while Yvka sat in the pilot's seat, steering the vessel and keeping the elemental active. Ghaji would've preferred to be back there with her, especially after their "rest break" in the cabin earlier, but he wasn't on this voyage to enjoy himself, though he had, and quite a bit at that. He was here because he had a job to do, so he kept his gaze forward and took his first good look at the island prison of Dreadhold.

Ahead of them a desolate mass of rock rose out of the sea. On its surface was a forbidding stone fortress that looked as if it had grown out the rock instead of having been purposely constructed. Dreadhold was legendary throughout Khorvaire as the place where the most dangerous criminals were incarcerated, including a number imprisoned for wartime atrocities. The prison was managed by the dwarves of House Kundarak, which carried the Mark of Warding. House Kundarak contained two major organizations: the Banking Guild and the Warding Guild. It was the latter—experts in both magical and mundane security—that operated and maintained Dreadhold. The prison had the reputation for being inescapable, and it was easy to see why. The island itself was completely barren—no grass, no trees, not even any gulls in the vicinity. Thus if by some miracle a prisoner did manage to get out of the main cellhouse, there was nowhere to hide, making him or her an easy target for the archers stationed atop the cellhouse roof. In the extremely unlikely event an escapee made it to the shoreline alive, where would he or she go? The nearest land was Cape Far, miles to the south, and the water here was too cold to swim in for more than a few minutes without freezing. Add to that all the regular patrols of sailing vessels in the area whose task it was to keep potential escapees in and potential raiders out, and it was clear that Dreadhold's fearsome reputation was well earned.

The main cellhouse was a long rectangular building two stories high without windows. The front entrance was the only way in or out of the prison—at least, that's what Yvka had told them. Ghaji had a difficult time believing it, though. The warden and guards had to have an alternate means of getting out of the cellhouse in case of emergency, though such an exit was bound to be well hidden. Near the cellhouse was a walled-in enclosure that served as an exercise yard, and next to that stood a high water tower, also with archers stationed on a walkway circling the top. In front of the cellhouse entrance was a stone lighthouse, and not far from that was a small stone building that Yvka had said was the warder's house. A larger building sat off to the side, though it was still only a quarter the size of the main cellhouse. These were the staff quarters, and downshore from there was the boat dock, though no craft were berthed at present. Probably to avoid providing any temptation for the prisoners to attempt escape, Ghaji thought.

"Everyone ready?" Yvka called out.

Ghaji looked at Diran, who'd been intently studying the layout of the island ever since it had come into view. Without looking at his half-orc companion, the priest nodded.

"As ready as we're going to get!" Ghaji called back.

Yvka gave no spoken command or made no gesture, but the *Zephyr* angled toward the dock and surged across the slate-gray waves. As the island grew steadily closer, Hinto said, "Do you really think this is going to work?"

"I have no idea," Diran answered. The priest looked down at the nervous halfling and smiled. "But we'll soon find out."

Hinto looked up at Ghaji for reassurance, but all the half-orc said was, "Welcome to my world."

❋ ❋ ❋ ❋ ❋ ❋ ❋

Yvka maneuvered the *Zephyr* into a berth and commanded the elemental to bring the vessel to a gentle stop. She then removed her hand from the arm of the pilot's chair, and the elemental's glow dimmed as the containment ring once more became nothing more than a circle of metal. Hinto vaulted over the starboard railing and landed on the dock. Ghaji tossed him a line, and the halfling quickly and skillfully tied the rope to an iron cleat bolted to the dock. He then moved over to the port side, and he and Ghaji repeated the procedure. Diran lowered the anchor.

When they were finished, Yvka unlocked a section of the railing on the starboard side and swung it inward. She then lowered a small gangplank and Hinto came back onboard. The four companions then stood in front of the gangplank as Diran and Ghaji made ready to depart.

"Be prepared to cast off at a moment's notice," Diran said. "If something goes wrong—"

"Which it usually does," Ghaji interrupted.

"—we'll need to make a swift departure," Diran finished.

"Are you sure it's wise to go ashore unarmed?" Yvka asked.

Ghaji had left his axe in the cabin, along with Diran's cloak of daggers. Diran had several blades concealed in his boots; those were the only weapons between them.

"It's better that we avoid any appearance of hostile intent," Diran said. "Besides, a few more daggers and one axe wouldn't be enough to help us against all the guards in Dreadhold."

"I suppose not," Yvka said, though she clearly wasn't happy about it. Truth to tell, neither was Ghaji, but he knew it was a necessary precaution.

Hinto gave them a salute. "You can count on us, Captain! Try not to scowl so much, Greenie. You'll put the guards into a worse mood than they already are."

"Come here, Hinto," Ghaji growled. "Let me give you a good-bye hug."

The halfling took a step backward and half hid behind Yvka. "Thanks, but I'm not really one for hugging."

"I am," Yvka said, smiling at Ghaji. "Though perhaps this isn't the best time or place."

Ghaji felt his cheeks burning and Hinto laughed.

"Maybe I should start calling you Reddie!"

Diran took hold of Ghaji's arm then, which is the only thing that saved Hinto from acquiring any number of broken bones.

"Let's go, my friend," Diran said. "Makala and the others are counting on us."

Ghaji glared one last time at Hinto, gave Diran a nod, then they started down the gangplank. They'd barely set foot upon the dock before a dwarf came hurrying to them, a trio of guards following in his wake. The leader was no doubt the dockmaster, and he was clearly not pleased to see unexpected visitors to Dreadhold, but he'd only brought three guards with him, so it didn't appear that he considered the *Zephyr*'s crew much of a threat.

"Stop right where you are!" the lead dwarf commanded. "You have not been authorized to disembark!"

The man was squat, broad-shouldered and muscular as was

common for his kind. He stood three feet tall, a bit short even for a dwarf. His head was bald, but he sported a neatly trimmed salt-and-pepper beard. He wore a purple jacket with fur trim over a white shirt. Brown leather pants and black boots with gold buckles completed his outfit. The dwarf appeared to be unarmed, but then he didn't need to carry weapons, not when he was accompanied by three guards in full armor. And what armor it was! Crystalline structures appeared on various areas of the metal, and Ghaji knew that meant it was Stonemeld armor. A Khyber dragonshard had been implanted in the armor, the mystic crystal allowing an earth elemental to be bonded to the metal, in much the same way the air elemental was bound to the containment ring aboard the *Zephyr*. Ghaji had never worn Stonemeld armor himself, but he'd seen it in action during the Last War. It gave its wearer extra resistance to physical attacks, as well as the ability to merge his or her body with stone. Such an ability seemed perfectly suited for dwarves, let alone ones working in a stone fortress on an island of rock. Of course there were the rumors, which Yvka had refused to confirm or deny, that House Kundurak operated a secret mining facility beneath the prison to harvest Khyber dragonshards.

Ghaji exchanged a look with Diran, and the half-orc knew his friend's thoughts were running on a similar track. What better place to operate an illicit mine than beneath the most secure site in Khorvaire?

Each of the dwarf guards carried a weapon—all three axes, Ghaji noted with approval. Unlike his, these axes had Khyber dragonshards set into their pommels. The presence of the smoky-colored crystals with dark blue veins meant the guards' weapons were magical, though Ghaji couldn't tell what specific properties the axes might possess simply by looking. Ghaji tried not to stare at the axes with obvious envy. He'd wielded elemental weapons on the battlefield during his years as a soldier, and he'd often thought how useful one would be in his current line of work. Too bad neither he nor Diran was wealthy, else they might have been able to purchase one, but as it was, he'd have to make do with his own mundane axe.

When the dockmaster and his guards reached them, Diran executed a small bow. "Good day to you, sir. My name is Diran Bastiaan, and this is my associate, Ghaji. To whom do we have the honor of speaking?"

"I am Bersi, dockmaster of Dreadhold," the lead dwarf said in a low bass, "and as I said, you two have *not* been given permission to leave your vessel."

The guards gripped the hafts of their axes more tightly, and Ghaji thought he detected a faint burning smell in the air. The axes were flaming weapons then, and the guards were more than ready to give their two unscheduled visitors a close-up demonstration of how they worked.

"Our apologies, Master Bersi," Diran said. "This is our first time visiting Dreadhold, and we were unaware of the proper procedures."

Bersi looked them up and down, scowling all the while. "I don't see any weapons on you."

Diran smiled. "We're scholars. We don't normally have much call to use weapons. Besides, it didn't seem prudent to attempt to enter Khorvaire's most formidable prison armed."

Bersi let out a short bark of laughter, though the trio of guards remained grim-faced. "You got that right! You'd have been dead before you set foot on shore." He frowned then.

"Scholars, you say? What would a pair of *scholars*—" at this the dwarf glanced at Ghaji as if he couldn't imagine a half-orc reading, let alone being a scholar—"want here?"

"Our research interests lie in the field of history and folklore," Diran said. "We have a letter of introduction from the chancellor of Morgrave University." Diran started to reach for his shirt pocket, and the guards' axes burst into flame.

"Go easy," Bersi warned.

Diran nodded. With exaggerated care he reached into his pocket and pulled out a small leather wallet. Holding it between his thumb and index finger, he held it out for Bersi to take.

One of the guards stepped forward and examined the wallet closely. When he was satisfied, he stepped back and all three of the guards relaxed, though not much.

Bersi shook the wallet, opened it, and withdrew a folded sheet of vellum. He handed the empty wallet to a guard, then unfolded the letter and read the words written thereon in the chancellor's ornate script.

The letter was legitimate, after a fashion. Chancellor Luchjan had indeed penned a general letter of introduction for them, but only because they'd helped save the life—not to mention the soul—of one of the university's true researchers who'd gotten herself into a bit of trouble in Q'barra a while back. More than once this letter had smoothed the way for Diran and Ghaji when, for whatever reasons, it was better not to let people know what their true purpose was.

Bersi read the letter over several times before handing it and the wallet back to Diran. As the priest replaced the letter and tucked the wallet back into his pocket, the dockmaster said, "The letter appears legitimate. From time to time institutions of learning do send representatives here for various reasons. I've seen Chancellor Luchjan's seal before, and I recognize it on your letter."

Ghaji felt like grinning but wisely restrained himself. It looked like the letter was going to work its own special brand of magic for them again, but then Bersi gestured at the *Zephyr* and said, "Tell me how a pair of university scholars can afford passage on an elemental vessel?"

Diran and Ghaji exchanged looks, then Diran said, "Research grants, of course. The university is fortunate to have a number of wealthy patrons who are only too glad to fund expeditions like ours." He leaned closer to Bersi and lowered his voice, as if about to share a secret. "Armchair adventurers for the most part, you know, but their money certainly comes in handy, right, Ghaji?"

Ghaji hated it when Diran decided it was his turn to talk during these sorts of deceptions. He could never think of anything to say.

"Money is good."

The dwarves looked at him as if he were feeble-minded, and Ghaji kicked himself mentally for playing to their stereotype of a dumb orc.

Bersi turned to Diran once more, as if deciding it would only be a waste of time to speak with Ghaji. "What is the specific purpose of your visit?" the dwarf asked.

"We're in the process of compiling a new biographical study of the life of Erdis Cai," Diran said. "We've been led to believe that one of his former crewmembers lives and works here, an artificer by the name of Tresslar."

Bersi's only reaction to hearing Tresslar's name was a slight narrowing of the eyes, but that was enough to tell Ghaji that the dockmaster was surprised, and Bersi didn't strike Ghaji as a man who was overly fond of surprises.

"An artificer named Tresslar does indeed work here and has for forty years or more," Bersi said. "He's nowhere near as skilled as the artificers of House Kundarak, of course, but he makes himself useful by helping to maintain the enchantments on the inmate cells. I'm not aware that the man was ever a sailor, let alone that he traveled with someone as famous as Erdis Cai."

The dockmaster exchanged glances with the three guards, and it was clear they found the notion of Tresslar being a former adventurer amusing.

"Perhaps the information we gathered was incorrect," Diran said. "Even so, we'd still very much like to speak with Tresslar. We've come a long way to do so, and research is about uncovering the truth, whatever it might be. If it turns out we confirm that the man never sailed with Erdis Cai, then we will have learned something of value from this trip."

Bersi looked at Diran for several moments, as if considering the "scholar's" words. Ghaji was beginning to think that the dockmaster was going to deny their request, when the dwarf reached into his jacket pocket and removed a metal token embossed with the seal of House Kundarak—a winged manlike beast flanked by flames. The dockmaster handed the token to Diran, who accepted it with a gracious bow.

"The guards will escort you to the main entrance. This token will gain you passage into the cellhouse. After that, you'll have to show both the seal and your letter to the sergeant. He'll be the one to decide whether or not you'll be able to make your request directly to Warden Gizur. It shall be he who ultimately approves or denies your request to speak with Tresslar."

"You have our utmost thanks, Master Bersi," Diran said. "You've helped make a significant contribution to the always vital pursuit of knowledge."

The dwarf waved Diran's words away. "Just doing my job." From the tone of his voice, Bersi sounded secretly pleased.

Diran and Ghaji then fell in with the guards—one in front of them, two behind—and the armored dwarves began escorting them to the cellhouse. It looked as if they'd found their way in, Ghaji thought. He just hoped they'd be able to get out again.

CHAPTER

SEVENTEEN

Tresslar?" Diran asked.

The man was middle-aged and thin, almost painfully so, with shoulder-length white hair and a close-cropped beard. He wore a gray tunic with a black belt and sandals, the standard uniform for prison staff who didn't serve as guards. He was kneeling before a cell door, running his hands across the bars and frowning in concentration. A dwarf guard stood next to him, holding onto a crossbow that was cocked and ready. Inside the cell, a tall broad-shouldered man with black hair and sky-blue eyes sat cross-legged on a sleeping pallet, glaring at the older man as he went about his work. The prisoner wore a tunic that was so white it nearly glowed. All the prisoners in Dreadhold wore the same uniform, the bright color making it both easier to spot inmates and far more difficult for them to hide.

The older man didn't respond to Diran's question. He continued moving his hands over the bars and softly muttered to himself.

The guard that the warden has assigned to escort Diran and Ghaji during their stay in Dreadhold cleared his throat. "Tresslar, you've got visitors," the dwarf rumbled.

Still the man didn't look up.

"Tresslar . . ." the guard repeated.

"Yes, yes, I heard you the first time," the older man snapped, "but visitors or not, I'm in the middle of examining the ward-spell on these bars, and I'd appreciate it if you didn't disrupt my concentration any more than you already have."

"If you possessed more than a modicum of skill, Tresslar, you wouldn't be bothered so much by distractions," the prisoner taunted.

"Shut up, Jurus," Tresslar said through gritted teeth. "If brains were dragonshards, you wouldn't have enough to power an elemental nail trimmer."

The cell was standard size for Dreadhold, nine by five feet, with a sleeping pallet, a wash basin sitting on a small wooden table, and a chamber pot. Not exactly the most ostentatious of accommodations, Ghaji thought, but it was better than being executed, though perhaps not by much.

"Tresslar, these two have come all the way from Morgrave University to talk with you," Diran and Ghaji's guard said. "Why they'd bother I don't know, but they have, and the warden wishes you to speak to them. *Now.*"

Tresslar continued working for a moment before finally sighing and removing his hands from the bars. "As usual, when Gizur wants something done, he wants it done yesterday." The artificer stood, interlaced his fingers, and loudly cracked his knuckles. "Very well, then." He turned to the dwarf holding the loaded crossbow. "I'll return as soon as I can. If Jurus so much as takes a step off his pallet, skewer him."

"You don't need to tell me my job, artificer," the dwarf said, his gaze fixed on the prisoner.

"Just do what I say. Jurus, despite all his posturing, is a skilled artificer in his own right. We can't afford to give him the chance to neutralize the wardspells on his cell."

Without waiting for the guard to acknowledge his warning, Tresslar turned toward Diran and Ghaji. "Come with me, you two." He glanced at their escort. "I see only one guard has been assigned to you. Gizur must not consider you much of a threat if he only ordered the one guard to keep watch over you."

"Well, we *are* only scholars," Diran said.

Tresslar looked them up and down, truly seeing them for the first time. "Scholars, eh?" He then turned and started walking down the corridor at a brisk pace. After a moment's hesitation, Diran and Ghaji hurried after him. However, the guard assigned to them by the warden walked off in a different direction. Ghaji figured that now that they'd found Tresslar, there was no need for them to have a personal escort, not when the cellhouse was crawling with dwarf guards, all of whom were no doubt keeping sharp eyes on their visitors.

After gaining entrance to the cellhouse and being taken to see the day sergeant, Diran and Ghaji had been permitted to speak to Warden Gizur himself. The dwarf recognized not only the seal of Morgrave's chancellor but also his handwriting. Gizur granted them permission for a two hour stay at Dreadhold, after which the scholars were expected to promptly depart the island, and the warden had made certain to emphasize the word *promptly*. The time limit shouldn't prove to be a problem, Ghaji had thought at the time. After all, how long would it take to ferret out the location of Erdis Cai's location from Tresslar?

As it turned out, quite long.

Tresslar may have agreed to speak with his two visitors, but that didn't mean he intended to make it easy on them. He never once stopped working. He hurried down one corridor or another, checking bars, examining locks, running his fingers over the stone blocks of walls and floors, forcing Diran and Ghaji to keep up with him. Ghaji would have preferred to grab the front of the artificer's tunic, lift him into the air, and shake the location of Erdis Cai out of him, but the corridors of Dreadhold were continuously patrolled by dwarf guards who would no doubt take a very dim view of such an action.

As they scurried throughout the prison, Ghaji got a good look at the inside of Dreadhold. The prison had been designed for security and efficiency, not beauty. Gray stone walls, black iron bars, all straight lines and right angles. Everbright lanterns lit the prison, but no amount of light could lend warmth to these cold and forbidding stone corridors. The prison was solid, sturdy, grim, and implacable, just like the dwarves of House Kundarak who'd built it.

While the inmates of Dreadhold represented every race on Khorvaire, including some warforged, the prison staff was primarily made up of dwarves. Tresslar was one of the few non-dwarf staff members they'd seen, and from Tresslar's constant complaining, this was something of a sore point with him.

"This is what my life is like here, day after day, year after year. The artificers of House Kundarak think they're the finest in the world, just because their house carries the Mark of Warding.

They *are* skilled and powerful, I'll grant them that, but they lack subtlety, a feeling for the more delicate ways that spells function, as well as how they can be disrupted. Dreadhold contains the highest percentage of mystically abled prisoners in Khorvaire, like that braggart Jurus you saw me putting up with earlier. They're constantly testing the wardspells on the cells, trying to lift them or at least alter them enough so that they can escape. That means I constantly have to run around this gigantic stone tomb all day and double-check the dwarf artificers' work. I can't tell you how many escapes I've prevented over the years, but am I recognized for my contributions? No, I am not! *I'm* not a dwarf; *I'm* not a member of House Kundarak! Go back to Morgrave University and tell them that, why don't you?"

Tresslar was ranting through his third variation of this screed when Diran finally interrupted.

"It's obvious that you're an exceptionally busy man, Master Tresslar, so let me tell you the purpose for our visit. My colleague and I are doing research on the life of the explorer Erdis Cai."

Tresslar didn't move, and for the first time since they'd met the man, he didn't say anything. The old man's shoulders sagged in what seemed like defeat, but when he turned to face them he was perfectly composed.

"I don't see how I can help you. I'm an artificer, not a folklorist. Now if you'll excuse me, I really should get back to Jurus. While I enjoy making him sit on his pallet and wait for me, it's unwise to push him too far."

Tresslar started to walk past them.

"You *are* the artificer who sailed with Erdis Cai, aren't you?" Diran said. "We have only one question to ask you: where is Erdis Cai's home port?"

Tresslar stopped. His eyes went wide and he shook his head.

Diran stepped forward and gripped the man's shoulders. "You must tell us! People's lives are at stake, perhaps even their very souls!"

"Guards!" Tresslar shouted.

There was no need for the artificer to shout twice. A half dozen dwarves in Stonemeld armor came running toward them from all directions. Diran glared at Tresslar, but he released his hold of the man.

The artificer brushed the front of his tunic as if contact with Diran had somehow soiled it.

"What's wrong, Tresslar?" one of the guards asked.

"These two gentlemen were granted permission by the warden to speak with me." Tresslar fixed Diran and Ghaji with a steely gaze, but the half-orc detected more than a little fear in his eyes as well. "We're finished."

Ghaji was about to protest when Diran said, "We wouldn't want to overstay our welcome." He inclined his head to Tresslar. "You have our thanks for your time, Master Artificer. You've been most helpful."

Diran smiled at Ghaji, narrowing his eyes slightly to indicate he wanted Ghaji to speak. Ghaji turned to Tresslar, drew his lips back from his teeth, and without opening his mouth, growled. "Most helpful, indeed."

Tresslar's face turned whiter than his beard at the site of Ghaji's orcish teeth.

"Y-you're welcome."

● ● ● ◉ ● ● ●

Seaspray coated his greenish skin, and when the night wind blew cold across the island's rocky shore, Ghaji felt as if he were covered with a thin layer of ice.

So this is the Principalities in summer, he thought. I really hope we're not still here come winter.

Of course, if the four of them were caught sneaking onto Dreadhold without authorization, they might get the opportunity to experience many, many winters here.

After leaving earlier that afternoon, Yvka had circled the *Zephyr* back to the island, and by the time they'd dropped anchor offshore, full night had fallen. They'd been careful not to use the elemental close to the island, lest the night guards spot the glowing containment ring.

They kept low as they made their way across the barren black rock toward the stone building that served as the staff quarters. Diran and Ghaji were in the lead, with Yvka and Hinto following close behind. Ghaji had been reluctant to bring the halfling along, given his emotional instability, but Hinto refused to be left alone on the *Zephyr*—and more to the point, on the water in the dark. Their plan was as simple as it was foolhardy. Diran and Ghaji had scouted the basic layout of the island's facilities earlier, and Yvka knew enough about Dreadhold to confirm the location of the staff's quarters. Presumably, Tresslar lived here as, unfortunately, did the guards when off duty. The four companions intended to enter the staff building, find Tresslar's room, and urge him—forcibly, if need be—to tell them the location of Erdis Cai's home port. Diran had seemed to enjoy planning their nocturnal visit to Dreadhold. *It reminds me of old times,* he'd said. Ghaji hated it when Diran said things like that, but the priest's experience and training as an assassin came in handy far too often for Ghaji to complain.

Ghaji felt almost sorry for the artificer. Diran had been growing increasingly impatient in the hours before their return to Dreadhold. He was so close to finding out where the Black Fleet had taken Makala, and Ghaji knew that his friend wasn't going to be able to stand any more delays. One way or another, Tresslar was going to give them the information they needed.

The island's black surface seemed to absorb moonlight rather than reflect it, and the ground was uneven enough that four more irregular shadowy shapes in the darkness should go unnoticed. There was a paved pathway from the main cellhouse to the staff quarters, but they approached the building from the side, though even this carried risk. Unlike the cellhouse, the building containing the staff quarters had windows. Luckily, only a few lights burned behind closed shutters even though it wasn't all that late. Ghaji wasn't surprised. Dreadhold didn't exactly seem like the sort of place to support a thriving night life.

When they were within a dozen yards of the building, Diran approached while the others hung back. The priest moved silently and swiftly, comfortable in the shadows. He moved from window to window on the first floor, checking to see if any of the shutters were unlocked. After making a complete circuit of the building, he looked over to where the others waited crouched low to the ground and signaled for them to join him. They made little sound as they walked over to Diran, and what noise they did make was covered by the sound of the surf breaking on Dreadhold's shore.

Ghaji gave Diran a questioning look, but the priest shook his head, indicating that he'd found no unlocked windows. They'd anticipated that. This was, after all, Dreadhold, and though an inmate escape was unlikely, keeping the windows barred at night was a sensible precaution, but what about the windows on the second floor? That's where Yvka came in. She stepped up to the wall, removed her boots, then placed her fingertips in the almost invisible seams between the stone blocks. She then began climbing. The elf-woman moved with almost pre-ternatural grace, fingers and toes finding purchase where there should be none.

Yvka headed for a darkened window first because that had the greater likelihood of being an empty room. When she reached the sill, she tried the shutters, but they must've been locked because she abandoned it and moved on to another. She tried two more darkened windows, avoiding a third that had a light burning inside, before she found one with the shutters unlocked and open. She cautiously peered inside, a risky move since there were no clouds to cut off the moonlight shining behind her. After several seconds, she hauled herself over the sill and climbed into the room. The companions on the ground tensed, waiting to hear the room's startled occupant shout an alarm, but they heard nothing. A moment later, Yvka appeared at the window. She smiled, nodded, and held out her hand.

Ghaji tucked Yvka's boots beneath his belt. He then removed the coil of rope that he carried around his shoulder and took the grappling hook from his pack. He quickly tied the rope onto the hook then stepped beneath Yvka and tossed it up to her. The elf-woman caught it on the first try then disappeared back into the room. Several moments later, she returned and motioned that they could begin climbing. Trusting that she had found a sturdy place to anchor the grappling hook, Diran began scaling the wall, moving with a speed and grace that, while perhaps not elven, still surpassed that of any other human Ghaji knew. Once Diran was inside the room, it was Hinto's turn. Ghaji was supposed to keep watch while the others climbed, but he couldn't help sneaking a glance at the halfling to make sure he didn't begin panicking halfway up. Hinto made it without difficulty, and it was Ghaji's turn. The half-orc was more than strong enough to manage the task, and once he was inside the room, he hauled in the rope so there would be no sign of their entrance to alert any patrolling guards.

The room had a low ceiling, which made sense since most of Dreadhold's staff were dwarves, and Ghaji had to keep his head lowered if he didn't want to bash it on the stone ceiling. Though it was dark in the room, there was enough moonlight filtering through the open window to reveal that these quarters weren't all that much larger than the prison cells. A single dwarf-sized bed with a trunk sitting at its foot comprised the room's entire contents. The bed, which Yvka had fastened the grappling hook to, was empty and recently made, the room's occupant presumably on night duty.

Ghaji returned Yvka's boots to her, and as the elf-woman slipped them on, he leaned close to Diran and whispered in his ear. "Now what? We can't just go through the building, knocking on doors and asking if anyone knows where Tresslar's room is."

"We need to find someone to question," Diran said.

There was a sudden soft click followed by the creak of metal. Ghaji drew his axe and Diran's hands sprouted a pair of daggers.

"Hinto's just picked the lock on the trunk and is having a looksee at the contents," Yvka said.

"Hinto," Diran said, "we're here to find and question Tresslar, not to rifle through someone else's possessions."

"Who says we can't do both?" The halfling sailor—and occasional pirate—swiftly rooted through the open chest, but he evidently found nothing of interest, for he soon closed the trunk lid.

"Put the money back, Hinto," Diran said.

"What money? All that was in there were folded tunics and a pouch of smelly pipe tobacco."

"And a coin purse," Diran said, "which you palmed and stuck into the top of your left boot. I can fish it out with one of my daggers, if you like."

Hinto sighed. He took the pouch from his boot and was about to put it back in the trunk when Yvka said, "Wait a moment."

"You mean I can keep it?" Hinto asked, sounding like a delighted child.

"No." Yvka reached out and took the pouch from him. "I think I just came up with a way to find Tresslar's room."

* * * * * * *

Yvka had been gone a while now, and Diran was becoming concerned. Her idea had merit, which was why he'd agreed to let her try it, but just because an idea was good didn't mean it was flawless. Perhaps she'd been captured or delayed by some unforeseen circumstance. What if the room's occupant came back while they waited? Diran didn't know how often the staff of Dreadhold changed shifts, but each moment they remained here increased their chances of being discovered.

He could hear a voice whispering in his mind. *Patience, my boy, patience,* but Diran couldn't tell if it was Emon's voice or Tusya's. Perhaps this time it was a blend of both.

Ghaji sat cross-legged on the floor, axe resting on his lap, ready to spring into action at a moment's notice. Hinto had crawled into the bed, which was just the right size for him, stretched out, and from the sound of his deep heavy breathing, had dozed off. Diran tried to relax, but he couldn't. He paced back and forth, hands empty but itching to reach into his cloak and draw forth a dagger or three, so he might juggle them to help pass the time. It would probably annoy Ghaji, and if Hinto awoke it could possibly frighten the halfling into letting out a screech and giving them all away, so he just kept pacing and tried not to think about how good a blade would feel in his hand right now.

Diran knew that he was letting his emotions get the better of him, but he couldn't help it. It had been two days since the Black Fleet raiders had abducted Makala and the others from Port Verge, and there was every possibility she was already dead. Even if they did locate Tresslar's room and convince him to tell them where Erdis Cai laired, it might be too late to save Makala. Whether Makala was alive or dead, Diran intended to make damn sure that Erdis Cai and the Black Fleet never preyed on innocents ever again.

There came a soft knocking at the door. Three short raps, three long. It was Yvka. Diran opened the door, and the elf-woman came in. She was wearing a gray tunic they'd found in the trunk and holding the money pouch in one hand.

Diran quickly shut the door behind her, turned, and said, "Well?"

"Mission accomplished. Tresslar's room is on the first floor in the southwest corner."

Though Yvka was petite, as was common for a female elf, the dwarven-sized tunic didn't quite fit her. The result, a low neckline and a high hemline, looked most fetching, and despite the situation, Diran couldn't help but think how attractive the woman was. He had to force his thoughts back to the matter at hand.

"Did you have any difficulty?" he asked.

"No, but it took me a while to encounter someone." Instead of going around and knocking on doors, potentially waking the entire building, they'd opted to have Yvka simply "bump into" someone in the hall who was already awake. "I was on the first floor, near the entrance, when a gray-bearded dwarf came in. I said hello, and we made small-talk for several moments. He's one of the cooks for the day shift, but he was working half the night to fill in for another cook who's ill. I told him that I was looking for Tresslar because I had to pay him back some money he'd loaned me while we were playing cards a few days ago, but I didn't know where his room was. He told me what I wanted to know, but he snickered the whole time. I think given the lateness of the hour, and seeing how I was dressed, the old lecher figured I was going to repay my debt to Tresslar in a somewhat different currency."

Ghaji scowled at that but said nothing.

"As long as your ruse worked, that's all that matters," Diran said. "Do you think the cook was suspicious of you?"

Yvka shook her head. "I told him that I was new so he

wouldn't question why he hadn't seen me before. Since most of the staff, including the guards, only serve temporary tours of duty here, I would imagine it's not uncommon for staff members to encounter someone they've never met before."

"Good," Diran said. "Now all we have to do is go talk to Tresslar." He started for the door, but Yvka stopped her.

"Let me change back into my own clothes first. This tunic isn't exactly designed for battle. One wrong move, and the outfit will probably tear right in two."

"Really?" Hinto said, sounding as if he'd like to see Yvka give a demonstration right then.

"Whatever you're imagining, stop it," Ghaji said gruffly. "Now let's turn around and give the lady some privacy while she changes."

Yvka smiled. "Why Ghaji, who'd ever have guessed you were such a gentleman?"

"Don't call me names," he growled, though he didn't sound displeased by the compliment. The three males then turned their backs, and Yvka quickly took off the tunic and put her own clothes on once more.

When she was finished, Diran said, "Let's go."

The four companions left the room, closing the door behind them. They headed down a stone hallway, and then down a flight of stairs to the ground floor. Yvka led them to the southwest corner, and they stopped before what Diran hoped was Tresslar's door. Diran knocked, and when there was no answer, he knocked harder. They waited several moments, and just as Diran was about to knock for a third time, a muffled voice came from the other side.

"Who is it?" Tresslar's voice.

As an assassin, Diran had been trained to imitate voices, and though he was no genius at it, he was a passable mimic. He pitched his voice low, in a fair imitation of a dwarf's. "Gizur wants to see you. He's made an alarming discovery about those two visitors you had today."

Tresslar didn't respond right away, and Diran began to think they would have to force their way in and risk waking everyone up. Then came the sound of a lock being disengaged. The door swung open and Tresslar poked his head out.

"Who—" The artificer's question died away as Diran pressed to the tip of a dagger to his throat.

"Step backward slowly," Diran said, "and be careful not to stumble. You wouldn't want my hand to slip." Diran had no intention of hurting Tresslar, but he couldn't afford to let the artificer cry out for help.

Tresslar nodded, his eyes nearly crossing as he tried to look down at the blade being held to his throat. He did as Diran commanded, taking slow steps backward into the room. Diran followed, keeping the point of the dagger pressed to the artificer's neck, not hard enough to draw blood, but hard enough so that the man couldn't forget it was there.

As they backed into the room, the others followed, and when they were all inside, Yvka closed and locked the door. Tresslar's room, while no larger than the one upstairs, had a human-sized bed, a desk and chair, and a small bookcase filled with volumes. A lantern on top of the desk lit the room with a soft orange glow. A book lay open on the desk, and the chair was pulled back and sitting at an angle. It appeared Tresslar had been doing some reading.

Tresslar frowned when he saw Yvka and Hinto. "Let me

guess. These are your apprentices." The artificer's joke was belied by the quaver of fear in his voice.

"As you've undoubtedly guessed by now, we aren't scholars. I am Diran Bastiaan, priest of the Silver Flame, and the man carrying the axe is my companion, Ghaji. The others are Yvka and Hinto. We regret the necessity of invading your quarters like this, but we are on a rescue mission, and it's vital that we discover where Erdis Cai makes his home port."

Diran went on to give Tresslar a truncated version of the Black Fleet's raid on Port Verge, along with their belief that Erdis Cai, now a vampire lord, was the one ultimately behind it. Diran kept the dagger against Tresslar's throat the entire time he spoke, but when the priest was finished, he pulled the knife away and returned the blade to its sheath on his hip.

"Now that you know the truth," Diran said, "will you help us?"

Tresslar stood there for a moment, moving his gaze back and forth between his four visitors. Finally, he walked over to the edge of his bed and sat down. He hunched over, hands clasped beneath his knees, and stared down at the floor.

"For forty years I've lived and worked on this island without once setting foot off it. I came here to hide . . . from *him*. I figured if there was anywhere in the world where I'd be safe, it would be within the walls of Dreadhold." He looked up at them. "So the captain became a vampire, eh? And Onkar too. I've heard rumors about the Black Fleet, and I'd wondered if it might have some connection to Erdis. Now I know."

"If you didn't know what Cai had become, why did you feel the need to hide yourself from him?" Diran asked.

"I might not have known the captain's exact fate, but I

knew the last time I saw him that if he survived his final quest he would become a creature of evil. I feared he would come in search of me because the captain didn't take kindly to deserters. Not at all.

"I was a young man when I joined the crew of the *Seastar*. I was already a skilled artificer, but I was a callow youth with much to learn about the ways of the world, and Erdis . . ." Tresslar shook his head but fondness came into his tone. "Erdis was like something out of a folktale. Larger than life. Confident, daring, brave. He was everything I wanted to be. Erdis took me under his wing, and I became like his younger brother. The adventures we had . . . let me tell you, I've read most of the accounts of our voyages that have been penned since, and none of them come close to the reality. My time on the *Seastar* was wondrous beyond belief."

"What happened? Ghaji asked. "How did someone like Erdis Cai become what he is now?"

"It was his appetite for adventure," Tresslar said. "He'd done so much in his life that by the time he reached his forties, he'd become jaded. He began seeking out new and more dangerous challenges. He became rash and gambled with his life and the lives of his crew simply to stave off boredom for another day, but Erdis's boredom wasn't solely to blame. The Last War had been going on for nearly eighty years by that point, and while the *Seastar* never fought on behalf of any nation, we saw a fair bit of action. The senseless ravages of war began to wear on Erdis's spirit, and he became disillusioned and filled with despair. No longer able to believe in the goodness of mortals or the presence of beneficent gods, he began searching for *anything* to believe in, and one day that search led him and the crew of the *Seastar* north to the frozen isle of Farlnen. Erdis had heard stories that a dark goddess lived there, and he was determined to find out if they were true."

Diran knew what goddess Erdis Cai had found on Farlnen.

"Vol," Diran whispered.

Tresslar nodded. "The closer we came to Farlnen, the more frightened I became. From some time I'd been concerned about the change that had come over Erdis, but whenever I tried to speak to him about it, he'd wave the matter aside. So many of the crew had perished during those last few months, and I began to fear this would be the final voyage for Erdis Cai and the *Seastar*. I decided I had to jump ship, but when I spoke to some of the other crew to see if they felt the same way, they hinted that I was talking mutiny. I rigged a longboat for myself, attached firestones to keep me warm, a lodestone compass, and bound a small water elemental to the stern for propulsion. Then one night I took some food and water, got in the boat, lowered it over the side, and watched the *Seastar* continue northward while I began slowly heading south. That was the last I saw of Erdis Cai.

"During the voyage back to the Principalities, I had time to think. I knew that if Erdis survived, he might come after me one day to punish me for deserting him, and that he might be . . . changed. I decided to come to Dreadhold and offer my services as an artificer. Luckily, the warden at the time took me on. I never told him or anyone else on Dreadhold about my time with Erdis. I honestly never expected to remain here for so long, but one year led to another, and now I've served on Dreadhold longer than anyone else. Forty years."

Tresslar shook his head as if he couldn't quite believe it.

Diran felt sorry for the man. What was it like to be so afraid of something that you would isolate yourself from the rest of the world—in effect, sentence yourself to exile—for four decades?

"Tell us where Erdis Cai is," Diran said, "and I promise as a priest of the Silver Flame that I will slay him, and you will never again have to live in fear."

Tresslar leaned back on his bed, palms on the mattress, arms held straight to prop himself up. He smiled in amusement. "While he was mortal, Erdis Cai was a legend. Now that he's immortal, no one can stop him. If I tell you where he is—or at least, where I *think* he is—he'll know who gave him away, and then he'll seek me out for certain. That's something I'd prefer to avoid, if it's all the same to you."

As Tresslar spoke, his left hand had inched closer to his pillow, and now he reached under it and pulled out a metal wand with a golden dragonhead on the tip. The dragon's eyes were made from red rubies, and its teeth from glittering crystal.

"Now maybe you people are who you claim you are, and maybe you aren't." Tresslar's gaze flicked back and forth between them, and a line of sweat beaded his forehead. "Either way, I can't risk having Erdis find me, especially if he's become—" Tresslar shuddered—"what you say he's become. I'd prefer not to hurt any of you, but I will if I have to. If you're sincere about rescuing those people from Erdis, then I wish you luck. I truly do. Now go, before you're discovered. You don't want to spend time with the master interrogators in the dungeons below Dreadhold, believe me, and that's where they'll take you if you're captured."

"We can't leave," Diran said, "not until we know where we can find Erdis Cai."

He felt his frustration beginning to edge over into anger. Emon Gorsedd taught his students many ways to extract information from someone who was reluctant to talk. When Diran had made the decision to become a priest, he'd vowed never again to use such aspects of his training as an assassin, but he was sorely tempted to return to them now.

Ghaji took a step forward, hands raised to show he wasn't holding any weapons. "Look, whatever that stick of yours does, why don't you just put it down? We don't want to hurt you, and you don't want to hurt us, right?"

Ghaji took a second step forward, and Diran knew his friend was getting ready to make a grab for Tresslar's wand, which Diran thought would be a terrible and quite possibly fatal mistake. Before Diran could intervene, Tresslar's eyes widened in panic as he realized what Ghaji planned, and he aimed the dragonwand at the half-orc. Diran drew a dagger and threw it hilt-first at the artificer's wrist. Tresslar managed to keep hold of the wand, but his hand was knocked to the side, spoiling his aim. A crackling bolt of miniature lightning blasted out of the dragon's mouth, sizzled through the air past Ghaji, and struck the stone wall with a loud booming sound. The stone blackened where the lightning hit, and the room filled with the acrid smell of released ozone.

Diran knew he couldn't give the artificer the chance to use his weapon again. The priest drew another dagger and hurled this one hilt-first toward the space between Tresslar's eyes. The dagger hit, Tresslar let out a soft moan then fell back onto the bed, unconscious, but even though he was knocked out, the man still retained his grip on the dragonwand.

As Diran retrieved his two daggers, Ghaji said, "Thanks."

Hinto had cringed when the lightning blast erupted, and now he lay on the floor, curled into a ball and shivering uncontrollably. Ghaji looked down at the terrified halfling and rolled his eyes. "Great. Now what do we do?"

"We take Tresslar and Hinto and get out of here before—" Diran was interrupted by a loud pounding on the door. "*That* happens."

"Tresslar, what's going on in there? Are you hurt? You're not experimenting in your room again, are you?" Whoever it was tried to open the door but found it locked

Diran motioned for Yvka to unlock and open the shutters covering Tresslar's window, and the elf-woman nodded and hurried to do so.

"Of *course* I'm fine!" Diran called out, imitating Tresslar's voice, and more importantly, his perpetually irritated tone. "Just had a little mishap is all. Nothing someone of your limited intellect would understand."

As Diran talked, Ghaji bent down to pick up Hinto, but the moment the half-orc touched the shivering sailor, the halfling let out a shriek of terror. In response, something slammed hard into the door, and a splintered crack appeared in the middle of the wood.

"Over here, Ghaji!" Yvka shouted now that there was no longer any point in remaining silent. The shutters were open, and she held out her arms. Ghaji scooped up the shrieking halfling and tossed him to Yvka. Despite her slender frame, the elf-woman caught Hinto easily, then she turned, and still holding onto the halfling, did a forward flip through the open window.

Another impact struck the door, and the crack widened.

One more blow, and the door would surely fall. If it hadn't been built on Dreadhold, it probably would've collapsed at the first strike, Diran thought.

"Get Tresslar outside!" Ghaji said, drawing his axe. "I'll slow down whoever it is!" He took up a position to the right of the door and flattened himself against the wall.

There was no time for Diran to argue with his friend. He pulled Tresslar off the bed and began hauling the artificer over to the window, the man still holding tight to his dragonwand with a death-grip. Diran laid Tresslar on the windowsill, half in and half out of the room, but before he could do anything else, the door burst inward in two large pieces and a shower of splinters. A dwarf stepped into the room, dressed only in a breech cloth and carrying an axe wreathed in flame. The dwarf, whom Diran assumed was one of Tresslar's neighbors, laid eyes on the priest.

"Who are—" was all the dwarf managed to get out before Ghaji swung the flat of his axe hard into his face. The dwarf stood there for a moment, smoke curling up around him from the charred remains of the door. Then he pitched forward, releasing his grip on the axe as he fell. The flames surrounding the weapon extinguished as both it and its bearer hit the stone floor.

There was shouting out in the hall now, and Diran knew their time had run out.

"Ghaji, move!"

Diran could no longer afford to be gentle with Tresslar. He shoved the man the rest of the way out the window and climbed through after him. Outside, Yvka and Hinto were nowhere to be seen. Diran guessed the elf-woman had already started back to the *Zephyr*, carrying the halfling with her.

Diran bent down and started to lift the still unconscious artificer, but then Ghaji leaped through the window and landed beside them. He took Tresslar and threw him over his shoulder as if the man weighed nothing. Then the priest and the half-orc started running toward the shoreline, heading for the spot where they'd left the *Zephyr*.

As they ran, Diran said, "I notice you've got two axes tucked into your belt now."

"I figured that if we're going to be walking into a nest of vampires soon, I could use a flaming weapon. Think Warden Gizur will mind that I borrowed it?"

Diran grinned.

CHAPTER

EIGHTEEN

Sunlight glittered off the waves as the *Zephyr* sailed beneath a clear blue sky. Tresslar stood at the railing looking out over the water.

"I never realized how much I missed being on a ship."

Ghaji and Diran stood nearby. They'd been keeping an eye on the artificer since he'd awakened several hours ago. Despite having been struck between the eyes by the hilt of a dagger, Tresslar had no bruising or swelling, for Diran had healed the man's minor wounds while he'd slept. Yvka sat in the pilot's chair, Hinto at her side, attempting to show her a card trick that he couldn't get right. The halfling laughed with good humor as he struggled to complete the card trick, showing no aftereffects of the panic that had seized him in Tresslar's room last night.

Taking the artificer's statement as an invitation, Ghaji and Diran joined him at the railing, Ghaji standing on his right, Diran on his left.

Tresslar ran his hand over the smooth soarwood surface

of the railing. "This is a most impressive vessel indeed. Oh, I could make a few alterations to it here and there, improve the efficiency of the runners, increase the elemental's output by a few knots, but still, she's quite a ship. If the *Seastar* had been an elemental vessel, who knows how many more places we might've been able to travel to, how many more wonders we might've discovered?"

"It must've been difficult for you, being landbound all those years on Dreadhold," Ghaji said.

Tresslar smiled. "I didn't think so at the time, but now . . ." He let the thought go unfinished. "I suppose my wand was left behind."

"No," Diran said. "You held tight to it all the way to the ship."

Tresslar nodded. "Then you're hiding it from me. Can't say as I blame you, considering I used it against you last night."

"What is it?" Ghaji asked.

"A spell collector," Tresslar said. "It's able to absorb and store magic until the user wishes to release it. I made it myself. Considering how mobile we needed to be on the *Seastar*, it came in handy on more than a few occasions."

"I apologize for abducting you," Diran said. "I fear it makes us no better than the raiders we seek."

"You did what you felt was right at the time," Tresslar said. He grinned. "Just like we used to do on the *Seastar*." He then turned back to gaze out across the sea.

"Forty years is a long time to be afraid," Ghaji said.

"Yes, it is," Tresslar agreed. He was silent for a time before finally saying, "The place you seek is called Grimwall. It lies within a hidden cove on the northern side of Orgalos."

Diran's face betrayed no emotion, but Ghaji could hear the repressed excitement in his voice as he said, "Thank you, Tresslar." The priest then hurried to inform Yvka that they needed to change course.

Ghaji said, "That was a brave thing you did."

"Perhaps," Tresslar said, "or very foolish. I suppose we'll soon find out which."

Ghaji nodded. "I suppose we will."

They felt the deck shift beneath their feet as the *Zephyr* began to tack northward. Ghaji went off to attend to the sails, leaving Tresslar looking out at the waves, alone with his thoughts.

● ● ● ◉ ● ● ●

While Ghaji took care of the sails, now with Hinto's help, Diran returned to the railing to stand once more beside Tresslar.

"Why has Erdis Cai been abducting people?" Diran asked.

Tresslar shrugged. "Since you told me that he's become a vampire, I assume he's been gathering them for food." The artificer grimaced.

"That's what I thought as well, until you told us the location of Grimwall. There's a sizable population on Orgalos. If all Erdis Cai needed was food, he could find it easily enough there. Vampires tend not to range very far from their lairs. They have great difficulty crossing running water, except in a craft of some sort, and even then it isn't comfortable for them. Can you think of any other reason Erdis Cai would need to abduct so many people?'

"Maybe he's creating an army."

"I'd considered that possibility, but as I mentioned before, while vampires possess great power, they also have a number of weaknesses that make them less than effective warriors. Sunlight, silver, running water, holy symbols . . . and while as their 'father' Erdis Cai would be able to dominate and control his army, vampires tend to be solitary predators, preferring little to no competition for prey."

"Then maybe Erdis is training his captives to be a mortal army. Presumably, that's how he came by his Black Fleet raiders in the first place. How am I supposed to know? I haven't seen the man for forty years, and the last time I saw him, he *was* a man! Now that he's a vampire, I don't . . ."

Tresslar broke off his rant, eyes widening as a new thought occurred to him. "No, it couldn't be that . . . could it?"

"Couldn't be what?" Diran asked.

"It happened several years after we'd discovered the abandoned underground city and took it over as our base. Whenever we were home, I'd spend my spare time exploring the city and the levels below, trying to uncover its secrets. One day, I found a hidden door that led to a chamber we'd never seen before. It was a burial chamber of a sort that held the desiccated bodies of hobgoblin warriors . . . two thousand of them. There was a large depression in the middle of the chamber with a stone dais rising in the middle. Runes had been engraved into the dais, and I translated them. The runes explained who the warriors were and why they had voluntarily chosen to die and be interred in the catacombs. There were also instructions for reviving them."

Diran felt a cold emptiness in the pit of his stomach. "Let me guess what the main ingredient for reviving the warriors is: blood."

Tresslar nodded, his face had gone pale. "And lots of it."

So Erdis Cai *was* trying to create an army, but not one comprised of vampires or humans. He was raising an army of undead hobgoblin warriors. Once he'd resurrected the goblinoids and they were under his control, he would use them to wreak havoc throughout the Principalities and beyond in his mistress' foul name. Their rescue mission had just become far more complicated and the stakes infinitely higher. Erdis Cai had to be stopped before he could resurrect his undead army—no matter the cost.

* * * *

Jarlain opened the door of her bedchamber, intending to check on Makala. She hadn't been thrilled when Erdis had commanded her to give over her room to the unconscious woman. After all, the other two candidates for tonight's sacrifice—both of whom Erdis had also entranced—were sleeping on the cold stone floors of separate cells. What made *this* woman so special? Despite her feelings, Jarlain had smiled and agreed to give up her room. Erdis was her master, after all. She was glad the bitch was going to die tonight, though. Erdis had displayed entirely too much interest in the former assassin. As far as Jarlain was concerned, there was room for only one woman in Erdis's inner circle, and that was her.

When she walked into the room and saw Erdis sitting next to her bed on her dressing table chair, looking down at Makala slumbering beneath *her* silken sheets, Jarlain experienced a surge of jealous anger.

"How long have *you* been here?" The words were out of her mouth before she could stop them.

"Since I woke from my day's rest," Erdis said without taking his gaze from Makala. "I've been thinking."

His voice held that distracted, dreamy tone she'd heard too often of late. She feared that there was less and less within him of the man Erdis Cai had once been, but what that personality was being replaced with, she didn't know.

"About what?" Jarlain asked, though she wasn't certain she wanted to hear his answer.

"Whether it might not be better to sacrifice the other two worthy ones tonight and save this one for . . . other purposes."

Erdis reached down and brushed a lock of blond hair off Makala's face. Jarlain didn't need to ask what those "other purposes" were.

"You've worked four decades to reach this night," Jarlain reminded him.

"So what will a few more weeks matter?"

Jarlain ground her teeth together in frustration, knowing that with his enhanced senses, Erdis would hear but not caring if he did. Ever since Onkar had captured her during a raid fifteen years ago on Lorghalan, where she'd been using her mental powers in the employ of a minor Lhazaarite prince, she'd served Erdis Cai and served him well. With her abilities, they'd been able to identify worthy sacrifices far more swiftly, thus speeding up the timetable for the completion of Erdis's plan. If it hadn't been for her, he might still be struggling to reach his first thousand sacrifices, instead of being on the verge of two thousand.

"When one nears the culmination of such a long project, it's only natural to start having second thoughts."

Erdis Cai's head snapped around so fast that if he'd been

mortal, he might've snapped his own neck. "I'm not having second thoughts. My mistress shall have Her undead army soon enough. But it would be a shame to allow this woman to die. She is a warrior with a spirit of fire and determination—a spirit strong enough to match my own."

Jarlain couldn't believe what she was hearing. "You're not thinking about *turning* her, are you?

"Why not? You saw how she handled herself in the amphitheater." He turned back to look at Makala with an expression that was almost tender. "She'd make a magnificent vampire, an immortal consort to spend eternity by my side."

"No!" Jarlain rushed over and knelt next to Erdis. "You can't mean that! I've served you well and loyally all these years! If you're going to make anyone a vampire, it should be me!"

"*You?*" Erdis Cai looked at her with an expression of almost comical surprise. "You serve me because it is your honor to do so. You are not owed any imagined reward. Your continued existence should be reward enough." He paused, as if deciding whether to go on. "To tell you the truth, at one time I did consider granting you the dark gift of eternal life. A vampire possessing your psychic powers would make a most formidable servant, but in the end, I realized you might become *too* powerful, perhaps even strong enough to resist the commands of your maker. That is why I shall never grant you immortality, Jarlain. You're powerful enough as you are."

Though she fought to hold them back, she couldn't stop the tears from falling. "I thought that you . . . that we . . ."

Erdis Cai threw back his head and laughed, the brittle sound piercing Jarlain's heart like a spear made of ice.

"You thought that I had *feelings* for you? I am a vampire,

Jarlain. I have feelings for no one and nothing. My only desire is the appeasement of my appetites. Anything else you might have thought you saw in me was merely an echo of the mortal man I used to be. Nothing more."

Jarlain's sorrow began to give way to rage, and she reached up and grabbed Erdis's wrist. She concentrated the full force of her power on him, intending to instill within his mind fear such as no one had ever experienced before, enough fear to drive him mad at the very least, and if she was lucky, perhaps destroy him from the inside out.

Instead Erdis lashed out with his free hand and struck her across the face. Pain exploded in her jaw and white light flashed behind her eyes. Her grip on Erdis was broken, and she fell back onto the stone floor.

Erdis rose from the chair and stood over her. When he spoke, his voice was cold and emotionless. "You are fortunate that I am in a good mood tonight, Jarlain. Otherwise I would take you to the amphitheater and let my crew have their way with you. I want you and Onkar to see to it that our sacrifices are ready for tonight's festivities, including Makala. Your sickening display has convinced me that a consort, even one as magnificent as she, would be more trouble than she's worth in the long run. And Jarlain? If you fail me in even the smallest of tasks tonight, I *will* feed you to my ghouls. Do you understand me?"

Through her sobs, Jarlain managed to gasp out, "Yes."

Erdis raised his foot, put it down on her side, and shoved her down against the floor. He then began putting his full weight on her.

"Yes, what?"

Jarlain had a difficult time drawing in enough breath to speak, and when she did, her answer came out as a soft exhalation.

"Yes . . . master."

"Much better." Erdis removed his foot and stepped over her. As he walked to the door, he said, "Be ready by midnight, Jarlain. I'll be spending time with my collection until then." He opened the door and stepped into the hallway, not bothering to close the door behind him.

Jarlain lay on the floor and sobbed while Makala, still deep in the somnambulant trance Erdis had put her in, continued sleeping as she had for the last two days, oblivious to the humiliation the woman had just suffered.

❂ ❂ ❂ ❂ ❂ ❂ ❂ ❂

As the *Zephyr* drew near Orgalos, her crew made their plans. First, Tresslar walked them through the basic layout of Grimwall. The dock entrance opened straight onto a wide passage that forked into two narrower curving corridors. The left corridor led to large chambers that the sailors had used to store supplies in Tresslar's day but which now seemed to be the most likely place to house prisoners. The right corridor led to a series of smallish rooms that the *Seastar*'s crew had used as personal quarters. At the end of this corridor lay a set of stairs that led to the upper level where the ancient goblinoid civilization had built a city of domed buildings. The *Seastar* crew hadn't made use of the abandoned city, for they feared whatever ghosts might linger there. On the far eastern side of the city lay a secret passage leading to the catacombs, concealed behind what appeared to be a section of the cavern wall.

"Once we're inside Grimwall, Ghaji and I will seek out the

catacombs, stop the sacrifice, and slay Erdis Cai," Diran said.

"Don't forget Onkar," Ghaji said, tightening his grip on his flaming axe. "I can't wait to show the bastard my new toy."

Diran turned to Ykva. "While Ghaji and I go about our work, you and Hinto will find the prisoners and free them."

"The *Zephyr* can carry only so many more passengers," Yvka said. "There are bound to be more prisoners than we can safely hold."

Diran smiled. "That's why in addition to the *Zephyr*, we're going to take one of the Black Fleet's vessels. Once you and Hinto free the prisoners, bring them to the dock, and get them aboard the ship. Then, after Erdis Cai has been stopped, we'll sail her out of here."

"We'll need a larger crew than the five of us to sail both a galleon *and* the *Zephyr*," Hinto said.

"Some of the prisoners are bound to be sailors," Diran said, "or at least have enough knowledge to help crew a ship." He smiled. "These are the Principalities, after all."

"What's to prevent the raiders from pursuing us in the other two ships?" Tresslar asked.

Ghaji bared his teeth in an orcish smile. "What makes you think there'll be anyone alive to give chase after we're finished in Grimwall?"

Tresslar paled at the sight of Ghaji's lower incisors.

"*You'll* prevent anyone from following us, Tresslar," Diran said. "You can use your skills to disable the elemental containment rings aboard the other vessels. Without the air elementals to power their sails, the raiders will never be able to catch up to us."

Tresslar nodded. "I can do that."

"Maybe Tresslar should go with you and Ghaji," Yvka said. "If he can nullify the containment rings, maybe he can use his knowledge of magic to prevent the resurrection of the goblinoid army."

Tresslar shook his head. "My skills, extensive as they are, don't extend to that sort of magic. Spiritual energy is entirely different from elemental magic. I can no more counter the enchantment on the hobgoblin warriors than I can repel the undead or exorcise demons."

They talked a bit more after that, but soon they reached the shoreline of Orgalos, and the time for talk was over.

❂ ❂ ❂ ❂ ❂ ❂ ❂

The *Zephyr* sailed into the hidden cove, moving silently across the still black water. Yvka had deactivated the elemental as they'd drawn close to Orgalos, so the glowing light generated by the containment ring wouldn't alert anyone to their approach. The rocky cliffs that formed the winding passage from the sea into the cove cut off most of the wind, so Ghaji and Diran rowed while Yvka worked the tiller. Hinto and Tresslar stood at the railing, keeping watch as they drew near Grimwall.

Ghaji was concentrating on rowing, but there was enough light from the moons to illuminate Tresslar's face, especially for someone possessing orcish night vision. Tresslar was looking up at the night sky, index finger weaving through the air, as if the artificer were drawing imaginary lines between the moons and stars. Then Tresslar stopped, and a look of grave concern came over his face. He hurried across the deck and sat down next to Diran.

"I'm not certain," Tresslar said in a near whisper. "After all, it's been forty years and more since I translated the runes in the catacombs, but I believe tonight's celestial configuration is conducive for the rite of lifeforce transference."

"How about translating that into common for the rest of us?" Ghaji asked.

Diran answered for the artificer, his tone grim. "He means that Erdis Cai is going to perform sacrifices tonight." He turned to Tresslar. "How much time do we have, assuming we haven't arrived too late."

"We have until half past midnight," Tresslar said. "I remember that detail very well because it seemed like such an odd time to me. Why not midnight? I've always wondered if it were due perhaps to some slight difference in the way the ancient goblinoids calculated the hours of the day."

Ghaji glanced up at the sky. He'd spent his childhood living in the wild, and he needed nothing more than the heavens to help him tell time. "That gives us about an hour, Diran, if that."

"Then we'll just have to work fast, won't we?" Diran said.

Hinto came over to join them then, the halfling trembling, and though the night air held a chill, Ghaji didn't think that was the sole reason Hinto shuddered.

"An hour? Is that enough time?" Hinto asked.

"It's going to have to be," Diran said and put his back into rowing.

The halfling looked at the priest for a moment with wide fear-filled eyes, then Hinto sat down next to him, grabbed hold of the oar and helped row.

The *Zephyr* rounded a last bend in the passage, and Tresslar said, "That's it. Grimwall."

Ghaji, Diran, and Hinto stopped rowing for a moment and turned to look forward. In the dark, the cliff face rose from the ebon water like a wall of solid shadow. A long wooden dock stretched forth from a semicircular opening carved into the base of the cliff, and berthed at the dock were three galleons, all painted black. Ghaji needed no further proof that Tresslar hadn't been lying to them than seeing the Black Fleet at anchor.

"Go easy," Yvka said in a loud whisper from the stern. "I'll take us in."

Ghaji, Diran, and Hinto slowed the pace of their rowing, and Yvka guided the *Zephyr* toward a berth at the end of the dock. Smart move, Ghaji thought. In the event that they'd need to make a quick getaway, they'd have no obstacles in their way to slow them down when they departed.

"Stop rowing," Yvka said.

Ghaji and Diran pulled their oars out of the water and hooked them into the oarlocks. The *Zephyr* then drifted slowly toward the dock and into a berth, the bow thumping into the wooden dock with the merest of impacts. Since Ghaji was no longer needed to row, he stood up and tapped Hinto on the shoulder.

"Come on, let's go tie us down."

Hinto gave the half-orc a smile, trying to be brave despite his fear, then rose and followed Ghaji. They vaulted over the starboard railing and landed lightly onto the dock. Diran and Tresslar tossed lines to each, and a moment later the *Zephyr* was lashed to the dock. They had no intention of dropping anchor here. It was too heavy and would make too loud a splash, and pulling it back up would slow them down if they needed to leave in a hurry. The rope lines would serve well enough.

Yvka locked the tiller then came forward to let the gang-plank down. Ghaji caught the other end and made sure the plank made no sound as he lowered it to the dock. As Diran, Yvka, and Tresslar disembarked, Ghaji drew his new fire axe and looked around. Though there didn't seem to be any guards stationed at the dock or on any of the elemental galleons, it paid to be cautious. In addition to his fire axe Ghaji carried his old axe tucked into his belt. Diran, as always, was fully armed, though he'd spent some time making certain the daggers hidden in his cloak would prove effective against vampires. Hinto had his long knife, and Tresslar carried his wand, which Diran had returned to him after they'd first sighted Orgalos. Yvka . . . well, Ghaji was confident she had one or two surprises in the bag of tricks hanging from her belt.

"Looks like no one's about," Yvka whispered, careful not to make any more noise than necessary.

"This cove is so well hidden that they don't need to guard the dock," Diran said. What he didn't say, but which Ghaji knew he was thinking, was that there was a good chance the denizens of Grimwall were all inside preparing for tonight's sacrifice.

Tresslar stood staring at the cliff face. In the dark, the artificer could make out few details, Ghaji guessed, but then the older man was probably remembering more than he was seeing.

"Tresslar," Diran said, but the artificer didn't reply at first, and Diran took hold of the man's shoulder and shook him gently.

"Hmm?" The artificer turned to Diran with an apologetic smile. "Sorry, it's just . . . been a long time. I never thought I'd be standing here again." Tresslar's tone was both wistful and frightened as memories of the past and fears about the present collided.

The five companions walked down the dock toward the entrance to Grimwall. As they passed the elemental galleons, Ghaji wished there was time to do a proper reconnaissance. Any number of raiders could be onboard any or all of the ships, ready to rush down the gangplanks and attack the intruders. If they were to have any chance of stopping Erdis Cai from sacrificing innocents, perhaps including Makala, they had to move swiftly and trust to luck. Diran, however, would say that they should trust in the power of the Silver Flame. That was all well and good, Ghaji supposed, but the half-orc warrior preferred to place his faith in a well-honed axe-blade.

They were three quarters of the way to the entrance when something splashed in the water off to their left.

"What is it?" Hinto said in a shaking voice. "Do you think it's . . . *them?*"

"We're leagues away from the Mire," Diran said. "There's nothing to fear from it."

"What if it's followed us?" Hinto said.

They stopped and listened, but the sound didn't come again. They started walking once more, but there was a second splashing sound, this time followed by the soft scratching of something climbing up onto the dock behind them. They spun around to behold a squat dark shape the size of a large dog crouching on the dock. Whatever it was, Ghaji decided it was best to kill first and ask questions later, if at all. He stepped forward, willing his axe to activate. The dragonshard embedded in the weapon's pommel glowed and the metal was wreathed in flame, though the haft remained cool to the touch.

The light revealed a mottled green-gray crab large as a mastiff. The sudden burst of illumination caused the creature to retreat several paces, its segmented legs making soft clack-clack-clack sounds as it scuttled back, large front claws waving back and forth in a defensive posture.

Ghaji was about to step forward and split the crab's shell in two when Hinto stepped past him, long knife in hand. The halfling waved his long knife in the air as he advanced on the beast, and the crab leaned left, right, then back again as it tracked the movement of Hinto's weapon. When the halfling was close enough, the crab lunged forward, ready to snap up the tasty morsel in its front claws. Hinto dodged to the side and smacked the flat of his blade hard against the one of the crab's eyestalks. The creature let out a hissing noise, scuttled to the edge of the dock, and flung itself into the water with a loud splash.

As Hinto rejoined the rest of them, he said, "It's just a dire crab, and a young one at that. They hate it when you hit their eyestalks. They're timid enough, until they smell blood. Then they can be downright nasty." Hinto chuckled. "Here I thought it was a monster."

Diran and Ghaji exchanged looks. It seems there was no predicting what would set off the halfling's panic.

"Right . . . the crabs," Tresslar said. "I'd forgotten about them."

Ghaji turned to the artificer. "Is there anything else you forgot? Sea dragons? Cannibalistic merfolk?" He concentrated and the flames flickering on the surface of this axe died out. "At least we know there's no one watching us. The light from my fire axe would've alerted them."

"Not to mention making us perfect targets for any archers," Diran said.

"I'm just glad you didn't set fire to the dock with that thing," Yvka said.

Tresslar, recovered from Ghaji's rebuke, sniffed. "Whoever attached the dragonshard to that weapon did a decent enough job, but if you want to see some *serious* flames . . ."

"I'll let you know," Ghaji said.

The five companions continued walking and reached the semicircular entrance to Grimwall without further trouble. The stone door was down, and there didn't appear to be any method of opening it.

Tresslar stepped forward. "It's been a while, but since I'm the one who constructed the locking mechanism on the door . . ." He leaned his face toward the stone surface of the door and pressed his lips against it. There came the sound of rock grating against rock, and the artificer quickly stepped back as the door began to rise. When the door had receded all the way and the entrance stood open, the others turned to look at Tresslar.

"It opens with a *kiss?*" Ghaji said.

"From one of the original crew of the *Seastar*, yes." Tresslar shrugged, his face coloring in embarrassment. "I used to have something of a whimsical nature when I was young."

The five companions paused at the threshold of Grimwall, as if something should be said. Good luck, perhaps, or as dangerous as their separate missions were, perhaps a tentative goodbye, but in the end they simply nodded to each other and went their separate ways.

CHAPTER

NINETEEN

Tresslar touched his wand to the containment ring's column, and the metal—painted black, of course—began to glow bluish-green. He could feel the vibrations as his device began absorbing the spells that other artificers had woven into the internal structure of both the column and the ring affixed on top of it. He didn't expect the process to take long. He'd already taken care of the elemental on the other ship without any difficulty. The spells the artificers had used, while serviceable, were crude and simplistic and presented no challenge to him. As the ships had been left unguarded, he'd faced no resistance.

Tresslar sighed. Forty years he'd been on Dreadhold, and if the spellwork he'd seen so far was any indication, artificers had become sloppy since he'd chosen to absent himself from the world. Perhaps the erosion of magical standards was an inevitable result of the Last War, when too many artificers had been forced to do rushwork out of necessity, but the war was over now, and there were no longer any excuses for such shoddy craftsmanship as far as Tresslar was concerned.

After a few moments, the greenish-blue glow where the golden dragonhead touched the column subsided, and it was done—no flash of light, no crackle of discharged energy. Tresslar preferred to avoid showiness in his work whenever possible. Restrained elegance was the hallmark of a true master of spellcraft, though in truth he couldn't take full credit for his wand's performance. He'd discovered the golden dragon's head during a voyage to Trebaz Sinara with Erdis Cai. The uninhabited island held many wonders and even more mysteries, and the origin of the dragon's head as well as its intended purpose was one of the latter. Tresslar had understood the dragonhead's power well enough to use it to create his spell-absorbing wand, but he didn't fully fathom the artifact's nature—not that he'd ever admit it to anyone.

His task was complete. Two of the Black Fleet's three galleons no longer possessed air elementals to fill their sails. With nothing else to do, he supposed he should disembark this vessel and board the ship he'd spared and wait for the others to finish their work.

Yet . . .

Tresslar turned and looked toward the open entrance to Grimwall. It had been four decades since he'd set foot inside, over half his lifetime. He knew it wasn't the same place that he remembered from his youth and that terrible things walked its corridors now. Still, he felt a powerful urge to walk down the ship's gangplank and head across the dock to the entrance and go inside. More than simple nostalgia, it was almost a compulsion, but he really didn't want to simply revisit Grimwall, did he?

What he really wanted—what he *needed*—was to see Erdis again. Perhaps Tresslar wanted to see if any trace of the great explorer he'd once revered remained inside the undead creature that now ruled Grimwall. Perhaps, as Diran suggested, Tresslar had been afraid for too long, and it was time that he faced that fear, looked it straight in the eyes, for better or worse.

Tresslar continued standing and gazing at Grimwall's entrance for several more moments before finally reaching a decision. Gripping his dragonwand tight, he headed for the gangplank.

● ● ● ◉ ● ● ●

Yvka and Hinto moved down the corridor with silent ease. Both of them possessed excellent night vision as well as nonhuman dexterity and grace, though Yvka might have made somewhat better time if she hadn't needed to shorten the length of her stride so the halfling could keep up. The greenfire torches which lit the corridor provided enough illumination to make it seem bright as day to elven and halfling eyes, and from what they could see, Grimwall—at least this section of it—was deserted. Whatever the grisly nature of the rite Erdis Cai was preparing to conduct this night, it appeared his people were in attendance as well. All to the better; it would make Hinto's and her task much easier.

The corridor they traveled curved slowly to the left, and Yvka saw that she'd allowed herself to become overconfident. Two male guards dressed in the familiar garb of the Black Raiders stood in front of a larger wrought-iron gate with burning braziers of greenfire mounted on either side. Despite the guards' bald heads and false vampire teeth, Yvka knew they were human, or at least she hoped so, and that meant there was a chance they hadn't spotted Hinto or her in the corridor's gloom. She stopped and crouched down, putting one hand on Hinto's shoulder to stop him and another over his mouth to prevent him from making any noise. Hinto must've already seen the guards, for he nodded, showing no surprise at Yvka's actions.

The elf-woman removed her hand from the halfling's mouth and motioned for him to retreat a bit down the corridor. He nodded again, turned, and moved off without a sound. Yvka followed, equally as silent. When they'd put a few dozen extra yards between themselves and the raiders, and the curve of the corridor wall hid them from view, Yvka caught up to Hinto and motioned for him to stop. The elf-woman knelt next to the halfling and whispered close to his ear.

"That looks like one of the storage areas Tresslar described," she said.

"Maybe," Hinto replied, "but that doesn't mean it's the place the raiders keep the prisoners."

"True, but if it was merely a storage area for supplies and such, why would they guard it, especially this night, when they've left so much of the rest of Grimwall unguarded?"

"Good point. What do we do now?"

Yvka thought for a moment. She still had a few tricks in the leather pouch dangling from her belt, provided by the ever-inventive and oh-so-devious wizards and artificers employed by the Shadow Network, but she wasn't certain any of her toys would prove useful in this situation. Then again, sometimes the simple ways were the best.

"Here's what we're going to do."

● ● ● ◉ ● ● ●

The halfling walked down the corridor toward the two guards, weaving with an unsteady gait. At first neither noticed him in the dim light, but as he drew closer, one of the guards whirled around to stare at the halfling.

"Hey, what are you doing here?" the man shouted, sounding more bemused than angry.

The halfling didn't answer. He took a couple more weaving steps, stopped, stiffened, then collapsed to the floor. Both guards stared at him for several moments, as if they expected the half-ling to leap up any moment and yell, "Surprise!" The small man just lay there, unmoving.

The guard who'd shouted at the halfling drew his sword and walked forward, keeping his gaze trained on the seem-ingly unconscious little man, alert for even the most subtle of movements. The guard reached the halfling and was just about to prod him with his sword when a blur of motion emerged from the corridor's gloom. The Black Fleet raider looked up to see a woman come cartwheeling toward him, but before he could fully understand what he was seeing, let alone react, he felt a sharp piercing pain in his side. He looked down to see the halfling sitting up and holding onto the hilt of the long knife that had been thrust into his gut. Confused and feeling the first numbing touches of shock, the raider could only watch as the woman—an elf, he thought, though she was moving too fast for him to be sure—tumbled past him. She leaped into the air and delivered a spinning kick to his partner's head before the other guard had gotten his sword even halfway clear of its scabbard. The other raider's head spun to the side, the motion accompanied by the sickening sound of snapping bone. The man was dead before the elf-woman landed on her feet, but it took his body an instant longer to realize it and topple to the floor.

The surviving guard looked back down at the halfling, and the little man gave him a savage grin before shoving the long knife farther in and twisting it around. Agony exploded in the raider's abdomen and chest, but darkness rushed in to sweep away the pain.

● ● ● ◉ ● ● ●

Yvka was examining the lock on the gate as Hinto wiped his long knife clean on the shirt of the downed raider. The halfling sheathed his weapon and came over to join her.

"How's it look?"

"Old and sturdy," she said, "but I think I can open it."

"Hello?"

Both Yvka and Hinto started at the sound of the voice. It belonged to a small girl child, and it came from the other side of the gate. With the light from the greenfire braziers so close, it took a moment for their vision to adjust before they saw the child standing a dozen yards behind the gate. She was dressed in ragged dirty clothing, barefoot, and her hair was scraggly and matted. She was also pale and far too thin.

Yvka gave the girl what she hoped was a reassuring smile. "Hello."

The girl hesitated then took a few steps closer. "The others don't want me to talk to you. They're afraid you've come to do bad things to us, just like you did to *them*." She pointed at the prone form of the guard whose neck Yvka had broken. "Have you?"

Yvka tried to peer past the girl to see the other prisoners, but the brazier light interfered too much, and she could only make out shadows behind the girl that might or might not be a huddled mass of frightened people. She sniffed the air and smelled unwashed bodies, urine, and feces. She then recalled what Tresslar had told them about the storage areas. *They're really just large caverns that the goblinoids didn't do much with, except smooth out the floors some. I can't imagine it would be a very comfortable place to have your quarters.* Considering the girl's appearance and the smell emanating from the cavern, Yvka thought the artificer had made a huge understatement.

"We've come to set you free," Hinto said.

"Free?" The girl came yet a few steps closer. "What's that?"

Yvka felt a rush of sorrow at the girl's question. "It means that you can go wherever you want, do whatever you want. It means that you'll never have to serve in Grimwall again, and you won't have to fear Erdis Cai any more."

The girl was still a few yards away, but she was close enough now for Yvka to see her clearly. The elf-woman sometimes had trouble telling how old humans were, for they aged so much more rapidly than elfkind, but she thought the girl was five, six at the most. Yvka wondered if the poor thing had been brought here so young that she had no memory of the outside world or worse, that she'd been born here and never been beyond Grimwall's tunnels and chambers. Either way, it was a tragedy. A human lifetime was brief enough as it was without having to waste any of it trapped in a place like this.

The girl kept coming toward them until she stood just on the other side of the gate. "Promise?" she said.

Yvka smiled though she felt tears threatening. "With all my heart."

The girl looked into the elf-woman's eyes as if trying to gauge her sincerity. Finally, the girl smiled, then turned to back over her shoulder. "Everyone! This lady is going to help us!"

At first there was no response, but then the shadowy forms began to come forward from the darkness, resolving into men and woman, children and oldsters, dozens upon dozens of them. Some were wearing simple brown tunics woven from coarse cloth, while others were garbed in tattered scraps no more substantial than what the little girl wore. Many were stooped and hunched over, or walked with a limp or held an arm at their side at awkward angle, the legacy of old injuries that had never healed properly. Worst of all were the gaunt ones with a white pallor and bite marks—some of them fresh—on every inch of their exposed skin.

Yvka hadn't told anyone, but once she'd learned Erdis Cai was behind the Black Fleet, she'd decided her employers would want to establish a trading relationship with the undead explorer in order to gain access to the treasures, both material and mystical, that he'd acquired during his mortal life. After seeing these poor wretches, she hoped Diran would destroy the bastard and send his soul straight to the worst afterlife the planes had to offer.

Yvka reached into her pouch, removed a pomegranate seed, and inserted it into the keyhole of the gate's lock. "Everyone stand back," she said. "This tiny seed is a magical explosive, and it packs a wallop when it goes off."

The prisoners shuffled backward but not too far, as if they couldn't bring themselves to move any real distance from the gate and their promised freedom. Yvka figured they were far enough away. After all, it wasn't *that* powerful an explosive. She looked down at Hinto.

"We need to move."

The halfling nodded and together they stepped several paces away from the gate. Yvka was just about to turn back around and speak the three words that would activate the magic seed, when her foot came down on something slick and almost slid out from under her. She gazed downward and saw a pool of blood on the floor, along with a line of thick drops stretching off down the corridor.

The guard whom Hinto had stabbed was gone.

● ● ● ◉ ● ● ●

Ghaji and Diran jogged through the domed city. They'd found their way here easily, thanks to Tresslar's directions, but the place was deserted. The half-orc ran with an axe in each hand, keeping a sharp eye out in case something should be hiding inside the domed buildings, ready to pounce on them.

A sound like breaking surf came from the direction in which they were headed. At first Ghaji wondered if the vast cavern that housed the domed city opened onto the sea, then he realized that what he was hearing wasn't the rise and fall of crashing waves but rather chanting. Ghaji glanced at Diran, and the priest nodded grimly. The companions increased their speed and ran as fast as they could toward the sound.

The chanting grew louder and the domed buildings fewer

and farther between. Then the buildings were gone, and the stone floor of the cavern sloped downward to make a large bowl-shaped depression in the ground. Bald-headed men and women garbed in black filled the amphitheater, sitting in descending rows. Now Ghaji understood why the city was deserted: everyone was here. Diran and Ghaji stopped at the top level of the amphitheater, hearts pounding and lungs heaving. The denizens of Grimwall were so engrossed in their chanting that they didn't notice the newcomers, though Ghaji didn't think they'd remained unnoticed for long.

He leaned close to Diran and spoke softly. "I thought the resurrection ceremony was supposed to take place in the lower catacombs."

"Tresslar was merely giving us his best guess," Diran said. "Perhaps Erdis Cai has made some changes to Grimwall in the last forty years."

The chanting, which was in a language Ghaji didn't recognize, grew louder still, rising to a crescendo. Diran gripped Ghaji's shoulder and crouched, pulling the half-orc down with him. Ghaji understood. Diran wanted to observe for a moment and remain unseen as long as they could.

A figure sitting on the bottom row stood and walked into the center of the amphitheater's stone floor. The audience was shouting now, some of them raising their fists in the air, though they stayed seated. The man was garbed in obsidian armor with jutting spikes at the shoulders and elbows, and he wore a broadsword belted at his waist. His head was uncovered, and even from this distance Ghaji could make out the man's chalky complexion and crimson-tinted eyes. This, at last, was Erdis Cai.

Ghaji glanced at Diran and saw that his friend's eyes had narrowed and his jaw was set in a determined line. This was the foul creature that had sent the Black Fleet out roving to capture and sacrifice who knew how many innocents over the years and who also held Makala prisoner somewhere within this ancient series of caverns and tunnels.

"Do you see the symbol on his breastplate?" Diran asked.

Ghaji's upper lip curled in disgust. "The Mark of Vol."

Erdis Cai raised his arms and the crowd fell instantly silent.

"My children," he began. The vampire lord didn't shout, but his voice filled the amphitheater. "All of you were either brought here over the yeas by my Black Fleet or are the descendants of those who were, and when the dark glory of Vol was revealed unto you, you chose to join me and enter into Her service."

Ghaji didn't have to wonder what happened to those captives who refused to worship Vol. They were pressed into servitude, sacrificed, or used as food.

"Most of you were not here at the beginning when the first sacrifice was made in our mistress' dark name, but you will all be here to witness the end, for only three more sacrifices are needed to restore the ancient warriors to life. Tonight we shall conduct all three sacrifices, and Vol shall have her army at last!"

The crowd roared with excitement, some people clapping, some stomping their feet, many doing both. Ghaji looked at Diran and saw that his frown had deepened into a scowl. Not only had they arrived on a night of sacrifice, they'd arrived on the *last* night, when Erdis Cai would complete the spell to restore the warriors to life and place them under his command.

TIM WAGGONER

Diran would have said that that the Silver Flame itself had led them here to this place and time in order to prevent such a monstrous evil from being unleashed upon the Principalities. Ghaji figured they'd just gotten lucky. Either way, it didn't matter. The two of them were here and there was work to be done—the kind of work they did best.

"Shall we?" Ghaji said.

A pair of silver daggers appeared in Diran's hands as if by magic. "Let's."

They stood and began making their way through the crowd toward the amphitheater floor. The crowd's exuberance drained away, and their cheers fell silent as all heads in the amphitheater turned to look at the priest and the half-orc. No one tried to stop them, perhaps because they were so surprised to find intruders in their midst. Then again, perhaps it had something to do with the way Ghaji bared his teeth at everyone as they passed.

If Erdis Cai was surprised to see the pair of newcomers striding through the crowed toward him, he gave no outward sign. The vampire lord simply stood, watched, and waited.

As Ghaji and Diran drew near the amphitheater floor, the half-orc spied Onkar sitting in the front row next to a beautiful raven-haired woman wearing a red bustier and a black skirt. The Black Fleet commander jumped to his feet, eyes blazing red and fangs bared in a hiss. Onkar reached for his sword, but Diran hurled one of his silver daggers and the blade pierced the vampire's hand. Onkar howled in pain and held his hand up to inspect it, as if he couldn't believe what had just happened. The dagger had completely penetrated his undead flesh and bone, the hilt pressed against the back of his hand and the blade emerging from his palm. Black ooze dripped from the wound, and a foul stench filled the air as Onkar's hand began to sizzle and burn. The vampire grabbed the hilt of the blade and attempted to pull it free, but the handle was also silver, and he yanked his hand away, the palm burnt and smoking. The hand impaled by the dagger continued to blacken until it was little more than bone covered by charred skin. Then the flesh on Onkar's wrist and forearm began to smoke as the silver poisoning started to spread.

Erdis Cai had only watched up to this point, but now he moved faster than Ghaji's eyes could track, becoming an obsidian blur as he drew his broadsword and sliced off Onkar's wounded hand before the infection caused by the silver dagger could spread any further. So swiftly did Erdis Cai move that he'd returned his sword to its scabbard before Onkar's severed hand hit the floor. The hand continued to burn until it fell away to ash, leaving the silver dagger, smooth and clean, lying on the ground.

Onkar stared at the stump where his hand had been, then he looked at Diran with hate-filled eyes. The vampire's body tensed, and Ghaji knew Onkar was going to attack.

The half-orc was about to activate his fire axe when Erdis Cai said, "Hold."

Onkar's body jerked backward as if he were a hound and his master had yanked on an invisible leash. He shot Erdis Cai a sullen glare but otherwise didn't protest.

"Welcome to Grimwall," Erdis Cai said to Diran and Ghaji.

He smiled, showing his fangs, but it was a cold smile devoid of any trace of humanity. His eyes glowed with the smoldering red flame common to all vampires, but beyond it Ghaji saw only a great vast nothingness, and this frightened him more than the fangs and crimson fire ever could. He'd seen similar empty gazes on the battlefield from men and women whose minds had retreated far inside themselves to escape the horrors of war. In Ghaji's experience, a person with such emptiness inside himself was capable of committing any atrocity without hesitation or remorse, or indeed, without any recognition that he was doing anything unusual at all. It was this emptiness far more than Erdis Cai's undead state and whatever dark magic he might command that made the vampire lord so very dangerous.

"I am Erdis Cai. This is my home and these," he gestured at the crowd, "are my children. Who are you?"

Before either of them could answer, the raven-haired woman stood. Up close, Ghaji could see that the woman's beauty was marred by a swollen, bruised jaw, as if she'd been recently struck. "These are Makala's companions, Diran Bastiaan and Ghaji, a priest and a half-orc warrior."

"A priest, eh?" Erdis Cai said. "How amusing."

"Where is Makala?" Diran demanded. "What have you done with her?"

"Up to now, I've done very little with her," Erdis Cai said, "but that's going to change shortly, for she has a very special role to play tonight."

Ghaji's blood ran cold. Was Makala to be one of the final three sacrifices? He looked at Diran, and he could see his friend was struggling to maintain control of his emotions.

"We know all about your plan," Diran said, "and we're going to stop you."

Erdis Cai sounded bored as he replied. "Yes, that's what I'm going to do, and no, you're not going to stop me."

Erdis Cai flicked his gaze toward Onkar, and though the vampire lord spoke no words, Ghaji sensed a message pass between master and servant.

Onkar bared his fangs like a serpent about to strike, then he rushed Diran. Ghaji started forward, intending to intercept the vampire before he could reach Diran, but even as he began to move, Ghaji knew he couldn't match Onkar's speed. Just before the Black Fleet commander reached Diran, he stopped and shielded his eyes with his remaining hand.

Diran was holding up the metal arrowhead symbol of the Order of the Silver Flame.

Onkar hissed in anger, but he continued to shield his eyes as he backed away from Diran. Erdis Cai looked on in amusement, seemingly unaffected by the sight of the holy symbol. Ghaji noticed the vampire lord made no move to get closer to Diran, however.

"You might have a few tricks priest," Erdis Cai said, "but what good will they do you and your," he sneered, *"associate* against all of my children?" The undead explorer gestured at the crowed that filled the amphitheater and they shouted their support of their master.

"We didn't come here to kill them," Diran said. "We came here to kill you."

Erdis Cai's smiled fell away, and he looked at Diran, his eyes pulsing with inner fire. Ghaji had fought enough vampires during his time with Diran that he knew what was happening: Erdis Cai was attempting to use his hypnotic abilities to dominate Diran and enslave the priest's will to his own. Ghaji looked away from the vampire lord, lest he be caught by the monster's mesmeric gaze. Diran scowled, teeth clenched, a line of sweat trickling down the side of his face as he matched wills with Erdis Cai. Then Diran slowly began to raise his hand until he held the silver arrowhead in front of his eyes, blocking the vampire lord's gaze.

Erdis Cai snarled and averted his eyes. "So you have a measure of power after all, priest." The vampire lord turned to face Diran once more, but he looked off to the side, unable to gaze directly at the holy symbol. "Let us see how strong you really are." He reached for the hilt of his broadsword and steel hissed as he drew the blade from its scabbard, but before he could free his weapon, a shout came from the uppermost level of the amphitheater.

"My lord!"

All heads turned to see who had cried out, all heads save Diran's, that is. He never took his gaze off Erdis Cai.

Ghaji saw a Black Fleet raider standing on the highest row of seats. The man's face was ashen, and he clutched his abdomen with blood-slick hands.

"Grimwall is under attack! Invaders are freeing . . . the servants . . ." The man staggered then fell forward, the people seated near him scrambling frantically out of the way as he smacked lifeless onto the stone steps.

Erdis Cai's upper lip curled away from his teeth in a bestial sign of displeasure. "Enough of this foolishness." He raised his voice. "Men and women of the *Nightwind*'s crew: go see what's happening with the servants. If you find any invaders, slay them!"

Several dozen raiders rose from their seats and dashed out of the amphitheater to do as their lord commanded. As Ghaji watched the raiders go, he hoped Yvka and Hinto had already freed the prisoners and gotten them aboard one of the elemental galleons. If not . . .

Erdis Cai continued. "Our dark mistress will just have to forgive us for dispensing with the formalities this evening. Jarlain, Onkar, come with me." He replaced his sword in its scabbard, turned, and began walking across the amphitheater floor away from Diran and Ghaji. Diran raised the hand holding a silver dagger and was about to throw it at Erdis Cai, presumably at the vampire lord's unprotected neck, when Cai said, "Tear them apart, my children."

The crowd roared and rushed forward.

"Stay close!" Ghaji shouted and activated his fire axe. Flames rose from the weapon, and the half-orc warrior began sweeping the axe in wide arcs in front of him to keep the onrushing citizens of Grimwall at bay. Diran stepped to Ghaji's side, holy symbol exchanged for another silver dagger. The metal wouldn't provide any special defense against these men and women since they were mortal, but a sharp blade was a sharp blade, regardless of what substance it was made from.

"We have to follow Erdis Cai before he can conduct the sacrifices!" Diran shouted.

Before he kills Makala, Ghaji translated. He nodded, and still wildly sweeping his fire axe with one hand and his mundane axe with the other, as a mob of black-garbed men and woman with clean-shaven heads and bloodlust in their eyes came at them. Erdis Cai's "children" held back at the sight of the flames trailing from Ghaji's mystic axe, none of them eager to be set afire.

Erdis Cai, Onkar, and Jarlain quickly reached the uppermost level of the amphitheater. Erdis Cai gestured over his shoulder, and the ground began to tremble. Immediately the bald cultists backed away, terror in their eyes. A seam appeared as the floor split into two separate sections that began to slide away from each other with a loud rumbling sound. The floor shook as its sections retracted, and it was all Diran and Ghaji could do to maintain their balance.

Erdis Cai and his two servants were no longer in sight.

"What's happening?" Ghaji shouted over the noise.

"Erdis Cai must've activated some sort of trap!" Diran said. "Whatever it is, it's terrifying our attackers!"

The black-clad men and women had lost all interesting in fulfilling their master's command. They turned away from Diran and Ghaji and frantically tried to get off the retracing floor, shoving, hitting, and clawing at one another in their fear. Ghaji and Diran were only a few yards from the edge of one of the sections, and the half-orc could see iron grating being revealed as the two halves of the stone floor pulled back. Then the floor stopped retracting with a sudden jerk, knocking many of the fleeing crowd off their feet. Diran grabbed Ghaji's arm to steady himself, and the half-orc braced his legs and managed to maintain his footing.

All was silent for a moment, and though many of Erdis Cai's children continued fleeing, a number stopped, puzzled looks on their faces. The silence was broken by a series of soft snicks, as of latches being released. A rectangular section of the iron grating dropped away and fell to the floor below with a loud clang. A moment later a mottled-fleshed hand with long black claws gripped the edge of the amphitheater's partially retracted floor. It was followed by many, many more, and then the owners of those hands hauled themselves up and dozens of naked forms with discolored flesh, burning eyes, and froth-flecked fangs scuttled onto the separate sections of the amphitheater's floor.

"Ghouls," Ghaji said. "If there's one thing I hate more than vampires, it's ghouls."

Those Grimwall citizens still standing on the floor screamed in abject terror and fled for their lives. The ghouls, nearly forty of them in all, Ghaji judged, shrieked in dark delight and began attacking whatever mortals happened to be nearest, including Diran and Ghaji.

CHAPTER

TWENTY

Yvka and Hinto were urging the first of the prisoners through Grimwall's entrance and onto the dock when they heard shouting behind them.

"They're coming!"

"The raiders!"

"Erdis Cai knows, he *knows!*"

Yvka swore. It seemed the wounded guard who'd gotten away had managed to sound the alarm. She knew they had only seconds before the prisoners' fear overwhelmed them and they panicked.

"Hinto, lead the prisoners onto the galleon. I'll slow down the raiders!" She had no idea if the halfling would be able to maintain control of his emotions long enough to complete the task, but she had no choice but to trust him.

A flicker of nervousness passed across the halfling's features, but he nodded and began shouting for the prisoners to follow him. Yvka plunged back through the entrance, shoving through the mass of frightened men, women, and children.

"Which way are they coming from?" she demanded, and several people pointed to the left-hand branch of the corridor. The elf-woman turned and saw the raiders running toward them, swords drawn, false teeth bared to inspire maximum terror in the prisoners.

"Go!" Yvka shouted. "Follow the halfling!"

The prisoners mulled about, uncertain and afraid, and Yvka had to yell at them to go one more time before they finally started moving.

Yvka stepped forward, placing herself between the fleeing prisoners and the oncoming raiders. She reached into her leather pouch and grabbed hold of a handful of objects. She didn't have time to select carefully, and she hoped that whatever she brought out would at least be enough to buy the prisoners enough time to get aboard the remaining functional galleon. She pulled her hand out of her pouch and hurled the items she'd grabbed toward the raiders. She caught a glimpse of the items as they flew through the air—crystalline pebbles, a dried cicada husk, tiny rodent bones, and a mummified frog's leg. Just as the first of the objects was about to hit the floor, Yvka spoke a single word in Elvish and averted her gaze. There was an explosion of light, smoke, fire, and wind, and the raiders cried out in pain and confusion. Though Yvka couldn't see through the smoke, she guessed that some of the raiders had been injured, though not all.

"Be careful to hold your breath until you're outside!" Yvka shouted. "That gas is deadly!"

It wasn't, of course, but there was no reason the raiders needed to know that. She turned to check on the prisoners' progress and saw that the last of them were hurrying through the entrance, perhaps spurred on by her false warning. The elf-woman sprinted after the prisoners, already hearing several raiders shout that it was just a trick and there was no poison gas.

Once outside Grimwall, Yvka saw a line of prisoners running down the dock and up the gangplank of the elemental galleon that Tresslar had spared. Hinto stood on the ship's deck, urging the prisoners to move faster. Of Tresslar, Yvka saw no sign. That struck her as ominous, though most likely the artificer was simply hidden from her view at this distance.

"Go, go, go!" Yvka shouted as she brought up the rear.

The prisoners, most of whom she guessed hadn't been outside of Grimwall in a very long time, picked up speed as they tasted the sweet salty air and saw the stars and moons shining down on them. They cried out in delight as they ran, and more than a few had tears of joy streaming down their faces.

The last of the prisoners reached the gangplank and were pushing and jostling to start climbing when the first of the raiders emerged onto the dock.

"Hinto, as soon as the last person's aboard, dislodge the gangplank!" she called.

She had a few toys left in her pouch. She hoped they'd be enough to slow down the raiders long enough for all the prisoners to board the ship.

"Miss, are you talking to the halfling?" It was the girl who'd been the first to speak to them through the bars of the gate that had kept the prisoners trapped in their squalid quarters.

Yvka turned and saw the girl standing at the ship's railing, looking down at her. "What's wrong with him?" she shouted back.

"He's lying on the deck, shivering as if he's got a fever, though his forehead's not warm!"

Great. Hinto had picked a most inopportune time to surrender to his fear. "I don't care who does it, but make sure to push the gangplank away from the ship!"

"What about you?" the girl asked.

Yvka didn't have time to answer, for the raiders came rushing at her then, weapons drawn and eager to use them. Yvka knew that neither acrobatic maneuvers nor what remained in her pouch would be enough to stop all the raiders, but if she could stay alive long enough, she might be able to—

"Crabs, Miss!" the child cried out. "Hinto says to tell you to remember the crabs!"

Yvka smiled. Even caught in the throes of his panic, the little pirate hadn't abandoned them.

As the first raider drew near, Yvka performed a forward handspring and slammed her heels into the man's jaw. He stumbled backward, dropping his sword. Yvka landed in a crouch, caught the sword before it could hit the dock, and swept it around in an arc that sliced open the raider's belly. The man shrieked as blood and intestines spilled out of the wound and splattered onto the dock. Yvka used the sword's momentum to bring the weapon around for another strike, gripping the hilt with two hands and angling the blade so the flat struck the screaming raider on the shoulder. The man staggered to the edge of the dock, slipped on his own blood, and tumbled into the water with a loud splash.

The rest of the raiders froze where they stood and stared at the water where their comrade had disappeared. For a moment nothing happened, but then the water erupted in a churning froth as dire crabs began fighting over the remains of the raider Yvka had gutted. Drawn by the blood and bits of viscera smeared on the surface of the dock, a crab climbed out of the water and scuttled toward the nearest tasty morsel, which happened to be another of the raiders. The woman cried out and swung her sword at the advancing crab, but the creature batted away the blade with one of its huge foreclaws and moved in for the kill. The raider screamed in agony as the crab began feeding, and her screams attracted the attention of more crabs. Within seconds the dock was swarming with dire crabs ranging in size from several feet wide to some large as horses. Some raiders fought while others tried to flee, but it was no use. There were simply too many crabs, and soon the dock was covered with blood, scraps of meat, and fragments of splintered bone.

The crabs didn't ignore Yvka. They came for the elf-woman too, and she leaped and tumbled to avoid their snapping claws. Yvka started to make her way toward the gangplank just in time to witness a group of prisoners dislodge it and shove it away from the ship. The gangplank bounced against the side of the dock several times, scraping the wood as it fell half onto the dock and half into the water. Yvka didn't blame the prisoners. She'd told them to do it, and though they no longer had to worry about the raiders, they couldn't afford to let any of the crabs scuttle up and onto the ship. That left Yvka with a dilemma: how was she going to get away from these damned crabs and onboard the galleon? She continued dodging snapping claws, but she knew she couldn't keep doing so for much longer. There were too many crabs and not enough raiders to feed them all. More and more would turn their attention to her, and when that happened she would be overwhelmed.

She saw the end of the gangplank that was in the water shudder, then a crab surfaced, crawling along the gangplank toward the dock. The crab was too heavy and the wood began to tilt beneath its weight, raising the opposite end into the air. Yvka saw her chance. She leaped into the air and ran across crab shells toward the rising gangplank. She launched herself off the back of a particularly large crab just as a gigantic shape rose forth from the water next to the gangplank. It was another crab, but far larger than any Yvka had seen so far, nearly half the size of a galleon, if not bigger. As Yvka soared toward the top of the rising gangplank, one of the monster crab's claws swept at her. Yvka's feet landed on the gangplank's edge, and she pushed off just as the monstrous claw came for her. She passed between the pinchers just as they snapped together, missing her by only a hair's breadth.

She flew toward the ship's railing, but the wave caused by the gigantic crab's emergence had caused the rising end of the gangplank to wobble as it sank, throwing off Yvka's trajectory. She had intended to grab hold of the ship's railing as she descended, but it was clear that now she was going to fall short. As she drew near the railing, dozens of hands reached out for her, and enough of them caught hold of her hands and forearms to keep her from falling. The prisoners who, thanks to her and Hinto were captives no longer, hauled her over the railing and onto the deck. The discarded gangplank fell into the water, and the monster crab, as if frustrated at losing its snack, tore the gangplank apart with its huge claws.

Yvka thanked her rescuers then hurried over to where Hinto lay shivering on the deck. The little girl sat next to him, holding his hand and telling him that everything was going to be

all right. As Yvka knelt by the halfling's side and took his other
hand, she didn't know if the girl's soothing words would turn
out to be prophetic, but at least now they had a chance. It was
all up to Diran and Ghaji.

She smiled down at the trembling halfling. "Thanks."

"You're . . . you're . . ." Hinto gritted his teeth and forced out
the last word. "Welcome."

As Yvka stroked Hinto's hand, she looked around for
Tresslar, but she didn't see the artificer. She wondered what
had happened to the irritable old man. Wherever he was, she
hoped he was safe and not doing anything foolish. Yvka and
the girl continued tending to Hinto, trying to restore him to a
state of calm, while below them the multitude of crabs finished
what remained of their grisly repast. Now all that remained
was for them to wait and see if Diran and Ghaji succeeded.
Yvka prayed that they would.

Diran held the arrowhead of the Silver Flame in his left
hand while he threw daggers with his right. Ghouls shied away
from the holy symbol, its power preventing them from getting
too close. A single bite or scratch from one of the loathsome
creatures was enough to cause paralysis, or worse, ghoul fever.
Diran could heal either Ghaji or himself if they were struck,
but they couldn't afford to waste the time.

Ghaji wielded his new flaming axe to devastating effect,
hacking off heads, arms, and legs, and setting ghouls afire in the
process. In his left hand, Ghaji gripped his old axe, and though
it was smaller and lacked the enchantment of his more recently

acquired weapon, the half-orc warrior still caused quite a bit of damage with it.

Diran was rapidly using up his supply of daggers. He sent blades hurtling into ghoul eyes, throats, and hearts with lightning speed and deadly accuracy, but only the silver daggers struck with mystical effect, the ghouls' mottled hides blackening and rotting away where they'd been wounded. Diran could summon forth the pure essence of the Silver Flame to repel the ghouls, but he feared if he did so, he might not be able to draw on that power again in time to use it against Erdis Cai.

Fortunately for the two companions, if not for the denizens of Grimwall, the ghouls attacked anything that moved and preferred easy prey. Since most of the black-clothed men and women put up no resistance as they attempted to flee, the ghouls fell upon them like ravening hounds on rabbits, raking flesh with black claws, and tearing off chunks of meat with razor-sharp teeth. He felt pity for the men and women who died at the savage claws of the ghouls. Few deserved such a hideous death as many of Erdis Cai's followers now suffered.

Diran and Ghaji had thinned the number of ghouls considerably by the time they reached the opposite side of the amphitheater floor, and those men and women who hadn't died or been injured by the ghouls' attack had fled, a number of the cannibalistic undead racing after them. Ghaji split the skull of one last ghoul with his fire axe, and the creature burst into flames and collapsed in a heap of burning flesh. The two companions then sprinted up the amphitheater's steps as they went in pursuit of Erdis Cai.

● ● ● ◉ ● ● ●

Makala didn't want to leave the darkness—not because it was pleasant or comforting, but because she suspected that cold and lonely as it was, it was still preferable to what waited for her on the other side of consciousness.

She opened her eyes anyway.

Stalactites hung above her like spears of rock, poised to fall and impale her any moment. Flickering green light illuminated the stalactites, casting dancing shadows on the cavern ceiling. Makala was lying on a smooth hard surface, and when she tried to sit up, she found she couldn't move. She could feel that her wrists and ankles had been bound by what felt like rope, but that was not what prevented her rising. She wanted to sit up, but her body refused to obey her commands.

You're still under Erdis Cai's spell, she told herself, at least partially.

Her mind began to clear then, and she realized where she was and what was happening. She was lying on the stone dais in the center of the blood pool, in the catacombs where the corpses of the ancient goblinoid warriors awaited the final three sacrifices that would restore them to life.

"I woke you, Makala, because I would not have you go to your death unaware. I would never dishonor your warrior's spirit like that."

Though she was unable to move the rest of her body, she was able to turn her head in the direction of Erdis Cai's voice. In doing so, however, she saw the two others who shared the dais with her. One was a young man who looked to be in his early twenties, and the other was a woman about ten years older. Both were bound like Makala, and both were dressed in black tunics fashioned from thin, light cloth. Makala couldn't see how she was dressed, but from the feel of the cloth on her skin, she knew she wore a similar tunic. The other two candidates for sacrifice lay still, eyes closed, lost in Erdis Cai's hypnotic trance, a trance from which neither of them would ever awaken.

Erdis Cai, Onkar, and Jarlain stood near the narrow walkway that stretched across the blood pool to the base of the dais. Jarlain smiled at Makala with smug satisfaction, her eyes gleaming in anticipation. Onkar glared at her, eyes burning with crimson fire as he cradled the stump where his right hand had once been. Makala didn't know what had happened to Onkar, but whatever it had been, she hoped it had hurt.

Erdis Cai had no expression on his face. His features were as cold and impassive as those of a marble statue. The vampire lord cocked his head to the side as if listening to a voice only he could hear.

He looked up at the cavern roof, his gaze seeming to penetrate the stone and see far beyond it. He lowered his head and though his expression didn't change, his voice held the merest hint of excitement as he said, "It's time."

He reached up to the crimson blood-drop symbol on his breastplate, grasped its edges, and plucked it free of the metal. As the Mark of Vol detached from the armor, a blade snicked out of the bottom and a handle jutted from the top. Erdis Cai wrapped his fingers around the handle and the Mark of Vol had become a sacrificial dagger.

The vampire lord stepped onto the walkway and began crossing the blood pool. The thick crimson liquid bubbled as if in excitement as he passed by.

Makala watched as her death drew closer.

● ● ● ◉ ● ● ●

"I don't suppose Tresslar told you how to find the entrance to this secret passage," Ghaji said as they ran through the outskirts of the goblin city.

"He gave me directions, but I don't think we'll need them," Diran said.

Ghaji frowned. "Why not?"

In answer, Diran pointed to a section of cavern wall where Tresslar stood, dragonwand tucked beneath his tunic belt. The artificer had his hand pressed to the stone, and when he removed it, a semicircular door swung open.

"At least he didn't have to kiss this one," Ghaji said.

Tresslar must've heard them approaching, for her turned, a wary expression on his face, but when he saw who it was, he relaxed.

Diran and Ghaji came to a stop as they reached the open passageway.

"What are you doing here?" Ghaji asked.

"I don't know," Tresslar admitted. "I . . . I just had to come."

Diran nodded to the open passageway. "This is it?"

"Yes. The catacombs lie at the bottom of the stairs."

"Ghaji and I will go first," Diran said. "Remember, whatever happens, Erdis Cai must not be allowed to gain control of those warriors." With that, Diran headed down the winding stairs into darkness, Ghaji and Tresslar following close behind.

● ● ● ◉ ● ● ●

Waiting for them at the bottom of the stairs was a scene out of nightmare. The chamber was just as Tresslar had described it: recessed areas housing the upright corpses of the ancient hobgoblin warriors carved into the circular wall, blood pool in the center of the room, stone walkway and dais rising out of the crimson liquid. Four braziers of burning green fire illuminated the chamber with eerie light, and the blood in the pool—the sheer volume of it was staggering—roiled and swirled around the dais as if alive. Onkar and the raven-haired woman stood at the edge of the pool, gazing upon their master. Erdis Cai stood on the walkway next to the dais, holding in one hand a knife formed from the Mark of Vol, its blade dripping crimson. In his other hand, he held a young man upside down by the ankle. The youth's throat had been slashed open and blood gushed from the wound, raining down to join the swirling mass of liquid in the pool. When the flow diminished to a trickle, Erdis Cai gave the youth's body a shake, like a man determined to get the last few drops from a bottle of wine. Then with an ease that was horrible in its casualness, the vampire lord tossed the drained corpse to the other side of the chamber where it fell to the floor, joining the body of an older woman who'd already been bled.

Two of the final sacrifices had been completed. The last lay bound hand and foot atop the dais, still very much alive. Makala.

Though Diran wanted to call out her name, let her know that help had arrived at last, he didn't waste time on talk. He drew one of his few remaining daggers from his cloak, a silver one that he had saved especially for Erdis Cai. The removal of the Mark of Vol from the vampire lord's breastplate had left an open gap in his obsidian armor, an opening Diran was determined to exploit. He hurled the dagger, but just as the blade was about to strike its target, Erdis Cai deflected Diran's dagger with his blood-smeared sacrificial knife. The silver dagger flew to the other side of the chamber, struck the stone wall, and fell to the ground.

The vampire lord smiled. "A gallant attempt, priest. You're fast—for a mortal."

Onkar snarled and started toward Diran. "I owe you for what you did to my hand, priest! I'm going to enjoy—"

The undead sailor never got to finish his sentence. Diran drew the silver arrowhead symbol of his order from his shirt pocket, and with a flick of his wrist, sent it spinning toward Onkar. The holy object wasn't a dagger, but it *was* silver, and what's more, it was consecrated in the name of the Silver Flame. The arrowhead flew into Onkar's open mouth, and its sharp edges sank into the flesh in the back of his throat. The vampire let out a gurgling scream as smoke curled forth from his mouth, immediately followed by a gout of black blood. Onkar clawed at his throat with his remaining hand, tearing away chunks of his own flesh as he desperately sought to remove the holy object. Eyes wild with panic, the undead sailor flew toward the stairs, tendrils of smoke trailing from his mouth, and black blood spilling over his charred lips.

As Onkar rushed past them, Ghaji swung his flaming axe, but the vampire was moving so swiftly that all Ghaji managed to do was lop off his good arm. Onkar staggered under the blow as his severed arm flopped to the ground, but he kept going, now entirely bereft of hands. He gained the stairs and rapidly ascended them, howling in pain all the way.

Erdis Cai showed no reaction to his second-in-command's

agonized flight. He was too busy staring past Diran and Ghaji with a puzzled expression.

"That old man with you . . . he seems somewhat familiar to me," the vampire lord said.

"That because I used to sail with you, Erdis."

The undead explorer's eyes widened in recognition. "Tresslar? Is that really you?"

"It is."

Erdis Cai grinned in delight, and when he next spoke, his tone was warm and filled with affection. "By the Sovereigns, how you've changed! But then, it's been quite some time since we saw each other last, eh, lad? Now I understand how the priest and the half-orc found their way here. They had you for a guide."

"You've changed, too, Erdis," Tresslar said sadly.

Erdis Cai's grin relaxed and some of the former coldness crept back into his voice. "It's a pity that you jumped ship when you did. You missed out on the greatest adventure of all."

"What adventure?" Tresslar challenged. "Becoming a monster? Serving a goddess of evil?"

Erdis Cai's smile disappeared and his voice was now devoid of emotion. "For an artificer, you always did display a surprising lack of imagination. I've become something more than human, Tresslar—something *better*. I found what I had been searching for all those long years that I sailed the world's seas: something greater than myself to believe in."

"Spare us your rationalizations," Diran said. "You're not more than human. You're nothing but a dead shell that contains only faint traces of the man called Erdis Cai. You're a vessel for Vol's evil, nothing more."

The raven-haired woman spoke for the first time. "Spare *us* your hypocrisy, Diran Bastiaan. In the process of determining whether Makala's mind and spirit were strong enough to make her a suitable sacrifice, I learned all about you, priest. You are a killer at heart, a predator in cleric's clothing. You may pretend that you slay those beings you deem 'evil' in order to protect the innocent . . . whoever *they* are, but deep down you're no different from Erdis, Onkar, or me." As she spoke, Jarlain began walking toward Diran, reaching out as if she wanted to take his hands in hers. "You kill because it's your nature . . . because you're good at it . . ." The woman was almost close enough to touch Diran now. "Most of all, because you *love* it."

Diran wanted to deny Jarlain's words, but how could he when at times he'd thought the very same thing himself?

Jarlain reached out to touch him, but before her hand could make contact, Ghaji stepped between them.

"Shut up," the half-orc growled and swung his axe in a flaming arc toward the raven-haired beauty.

Diran saw the surprised look in Jarlain's eyes for only an instant, then her severed head flew away from him. Blood fountained upward from the stump of her neck, and her body slumped to the ground, lifeless. Blood continued to gush from her corpse, spreading toward the edge of the pool.

Tresslar ran to Jarlain's body, grabbed it by the ankles, and began pulling it away from the pool. "We have to move her before—"

It was too late. Jarlain's blood ran over the edge and poured down into the pool where it merged with the roiling mass of liquid. The pool's level rose only the merest fraction of an inch, but that was enough. Blood began flowing along the twenty-five runnels toward the alcoves where the withered corpses of the goblinoid warriors stood waiting. The corpses' desiccated feet stood in the runnels, and as the blood flowed around their ankles, the first of them began to move.

Diran looked at Ghaji.

"Damn," the half-orc said.

CHAPTER

TWENTY-ONE

The undead hobgoblins opened their eyes, revealing empty sockets— no, not empty, rather filled with pulsating shadow. Arms that were little more than bone covered by dried parchment-like skin lifted swords, spears, halberds, and war hammers, dark magic supplying the strength their withered muscles couldn't provide. The goblinoid warriors stepped forth from the stone alcoves where they had stood throughout the long years waiting with the patience that only the dead can know. Leathery lips parted for the first time in centuries as the living corpses let out silent battle cries.

Erdis Cai laughed. "You've failed, priest!"

The vampire lord turned his back on them, and still holding onto his sacrificial blade, he stepped closer to the dais where Makala lay staring at him with wide, fear-filled eyes and shaking her head in denial. As if it were an afterthought, he said, "Slay the intruders, my warriors, while I tend to more

. . . pleasant matters." His teeth drew back from his fangs in a hideous parody of a smile and Makala screamed.

Diran turned to Ghaji.

"Tresslar and I will deal with the goblins," Ghaji said. "Go save Makala."

Diran nodded, drew the last wooden dagger from his cloak, and ran for the walkway that crossed over to the dais. Behind him, he heard Tresslar said, "What do you mean *we?*"

"Be quiet and put that dragon-stick of yours to work, old man!" Ghaji shouted, then Diran heard the sound of clashing metal and he knew the battle had been joined.

"Old?" Tresslar sounded quite affronted, then there came the crackle of released mystic energy as the artificer did as Ghaji advised.

Trusting his companions to take care of the resurrected hobgoblins, which were now striding forth from their alcoves by the dozens, Diran ran across the walkway toward the dais. Erdis Cai leaned over Makala, clearly intending to sink his teeth into her neck and infect her with his vampiric contagion. Though she looked terrified, Makala remained motionless as the vampire lord bent down over her. Diran guessed that Erdis Cai must have placed her in some sort of paralytic state, for such simple bonds as those encircling her wrists and ankles would never have prevented her from fighting otherwise. Diran held his wooden dagger in a tight grip, but Erdis Cai was standing at an angle to him, depriving Diran of a clear shot at the opening in his breastplate. He heard Emon Gorsedd's voice then.

If you can't take your best shot, take your second-best.

Diran hurled the wooden dagger at Erdis Cai's unprotected

neck. The blade severed the vampire's artery as it pierced his undead flesh, and black slime spurted from the wound. Erdis Cai spun around, eyes aflame, fangs bared in a feral snarl. He made no move to withdraw the dagger jutting out of his neck as Diran approached. Instead he raised his own knife, the one formed from the unholy Mark of Vol, and lunged forward to meet Diran's advance.

Diran stopped and raised his right hand. It was empty at first, but then a glimmer of silvery light appeared. The glimmer burst into brilliant radiance and Diran Bastiaan held the power of the living Silver Flame in his hand.

Erdis Cai broke off his attack and raised an arm to shield his eyes, dropping the sacrificial blade as he did so. The weapon fell into the roiling blood pool, which was slowly draining, its thick crimson liquid flowing up the sides of the pit and into the runnels as it continued to restore life to the hobgoblin army.

"It's over, Cai!" Diran said. Energy blazed through every fiber of the priest's being, but there was no pain, only a sensation of strength and rightness as the Silver Flame did its holy work through him. He was the weapon, and the Silver Flame, which was the power of Life itself, was the hand wielding him. Some called Diran the Blade of the Flame, and that title was never more appropriate than at this very moment. "Surrender, and I promise your destruction will be swift and merciful!"

Erdis Cai cringed from the intense illumination radiating from Diran's hand, and the priest stepped closer, reaching back into his cloak for a dagger—any dagger—that might end the vampire's foul existence, but before Diran could locate a suitable blade, Erdis Cai turned and clamped his gauntleted fingers around Makala's throat.

"Extinguish your light, priest, or I'll close my hand and pop off her head like the bloom of a dandelion!"

"Don't—" Makala started to say, but the vampire lord tightened his grip, choking off her voice.

Diran knew what his former lover had intended to say, for he would've said the same in her place. *Don't worry about me—kill him!* Diran also knew that as a priest of the Silver Flame, it was his sworn duty to destroy creatures like Erdis Cai, regardless of the personal consequences. Diran knew then what he had to do.

He closed his fingers around the silver flame burning in his hand, extinguishing it in his fist.

The blinding holy light gone, Erdis Cai released his grip on Makala's throat and whirled around to face Diran once more. His armored hand lashed out and fastened around Diran's neck. The priest felt a jolt of freezing cold as the metal came in contact with his skin, and a numbing sensation became to spread outward from his neck into the rest of his body. He felt weary, listless, drained of energy, then he understood what was happening. Erdis Cai's obsidian armor was enchanted, and the vampire lord was using it to absorb Diran's lifeforce.

Erdis Cai's inhuman gaze bored into Diran's eyes. "You put up a good fight, priest, I'll give you that much. In fact, it was the most fun I've had since I became immortal, but the game's finished and I'm the victor. Go to your death knowing that your strength will be added to my own, and your woman will join me in the dark glory of undeath. Farewell, Diran Bastiaan."

Diran caught a flash of orange-red out of the corner of his eye, and Erdis Cai's head snapped back as Ghaji's fire axe bit into his skull. The vampire lord screamed as his head burst into flame, and he loosened his grip on Diran's throat—not much, perhaps, but enough. Diran felt the transference of his lifeforce cease, and he opened his hand to reveal a still-glimmering flicker of the Silver Flame. The flicker grew and lengthened until to became a dagger of pure energy, and then Diran rammed the blade of silver fire through the opening in Erdis Cai's breastplate.

The vampire lord opened his burning mouth to scream anew, but all that emerged from within was a shaft of bright silvery light. Other shafts burst forth from his eyes, ears, and even his nostrils, the light spreading, merging, until it covered Erdis Cai's entire body. Diran pulled his empty hand free of the vampire lord's chest. The silver light dimmed and the flame surrounding Erdis Cai's head slowly died away as Ghaji's fire axe deactivated. All that remained of the undead explorer was a suit of armor and an ash-flecked skull with an axe embedded in it. For an instant, the skeletal remains continued standing, as if held upright by the obsidian armor encasing them, then Erdis Cai's remains collapsed to the walkway, his armor striking the ground with a loud crash.

Diran felt like collapsing himself, but Ghaji shouted, "Do you mind tossing my axe back to me? I could really use it right about now!"

Diran turned to see that Ghaji and Tresslar stood on the walkway, battling the undead warriors as they came one and two and a time. Ghaji was forced to make do with his old axe, hacking off desiccated arms and legs, while Tresslar's dragonwand had conjured what appeared to be a gaseous reptilian claw from its tip. The claw was solid enough, though, for it gouged out large chunks of undead flesh from one hobgoblin after another. The destruction of Erdis Cai appeared to have had no effect on the undead goblinoids. They continued to fight, and though Ghaji and Tresslar had taken out a number of the creatures, more were being resurrected by the moment.

"Forget the axe!" Tresslar said. "Throw Onkar's arm into the pool!"

Diran recalled how his poison-coated daggers had affected the Mire, and he thought he knew what the artificer had in mind.

"Do it, Ghaji!" he shouted.

The half-orc dispatched another hobgoblin then raced across the walkway, weaving between more of the undead warriors. He reached Onkar's severed arm with its bloody, ragged stump and kicked it into the pool. Immediately, the blood remaining in the giant basin turned black, and the ebon color rapidly spread along the upward flowing streams of liquid and down the twenty-five runnels and back into the alcoves where the rest of the hobgoblins waited to be restored to life. A rank stench of rotting meat and sewage wafted from the openings, and a flood of brackish liquid gushed out, flowing back into the basin and filling it almost to the brim once more. Skeletal fragments bobbed in the horrid soup, but they quickly dissolved and were gone.

Diran smiled grimly. Onkar's arm had poisoned the blood his master had harvested over the course of four decades, destroying those warriors that had yet to be resurrected. Unfortunately, it hadn't done anything to stop those hobgoblins that had already been reanimated, but at least no more would be replenishing their ranks.

Diran pried Ghaji's axe out of Erdis Cai's skull and tossed the weapon to his friend. The half-orc caught the axe easily, and the metal burst into flame once more. Ghaji then returned to doing what he did best—hacking things to pieces. Diran turned, stepped over Erdis Cai's armor, and went to Makala's side. With the vampire lord dead, her paralysis had been lifted and she sat up.

"I'd say it was good to see you, but that would a monumental understatement."

Diran smiled and leaned forward to kiss her. When they parted, Ghaji said, "If you two are finished, Tresslar and I could use a little help over here! Too many remain for us to deal with alone!"

Diran bent down and picked up the wooden dagger that had been embedded in Erdis Cai's neck. He cut the ropes binding Makala's wrists and ankles, then offered her the blade.

"No thanks," she said. "There are plenty of weapons lying around." This was true; the chamber was littered with mutilated hobgoblin corpses and the weapons they'd wielded. "Nothing personal, but I'd rather use something a bit more substantial than a dagger."

"Suit yourself," Diran said. "Ready?"

Makala grinned. "Try and stop me."

Together they ran down the walkway.

❋ ❋ ❋ ❋ ❋ ❋ ❋

"I never thought I'd say this, but I think I've killed enough undead monsters to last me for a while," Ghaji said.

Ghaji, Diran, Makala, and Tresslar walked through the domed goblinoid city on their way to the dock. They moved cautiously, for while they'd escaped the sacrificial chamber, a number of the undead warriors yet survived and might still prove a threat. So far, it seemed as if the ancient hobgoblins had no intention of leaving the chamber, but they kept careful watch just the same.

"Where is everyone?" Makala asked.

"Hiding," Diran said, "or perhaps with their master gone, they've abandoned Grimwall."

"There *are* several passages that lead to the surface," Tresslar said.

"I take it you don't want to hunt them down," Makala said.

"Erdis Cai, Onkar, and Jarlain are dead. The prisoners are free—assuming things went well for Yvka and Hinto—and the Black Fleet is no more," Diran said. "I think that's enough for one night, don't you? I doubt the others will return to Grimwall, and perhaps knowing their master has been defeated will convince them of the folly of worshipping Vol. Perhaps some of them will even cross over to the side of Light."

"I think you're being overly optimistic," Tresslar said.

"Oh, I don't know," Makala countered. "I can think of a time or two that it's happened before."

Diran smiled at Makala and reached out to take her hand, but before their fingers touched, a quartet of naked figures came rushing out of one of the domed buildings in front of them.

"Ghouls!" Ghaji shouted.

The undead cannibals come running toward them, eyes burning with hunger, tongues lolling out of their mouths. Ghaji, Diran, and Tresslar stepped forward to deal with the creatures, Makala still had the sword she'd taken from one of the dead hobgoblin warriors. She reached for it now, intending to help slay the ghouls, but she froze as a horribly distorted voice whispered in her ear.

"Hello."

A handless forearm pressed against her mouth, and Makala struggled as Onkar pulled her back through the open doorway of another domed building. There, in the darkness, she felt charred lips press against her throat and sharp fangs sink into her neck.

CHAPTER

TWENTY-TWO

When the last ghoul was dead, Diran took a quick look around and realized that Makala was missing.

"Makala?" he called, but there was no answer. He turned toward Ghaji and Tresslar, but the worried expressions on their faces told him that they had no idea where she was.

Diran still held a silver dagger from their battle with the ghouls, and he gripped it tightly and starting running back in the direction from which they'd come. Part of him wanted to believe that Makala had simply gone off in pursuit of a fleeing ghoul, but he feared something else had happened—something bad.

As he drew near one particular building, he felt a dark presence emanating from within. He could almost see it, as if a shadowy cloud covered the domed structure. Without hesitation, he headed for the building and plunged through the open doorway.

Onkar crouched over Makala's prone form. Her throat had been torn to shreds and her blood was smeared over the lower half of the vampire's face. Onkar looked up with a feral snarl and his eyes blazed with red flame, as if he were a wild beast disturbed in the act of feeding. Thanks to the fresh infusion of nourishment Onkar had stolen from Makala, the battle wounds he'd sustained were already in the process of healing. A tiny hand no larger than an infant's now protruded from the stump where Ghaji had hacked off his arm. The hand possessed miniature claws and the slender fingers waggled, almost as if Onkar's new hand were waving to Diran.

Onkar grinned, displaying fangs slick with Makala's blood. "You're too late, priest. She's dead, but if it comes as any consolation to you, she was *delicious.*"

With the litheness of a jungle cat, Onkar sprang over Makala's body toward Diran, fangs bared and claws outstretched. Onkar slammed into Diran and knocked him to the ground. The vampire held Diran down with his good hand while he lowered his mouth toward the priest's throat.

For an instant, Diran considered letting the vampire have him. He'd fought so long against the darkness—both within and without—and his soul was weary. He'd come too far to give up now, and if he could reach Makala in time, there was a chance that he might be able to save her.

Just as Onkar's incisors dimpled the flesh over his artery, Diran brought the silver dagger in his hand up and rammed the blade into Onkar's left ear. The sacred metal burned its way through undead flesh and bone and lodged deep within the vampire's brain. Onkar threw back head and screamed. Blood gushed from his other ear, his eyes, nose and mouth. Makala's blood.

Diran shoved the shrieking fiend off him and quickly crawled over to Makala's side. As Onkar thrashed on the floor of the domed building, Diran closed his eyes and concentrated on breathing evenly.

Please, he prayed, and pictured a spark of silver fire appearing in the palm of his hand. He felt the holy power of the Silver Flame surge through his body, and when he opened his eyes, he saw that his hand was filled with a brilliant blue-white light. So strong was its illuminaton that Diran couldn't look directly at it. The light spilled over Onkar as well, and the wounded vampire's shrieks rose in volume and pitch, becoming so loud that Diran thought his eardrums might burst, but he didn't care about that. All that mattered was Makala.

Diran pressed his palm to Makala's savaged throat and willed the Silver Flame to enter her body, to seek out the foul corruption inside her and destroy it. How long he knelt there, channeling the power of the Silver Flame into Makala, he didn't know. At one point he became aware that Onkar's screams had stopped, and he knew that Ghaji and Tresslar had arrived and finished off the damned creature.

Finally, Diran felt the Silver Flame diminish, and the light slowly faded until it was gone. When he removed his hand from Makala's throat, he saw that the skin was smooth and unbroken, as if Onkar had never attacked her.

"Did it work?"

Diran glanced over his shoulder and saw Ghaji standing there, worry in his eyes.

Diran avoided his friend's question. "Where's Tresslar?"

"While you were . . . busy, I decapitated Onkar and dragged the two halves of his corpse outside. I used my fire axe to set the remains aflame. Tresslar's watching the body burn. We're going to make sure the bastard is completely destroyed."

Diran nodded. He'd been so focused on Makala that he hadn't noticed the foul stink of burning flesh, but he smelled it now.

Ghaji nodded toward Makala. "Is she hurt?"

Diran turned back to look at her. Though her body and clothes were stained with blood from Onkar's attack, she looked peaceful and relaxed, as if she were only sleeping.

"I don't know," Diran admitted. "What I tried has never been attempted, as far as I know. If I got to her in time . . ." He trailed off and reached into a pocket and brought forth the silver arrowhead that was the symbol of his faith. He reached out, placed the arrowhead in Makala's palm, and closed her fingers around it.

At first nothing happened. Then came a soft sizzling sound, as of meat cooking over an open flame. Diran opened Makala's hand and removed the holy token.

On her palm was a scorch mark in the shape of an arrowhead.

Makala opened her eyes.

"Welcome back," Diran said.

She sat up and reached for her throat. She ran fingers over smooth, unbroken skin and sighed with relief. "Did you heal me?"

Only a few feet away, Diran sat cross-legged on the stone floor. The domed building contained a single large room, crudely furnished with a wooden table, chairs, and sleeping pallet set against a curved wall.

"I tried," Diran said, his voice hollow, "but we found you too late. Onkar hadn't quite . . . finished yet, and I destroyed him, but he'd nearly drained you dry by that point, and the vampiric contagion had already begun its work inside you. Despite my best efforts, I could not reverse its effects. I am . . . so sorry."

Makala stared at Diran, as if she couldn't comprehend what he was saying. Then she reached up and gingerly felt her elongated canine teeth.

"No . . . No!"

She began to cry, and cold tears trickled down her cheeks. She wiped the tears away with her fingers then looked at her hands. Her fingertips were smeared with crimson—the tears of a vampire. Without thinking, she started to bring her hands to her mouth to lap up the blood, but when she realized what she was doing, she shuddered in disgust and wiped her hands on the dirt floor.

Diran reached out to embrace her, but she scuttled away from him. She wanted Diran to hold her, but at the same time she feared his touch. The hurt Diran felt at seeing her recoil from him was plain in his eyes, but she couldn't control herself. It was as if she were an animal acting on instinct. She was now an unholy thing, and Diran was a priest. No matter how much she wanted to, she couldn't bring herself to go near him.

"It took a day for the transformation to complete itself. I've sat here the entire time, waiting."

"Waiting for what? To destroy me?"

"If that's what you wish." Diran lifted his hand and showed Makala the wooden stake he held.

"I don't understand."

"Remember what you said just before Onkar attacked you?

You were telling Tresslar that you knew two examples of people crossing from darkness over to light, from evil to good. You were talking about us, Makala."

"Yes."

"We both found the strength to do without our dark spirits, and we both stopped killing people for profit. If you could do those things, perhaps you will be able to resist the darkest aspects of your new . . . condition. You may carry evil's taint within your blood now, Makala, but that doesn't mean you have to let it control you. I will not slay you, not unless you want me to."

A silence fell between them then, and it was some time before Makala finally broke it.

"I can hear the blood pulsing in your veins, Diran. I can *smell* it. The thirst is so strong . . ." She began crawling toward Diran, the first flickers of red flame dancing in her eyes. As she drew near, she pulled her lips back from her teeth and opened her mouth wide.

Diran made no move to stop her. He simply sat and waited for whatever would happen next.

Makala paused. Slowly, the crimson light in her eyes dimmed and she closed her mouth. "I don't want to live like this," she said, "yet . . . Sovereigns help me, I don't want to die, either." She forced a laugh. "Emon would be proud of me, don't you think? I've become the ultimate assassin. I no longer need another spirit to share my body—I *am* an evil spirit all by myself." She felt as if she was going to cry again, but she fought back the tears. She didn't want Diran to see her weep blood.

"No matter what else you have become," Diran said, "you are still Makala, and I will always love you."

Makala gave Diran a sad smile, then came forward and pressed her cold lips to Diran's.

"Farewell, my love."

Her form blurred then, and with a sudden rush of wind, she was gone.

Diran remained sitting there, alone, for quite some time.

● ● ● ◉ ● ● ●

"Is it done?" Ghaji asked as Diran stepped onto the deck of the *Zephyr*.

Diran didn't answer, and Ghaji decided not to press the matter. Whatever had occurred, Diran would share it in his own good time.

The priest stepped over to the starboard railing and looked out upon the moonlight reflecting silver off the water. Ghaji walked over and joined him.

"The *Nightwind* is ready to sail, but Hinto thinks we should wait until daylight to depart. It'll be easier to navigate the winding passage out of the cove then."

Diran nodded, though Ghaji didn't think his friend had really heard him.

Their plan was simple. The *Zephyr* would lead the *Nightwind*—piloted by Hinto and Tresslar and crewed by a number of former prisoners—along the shoreline of Orgalos until they found a suitable place to set anchor. They would then begin ferrying the freed prisoners onto land.

The half-orc wasn't certain what would become of Grimwall. Tresslar wanted to pick through Erdis Cai's collection to retrieve whatever magic items might be of interest, while according to Yvka, her employers in the Shadow Network would most likely wish to do the same. Hinto wanted them to take over Grimwall and use it as their base of operations, just at the crew of the *Seastar* had so many years ago. Ghaji had tried pointing out to the halfling that there was no *them*, and thus they had no need for Grimwall—not to mention there were still undead hobgoblins lurking about somewhere—but Hinto had ignored him.

"How much longer until sunrise?" Diran asked.

Ghaji looked up at the sky. "A little less than two hours."

"Where's Yvka?"

"In the cabin, meditating."

"Why don't you go join her and get some rest," Diran turned to Ghaji and managed a smile, "or whatever. I think I'll stay here and wait for dawn."

"If it's all the same to you, I'd rather let her be. Though she won't admit it, piloting the *Zephyr* takes a lot out of her, and she'll need her rest for tomorrow."

"As you wish," Diran said.

The two companions stood silently side by side as they waited for the first rays of sunlight to come chase away the darkness.

Preview chapter for

VOYAGE OF THE MOURNING DAWN

Book 1 of the Heirs of Ash

By Rich Wulf

Avaliable June 2006!

Chapter One

As far as Seren Morisse was concerned, Wroat wasn't the sort of place people lived on purpose. It was just where you ended up. There you were, living a normal life, minding your own business, and one day you found yourself in Wroat. Didn't matter if you were rich or poor, Wroat just sort of snuck up on you. You came here thinking it might be a good idea to visit for a time, maybe make money or contacts before moving on to somewhere better, but the city found a way of sinking its hooks into you. Wroat made you need it. It made it easier to stay than to leave, and every day you stayed, the city got a little less pretty. The flaws became a little more apparent. The stink became a little more cloying. The people showed you who they really were, and by then it was too late.

Wroat became a part of you, and you were a part of Wroat.

The King of Breland lived in Wroat. As Seren hauled herself onto the rough stone ledge, she looked at the towering spires of the palace and wondered if the King ever felt the same way. He probably did, maybe even more so than anybody. After all, who had less say in his own future than a king? Maybe she wasn't that different from old Boranel. Let him enjoy his prison of silk, jewels, and fine food. At least Seren had her freedom . . . precariously huddled on a loosely tiled ledge on the second floor of the d'Cannith guild house with rain pouring down around her.

Seren sighed deeply.

No, on second thought, she would most certainly trade him.

Seren peered over one shoulder, around the edge of the window. Within, she saw a richly appointed study, illuminated by a roaring fireplace and a single lamp. A large wooden desk stood near the window, buried under heaps of unfurled scrolls and books, left lying open and stacked in heaps. The walls were lined with shelves stuffed with even more volumes. The number of books was somewhat surprising considering the inhabitant's reputation; he didn't seem the scholarly type. A few plates of half-eaten food and glass tumblers, some still half-filled with wine, sat heaped on the desk and even scattered on the floor. Small models of airships, lightning rail engines, and even the adamantine faceplate of a warforged decorated the walls and shelves in a random, haphazard manner. The decorations were covered with dust, but the books were clean and well maintained.

Seren knew this house had plenty of servants—she had watched them enter and leave the house for the past four days to learn their routine—but they obviously had not touched this room in some time. Perhaps the things kept here were too valuable to trust in the presence of servants. If so, this was exactly what she was looking for. If not, then this was as good a place as any to start. Seren reached for the window, but she drew back as the door within opened. She huddled back against a nearby gargoyle, wrapping her arms around her knees to stay warm in the chilling rain. She tried once again to console herself with the fact that she was so much better off than King Boranel.

How did it happen? How did she end up here? Good question. Seren's answer was easy. Stupidity. Her father had been a soldier. The end of the War had been a good thing for a great many families—but not for Seren's. Other fathers returned to joyous reunions with loving families. Seren's family received only a black envelope delivered by an apologetic young messenger in a travel-stained uniform. Seren remembered her mother dropping the envelope and bursting into tears. She remembered how the messenger hurried away—he had many more messages to deliver that day.

The army had provided a small stipend to support the families of veterans who had died in the war—but it wasn't much, just enough to get a family back on its feet or support a single widow. Seren's mother never complained, but with each day that passed the worried lines around her eyes grew a little deeper. Finally, one night, Seren decided to set out and find her own fate. Her mother would miss her, that was certain, but she knew if she stopped to say good-bye she would lose her nerve, and the two of them would starve together.

In any case, running off to the city seemed a romantic enough notion. How could she fail?

Oh, she had heard all the stories, all the warnings. Her mother had always told her how it was dangerous for a young girl to find a life on her own. Her father, when he was home, always warned her how runaways ended up doing the most terrible things to survive. It wasn't that she didn't listen, or didn't believe them. Quite the opposite, she believed that sort of fate was exactly what could befall a foolish person, and she took their warnings to heart. Seren knew she was not a foolish person, so clearly she was secretly exempt. She ran away from Ringbriar to find a dazzling future somewhere, maybe as an artist or a diplomat. The fact that she had no talents in either art or politics was irrelevant. Those kinds of things weren't hard. It was all a matter of finding the right opportunity.

A tile slid under Seren's feet and she wobbled dangerously. Her hand squished something unpleasant as she clutched the edge of the gutter. She grimaced but didn't risk letting go. She watched the tile spiral downward, wincing as she waited for the shattering report on the street below. The sky flashed overhead, and a riotous peal of thunder filled the night. Seren finally breathed. No one would have heard the falling tile. She whispered a brief prayer of thanks to Kol Korran and, while she was praying, added a polite request that whichever member of the Host was in charge of the lightning this evening, please keep it in the sky until she was safely off this ledge.

In hindsight, she realized she'd been every bit as foolish as the girls in those stories. A big city like Wroat didn't have many uses for a girl on her own. Well, honestly, that wasn't exactly true. Seren was young and pretty, if in a tomboyish sort of way. She soon found quite a number of gentlemen (and one rather curious lady) with many helpful suggestions as to how she could earn her keep, but the prospect of earning a living on her back was not very appealing.

It wasn't until a particularly fat and odious fish merchant propositioned her at the Steaming Ferret that Seren learned her true calling. Seren enjoyed several drinks with the man, only sipping from her own cup as he threw back mug after mug. She entertained his suggestions with vaguely noncommittal flirtation and then excused herself to use the lavatory. While the drunken merchant sat heaped on his stool, waiting for her to return, Seren snuck out the back door with his belt pouch tucked in her skirt.

She was no artist or diplomat, but she had proven to be quite a talented thief.

Seren peered carefully through the window again. She now saw the back of a short, thick-bodied man dressed in a rich lavender suit and a peaked green cap. She couldn't see his face but recognized his build and clothing as that of the house's owner. The man sat at his desk, leaning back comfortably in his worn leather chair, holding a small frosted cake in one hand and chewing intently as he balanced a thick book upon his knee. Thunder cracked overhead again, and the rain came down even harder. Seren's long black hair was now plastered to her face and down her back. She scowled through the window, trying to compel the man to finish his reading and leave through sheer force of will. Not surprisingly, it didn't work. Seren settled back against the gargoyle, trying to find some shelter or warmth against its bulk. The statue stared blankly down at the street, showing no sympathy whatsoever.

Waiting was the most difficult part of being a thief, by far. The threat of punishment didn't frighten her. The excitement of a job well done balanced that. The danger made the job worthwhile. But this? She muffled a sneeze with one hand, her damp hair slapping forward and covering her face. Waiting was miserable. Where was Jamus? He was late, and she was going to kill him—if she didn't slide off the ledge or perish of pneumonia. Rain streamed down her back and shoulders. Seren wished that she had dressed a bit more warmly. Her short cotton breeches and leather vest offered mobility for climbing but little protection from the elements. The weather had been fair when she started climbing. It wasn't until halfway up the building that the clouds rolled in and the rain started. She should have climbed back down and put off the job until tomorrow, but Seren was a stubborn sort of person.

Carefully holding the gutter with one hand and the gargoyle's stone claw with the other, she leaned out and peered down. She couldn't give up, even if she wanted to. The climb back down would be far too dangerous in the rain. The only way out of here was through the house, and her distraction was taking an inordinate amount of time to arrive.

Almost on cue, a heavy banging sounded in the street below. Seren sat back against the wall again, peering carefully in the window to see the inhabitant's reaction. The fat man merely sat in his chair, chewing happily on his cake and reading his book, ignoring the commotion.

More banging followed, this time accompanied with a quavering voice calling out, "Hello? Master d'Cannith? Is anyone there?"

The man inside set his cake down and sighed heavily. He drummed his fingers on the desk, as if waiting for his visitor to go away.

Another round of heavy banging. "Master d'Cannith, my business is most urgent! If you are occupied, I understand, and shall take my business to Master d'Phiarlan. I had hoped to offer your guild this honor first, but such is life!"

Dalan closed his book with a snap, tossing it onto a nearby couch and stalking toward the study door. After several moments, she heard the iron squeal of old hinges below.

"What?" snapped a terse voice below.

"Ah, greetings and good evening to you, Master d'Cannith." She heard the reply, though she could not see either speaker beneath the sloping overhang. "I bring you greetings on behalf of the Lost Children of Wroat. Surely being a member of a household whose humanitarian actions during the Last War are so renowned, you would be eager to aid this prestigious charity? I ask only whatever you can spare to help us purchase food, medicine, perhaps even new toys to brighten what would otherwise be a bleak and hopeless . . ."

Seren could not help a smile. Jamus hadn't shared the full details of how he intended to distract their target, but she had trusted the old thief to be creative. She unhooked the metal sphere from her belt, cracking it open to reveal the glowing stone within. Such magic was expensive, but light without a spark was a useful investment in her line of work. She frowned as she studied the window, finding no lock. Holding the stone up to the window, she began tracing the edges of the sill with one finger.

"Orphans?" the other voice said below. "You roused me from my leisure to beg for charity?"

"Not just any charity, Master d'Cannith, the Lost Children of Wroat, a proud and well respected . . ." The sound of a slamming door connecting with the toe of a boot interrupted his monologue. "Ahem. A proud and respected charity with, as I am sure one of your impressive social connections is aware, a sterling reputation for . . ."

"I have never heard of you and I can assure you I give quite generously to several *legitimate* charities. Now get your foot out of my door."

"I can understand your reluctance, Master d'Cannith, for there are many opportunistic souls who seek to twist the generosity of those touched by the War," Jamus said, accompanied by the rhythmic sound of a door repeatedly hitting a foot. "I assure you, however, that we are legitimate. Look only to these beautiful glass marbles, painted by the children . . ."

"Leave before I call the Watch."

"Please, master, look at these marbles," Jamus continued, "each hand-painted in exquisite detail by the very innocents whom your money will support.

"I am not interested. Return when it is daylight and take up your begging with my servants if you must."

"But please, good master, just examine one and see the simple beauty . . ." A wracking cough resounded from below, followed by the sound of a bag of glass marbles striking a wooden floor and scattering its contents.

"Oh, drat," Jamus said.

This was followed by the other voice swearing urgently in several languages.

"I apologize, good master. This chill rain has left me with trembling hands."

"Just pick them up and go!"

There, Seren found what she sought. What appeared to be

a flaw in the grain was actually a mark, painted in dark brown ink, in the upper corner of the window. It formed a figure eight pattern between the sill and the wood. She didn't recognize the rune; perhaps it simply held the window sealed unless the proper word was spoken. Perhaps it would raise an alarm, or worse, explode and hurl Seren into the street. The d'Canniths were artificers and magewrights, and though the man who lived here reputedly possessed no magical training, it was no surprise to find his home was protected. Seren rose from her crouch as much as she dared, studying the ward further.

In a city as large as Wroat, magic was fairly common. The city drew wizards as surely as it drew everyone else. Seren avoided stealing from wizards or magewrights, not out of any fear of magic but simply because they were more trouble than they were worth. Jamus taught her that magic was no different from any other form of power—worthy of respect, but no more frightening than the flawed men and women who used it. Even if you couldn't learn to use magic, you could learn to deal with it. Seren couldn't build a lock, but she could pick one with a bent wire. Magic was the same. There was always an answer.

Seren drew a small tin and brush from her belt pouch. Shielding the tin from the rain, she opened its lid and wrinkled her nose at the harsh smell of its contents. Carefully, she brushed the thick, clear paste over one of the glass panes, coating it entirely, then closed the tin and put it back in her pouch. Next she drew out several strips of thick felt and pressed them against the glass, then bound another around her right hand. Taking a deep breath, she punched the glass as hard as she could where she had glued the felt over its surface. She heard only a muffled crack in reply. She peeled the felt away in a single piece, removing the broken pane in one neat sheet, which she carefully folded and stuffed into the gargoyle's open beak.

Next she produced a small mirror with a sharp pin on one side and a long stick of charcoal. Careful to avoid the broken glass, she reached through the window and pinned the mirror to the sill inside, facing her. She adjusted it until she could see the rune pattern on the inside and then carefully began work on the rune with her charcoal. It was the same sort of pigment most mages used to complete such wards, and if she was careful enough she could isolate the pattern on each side and disable the ward, at least for a short time. Finishing the pattern on the inside, she paused only long enough to sharpen her charcoal on a shard of broken glass, then do the same on the exterior. Tucking the tools back in her pouch, she looked at her work cautiously. There was only one real way to tell if it worked. She closed her eyes, took a deep breath, and opened the window with a quick heave.

Seren opened her eyes to discover, quite happily, that the window was open, there was no alarm, and she was still alive. She could still hear voices downstairs, one swearing in a rage and the other apologizing obsequiously as he continued to clumsily lose his marbles. With no sign that she had been discovered, Seren plucked up her mirror, nimbly hopped into the study, and closed the window behind her.

The thick smell of incense and woodsmoke hung heavily in the air, barely covering the more cloying scent of old sweat. This was clearly one man's private refuge, and she would be glad to be out of it. She looked down with a start as something wet touched her shin. A squat, shaggy black hound, its fur shot through with gray, looked up at her mournfully. Its tail thumped the side of the desk when she looked at it.

"Some watchdog you are," she whispered.

The old dog's ears perked up. It glanced up at the desk, then back at her. A low whine began to rise in the dog's chest, and it opened its mouth as if to bark. Seren quickly snatched Dalan's half-finished cake from the desk and tossed it to the dog. The animal caught the cake in midair and flopped on the floor, consuming the sweet bribe contentedly.

Seren stepped past the dog, eager to find what she sought and leave before the dog reconsidered its treachery. She drew a scrap of paper from her pocket and glanced at the illustration as she scanned the shelves. The paper bore an illustration of a small journal with a black cover, emblazoned with the d'Cannith gorgon crest above the image of an albatross in flight. Seren scowled in irritation as she looked at the countless books that lined the shelves. The house's owner had a reputation for being indolent and lazy; he was not known as a scholar. She had thought one book would be easy to find in his house. Now she realized she might search all night and never find the right one. She tested the nearest bookcase, hoping against hope that they were the false vanity books that many nobility favored. They were genuine enough, unfortunately, and focused on a variety of eclectic subjects from magic to history to music and even exotic cooking. All looked well read. She would never find the book she wanted before the guildmaster returned to find his broken window, missing cake, and the small river of rainwater she'd leaked on his floor.

As she stepped back to give the bookcases a better look, Seren stumbled over a book discarded on the floor. She glanced down to see the gorgon and albatross looking back at her impassively. Seren blinked in disbelief. She looked back at the dog. It only watched her with soulful black eyes, nose buried between furry paws, mourning the untimely demise of the cake. Rather than dwell upon her uncanny luck, Seren snatched the book and tucked it into the sack at her belt.

The study door no doubt bore wards like the window, but fortunately it had been left open. Seren hurried out and down the stairs, tiptoeing with a silent grace. To her right, she could see the two men. Jamus stood near the door, playing the part of the lost and confused old man as he apologized repeatedly, stroking his long white beard with one hand. The guildmaster, apparently tired of the crazed beggar's floundering, had snatched the marble bag and was now picking up the marbles himself.

"Here, take the accursed things, and do not drop them again or you shall return to the orphans without them."

"Are you certain you found them all?" Jamus asked, blinking foolishly. "I think I saw one roll under the clock in the corner . . ."

"Then here!" The man snapped. He rummaged in his pocket and held out a handful of silver. "To pay for your lost marbles."

Jamus opened his mouth to demur again, but his sharp eyes focused squarely upon Seren in the shadows of the stair. He gave a slight nod and reached for the bag and coins, clasping the guildmaster's hands with both of his own in a gesture of exaggerated gratitude. Seren made her way to the back door, quietly unlocked the latch.

"I thank you, Master d'Cannith," Jamus said, bowing repeatedly as he clasped the man's hands. "The orphans thank you as well."

"Yes, the orphans," she heard the other man growl as she

slipped out into the alley. "Give them my regards. Now go!"

Closing the door gently, Seren broke into a sprint. Darting between the puddles and strewn garbage of the alleys, she stopped at a particular abandoned house after several minutes of running. Looking back to make certain she wasn't followed, she pulled a loose board aside and stepped through the wall. The interior was lit by a single candle. An older gentleman dressed in a sleek black jacket and trousers reclined on a tattered couch. A long white beard lay discarded on the floor. He toyed with a pair of painted glass marbles, rolling them between his fingers idly.

"Did you find the book?" he asked, looking up at her with a faint grin.

She stared at Jamus blankly. "How did you get here first?" she asked.

"Rather I should ask why it took you so long," he said, though his smile took the barb off his words. He fell to a fit of coughing for several seconds and then looked up at her with a forced grin. "So. Find the book?"

Seren nodded, patting the bag at her hip. She picked up her cloak from where she had left it folded on the floor earlier in the evening and began using it as an improvised towel, drying herself as best she could.

"May I see it?" Jamus asked patiently.

"After you tell me why you left me up on that ledge in the rain for so long," she said tartly.

"Because I didn't think you'd be foolish enough to keep climbing when the storm began," Jamus said. "I thought you would come back down and we'd try another day."

She shrugged. "Can't turn back once you start or you'll never finish," she said.

"Of course," he said. "I underestimated your stubbornness, as always. It is your second most endearing and maddening trait."

"Second?" she asked, "what is the first?"

"Your infuriating willingness to speak your mind," he said. "You remind me a great deal of my daughter, Seren. I suppose before you give me the book I shall be subject to another lecture on my questionable wisdom of undertaking this mission."

Seren folded her arms across her chest and frowned. "I did the job, Jamus, but my opinion stands," she said. "I don't think it's smart to cross the dragonmarked houses. I don't care what the pay is. It's going to be trouble."

"Afraid of magic, Seren?" he asked. Jamus rose from his couch and walked toward her. "I thought I taught you better than that."

"You taught me to respect power," Seren said. "The d'Canniths are powerful. If they find out what we've done . . ."

"They simply won't care," Jamus said. He rested one hand on her shoulder, looking down at her like with the expression of a parent soothing a frightened child "Dalan d'Cannith has a checkered past. He may be a local guildmaster, but he is not particularly liked or respected among his family. His power is limited outside of Wroat. Our payment for this job will place us far beyond his grasp."

Seren's eyes widened. "We're leaving Wroat?" she asked, excited. "You never told me that."

Jamus nodded, though he glanced away as another fit of coughing shook his spare figure. "I didn't want to distract you before the job," he said. "Our employer guaranteed future opportunities beyond the city when she gave me our advance."

"There's an advance?" she asked with a small grin. Jamus hadn't mentioned that either. "Where's my share?"

The old thief smiled slyly. "Right here," he said, tossing her the bag of marbles. She caught it in one hand and favored him with a sour look. "No worries, Seren, you'll be paid when we deliver. Only the most difficult part remains."

"The most difficult part?" she said, bewildered. "What can be more difficult than what we've just done?"

"Don't ask that question," Jamus said with a chuckle. "Never ask that question, lest it be answered sooner than you'd like."

"I'm serious, Jamus," she said. "What else is left? We already have the book. All we need to do is deliver it. Are you afraid the Watch will find us, or do you not trust our employer?"

"I *never* trust my employer as a matter of course," Jamus said. "Anyone who enters our line of work, as a client or a professional, is untrustworthy by definition."

"But we trust each other," she said. "Don't we?"

He leaned forward and kissed her forehead, then made his way toward the door. "Only because we both have something to gain," he said. "Ours is a relationship of mutual benefit, teacher and student. Trust is born from mutual benefit. We trust our employer because we are offered payment in return for our services . . . mutual benefit—but we do not trust foolishly."

"So what do we do if our employer decides there's greater benefit in not paying us?" she asked. "What then?"

"In this case such a betrayal would be foolish," Jamus answered. He pushed the loose board aside, studying the street to make certain no one was outside. "I have a reputation in this city. Were I to disappear, questions would be asked, and I have arranged for answers. I have written speaker posts addressed to certain allies, describing the details of our work here. If I do not arrive to cancel the deliveries, the Sivis messengers will whisper into their speaking stones and the truth will fly upon the winds of Khorvaire. Within hours, friends as far away as Fairhaven will know the truth."

"That doesn't make me feel much better," Seren said. "If we die, we're still dead, no matter who knows what happened."

"Then ignore the negative and focus on your goals, Seren, dear," he said, stepping out into the street. "Think about leaving this place far behind, and it will be. Until then, be safe. Stay out of sight. The town guards will be suspicious of anyone on the streets on a terrible night like tonight. I will meet you back at the house."

The old thief slid the board back into place behind him. She could hear his wet footsteps and quiet cough recede into the distance. Dalan d'Cannith would have summoned the Watch by now, searching for the thief and his beggar accomplice. It was safer to wait, to move separately.

Seren would have preferred Jamus carry the book, at least. It was his idea to steal it, after all. She took the book out of the sack and studied its cover. She recognized the Cannith crest; she had seen it in the city often enough. Beneath a small hammer and anvil design, the snarling metal bull's head of a gorgon glared up at her. The relatively indifferent albatross beneath it was not typically part of the crest. It must be some sort of personal seal. Seren opened the book and flipped through the pages cautiously. She told herself she was merely checking to make sure that the book hadn't been damaged by the rain. In reality she wanted to know what was so important about it. Diagrams covered the pages within, depicting airships, clockwork mechanisms, and other artifacts whose purpose Seren could not comprehend. The writing was in a strange, arcane cipher. It told her nothing, nothing that would explain why it was important enough to make enemies of House Cannith.

The Canniths were one of the twelve dragonmarked houses, powerful organizations ruled by individuals born marked by hereditary arcane symbols. Seren didn't really understand what the Prophecy was, nor did she really care. All she knew was that the Prophecy gave incredible powers to those marked by it. Each of the dragonmarked houses boasted magical abilities and had used those abilities to cultivate great wealth and political influence. Each house was as powerful as a country, the services they offered so valuable that their power transcended international boundaries.

House Cannith bore the Mark of Making, which granted the ability to repair what had been broken or to create new things. They were engineers, artificers, and weaponsmiths. Many of the most incredible inventions in all of Eberron—the lightning rails, the airships, and even the mysterious war-forged soldiers—bore a Cannith artisan's seal. Many of the most ferocious battles in the Last War had been fought with Cannith weapons, and Breland was not the only nation that still owed them a great debt. If this book was as valuable as Jamus claimed and the Canniths realized who had stolen it from them . . . well, making two thieves in the slums of Wroat disappear wouldn't be such a difficult task for a house that commanded the loyalty of kings.

Seren pushed the book back into the sack and pushed such

thoughts away with it. Her own words returned to her—can't turn back once you start or you'll never finish. There was no option now but to see the job through and try to make a profit. If this really got her out of Wroat, then maybe it was worth it.

But she hated waiting the most.

EBERRON

During the Last War, Gaven was an
adventurer, searching the darkest reaches
of the underworld. But an encounter with
a powerful artifact forever changed him,
breaking his mind and landing him in the
deepest cell of the darkest prison in
all the world.

THE DRACONIC PROPHECIES

BOOK I

When war looms on the horizon, some see it as more
than renewed hostilities between nations. Some see the
fulfillment of an ancient prophecy—one that promises
both the doom and salvation of the world. And Gaven may
be the key to it all.

THE STORM DRAGON

The first EBERRON hardcover by veteran game designer and
the author of *In the Claws of the Tiger*:

James Wyatt

SEPTEMBER 2007

EBERRON

Land of intrigue.
Towering cities where murder is business.
Dark forests where hunters are hunted.
Ground where the dead never rest.

To find the truth takes a special breed of hero.

THE INQUSITIVES

BOUND BY IRON
Edward Bolme
Torn by oaths to king country, one man must unravel a tapestry
of murder and slavery.
April 2007

NIGHT OF THE LONG SHADOWS
Paul Crilley
During the longest nights of the year, worshipers of the
dark rise from the depths of the City of Towers
to murder . . . and worse.
May 2007

LEGACY OF WOLVES
Marsheila Rockwell
In the streets of Aruldusk, a series of grisly murders has rocked
the small city. The gruesome nature of the murders spawns
rumors of a lycanthrope in a land where the shapeshifters were
thought to have been hunted to extinction.
June 2007

THE DARKWOOD MASK
Jeff LaSala
A beautiful Inquisitive teams up with a wanted vigilante to take
down a crimelord who hides behind a mask of deceit, savage
cunning, and sorcery.
November 2008

HEIRS OF ASH

RICH WULF

The Legacy . . . an invention of unimaginable power. Rumors say it could save the world—or destroy it. The hunt is on.

Book 1
VOYAGE OF THE MOURNING DAWN

Book 2
FLIGHT OF THE DYING SUN
February 2007

Book 3
RISE OF THE SEVENTH MOON
November 2007

BLADE OF THE FLAME

TIM WAGGONER

Once an assassin. Now a man of faith. One man searching for peace in a land that knows only blood.

Book 1
THIEVES OF BLOOD

Book 2
FORGE OF THE MINDSLAYERS
March 2007

Book 3
SEA OF DEATH
February 2008

THE LANTERNLIGHT FILES

PARKER DEWOLF

A man on the run. A city on the watch. Magic on the loose.

Book 1
THE LEFT HAND OF DEATH
July 2007

Book 2
WHEN NIGHT FALLS
March 2008

Book 3
DEATH COMES EASY
December 2008

WELCOME TO THE

WORLD

Created by Keith Baker and developed by Bill Slavicsek and James Wyatt, EBERRON® is the latest setting designed for the DUNGEONS & DRAGONS® Roleplaying game, novels, comic books, and electronic games.

ANCIENT, WIDESPREAD MAGIC

Magic pervades the EBERRON world. Artificers create wonders of engineering and architecture. Wizards and sorcerers use their spells in war and peace. Magic also leaves its mark—the coveted dragonmark—on members of a gifted aristocracy. Some use their gifts to rule wisely and well, but too many rule with ruthless greed, seeking only to expand their own dominance.

INTRIGUE AND MYSTERY

A land ravaged by generations of war. Enemy nations that fought each other to a standstill over countless, bloody battlefields now turn to subtler methods of conflict. While nations scheme and merchants bicker, priceless secrets from the past lie buried and lost in the devastation, waiting to be tracked down by intrepid scholars and rediscovered by audacious adventurers.

SWASHBUCKLING ADVENTURE

The EBERRON setting is no place for the timid. Courage, strength, and quick thinking are needed to survive and prosper in this land of peril and high adventure.